ALLAN MASSIE

The author was born in Singapore in 1938, brought up in Aberdeenshire and educated at Glenalmond School and Trinity College, Cambridge, where he read history.

His previous novels include THE LAST PEACOCK, which won the Frederick Niven Award in 1981, THE DEATH OF MEN, A QUESTION OF LOYALTIES, Winner of the Saltire Society/Scotsman Book of the Year Award, and AUGUSTUS, the first of a trilogy of 'Roman' novels of which TIBERIUS is the second. His non-fiction includes a work on Muriel Spark, a study of crime in nineteenth century Edinburgh, ILL MET BY GASLIGHT, a historical work on the twelve emperors of Ancient Rome, THE CAESARS, and his acclaimed GLASGOW: PORTRAITS OF A CITY.

Allan Massie is a Fellow of the Royal Society of Literature and has been a Booker Prize judge. He is *The Scotsman*'s lead fiction reviewer, and *The Sunday Times*'s Scottish columnist, as well as being a regular reviewer for the *Sunday Telegraph* and contributor on Scottish affairs for *The Spectator*. He lives in Scotland with his wife Alison and their three children.

*Also by Allan Massie, and
available from Sceptre Books:*

AUGUSTUS
A QUESTION OF LOYALTIES

Allan Massie

TIBERIUS

The Memoirs of the Emperor

First published in Great Britain in 1990 by Hodder and Stoughton Ltd.

Sceptre edition 1992

Sceptre is an imprint of Hodder and Stoughton Paperbacks, a division of Hodder and Stoughton Ltd.

Printed and bound in Great Britain for Hodder and Stoughton Paperbacks, a division of Hodder and Stoughton Ltd, Mill Road, Dunton Green, Sevenoaks, Kent TN13 2YA. (Editorial Office: 47 Bedford Square, London WC1B 3DP) by Clays Ltd, St Ives plc. Photoset by Rowland Phototypesetting Ltd, Bury St Edmunds, Suffolk.

British Library C.I.P.

Massie, Allan
 Tiberius.
 I. Title
 823.914[F]

ISBN 0-340-56005-3

For Alison
again; of course; for ever

CHRONOLOGY

BC

63   Birth of Augustus.

49   Civil war, Caesar becomes dictator.

46   Caesar dictator and consul (second and third time respectively).

44   Caesar assassinated.

43   First triumvirate of Augustus, Antony and Lepidus established.

42   Birth of Tiberius. Brutus and Cassius commit suicide after defeat at Philippi.

41   Perusine war. Antony in Asia Minor, meets Cleopatra.

40   Agreement at Brundisium partitions Roman world. Antony marries Augustus' sister, Octavia.

39   Tiberius' family returns to Rome after expulsion for having supported Antony. Augustus makes peace at Misenum with Antony and Sextus Pompeius.

38   Augustus marries Livia.

37   Antony marries Cleopatra.

36   Tribunician power granted to Augustus. Sextus defeated. Lepidus ceases to be triumvir.

32   Antony divorces Octavia.

31   Augustus defeats Antony at Actium.

30   Suicide of Antony and Cleopatra.

29   Augustus' triple Triumph – consolidates power.

27   Augustus receives *imperium* for ten years. Tiberius taken to Gaul where he first learns of military matters. Augustus in Gaul and Spain until 25.

25   Tiberius marries Agrippa's daughter Vipsania; Marcellus marries Augustus' daughter, Julia.

23	Augustus ill. Conspiracy of Caepio and Murena, Tiberius prosecutes. Constitutional resettlement. Augustus resigns consulship and receives full tribunician powers. Death of Marcellus. Agrippa sent to East.
21	Agrippa marries Julia.
20	Tiberius, first military command – great acclaim in Parthian campaign where he returns standards. Enters Armenia and crowns Tigranes.
18	Augustus' *imperium* renewed for five years. Agrippa coregent with *maius imperium* and *tribunicia potestas*.
17	Augustus adopts Gaius and Lucius, his grandsons.
15	Tiberius and Drusus defeat Raeti and Vindelici and reach Danube.
13	Augustus' *imperium* renewed for five years. Tiberius becomes consul.
12	Augustus becomes Pontifex Maximus. Agrippa dies. Tiberius in Pannonia. Drusus campaigns in Britain and Germany.
11	Tiberius compelled to divorce Vipsania and to marry Julia.
9	Death of Drusus near the Elbe. Tiberius takes fighting commands away from Rome.
8	Tiberius in Germany.
6	Tiberius given *tribunicia potestas* for five years. He retires to Rhodes.
5	Augustus' twelfth consulship. Gaius introduced to public life.
2	Augustus' thirteenth consulship. Julia disgraced and exiled.

AD

2	Tiberius returns to Rome from Rhodes. Death of Lucius.
4	Death of Gaius in Lycia. Augustus adopts Tiberius who receives *tribunicia potestas* for ten years. Tiberius adopts Germanicus and goes to German front.
5	Tiberius advances to Elbe.
6	Pannonian revolt begins, later suppressed by Tiberius.

9   Revolt in Dalmatia. Varus loses three legions in Germany.

12   Tiberius has total success in Germany.

13   Augustus' *imperium* renewed for ten years. Tiberius receives *tribunicia potestas* for ten years and proconsular *imperium* co-ordinate with that of Augustus.

14   Death of Augustus. Accession of Tiberius. Sejanus made Praetorian Prefect. Tiberius' son Drusus sent to crush mutiny in Pannonia. Germanicus crosses Rhine.

15   Germanicus makes further inroads into Germany.

16   Germanicus recalled after further invasion of Germany.

17   Triumph of Germanicus. Piso made legate of Syria.

18   Tiberius made consul for the third time, now with Germanicus, who goes to Egypt.

19   Death of Germanicus.

20   Trial and suicide of Piso.

21   Tiberius consul for fourth time, this time with his son Drusus. Tiberius retires to Campania. Revolts in Gaul; trouble in Thrace.

22   Drusus granted tribunician power.

23   Death of Drusus.

24–6 Trouble quelled in Africa and Thrace.

27   Tiberius withdraws to Capri. Sejanus' power increases.

29   Death of Livia. Banishment of Agrippina the Elder. Tiberius' health deteriorates. Rumours of monstrous acts engineered by him begin to circulate.

31   Tiberius becomes consul for the fifth time, now with Sejanus. Gaius (Caligula) receives *toga virilis*. Macro appointed Praetorian Prefect. Death of Sejanus under Tiberius' orders, with the aid of Macro. Senate complies.

33   Death of Agrippina on Pandateria. Caligula becomes a quaestor. Financial difficulties in Rome.

36   Tiberius' reputation worsens: he is accused of numerous murders.

37   Tiberius takes ill and Caligula is named his successor, supported by the Praetorian Guard. Tiberius recovers, panic ensues but he is smothered by Macro, the Praetorian.

LIST OF PRINCIPAL CHARACTERS

TIBERIUS	born Tiberius Julius Caesar Germanicus

His family and their relation to him

AUGUSTUS	stepfather and adoptive father
LIVIA	mother and wife of Augustus
DRUSUS	brother
VIPSANIA	first wife and daughter of Agrippa
JULIA	second wife and daughter of Augustus
GERMANICUS	nephew and adopted son, husband of Agrippina the Elder and father of Caligula
AGRIPPINA THE ELDER	stepdaughter, daughter of Agrippa and Julia, wife of Germanicus, mother of Caligula
CALIGULA	great-nephew and successor to Tiberius
ANTONIA	sister-in-law, wife of Drusus and daughter of Mark Antony and Augustus' sister Octavia
AGRIPPA	father-in-law, Augustus' greatest general and father of Gaius and Lucius, Augustus' grandchildren and also adopted sons, stepsons to Tiberius
DRUSUS	son by Vipsania
(JULIA) LIVILLA	daughter-in-law, wife of Drusus and daughter of Antonia and the elder Drusus, brother of Tiberius, and thus also his niece
DRUSUS AND NERO	great-nephews, sons of Germanicus and Agrippina, brothers to Caligula and Agrippina the Younger
TIBERIUS GEMELLUS AND LIVIA JULIA	grandchildren, children of Drusus and Julia Livilla. Livia Julia was married to Nero, son of Germanicus

OTHER CHARACTERS

(GAIUS) JULIUS CAESAR
Roman patrician, general and statesman. Sole dictator after his defeat of Pompey. Uncle and adoptive father to Augustus.

OCTAVIA
Augustus' sister, married to Mark Antony. Mother of Marcellus.

MARCUS ANTONIUS (MARK ANTONY)
Supporter of Caesar and consul with him in 44 BC. Joined Lepidus and Octavian (Augustus) to form a triumvirate and controlled the forces of the eastern empire. He was defeated at the battle of Actium and committed suicide in Egypt.

MARCELLUS
Augustus' nephew, later son-in-law after marriage to Julia. Octavia's son by her marriage to Gaius Marcellus, favourite of Augustus.

AGRIPPA POSTUMUS
Augustus' grandson and brother of Gaius and Lucius. Julia's son by Agrippa.

ANTONIUS MUSA
a doctor.

TERENTIUS VARRO MURENA
a consul, prosecuted by Tiberius for his conspiracy against Augustus.

FANNIUS CAEPIO
co-conspirator with Murena.

GNAEUS CALPURNIUS PISO
a consul, later governor of Syria, and one of Tiberius' closest friends until Germanicus' death when Piso was accused of poisoning him.

IULLUS ANTONIUS
SEMPRONIUS GRACCHUS   young noblemen and lovers of Julia.
MARCUS FRISO
TIMOTHEUS   a catamite and secret agent.
TITUS LIVIUS (LIVY)   Roman writer and historian.
PUBLIUS VERGILIUS MARO   Roman poet and mentor to Augustus.
  (VERGIL)
P. OVIDIUS NASO (OVID)   Roman poet, exiled for immorality.
SEGESTES   German prince "captured" by
                      Tiberius and later cared for by him
                      and brought to Rome.
SIGISMOND   German prince, captured by Romans
                      and saved from death in gladiatorial
                      combat by Tiberius who installed him
                      in his household. Cared for Tiberius
                      until the emperor's death.
LUCIUS AELIDS SEJANUS son of Lucius Seius Strabo, ex-head
                      of Praetorian Guard and Proconsul of
                      Egypt. Protégé of Tiberius, Prae-
                      torian Prefect, soldier and informant,
                      eventually the victim of a coup engin-
                      eered by Tiberius.
MACRO   Praetorian Prefect, in succession to
                      Sejanus.

CONTENTS

INTRODUCTION

by way of Disclaimer

I don't know when I have undertaken anything with more hesitation than this preface, which my publishers have demanded of me. They have done so because they don't wish, as they put it, "to be associated with anything which may turn out to be a fraud without making their doubts as to the authenticity of the publication known".

Fair enough, of course; but where does it leave me, for even the strongest disclaimer is unlikely to allay the reader's doubts? After all, if the book itself is not what it purports to be, why should the introduction be believed?

And yet I see why they want it. That is the irritating thing. It's the coincidence as much as anything which disturbs them.

Let me explain then, as far as I can.

In 1984 the autobiography of the Emperor Augustus was discovered in the Macedonian monastery of SS Cyril and Methodius (not St Cyril Methodius as erroneously stated by Professor Aeneas Fraser-Graham in his introduction to my English version of the book, an error which has persisted obstinately, despite my appeals, in British, American, French, Italian, German and, as far as I can determine squinting at uncut pages, Danish editions).

This autobiography, lost since antiquity, but attested to by Suetonius and other writers, was entrusted to me to translate. Mine was to be a popular edition published in advance of the great scholarly annotated edition which was being prepared and is still, as far as I know, being prepared, and indeed looks likely to remain in that state of preparation for a long time to come. That is no concern of mine however.

My translation attracted gratifying notice on the whole, also, of course, the attention of the odd lunatic; one such, for example, informing me that page 121 of the American edition disclosed the secrets of the Great Pyramid, which is surely unlikely.

Then, eighteen months ago, when I was visiting Naples at the invitation (as I supposed, though this was in fact an error on my part) of the British Council, I was accosted in the Galleria Umberto by a stout middle-aged man in a dingy suit. He was clutching a black book under his left arm. The way he held it drew my attention to a hole in the elbow of his jacket. He addressed me by name, according me, in the Italian fashion, a doctorate to which I am not entitled, owing (if I may digress) to a difference of opinion with the authorities of Trinity College, Cambridge in 1960.

Then he introduced himself to me as Count Alessandro di Caltagirone, a name the significance of which I did not immediately grasp. He told me he had been greatly impressed by my translation of the memoirs of Augustus, though he understood, of course, that they were not authentic.

"Why should you think that?" I said.

"That is no question to put to me," he replied, and called for a brandy and soda at my expense.

"Unlike what I can offer you," he continued.

"And what is that?"

"The authentic memoirs of the Emperor Tiberius," he replied.

"Come," I said, "this is too much of a coincidence . . ."

"On the contrary, it is only so much of a coincidence because it was written that it should so be . . ."

"Written?" I said.

"In your horoscope, which I cast myself, more than two hundred years ago."

By now, as you may imagine, I concluded that I was dealing with a madman, and tried to remove myself as inconspicuously as possible. But he would not be shaken off. He positively attached himself to my person, and, to cut a long story short, we eventually came to an agreement, the exact terms of which I am not at liberty to divulge. The long and short of it was that I came into possession of the Latin manuscript which I have now translated and present to you here.

I am not going to pronounce on its authenticity: that is for the reader to determine. If it convinces him or her, that is a testimony such as no scholar can gainsay. (And my own faith in scholarship has, I confess, been shaken in recent years. Scholars are like other people: they believe what it suits them to believe and then find reasons for doing so.)

But there are certain reservations which, to protect my good name, I wish to make.

First, the manuscript from which I worked is probably the only one in existence and is written on paper which dates only from the eighteenth century.

Second, Count Alessandro di Caltagirone is, I have gathered, a man with a dubious reputation. For one thing, this is certainly not his name, and it is doubtful if he is really a count. More alert readers will have made at once a connection which escaped me for some months. Caltagirone was the name of the monastery where Giuseppe Balsamo, better known as Count Alessandro di Cagliostro, was educated from 1760–69. Cagliostro of course – physician, philosopher, alchemist and necromancer – claimed to possess "the elixir of eternal youth", a phrase that has dropped also from my friend Caltagirone's lips, though I am bound to add that his appearance contradicts it.

When I asked him about the provenance of the manuscript, he was first evasive, then said he could certainly account for its whereabouts since 1770. What is one to make of that?

Even a cursory reading of the memoirs must inspire the critic with doubts. There are moments when Tiberius appears to have the sensibility which one associates with the eighteenth-century Enlightenment rather than with Ancient Rome. There is, too, a curious lack of detail about daily life in imperial Rome, and an absence of that awareness of religion which, despite other indications to the contrary, formed such an integral part of the superstitious Roman character. Such references as there are to this central experience of the Roman spirit are perfunctory, as if the author of the manuscript found the whole business a bore to which he nevertheless paid occasional heed. If one remembers that the eighteenth century saw the first revulsion from Tacitus, the traducer of Tiberius, a revulsion expressed, for instance, by both Voltaire and Napoleon, then it seems plausible to suggest that what we have here is an "Anti-Tacitus" composed by some mischievous intellectual of that time for his own diversion.

On the other hand, if one accepts the Caltagirone–Cagliostro identification (which I am loth to do), then it may contain some occult message which I have failed to decipher.

That is indeed a possibility, but if there be such a message, then it is likely to be understood only by the surviving lodges of Egyptian Freemasons which were founded by Cagliostro himself. There is one in Palermo, another in Naples itself, a third in St Petersburg (inactive, I am told) and a fourth, which is also the largest and most vocal, in Akron, Ohio. Yet even the Akron lodge has failed to respond to my appeals for help.

A week after Caltagirone pressed the manuscript upon me, his death was announced on the front page of *Il Mattino*, the principal Neapolitan daily. He was described in the frank manner of the Italian press as "a notorious swindler".

So I was left with the manuscript, and, intrigued, set to work on it.

Further discrepancies appeared, and it was soon clear to me that, whatever its provenance, whatever its element of authenticity, the memoirs had been the work of more than one hand, and at different periods. I became convinced that even the eighteenth-century paper was a blind or false trail or red herring. It seemed strange, for instance, that on page 187 of the manuscript Tiberius should be quoting Nietzsche. This, together with the tone of some passages, made me wonder whether a gloss had been put on the original (if it existed) by some resident of Capri in, perhaps, the first decade of this century. And this suspicion was intensified when my all-seeing agent, Giles Gordon, remarked that one incident seemed to be drawn from *The Story of San Michele* by Axel Munthe.

As against this, the coincidence is explicable if one remembers that the figure who appears to Munthe also claims to have appeared centuries previously to none other than Tiberius. It has always been assumed that Munthe invented this *genius loci*; but what, it occurred to me, if he had not? Might not such a supposition confirm the authenticity of the memoirs?

Then there is another story – about Sirens – which recalls one by Giuseppe di Lampedusa. That would place the concoction of the memoirs unacceptably late, I thought; besides, the Mediterranean lands are rich in Siren stories, and it is known that Tiberius took a particular interest in the myth. And then there is the postscript, which is decidedly rum, though it purports to account for the survival of the original memoirs in manuscript.

Ultimately I remain undecided. I do not assert that these are the memoirs of Tiberius, or not unequivocally so. I think the bare bones of the narrative may be authentic, but that subsequent versions have refined, expanded and glossed them.

And I find myself asking whether it matters. What we have here, persuasively and movingly in my opinion – else I should not have put myself to the labour of translating the work – is a remarkable portrait of one of the greatest, and certainly the unhappiest, of Roman emperors. In the end, I say to myself, fiction – if this is fiction – may offer truths to which neither biography nor even autobiography can aspire. Who knows himself or another man as thoroughly as the artist may imagine a life? Whose identity is fixed? A great and malignant artist, Tacitus, pinned a terrible portrait of Tiberius on the wall of history. If another hand has been moved to amend that picture, so be it. It was Napoleon, with his uncanny penetration of men's motives, who dismissed the great historian as *le poète*; yet Tacitus' lying truth held sway for centuries. The author of this autobiography, whoever he may be, is, I would claim, a poet himself at moments, and I trust that his version of the story, a version which is certainly the case for the defence, will work its influence also. Tiberius has waited long for justice; perhaps it is time that the deceptive bargain offered him by the divine boy in the garden, who promised the aged emperor peace of mind in exchange for the sacrifice of his reputation, should be expunged.

So I do not care whether these memoirs are authentic or not. They convince me that they contain important verities. *Basta!*

I had written this and left it to rest a week or two, to see if there was anything I wished to add.

No sooner had I concluded that I was satisfied, than I received a telephone call.

I recognised the voice at once. It was the Count. He reminded me of a bargain we had not made: that he should receive seventy-five per cent of translation rights, and twenty per cent of my English royalties. When I told him I had no memory of this, and had anyway thought him dead, he laughed.

"I have given Tiberius to drink of my elixir," he said. "Why should you suppose that either he or I can die?"

I had no answer to that. He promises to appear at the publication party. We shall see.

Allan Massie

PART ONE

PART ONE

ONE

That I relish dryness is not strange: I have campaigned too many years in the rains of the Rhine and Danube valleys. I have marched miles, ankle-deep, through mud, and slept in tents soaked through by morning. Yet my relish for what is dry is of another nature: I detest sentiment or displays of feeling; I detest acting. I detest self-indulgence, and that emotion in which one eye does not weep but observes the effect of tears on those who watch.

I take pleasure in language which is precise, hard and cruel.

This has made me a difficult and uncomfortable person. My presence makes my stepfather, the Princeps, uneasy. I have known this since I was a youth. For years I regretted it, for I sought his approval, even perhaps his love. Then I realised I could never have either of these: he responded to the false spontaneous charm of Marcellus, as he does now to that of his grandsons, Gaius and Lucius, who are also my stepsons.

Nothing has been easy for me, and it would not be surprising if I were to relapse into self-pity. It is a temptation, because my merits have ever been unjustly disregarded on account of my lack of charm. I have never been able to dispel clouds with a smile and a jest, and it is natural if I have experienced twinges of envy when I see my inferiors able to do so. Yet I am kept from self-pity by my pride. This is inherited. It is Claudian pride.

Augustus has always been rendered uneasy on account of the indignity of his birth. It is only by the accident of marriage that he has had a career; the accident of two marriages, I should say, for there can be no question that his own marriage to my mother smoothed his path to power.

It was, however, the marriage of his grandfather, M. Atius Balbus, to Julia, the sister of Gaius Julius Caesar, the future dictator, which raised his family from an obscure provincial station. The Princeps' own father was the first member of the family to enter the Senate. Contrast that with my heredity.

I shall not boast of the Claudian *gens*: our achievements glitter on every page of the Republic's history.

Mark Antony – a liar of course – used to delight in mocking my stepfather's antecedents. He would claim that the great-grandfather of his colleague in the triumvirate had been a freed-man and rope-maker, and his grandfather a dishonest money-changer. It is not necessary to believe such charges to understand why Augustus' attitude to the old aristocracy of Rome has been ambiguous: he is both resentful and dazzled.

I, being a Claudian, judge these things better. I know the worthlessness of my fellow nobles. I recognise that their deca-dence has made them unfit to govern, and so destroyed Liberty in Rome. Though the Roman Empire now extends over the whole civilised world to the limits of the Parthian Empire in the East, our great days are behind us; we have been compelled to acquiesce in the suppression of Liberty.

I write this in retreat in Rhodes, in the tranquillity of my villa overlooking the sea. My life is now devoted to the study of philosophy and mathematics, and to pondering the nature of experience. Accordingly it is not surprising that I should think to write my autobiography. There is good precedent for this, and any man of enquiring intelligence must frequently stand amazed before the spectacle of his own life and wish to make sense of it.

I am forty-two years old. My public life is ended through cir-cumstances and my own desire. I have been humiliated in my private life. I am disgraced through no fault of my own, rather on account of the schemes of others and my own indifference. I may, if the Gods will it, have as long to live again, though nightly I pray otherwise. Even from this distance I cannot contemplate the shipwreck of old age with equanimity.

*   *   *

My father was Tiberius Claudius Nero, dead now for more than thirty years. (I was nine when he died. They made me deliver his funeral oration. More of that later, if I can bring myself to write it.) My mother, who still lives, is Livia Drusilla. She was seduced by the triumvir, Caesar Octavianus, who is now styled Augustus. He was not deterred by the fact that she was pregnant. My brother, Drusus, was born three days after their marriage. He knew no father but Augustus, and our real father refused to receive him: he liked to pretend that Drusus was not his son. This was nonsense. Perhaps it salved his pride.

I used to go to stay with him on the estate in the Sabine Hills to which he had retired. I wish I could claim vivid memories. But I have few, except of meals. He comforted himself with gluttony; his dinner lasted the whole afternoon. He liked me, even when I was only six or seven, to drink wine with him.

"Don't water it," he said, "it delays the effect . . ."

As the sun set he would embark on long monologues, to which I scarcely listened and which I could not anyhow have understood.

He was an unlucky man, of poor judgment and some sense of honour. Fortune having dishonoured him, he sought refuge from the regrets which assailed him in eating and drinking. As the years have slipped away, I have come to understand him; and to sympathise.

"Why prolong life save to prolong pleasure?" he would sigh, raising a cup of wine; and a tear would trickle down his fat cheek.

A few years ago my father started to appear in my dreams. I would see him standing on a promontory looking out to sea. He was watching for a sail. I gazed at the blue water too, but did not dare to approach him. Then the sun was darkened, as if in an eclipse, and when light returned my father had vanished; in his place stood a white cockerel bleeding from the neck. This dream came to me, in identical form, perhaps seven times. At last I consulted Thrasyllus but even he, the most acute interpreter of dreams, was unable to supply an explanation.

Or perhaps dared not. In my position few, even among
trusted friends, have the courage to speak their minds.

Drusus, as I say, was never allowed to visit our father. Indeed
I do not think he ever thought of him, except when I compelled
the subject. But then he had no memories, and Drusus was
never introspective. I, on the other hand, can recall my father
on his knees clutching my mother's ankles and sobbing out his
love for her. She disengaged her legs: he fell prostrate on
marble; and I began to howl. I was three at the time.

I adored my mother for her beauty, and for being herself. She
would sing me to sleep with honied voice; the touch of her
fingers on my eyelids fell like rose petals. She would tell me
stories of my ancestors and of the gods, of Troy and of Orpheus,
and the wanderings of my forefather Aeneas. At the age of five
I wept for Dido, Queen of Carthage, and she said:
   "You are wrong to weep. Aeneas was fulfilling his destiny."
   "Is destiny so grim, Mama?"
   "Go to sleep, child."

Drusus would clamber all over our stepfather who would kiss
him and throw him in the air and laugh at his whoops. But I
kept my distance. My love was for Mama, whose favourite I
knew myself to be. That was important to me, and it confirmed
me in what may have been an instinctive conviction that the
world is ignorant of justice: for I knew Drusus to have a charm
that I lacked, and, moreover, I recognised in him a sunny virtue
which was absent from my character. His temper was benign.
Nothing alarmed him. He was always truthful and generous.
Even as a baby he would surrender a cherished toy with a happy
smile. But I was greedy, and untruthful, and afraid of the dark
places and of night. (Yet I also welcomed the night, and never
went reluctant to bed, because I knew that bedtime promised
me my mother's undivided attention, promised me stories, and
the cool touch of her sweet-smelling hand; I would lie waiting
for sleep in a world from which all but the two of us were
banished . . .)

Because I was her favourite she chastised me. She whipped me for my transgressions till I was within a few years of assuming the *toga virilis*. I recognised in her lashes, which bit with stinging joy into my flesh, the strange expression of her love: each blow sang out that I should be her creature, hers alone. We were joined together in a savage rite: Claudian pride flayed Claudian pride, and called for a cry of mercy, which never came. And then, afterwards, how sweet and honied the reconciliation!

We were joined in passion, all the more intense because we are both shy of speech. In public she sometimes liked to mock me; as I grew older she would upbraid me for a great clumsy oaf. We never referred to such outbursts when we were alone. I knew them to be provoked by the intensity of her love, which she resented. It annoyed her, no, infuriated her, to know how much she cared.

When I was a child she mocked and whipped me out of my stammer. "It makes you seem a dolt," she said. "Do you want the world to take you for a fool?" So, by willpower, I overcame my infirmity.

Her moods were as quick-changing as mountain weather. Her inconsistency was wild enchantment. When she smiled the world was spring sunshine; but her frowns darkened any company. Consequently we were engaged in endless warfare. I found her entrancing, but I declined to submit to her black moods. Yet it was in my reaction to Livia that I came to sense my superiority to my stepfather: he was afraid of her; I was not.

Of course he loved her, depended on her, could not – as he often exclaimed – imagine life without her. Very good, I don't dispute it. Yet he was always less in her presence, more timid, more circumspect, dreading that she should turn cold and refuse to speak to him. That was all Livia has ever had to do to bring Augustus to heel: refuse to speak to him. I, on the other hand, know myself her equal; and, in fact, since I grew up, Livia has been a little in awe of me.

*   *   *

I have run ahead of myself, ahead of my story. Yet it is hard to see how autobiography can avoid being discursive. Everything one recalls promotes reflection. I am writing of people without whom my life is unimaginable.

Perhaps it will be easier to keep to the point when I get beyond childhood. For, looking back on childhood, I see one thing clearly: there is no narrative there. Childhood is a state, not a story. Let me try to reveal my childhood in four distinct episodes therefore.

I was, as I said, nine when my father died. Naturally I did not weep.

"You are head of the family now," Livia said.

"What do I have to do, mama?"

"First, it will be your duty to pronounce your father's funeral oration . . ."

I don't know who wrote it, but I daresay its author made the best he could of it. These people have a certain professional pride after all. But there was not much to say about the poor man, and it was raining, a November day of thick cloud that obscured the houses on the Palatine Hill. I rehearsed the speech so well that I can remember parts of it to this day.

My father was a victim. I see that now, though in my adolescence I came to think harshly of him as a weakling and failure. His public history was undistinguished. He fought with Julius Caesar in the war against Pompey and commanded the dictator's fleet at Alexandria. But this association disgusted him, for he saw that Julius was an enemy of the traditional liberties of the Roman people. Too tender-hearted to join the conspiracy of the Ides of March and perhaps inhibited by his consciousness of what he had himself received from the dictator, he nevertheless rejoiced at its success. In the Senate he proposed that the Liberators be publicly rewarded. That suggestion was enough for him to earn my stepfather's undying hatred; not, you understand, that Augustus (as it is convenient to call him, though he had not yet been accorded that honorific title) had any affection for Julius himself; but because he knew it was expedient that he should pay public honour to his name. Otherwise, why should Caesar's old soldiers fight for him?

Reluctant to leave Italy, where he feared the confiscation of his estates, convinced anyway that the Liberators could never withstand the Caesarean forces, my father naturally adhered to Antony rather than to Augustus. Besides, he was an old friend – and personal loyalty meant much to him – of the younger Antony, Lucius, who had inveigled him into the campaign that was to end in the terrible siege of Perugia. He never forgot the rigours of that siege, and even the mention of Mark Antony's wife, the loathsome Fulvia, would make him shudder, right up to his death. Desperate now, he blundered again, joining himself with Sextus Pompeius, the unprincipled son of a dubiously great father. He was soon disillusioned, and rejoined Antony. Then came the Peace of Misenum. During the negotiations that led up to it, Augustus encountered Livia, fell in love with her, and carried her off.

How could such a life be eulogised? Only in empty, high-sounding phrases, obviously, with much talk of private virtues (which indeed the poor man did not lack) and with noble, not unveracious, platitudes about the malignity of fortune. These platitudes had nevertheless to be modified, since they should not in any wise reflect upon the victor and favourite of fortune, Augustus, his successor as Livia's husband, who would be standing on the speaker's right hand.

Accordingly, my introduction to the art of public oratory was to spout disingenuous rhetoric.

Cant.

I have distrusted rhetoric ever since, even while acknowledging that its mastery is a necessary part of education.

Four years later, after Actium, my stepfather Augustus prepared to celebrate the triumph granted him by the Senate and the Roman people in honour of his achievements in the war against Egypt. There was cant here too, for no one was allowed to remind us that Roman citizens had been the chief victims of his wars. Instead all attention was concentrated on Egypt.

"Will Cleopatra walk in chains, Mama?"

"What do you children know of Cleopatra?"

"That she'th a bad woman who seduteth Romans," Julia said.

"That's no way for a little girl to talk. Do you want your mouth washed out with soap?"

"It'th what I heard Uncle Marcuth Agrippa thay."

She gave a little pout, holding strawberry-pink lips open and thrust forward. I was twelve then, so Julia must have been ten. But she already knew – had always known as if by nature – how to act, tease and provoke. Augustus at that stage liked the three of us to behave as if we were indeed brothers and sister – Julia is of course the child of his second marriage to the appalling Scribonia, one of the few women I have ever met who is as disagreeable and generally awful as the reputation which precedes her. Livia was always less certain that we should be encouraged to think of ourselves as siblings.

"What does seduteth mean?" Drusus asked.

"It's seduces," I said. "Julia only says seduteth because she's lost a front tooth. Anyway, Julia, Marcus Agrippa isn't really our uncle, you know. He can't be because he's a plebeian."

"Quite so," Livia said, and changed the subject.

Augustus liked us, however, to speak of Agrippa as our uncle; he was always eager that his supporters should feel they were a family; later, when Livia wasn't about, he upbraided me for the way I had spoken of his friend.

"If you grow up to be half the man Agrippa is," he said, "you'll be twice the man your own father was. And don't speak of plebeians in that silly way. If it weren't for plebeian blood, Rome wouldn't have an empire . . ."

He was right of course, and I came to appreciate Agrippa later, but then I could only think that my stepfather himself was essentially plebeian. I took his irritation as further evidence of his inferiority to the Claudians and of his lack of true nobility.

He had his revenge in the arrangements of his triumph. His nephew Marcellus was granted the honour of riding on the leading trace-horse, while I was relegated to an inferior position.

Cleopatra did not of course walk in chains, as she deserved to do. She had escaped him, by means of the now famous asp.

Two years later Augustus declared that he had restored the Republic. (I shall treat of this more fully, and philosophically, at a more appropriate stage of my history.) Marcellus was ecstatic.

"There never was such a thing," he said, again and again. "Such a surrender of power."

"I don't understand why Daddy should choose to give up power," Julia said. "It seems strange to me, after fighting so long to win it." She had quite lost her lisp, you observe.

"Yes," I said, "very strange."

I look up from the terrace on which I am writing this, and gaze over the evening sea and it is as if I can see reflected there our childish faces, as we strove with the dawning of our political understanding. I see Marcellus, six months older than I – and how much younger? – candid, beautiful, insipid. He reclines on a couch, in languid attitude that cannot disguise his animal energy, and yet looks, as always, as if he has fallen into a pose to delight a sculptor. I see Julia, the childish gold of her hair already darkening to that colour for which I have never found the right epithet, her blue eyes set rather far apart and moist at the edges, her lips always a little open. (Livia used to say she had breathing difficulties but I have always thought that the habit indicated her greed for experience.) And myself? When I try to envisage myself a shadow falls, and my face withdraws into the dark.

So we argued the matter and I have forgotten what we said, but the impression of that evening remains warm. We could hear the din and bustle rise from the forum below. Julia was eating a peach, and the juice trickled down her chin, to be retrieved by that quick, pointed tongue. Marcellus strove to convince us of Augustus' nobility and generosity in handing the Republic back to the Roman people, and Julia laughed and said,

"Daddy's not noble, he's clever, he's much too clever to do that. I'm only a girl and my interest in these political affairs is strictly limited, but I know perfectly well that you don't fight

civil wars for fifteen years in order to give the dice back to your
enemies and tell them to play the game again in their own way.
If you take things at face value, Marcellus, you're a fool. Of
course, you are a fool. I'd forgotten that."

She was quite right. Marcellus was a fool, a beautiful fool certainly, but all the more fool for that, because he was eaten up
with self-love. "He's just like Narcissus, or Hyacinthus, isn't
he?" Julia once said to me. "One of these silly Greek boys who
fell in love with their own beauty." So from that day we called
him The Hyacinth.

"You're different," she said to me, and put her arms round
my neck. "You sit there like a wise man and say nothing.
Nobody knows what you think, do they, Tiberius? I think that's
clever."

And she kissed me. It wasn't a child's kiss. Or a sister's. It
lingered on my lips.

But Augustus did not think Marcellus a fool. He thought him
a golden youth and adored him. I believe Livia tried to warn
him that he was in danger of making an ass of himself, but he
was infatuated with the boy. Of course Marcellus was the son
of his sister Octavia, whom he had always thought perfect and
who now aroused feelings of guilt in him because he had compelled her to marry Mark Antony for political reasons; and the
boy's father, C. Claudius Marcellus, had been one of his earliest
supporters. (The Claudii Marcelli were, of course, cousins of
mine.) But this wasn't the real reason for the enthralment in
which Augustus was held by his nephew; and, despite the
sneers of Roman gossip, it wasn't a vicious attachment either.
The truth is that in Marcellus Augustus saw what he longed to
be, and knew, of course, that he couldn't: a natural aristocrat,
spontaneous, generous, idealistic; impulsive, a being born to be
adored. His stupid love for Marcellus represented his surrender
to a suppressed part of his character; it represented the wish
that life is not what it is but an idyll.

He took us on campaign in Gaul when we were both very
young. By this time – though I wasn't yet aware of it – he had
already decided that Marcellus and Julia should marry. In that

way he would, he fondly thought, continue to possess the two
people the immature side of his nature most adored. (It was a
different, and more worthy, side that loved Livia.) He was
asking for the impossible of course, forgetting that neither could
remain eighteen.

He loved to question us in the evening, to extract our views
on life, and then try to correct them; he has always been a
natural teacher. He told us that the business of government
was service. "The only satisfaction," he said, "is the work itself.
The only reward, the ability to continue the work. It is our task
to bring law and civilisation to the barbarians. The true heroes
of our empire are the countless administrators whom history
will never know . . ."

I was fascinated. This was a different Augustus I was seeing.
I realised for the first time how my mother diminished him; in
her presence he would never have dared speak as if he had
authority. Men, I said to myself, become fully themselves when
they are away from women: in the camp, at their office, feeling
responsible for action, for decisions which determine life and
death. But Marcellus was bored. He interrupted:

"Caesar invaded the island of Britain, didn't he?"

If I had interrupted in such a manner which showed that I
had paid no attention to what he had been saying, he would
have reproved me. But he beamed at Marcellus and laughed:

"You know he did. You've read his memoirs, haven't
you . . . ?"

Marcellus groaned.

"Not much of them. He's awfully dull, you know."

"I can see how you might think so," he stretched over and
rumpled my cousin's hair. "Is that your opinion too?" he asked.

"He's admirably lucid," I said, "and I've no experience of
course, but I find his descriptions of battles very convincing.
Except for one thing. He's always the hero. Was he really like
that, sir?"

He smiled at us, as if thinking. I nibbled a radish. Marcellus
took a swig of wine. Then, before Augustus could speak, he
said:

"I do like the sound of Britain, there are pearls there and

the warriors paint themselves blue. They must look funny, but despite that, it seems they can fight a bit. Why don't we carry on Caesar's work and conquer the island?"

"What do you think, Tiberius . . . ?"

I hesitated, to show that my opinion was well considered. But I had no doubt:

"It seems to me that we have enough trouble with the empire as it is. I think it may be big enough. Wouldn't we be best to consolidate before we bite off any more . . . ?"

And what was Marcellus' reaction to this good sense?

He called me an old woman. If we'd been alone I might have said that it was better to talk like an old woman than a silly girl, but in the circumstances I only smiled.

To my surprise, Augustus agreed with me.

"Caesar was an adventurer," he said. "I'm not. The conquest of Britain would be worthless, for the island is covered in fog and there's little evidence that the pearl fisheries are of much value . . ."

Marcellus sighed. "It would be such an adventure," and Augustus laughed and rumpled his hair again.

TWO

Augustus was from the first, by nature, a dynast. The word is Greek and means a man of power. It was on account of his single-minded pursuit of power that he triumphed in the civil wars; it was that pursuit which forced the war against Antony and Cleopatra on the Roman people. Yet he was never even a competent soldier. He owed his victories to Marcus Agrippa, and to the goddess Fortune.

I didn't appreciate Agrippa till he became my father-in-law. I can't reproach myself for failing to do so. It would have been more remarkable if I had understood his genius, for he was everything I distrusted by nature: rough, uncouth, with a strong provincial accent, and given to laughing loudly at his own (poor) jokes. He had that taste for bawdy stories which is such a useful means of creating good-feeling between men; it is my ill-fortune that I am fastidious and detest such ribaldry.

Augustus relied on him utterly. They were complementary. Neither would have been capable of the other's achievement. Nevertheless, as children, we used to mock him, Julia especially. I didn't realise then that Augustus had already arranged that I should marry Agrippa's daughter, Vipsania. I would have been extremely offended, for I found her insipid.

Certain scenes of youth stand out with the clarity of wall-paintings. A summer evening in the gardens of a villa overlooking the sea, Naples some twenty miles distant. I am reading Homer and listening to a nightingale, for it is almost too dark to read the words. A hand is slipped across my eyes from the rear. I have heard no one approaching. The hand is cool and dry.

"Julia," I say, without moving, and feel the fingers move down to stroke my cheek.

"I wish you weren't always reading. I don't know what you see in books."

"They tell us," I say, "how life . . ."

"Now, darling," she says, "don't be pompous . . ."

Even at that age – what, thirteen? – when most of us are shy and awkwardly aware of ourselves, Julia could employ the word "darling" as naturally as a child or a lover.

But she was perturbed that summer, that evening.

"Put your book away," she said. "I want to speak to you."

"Well, it's too dark to read . . ."

"Please be serious."

"What is this? You ask me to be serious?"

"I've got some news. Daddy says he wants me to marry The Hyacinth."

"Congratulations."

"Don't be silly."

"I'm serious. Marcellus is going to win great glory. Your father will see to that . . ."

"That's what I mean. I should prefer my husband to be a man who will win glory for himself. Or perhaps not? What is glory after all?"

"But Marcellus is charming also," I said. "Everyone agrees on that."

"Oh yes," she said, "but I don't want him . . ."

She leaned forward, kissed me on the lips, and ran away, laughing.

She would laugh – at intervals – all through her marriage to Marcellus, and he took it as a tribute to his charms. But laughter in Julia was not necessarily a sign of happiness.

As it happened, my mother also was opposed to the marriage. She made her view clear, but this was one of the few battles with Augustus which she lost.

"He was besotted with the boy," she told me later. "It blinded his judgment and made him obstinate as a pig."

Curiously, Marcellus' own mother, Augustus' sister, Octavia,

also disapproved of the marriage. She feared that it would
expose her son to the jealousy of more capable and more ruthless men. She knew he was a lightweight, even if she adored
him. Indeed it is quite possible that Marcellus commanded the
adoration of his mother and uncle precisely for that reason.

Nevertheless the marriage went ahead. Augustus was silly
with joy. Marcellus preened himself. Julia sulked. She soon
found however that there was something to be said for her new
state. As a married woman she had privileges denied a virgin.
She had her own household and discovered that she enjoyed
the freedom and the opportunities to command which this
afforded her.

But she was not happy and she had reason for discontent.
One evening she invited me to supper. I was surprised to discover that we were alone together.

"Don't be silly, my old bear," she said. "After all we're practically brother and sister."

She toyed with her food, nibbling a little dried fish and some
green grapes, a slice of smoked ham and two purple figs, which
she held up between thumb and forefinger before putting them
whole into her mouth. She drank two or three goblets of wine,
and urged me on. Then she dismissed the slaves and we were
alone.

She stretched out on her couch, holding up her arm to admire
the shape of her hand, and let me have a glimpse of her breasts.
She pulled up the skirts of her gown to display her legs.

"They're improving, aren't they?" she said. "Only a few
weeks ago they were still fat. What do you think of them, old
bear?"

"Stop it," I said.

"Why?"

"Because it's not right . . ."

"It's not my fault if I fancy you and not my husband. Is it
now?"

She stroked her thighs and smiled.

"Cat," I said; but didn't move.

"Old bear. Are you a virgin, old bear?"

I'm sure I blushed.

"As a matter of fact, no," I said.

"Oh good. The Hyacinth can't do it," she said, "not with me anyway. I think he needs people to tell him how pretty he is, and I won't do that. Do you know where he is tonight, actually . . . ?"

I shook my head. I couldn't take my eyes off her legs and the movement of her hands . . .

"He's having supper with Maecenas," she said.

"Won't the conversation be rather over his head?" I asked, for Augustus' Etruscan minister was celebrated as the patron of poets and artists.

Julia giggled.

"Maecenas gives other kinds of parties, you know. With dancers and painted chorus-boys. That's the kind he invites Marcellus to. He's been doing it for years and nobody dares tell my father, not even his paid spies."

She sat up.

"Look at me. I'm a beautiful girl, the daughter of the most powerful man in the world, and the husband my father has forced on me would rather have any Phrygian boy who wiggles his bum at him."

She threw herself down sobbing. I watched her shoulders rise and fall, and felt my mouth dry. I touched cracked lips with my tongue. I moved to comfort her. In a trice her arms were round my neck, her tongue seeking mine. I tasted tears, wine and warm, eager, scented flesh; she was soft as rose petals and firm as a galloping horse. She cried aloud with joy-filled pain, and I sank into unimaginable delight . . .

"Old bear, old bear, hairy beast . . ."

"Lascivious cat . . ."

It was like that then. The night dies over the ocean. The moon swells behind the mountains of Asia which roll back, wave upon wave, to the confines of empire. I pour myself more wine and gulp it, seeking fierce oblivion that will not come.

THREE

The following morning my mother summoned me to her apartments. She gave me what Drusus and I called her Medusa look.

"You're a fool," she said, "and you look awful . . ."

"I'm afraid I drank too much wine last night . . ."

"That's not all you did last night. I suppose you're too old to whip . . ."

"Yes," I said, "that must be a matter of regret for you, but I am indeed too old to whip."

"Then I shall have to employ my tongue. I didn't ask you to sit down."

"No, you didn't. Nevertheless . . ."

"Don't be insolent. Don't add insolence to your other folly."

"If I knew what you were talking about . . ."

"You know very well . . . And don't smile. You have put yourself, and everything I have worked for on your behalf, at risk, for a little honeypot with the morals of an alleycat . . ."

"Ah," I said, "I should have realised, Mother, that you would have an informer in Julia's household . . ."

"You should indeed. Shall I tell you something which you should never forget? Success in life and politics, which for people like us amounts to much the same thing, depends on information. Naturally, therefore, one takes steps to obtain it. I hadn't thought you could be such a fool."

I picked up an apple and bit into it. I knew that a show of unconcern would screw Livia to still more intense fury, but I had long ago found that apparent indifference was my surest weapon against her. Or if not a weapon, at least a shield.

She said, "Tiberius, I wonder if you realise what the Princeps would do if he found out what I know . . . ?"

It irritated me when she referred to him in that way.

I said, "He ought to be grateful to me for making his daughter happy. It's more, it seems, than his beloved Marcellus has been able to do . . ."

"Do I care if she is happy?"

"Do you care if anyone is happy, Mother?"

"Don't be foolish. You know that my constant concern is for your future, and that of Drusus. But, unlike you, I know the world. You can't be blamed for your ignorance. You haven't seen the best part of a generation destroyed as I have. Therefore you don't realise how necessary it is to be circumspect, to plan every action, to eschew all folly, especially such as you have been guilty of. You don't realise that the life of a public man, that is to say of anyone who belongs to the Roman noble class, is perilous. Do you think you are safe in a world in which Caesar, Antony, Pompey, Cicero, Marcus Brutus all found themselves powerless in the end against the malignity of fate? Can you imagine that? I took you for someone more intelligent."

"But, Mother," I said. "I am protected surely. The love the Princeps bears you is my shield . . ."

The irony in my tone annoyed her. Livia has always been sensitive to irony. She resents its assumption of superiority.

"Of course he loves me," she said, "and I love him myself. That's not the point. We are not private people and we have different ambitions for our own children. Don't think the Princeps' love for me will protect you if you disturb his arrangements. He is quite capable of operating in a secret world from which I am excluded, and then of being full of regrets if his actions distress me. A dynast, a man of power like your father . . ."

"My stepfather, Mother . . ."

"Very well, your stepfather, if you insist, lives on two distinct planes, both real enough. There is the family man who is all concern and warm affection, and there is the politician who has no affections, no loyalty, no scruples. He loves his sister Octavia. That didn't prevent him from forcing her into marriage with Mark Antony, though he knew precisely how cruelly Antony would treat her. And, since you insist on it, remember always he is indeed your stepfather, not your father. He has no natural affection for you any more, since I am being frank, than I have for that little hussy, his daughter. Moreover, I must tell you that she is quite capable of destroying herself. I don't choose that she should pull you down with her . . ."

I cannot of course be certain that, at this distance of time, my memory restores to me the precise words of our conversation. Our own past, it sometimes seems to me, is a species of dream, just as dreaming so often reveals to us glimpses of the future which we cannot recognise till we find ourselves enacting those heralded moments. Experience is like a journey along a foggy river valley: for brief moments the line of the hills may be seen; then the mist hides them. We never know quite where we are or what surrounds us. Even the sounds we hear are deceptive. Our life is composed of a series of illusions, some of which we dignify by the name reality, but our perceptions are never more truthful than the shadows flickering on the wall of Plato's cave.

The successful man is often the sleepwalker. Augustus believed in his destiny. This freed him from the self-examination with which I have perplexed myself.

What he remembers becomes true for him. I sit here wondering if I have only dreamed this conversation with my mother.

But did I dream her last sentence?

"Believe me, my son, your stepfather's love for me secures you no more protection than Thetis obtained for her beloved Achilles . . ."

And if I dreamed it, wasn't my dream a true warning?

FOUR

I entered public life in my twentieth year when I was elected quaestor. I had been granted the right to stand for each magistracy at five years below the legal limit. In retrospect I deplore this example of favouritism, though I am bound to point out that I was less favoured than Marcellus, who was excused ten years' seniority. Nevertheless, despite my disapproval, I understand Augustus' decision. Two reasons may be advanced. First, it is always difficult to find reliable men to undertake necessary work and it was natural for Augustus to seek them among the members of his own family, whom he believed he could trust. Second, as Agrippa remarked in his crude vernacular, "You young buggers are best kept busy. It keeps you out of mischief."

The quaestorship was no empty honour. As every schoolboy knows, this office is an essential but unglamorous part of our body politic. It may be compared to the post of quartermaster in the army: he directs no strategy, wins no glory, but the army cannot function without him. Those ignorant of military affairs think of the quartermaster, if they think of him at all, as a dull fellow doing a dull job. Every serving soldier, however, knows that his comfort and safety depends on the efficiency with which this dull fellow works.

My first task as quaestor was to investigate irregularities which were occurring at the port of Ostia in the supply of corn to Rome. The assurance of a regular supply of grain for the capital is one of the most necessary tasks of government; if the supply fails, then there can be no guarantee of civil order. Augustus impressed upon me the importance of the task with which he had entrusted me.

"I know you are young," he said, "but you have this advantage: you have not been corrupted by experience. I have found that any man who has been long engaged in this business comes to accept the arguments of the middlemen and monopolists."

I soon discovered that it was the practice of certain shipowners' agents at Ostia to delay the transmission of cargoes from the port to the city till they had assured themselves that the price was satisfactory. If anyone tried to persuade them to move more quickly, they would only do so on payment of a personal commission. Moreover, the overseers at the docks, generally freedmen, were likewise prepared to delay the unloading of a ship at their own pleasure. In short, there was a chain of corruption which, in being worked to the advantage of numerous distinct individuals, amounted to a conspiracy against the public interest.

Yet I was uncertain how to proceed. It is one thing to identify the cause of some malfunctioning, another to remove it. One of my fellow quaestors suggested that we should arrange to pay a bounty to any grain merchant who delivered corn from Ostia to Rome within a given period.

"In this way," he said, "we shall accelerate the period."

I did not dispute his argument, but I had seen him engaged in close conversation with a number of merchants whom I deemed among the most corrupt, and it seemed to me likely that a portion at least of the bounty would find its way into his own coffers. Moreover, it seemed to me wrong, as a general principle, to attempt to check corruption by actions which were themselves in essence corrupt.

Not wishing to trouble Augustus with my problem, for I was convinced that to do so would lower his estimate of my capacities, I approached Agrippa. In retrospect, I find this significant. Despite my juvenile prejudice against him, I recognised in the imperial coadjutor a man devoted to efficiency.

He received me in his office, where he was surrounded by maps and plans of the water system for Rome which he was then attempting to reorganise. I outlined my problem as I saw it. He listened in silence, something Augustus could never have done.

"What is your own inclination?" he said. "Since you dislike your colleague's suggestion."

"I've already explained my reasons for that," I said. "But it seems to me one has a choice in these matters. You can reward or you can punish. My colleague proposes what is in effect bribery. I would rather impose penalties."

"Why?"

"I do not believe you can make men good, but I believe it is possible to make them behave well."

"And you consider fear of punishment more efficacious than the promise of reward?"

"Yes, when the reward is offered as a sort of condonement of the offence."

"You are quite right."

He tapped his nose.

"I'm a soldier," he said, "and I believe in discipline. Perhaps you have the makings of a soldier yourself. It would be a change in your family."

Fortified by his approval, I drew up a code of penalties to be imposed for any delay in the transmission of grain. My colleague was horrified; he saw his own prospect of a reward draining away. I stood firm. The code was enacted. For a short while the blockages were cleared. But I am afraid that old practices were soon resumed when my responsibilities took me elsewhere.

Nevertheless I have never forgotten this experience. I am very conscious that Rome is dependent on supplies from abroad, and that the life of the Roman people is every day tossed about not only at the mercy of wind and wave but at the greedy whim of the merchant classes and their underlings. These drive the price up, and so threaten popular insurrection. If the state is to remain orderly, as all good men must devoutly wish, then the grain supply must be assured. The popularity of government rests on full bellies. A hungry people does not listen to reason.

I was then given another task of extraordinary interest and importance. At Agrippa's suggestion, as I believe, I was put at the head of a commission charged with investigating the condition of slave barracks throughout Italy.

("How disgusting," Julia said, when I told her of my appointment. "When you've finished you'd better not approach me till
you have had a good many baths. Everyone knows we have to
have slaves, but we don't have to think about them as well,
surely.")

The immediate purpose of the commission was, as I discovered when I read the brief prepared, to determine whether
freemen were being held illegally in these barracks and whether
they were harbouring military deserters. But I soon found it
necessary to go beyond this brief, and my eventual report was
to mark a new chapter in the history of this unfortunate but
necessary institution.

What can we say of slavery? It is an institution common to
all people, and certainly to all civilised people. (There are, I
believe, a few barbarian tribes amongst whom it is unknown,
on account of their poverty or feeble character.) Nevertheless
it must also be admitted that slavery violates the law of nature.
Our ancestors did not think so; Marcus Porcius Cato, most
disagreeable of men, considered that the slave was no more
than a living tool. Those were his precise words. They disgust
me. A slave has the same limbs and organs as a freeman; the
same mind, the same soul. I have always been careful to treat
my own slaves as human beings. Indeed I think of them as
unpretentious friends. There is a proverb: "As many enemies
as you have slaves". But they are not essentially enemies. If
slaves feel enmity towards their masters, then it is generally
the masters who have provoked it. Too many Romans are
haughty, cruel and insulting to their slaves, forgetting that like
themselves the poor creatures breathe, live and die. A wise
man, which is also to say a good man, treats his slaves as he
would himself be treated by those set in authority over him. I
have always experienced a mixture of amusement and contempt
when I have heard senators complain that liberty has vanished
in Rome (which is unfortunately true) and yet have seen the
same men delight in humiliating and exhausting their slaves.

These are ideas which I have acquired over the years. I did
not hold them all when I was entrusted with this commission to
investigate the slave barracks. But their seed was there, and

that experience caused it to germinate. I saw in these barracks
the degradation of man.

I was learning men's nature fast, and almost always with disgust. The year after my quaestorship the uneasy stability which
had succeeded the civil wars was threatened by ambition and
discontent. Fannius Caepio, whose father had been an adherent
of Sextus Pompeius, was the author of a conspiracy against the
Princeps' life. His chief associate was Tarentius Varro Murena,
that year's consul. He was the brother-in-law of Maecenas.
Disaffection therefore infected the heart of the Republic. The
conspiracy was discovered by Augustus' secret police, themselves, by the mere fact of existence, evidence of how Rome
had changed for the worse. We had entered a time when, as
Titus Livius observed in the preface to his *History of Rome*,
"We could endure neither our vices nor their remedies". I was
myself called upon to prosecute Caepio, which I did with an
efficiency which was admired by many, at least in public, and a
dismay which I sought to conceal.

That year I married Vipsania. We had been betrothed for
many years and I had accustomed myself to the idea that we
would be man and wife. At one time I had rebelled against the
prospect. It seemed an unsuitable match for a Claudian. But I
had reconciled myself when I came to know her father Agrippa,
and was thus able to form a more just conception of his supreme
capabilities.

"I won't ask you how you are getting on," he said to me a
few days after the marriage. "But I want you to know that I
welcome you as an ally."

"An ally, sir?"

He sat back in his chair, his massively muscled legs thrust
out before him.

"Don't pretend you don't understand me. I've watched you
for years, ever since your mother and I agreed to this match.
Don't pretend to be an innocent or a fool. You know perfectly
well that a marriage such as yours is more than a family com-
pact. It's a political act. Of course I hope that you and Vipsania
will be happy together: she's my daughter and I'm fond of her;

but I also hope that this marriage will make it easier for you and me to work together. You're young, but you have a head on you, and I'm ready to swear that you have some understanding of how things stand. If nothing else, your experiences as prosecutor in the recent case should have opened your eyes. What sort of state would you say we live in?"

"My stepfather has often told me how proud he is to have restored the Republic."

"Balls. And you know it, don't you?"

"Well . . ."

"Precisely."

"Of course I realise it's not the Republic as it used to be, and that he doesn't deceive himself that it is."

"That's better. It's not the Republic, and the Republic will never be restored. Its time has gone. You can't run an empire on the basis of votes in the Roman forum, or of long-winded deliberations in the Senate either. So it's not the Republic. What is it then?"

"Let's say it's the empire, sir."

"Fair enough. But what's the empire? Is it a monarchy?"

"Not precisely."

"A dictatorship?"

"The office of dictator has been abolished, hasn't it?"

Agrippa laughed, drank some beer, fixed me with his eyes. His gaze was hard, heavy, imperious. I felt his power.

He waited. I held my peace.

"So what is the empire?" he said again.

"You are one of its two architects, sir."

"And even I am ignorant. But I can tell you this: only immature states can be either democracies or monarchies. We have grown beyond both these forms of government. The classic Greek delineation of types of state no longer applies, for we are not even an oligarchy as they understood the term. We are perhaps a constellation of powers . . ."

Agrippa had no reputation as a theorist. Indeed, to hear him speak, you would have thought him a mere force of nature, an exponent of brute strengths. Not so.

"The Princeps is a remarkable man," he said. "But you know

that. Nevertheless you must see that he doesn't owe his success to his own qualities entirely."

"I know that too, sir."

"And he has his faults."

Again I said nothing. We were in his villa by the sea, north of the city, in a garden apartment. The sun shone on a path beyond and a westerly breeze wafted in the scent of box trees and rosemary growing on the terrace. Below, in a sunken garden, there were mulberries and fig trees. I could hear, in the lacunae of our conversation, the sea lapping at the wall.

"His chief fault," Agrippa said, "is his affectionate nature. Often he allows it to dominate his intellect, warp his judgment. It's strange when he can be so ruthless at other times."

"Marcellus is very charming," I said. "It's no wonder that my stepfather is so fond of him."

"Yes," Agrippa said, "he's a delightful boy, isn't he?"

He got to his feet.

"We've said enough, haven't we? I'm glad it's you, not Marcellus, who is married to my daughter. Your mother is also concerned about the Princeps' fondness for the boy. She realises, like me, that it won't do for him to advance him further. Not too quickly. This isn't, as we agreed, a monarchy. We're a faction in power, a party. There are always those who would displace us if they could, like Caepio, whom you prosecuted so capably, and his friend Murena, and you know whose brother-in-law he was. That comes a bit near home. Marcellus sees too much of that bugger, my old friend Maecenas. That's enough, don't need to spell it out further, do I? One other thing. Remember: the basis of our power is the legions. Think you have the makings of a soldier. I'm bloody sure Marcellus hasn't."

I pondered that conversation.

A few weeks later Augustus fell ill. He was indeed near death. They said he raved in delirium. Livia fled from the chamber distressed by what he uttered in his madness. She retired to the Temple of Vesta to pray and sacrifice to the gods, that they might relent and restore her husband to health. In a brief moment of lucidity, fearing that he was on the point of death, he summoned Agrippa and Calpurnius Piso, who had replaced Murena as his consular colleague, and consigned to them the care of the Republic. A change of doctor and a change of treatment proved effective. He recovered and all was well.

But, though all was well, a secret had been revealed: the revolution he had accomplished depended on his life. The conspirators of the summer were posthumously justified. If they had killed Augustus, the régime would have crumbled.

It was for this reason that he remodelled it that autumn, obtaining a grant of *maius imperium* for himself from the Senate, and abandoning his practice of holding one of the consulships himself. More important, he associated Agrippa more closely in the government, granting him proconsular power over all the provinces of the empire, and, more important still, the *tribunicia potestas*, the tribunician power.

The will of Livia and Agrippa had prevailed over the inclinations of my stepfather. Marcellus was eclipsed. And that winter he died, suddenly.

FIVE

Julia had miscarried as her husband died, thus cheating her father of the grandson he so greatly longed for. But his grief for Marcellus for a time blinded him to this other loss. That was excessive. To please him, Vergil would incorporate a reference to Marcellus in his *Aeneid*, ridiculously exaggerated, I'm afraid.

But a curious thing: Julia also appeared to be overcome by grief. This amazed me for I had doubted whether the child she was carrying and had lost, was indeed her husband's. (Indeed I wondered if it might be mine; it was possible.) Livia of course dismissed Julia's display of emotion as playacting, but she was naturally volatile and might have been sincere. Vipsania said to me that while she realised there had been difficulties between them, it was her impression that they had been agreeing better in the last months. That might indeed be true; Vipsania was a good judge of these matters. On the other hand, I knew, as she didn't, how close Marcellus had come to being singed by the conspiracy of the spring. He hadn't been directly involved, but the conspirators had been his friends. He had had a fright, and it may have seemed prudent to give the impression of devotion to his wife. After all, since his talents were slight, Marcellus depended absolutely on his uncle's favour.

You wonder how I knew of his involvement? In two ways.

First, Fannius Caepio, under examination, tried to throw suspicion on him. I recognised this as a bargaining counter, when the "evidence" was brought before me in my capacity as prosecutor. Therefore I decided to have nothing to do with it and, to prevent any hint of the accusation from being brought before the court, I had it expunged from the record of the examination. But before I did so I confronted Marcellus with the charge. He came near to fainting. When I told him I didn't believe a word of it, and was going to make sure that Caepio's accusation didn't go any further, his relief and gratitude were pathetic, and repulsive. He fawned on me and I felt a certain thrill as I realised the depth of his terror and savoured the knowledge that he had confessed himself in every way my inferior. He hugged me with gratitude.

"How could he do such a thing to me?" he said again and again. "I've never even met him, except at a party."

"One of Maecenas' parties?" I asked.

It wasn't, however, only there that Marcellus had encountered the conspirators. This I learned from my second source.

One day while I was preparing the case against Caepio I received a message which puzzled me. Its substance was that its author had information relating to the case which he could only give me in person; however, he was reluctant to approach me openly. Now of course such messages are common in such circumstances, and my first inclination was to ignore it: if a man is frightened to give information openly, it is likely that he is untrustworthy and his evidence tainted. Yet I had an instinct that it might be otherwise on this occasion. I therefore consented to a secret meeting.

This took place, by night, in the back room of a low tavern in the maze of little streets between the Campus Martius and the river. Following instructions, I presented myself there heavily cloaked. The tavern was clearly a disreputable place, frequented by the scum of the city, prostitutes of both sexes and their panders. I was indeed glad that my face was concealed, and for a moment I wondered if I had been foolish to go there. However, I gave the password to the proprietor and was shown into the back room as arranged.

There was a man lying on a couch with a curly-headed boy sitting on his lap. Neither moved when I entered and I thought I had been deceived and was ready to burst out angrily. Then the man sat up, pushing the boy off.

"Time's up, darling," he said. "Fetch us wine."

He unfolded himself and rose to his feet.

"You're earlier than I expected, my lord," he said.

"I'm punctual."

"Oh dear, you are stiff."

He spoke with a lisp; a Greek a few years older than myself with scented ringleted hair and an effeminate manner. He was sweating, and smoothed his tunic and then busied himself sitting me at the table. The boy brought in some wine and departed with a saucy look over his shoulder. I felt a little sick.

"My name's Timotheus," the man said. "I do a lot of work for the Princeps, though you won't have heard of me, and I have a problem which I would like to discuss with you. It concerns the case with which you are occupied."

He smirked and wriggled his shoulders.

"I asked you here because I wanted to keep things dark. I'm in a quandary. I'm the Princeps' own agent and the information I have is such as I frankly don't dare to give him. Do you begin to see?"

"No, I don't. Perhaps you should begin at the beginning and stop talking in riddles."

"Riddles are often all it's safe to talk in these days."

"Listen," I said, "I am prosecuting in the case you refer to. If you have information then I can compel you – painfully – to divulge it."

He sipped his wine and pushed the jug across the table to me. I was surprised to see that I had already drunk my first cup. It was a sweet wine with a touch of resin, the sort of thing Greeks prefer.

"That wouldn't be wise," he said. "The Princeps would like that even less. He wouldn't want it to be known he employs types like me. Besides, I must tell you, if only to secure my position, that we began our connection in circumstances he wouldn't want to be recalled. Frankly, my dear, I know too much. So why don't you come off your high horse, and listen like a good boy? I'll begin at the beginning as you suggest."

His manner disgusted me. I longed to have him whipped; and yet I was curious. I raised my cup to my lips and nodded.

He told his story in an affected manner, with many digressions. But its essence was simple. He was a spy whose especial talent was what he described as provocation. "When I get a whiff of disaffection, I fan it . . ." The Princeps had been suspicious of his colleague, Murena, and had conveyed his suspicions to Timotheus, commanding an investigation. Timotheus had therefore introduced his agent into the consul's house, as a servant, "A regular Ganymede, *you* understand" – he fluttered his eyelashes at me. "But of course servants, however sweet, can't find out everything, though I let the Princeps think that all my information came from the boy." It didn't. He had also recruited a young nobleman called Fannius Cotta, a cousin of Caepio's. From his manner of talking I had no doubt that this Cotta was the wretch's lover. Cotta – who must, I thought, be practically half-witted to have fallen in with Timotheus' suggestion – had encouraged his cousin and the consul in their treason, all the while reporting every detail to the Greek. But now Cotta had been arrested with the other conspirators; I knew that of course, for I had arranged to examine him.

"So?" I said.

The Greek dabbed at his eyes, as though his narration had moved him. He wanted Cotta set free; that was obvious.

"I have only your word for the part he played," I said. "And in view of what you say about your relations with him, I see no reason why I should believe you."

"But I think I can persuade you," he said. "I have a letter written by a certain gentleman not unconnected with the Princeps. It is addressed to Cotta and unkind men might interpret it as offering encouragement to the conspirators."

"I see."

And I did. I had no doubt to whom he referred.

"Why don't you offer it to the Princeps?"

"Don't be silly, my dear. I wouldn't dare. For one thing, he would think it a forgery. For another, that wouldn't help my friend. And for a third, I'm a Greek, a poor freedman, and . . . well, we Greeks have always had dealings with the Persians, and you know the Persian way of treating the bearer of bad news. It would be as much as my life is worth. But it seemed to me, regarding the relationships within the imperial family, that it might be of some use to you . . ."

"I disapprove of the term, 'the imperial family'. Such a thing doesn't exist, and is offensive even as an idea."

"As you like."

"Do you have the letter here?"

"Don't be silly. I have a copy . . ."

"You speak confidently for a man in your circumstances."

He smiled. "That's your interpretation," and thrust his hand down into his tunic and produced the letter.

"This could be interpreted in more than one way," I said.

"Either way would be damning, wouldn't it? But you see my dilemma, which I'm now sharing with you. I want to save my friend, but I can't possibly pass on that letter to the Princeps."

"Isn't it your fault for having concealed that he was working on your behalf to provoke the conspiracy?"

"Perhaps, but there it is."

I was naïve of course. I saw that at once. Cotta was clearly a genuine conspirator, and perhaps his relations with the Greek had developed out of the conspiracy. Nevertheless I couldn't but admire the adroitness of the Greek's plan. And the letter was certainly – if indeed in Marcellus' own hand – damning. I would be pleased to have it. Arrangements, satisfactory to all parties, could therefore be made. I indicated as much.

"But I must still interrogate Cotta," I said. "You understand that? Nevertheless . . ."

Fannius Cotta was a tall, well-built young man with big eyes and a loose mouth. Terror had unmanned him, rendering him alternately sulky and abject. Twice during our conversation he threw himself down on his pallet bed sobbing. He wore a short tunic and the sweat sparkled on the back of his thighs as his shoulders heaved. He promised that he could incriminate Marcellus still further, if that was what I wanted.

"You mistake me," I said. "I want to bring this thing to an end. One means of doing so would be for you to meet with an unfortunate accident."

He threw himself on the ground before me, grabbing my ankles and begging for mercy.

"Get up," I said. "Have you no dignity?"

It went against my inclination, but I made arrangements for his release. I knew that Timotheus would destroy the letter rather than produce it if I broke our agreement. Loathsome though he was, I also realised that he had sufficient intelligence to have prepared for himself a defence against any action I might take to incriminate him. But I made two conditions: Cotta must leave Italy for a space of five years. He must never communicate with Marcellus. I issued threats, though I knew I would soon have no means of enforcing them. But I was certain that Cotta was such a coward that he would not dare to defy me.

I kept the letter secret. There might come a time in the future when it could be of more service to me than at the present. Timotheus' manner when he delivered it to me was disturbing: I saw that.

He had outwitted me. He had made me his accomplice in deception. Nevertheless he had put a weapon in my hand. I owed that to him.

Marcellus' death robbed me of the weapon, made it obsolete. I was still, however, in the Greek's debt.

One other thing: the doctor who treated Marcellus was one Antonius Musa, the same who had cured Augustus. He had been introduced to his household by Timotheus. A few years later he retired on account of ill-health and lived in a villa with Timotheus. Their conduct scandalised the local farmers, but Augustus protected them.

It was a pleasant irony to think how Timotheus had worked to destroy the Princeps' favourite, and how Musa may well have murdered him.

SIX

There are those who believe that character is constant. We become, they would insist, only what we already are; we can never escape our inherent nature. Any change that may seem to take place only reveals traits which the person has previously thought it prudent to conceal; conversely, it may result from the assumption of a hypocritical virtue. This is an argument which must perplex philosophers, and one to which there can be no certain answer. For example, Augustus showed himself ruthless in the pursuit of power; he shrank from no cruelty that seemed to him necessary for the achievement of his aims. So he sacrificed his mentor, Marcus Tullius Cicero, at the time of the proscriptions. Though he knew that he owed him much, he judged it more necessary to conciliate Mark Antony by bowing to the hatred Antony entertained for the veteran orator than to insist that clemency be extended to the man whom even Julius had described as "an ornament of the Republic". Likewise, Augustus loved his sister Octavia with a warmth such as he offered to few. (Had she been less ostentatiously virtuous, I have no doubt that the scandalmongers would have had much to suggest as to the nature of their relationship.) Yet he sacrificed her happiness to the demands of his alliance with Antony, forcing her to accept that brutal drunkard as her husband. Those who adhere to the opinion that character is constant must ask whether Augustus forced himself to practise a cruelty that his nature abhors or has since assumed a virtue which is no more than a manifestation of his innate hypocrisy.

For my part, I find this view of human nature false and inadequate. It seems to me that on the one hand there are depths of our character which we do not understand, which perhaps we fear, and which sometimes surface to take us by surprise; and that on the other hand, we are in a condition of perpetual creation. Heraclitus, you will remember, posed the question whether a man could ever bathe twice in the same river. His disciples assert this is impossible; everything is in a state of flux, the river is changing before our eyes. Others however, whom I will term the Common Sense school of philosophers, think this mere casuistry. They say that though the water changes the river remains; the enduring is more real than the changes which they term superficial.

It seems to me however that it is possible to grant justice to both arguments: to say that while everything changes, much that is contained in it remains the same. A man is always himself, but he is not necessarily the same man.

I am drawn into these reflections by memories of my marriage to Vipsania. I entered the marriage in obedience to my mother's wishes, understanding that her choice of my wife was politically astute. But I felt neither warmth nor enthusiasm. Moreover, in other respects, we were an awkward pair; Vipsania's chaste modesty made her as shy as my own reserve made me. Though we had known each other all our lives, we did not know how to converse. Perhaps we had never exchanged more than a few sentences over the years, and those of an insignificant sort. Now we were alone together as we had never been. Vipsania's submissiveness irritated me. She lay stiff in bed, the covers drawn up around her neck. I thought – how could I fail to? – of Julia caressing her thighs and drawing my gaze to her body. Vipsania received me as one having his will. Her sense of duty compelled her to yield to me, but as a victim, not a woman. For weeks we seemed frozen in immobility. I knew that she was unhappy and, being unhappy myself, resented her unhappiness. When I found her in tears, I was unable to take her in my arms.

I had no one to consult. The intensity of my relationship with Livia has always precluded discussion of emotional affairs. My brother Drusus, whom I loved for his spontaneity and virtue, would have been incapable of understanding my dilemma. Vipsania and I were locked in incomprehension of each other, both fearful to try to turn the key which anyway we did not perhaps recognise.

Yet now, more than twenty years later, I look back on the early days of our marriage with similar uncomprehending wonder. For everything changed. She became the medicine of my soul, the light towards which I turned. And I cannot say why or how. There was no single moment when the barriers yielded, no single moment when our personalities disarmed themselves. It was rather as if acquaintance made the ramparts crumble. Without my knowing it was happening, I was softened by her tenderness and virtue. The time came when the turn of her head, the cool touch of her flesh, her low voice, could appease any anxieties.

No doubt the birth of our son, young Drusus, contributed to this development. To see her with the baby in her arms, or leaning over his cradle lulling him to sleep with an old song, was to experience everything that over the centuries, it seems to me, men have come to desire; it was to feel myself enfolded in a love that was total.

Something else contributed to our developing intimacy: she respected my wish for secrecy. I have always felt uncomfortable with the expression of emotion, either by words or actions. She did not try to force my confidence, and in this way gradually won it.

Meanwhile Julia presented a problem. She believed she had a claim on me. She knew she could arouse me, and for that reason regarded me as her possession. My marriage meant nothing to her. "It's convenience, isn't it?" she would say; then, looking at me through her veil of eyelashes and touching her breast or stroking her thighs, "Of course, if you are going to take it seriously, it's an inconvenience. But only a trifling one. You couldn't prefer that insipid girl to me, could you?"

Put like that, she was quite right. Her body was to me as the wine-flask to the drunkard: a temptation that made me tremble. Half a dozen times, in the winter that followed Marcellus' death, I slipped into her bed, knew the intensity of delight, and then the pain of remorse and self-contempt. I have never been able

to regard the sexual act as something from which emotion can
be divorced.

Livia knew what was happening and reproached me.

"You are weak," she said, "contemptibly weak. Do you want
to destroy everything I had worked for on your behalf?"

There was no answer to that. Shame locked my tongue.

"Do you know," she said, "Augustus suggested to me that
you should marry her? I soon put a stop to that. Besides, he
must be mad to think of it, I said. How could he contemplate
so offending Agrippa, by dishonouring his daughter? And now,
you fool, you are risking just that. And for what? For a little
honeypot that needs her bottom smacked."

At that time Julia's behaviour stopped just short of being scandalous. All the same the spy Timotheus approached me, having,
as he said, my best interests at heart. I wasn't Julia's only lover;
she was the centre of a coterie of young nobles, some of whom,
he said, had "dangerous antecedents". I would do well to be
careful.

He left behind him a lingering scent of attar of roses and the
more enduring stench of moral corruption.

I was alarmed. I couldn't trust myself near Julia. I had the
sense to put in for an attachment to the armies.

I was assigned to Spain where the hill tribes were in revolt.
There is no glory in such warfare, which is a species of police
action. Yet it is the best training for a young officer: it teaches
him the true purpose of the army, which is the preservation of
Rome and all that is meant by Roman order. Furthermore, in
such campaigns, he learns the importance of care for his men.
That is the first rule of generalship: that the troops are properly
fed, clothed, armed and housed. We recruit soldiers and invite
them to risk death in defence of fat taxpayers. The least we
can do in return is to attend to the conditions in which they
have condemned themselves to live. Show me the general who
does not put his men's welfare first, and I shall show you a man
dominated by vanity. I have never pretended to military genius,
yet I have been successful because I have never neglected my
men, have never moved in defiance of intelligence reports, and

have never forgotten that the soldiers have entrusted me with their lives. It is a responsibility which some commanders delight to ignore.

Wherever I campaigned, I built roads. The road, which is unknown to barbarians, is the sign of Rome, civilisation and empire. It is by roads that the empire is joined together, by roads that trade is carried, by roads that barbarian tribes are subjugated. Wherever you seek the majesty of Rome, there you will find the road.

A letter from my mother:

Beloved son,

We hear good reports of your industry and efficiency. Bear in mind that you are a Claudian, and as such superior to all; therefore it behoves you to do men service. It is to accomplish this that the gods have created a superior breed of men.

The problem of Julia is solved. Amazingly it was Maecenas who persuaded your stepfather of the best course of action. She is to wed Agrippa. There, I knew that would take you by surprise. It will be strange for you to welcome her as your mother-in-law. But it is for the best. He may be able to control her. Moreover, it is prudent to bind him still more firmly in love and obligation to your stepfather. Believe me, great men like Agrippa are always subject to the temptation of ambition. All the more so, when they are not well born.

Vipsania tells me that she intends to winter with you in Gades. I am delighted to hear it. It is not good for husband and wife to dwell long apart. Moreover, I know only too well the temptations of the camp.

You have a difficult nature, my dear son. You require the support of a loving and virtuous wife.

I have always known that. It is why I promoted your marriage to Vipsania who is everything a mother could desire in her son's wife. I speak of her personal qualities. Despite her father's distinction, her birth would have disqualified her in normal times. But the times are not normal, and never will be again.

Both Augustus and I are in good health.

A letter from Vipsania:

Dearest husband,

I look forward eagerly to being with you. I have missed you. I do not dare to ask whether you have missed me, yet because I trust you, I hope that you have.

You will have heard the news about my father and Julia. It is very strange, but may work out well. Of course I am sorry for my mother who has had to be divorced. But she is well compensated, and, to tell the truth, has seen so little of my father in recent years that I think it likely she will feel the dishonour, but not the desertion. And, as you know, she is a devoted gardener, and the creation of her gardens on the Bay has been her chief interest. "Nobody," she once said to me, "can be unhappy planting flowers . . ."

Julia was furious when the match was first proposed. You can guess why. But she is now reconciled to it. She realises that my father is a great man.

"I am not going to ask you about Julia," Agrippa said to me, "because I don't think I would like the answer. But she'll behave herself now, you'll see. What she needs is authority . . ."

I didn't see her for two years.

SEVEN

It is not my intention in this brief memoir to dilate at length on my military exploits. I have observed that there is a sameness in accounts of campaigns and that it is almost impossible to differentiate between one year's service and the next. Indeed they blur in my mind. Yet in as much as the greater part of my adult life, till I retreated into philosophic retirement, has been passed in camps, completely to ignore my memories of soldiering would give a misleading picture of my life.

Yet I write this in no expectation of being read. Indeed in the hope that I will not. I write for my own satisfaction, in pursuit of my personal enquiry into the nature of truth; in an attempt to answer the two perplexing questions: what manner of man am I? What have I done with my life?

When my mind drifts back now, it is images rather than a coherent narrative which present themselves to me: mist rising from horse lines in the thin keen wind of a morning by the Danube; long marches, the men ankle-deep in mud behind creaking waggons, as the beech and ash woods of Germany enfold us; a hill-top in northern Spain, when snow fell below us in the valleys but we lay on dry, iron-hard ground under the stars; grizzled centurions lashing at the transport horses, yelling at the legionaries to put their shoulder to a wheel that was spinning as if in mockery of their efforts; a boy with blood oozing from his mouth as I rested his dying head on my arm and watched his leg kick; my horse flinching from a bush which parted to reveal a painted warrior, himself gibbering with terror; the sigh of the wind coming off a silent sea; the tinkle of the camel bell across desert sands. Army life is a mere collection of moments.

*   *   *

My first independent command was, however, glorious. I use
the word in full awareness that it can rarely be employed without
irony, even if the understanding of the irony is reserved to the
gods.

Everyone knows that the greatest power in the world after
Rome is Parthia. This vast empire extending to the boundaries
of India, and influential beyond them, is fortunately divided
from us by a wide and inhospitable desert. It was in that
desert that the millionaire triumvir, Marcus Crassus, seeking
to emulate the glory of his colleagues Caesar and Pompey,
suffered, thanks to his vanity and ineptitude, the greatest
disaster ever to befall Roman arms. His troops were cut to
pieces at Carrhae, all killed except those taken prisoner, his
standards captured, and he himself slain. (His head was
thrown on to the stage of the theatre in which the Parthian
Emperor was watching a performance of *The Bacchae*.) Later
Mark Antony led another expedition against Parthia, meeting
with almost equal disaster.

The desert divides the two empires, but in the north the
kingdom of Armenia serves as a buffer between them. In race
and culture the Armenians are closely allied to the Parthians, a
similarity which deepens the hatred they feel for them. But
Armenia is of great strategic importance, for it thrusts itself like
a dagger into each of the two empires. It is in Rome's interest
to control it, since by that means we can defend the security of
our empire; but the same consideration applies in reverse to
Parthia. Therefore the domination of Armenia is the chief point
of dispute between the empires, and a matter of prime importance to Rome.

This Augustus recognised. I have remarked before that his
acuity was admirable whenever he was able to disengage his
intellect from personal affections. Now it happened, when I was
twenty-two, that King Artaxes of Armenia was assassinated by
his fellow countrymen, whom he had shamefully abused. Roman
help was sought. I was surprised to be put in command.

"I have no fear as to your capabilities," Augustus said.
"Besides, these Orientals are all easily impressed by position.
They will know you are my son . . ."

I was intoxicated by the clear air of the mountains, the vigour of the highlanders, the beauty of the young women. I was revolted by the untruthfulness displayed by all with whom I had dealings. There was not a single man on whose word you could rely. We took advantage of the confusion of the situation to install the late king's brother, Tigranes, on the throne. He was a loathsome fellow who slept by choice with his sister, but he owed everything to us, and his terror of the Parthians and of his own subjects was such that he agreed willingly to the establishment of a legion in his capital. Meanwhile the position in Parthia itself was almost equally confused, for the coup d'état in Armenia had inspired an attempt there also. It so happened that the emperor's son had been sent to Rome as a hostage some years previously. I now called for him, and entered into negotiations with his father. They were prolonged, as negotiations with Orientals always are.

My purpose was adamant, and my understanding had been clarified in my journey through Syria. I saw how this rich and populous province depended utterly on the security provided by the legions. We had a garrison of four legions, more than twenty thousand men, held on standing watch, besides auxiliary troops scattered about the peel-towers which protected the crossings of the great river, Euphrates. Behind us lay Antioch, the sweetest city in the world, men said, with its flowered palaces, its streets lit even by night, its perpetual fountains, its marts and emporia. No one who has stood gazing over the black waters of the Euphrates, seeing the moon sink behind distant mountain ranges, can avoid feeling the majesty and benevolence of Rome.

My purpose was one of reparation. There was an old stain to be expunged. When the Parthian diplomats prevaricated, I swept the documents from the table before me and insisted. Phraates' son would not be restored. Instead, using Armenia as a base, which would enable me to avoid the desert route, I would strike deep down the river valleys into the heart of Parthia: unless I had my way.

My demands were simple. First, my settlement of Armenia would be recognised, and, as an earnest of their good intentions, new hostages would be delivered to me. Second, and more important, the standards taken at Carrhae would be restored.

Some may wonder why this was more important. Such questioners do not understand the Oriental mind, which is even more profoundly moved by symbols. These standards were the mark of Rome's failure, disgrace, inferiority on a particular historical occasion. By receiving them back, that memory would be wiped out, that emblem overthrown. I am not ashamed to confess that Augustus himself had insisted on the importance of my demand, had enlightened me as to the manner in which Orientals think.

At last, alarmed, they gave way. Having done so, they revealed something of which we were ignorant.

This is a curious trait of Orientals: when their obstinacy crumbles and they determine to let you have your way, their submission is complete, they go beyond what is necessary to do, believing that they thereby recover what they call "face" by laying you under an obligation. So their ambassador, a lean fellow whose name I forget, though I remember his oiled ringlets and the odour of mint which was diffused about him, said with a leer: "There are certain human trophies to be returned also."

I did not understand him immediately, but he clapped his hands, and a slave-boy departed to return after a few minutes leading a group of old men, several of whom at the sight of the Parthian lord fell to their knees.

"They have learned who their masters are," the ambassador said, "but now that there is peace and tranquillity between our two great empires, it is time that they should go home."

They looked up as if expecting a trick. They were soldiers from Crassus' army, men who had spent almost forty years in slavery. They crowded round me, babbling. I later discovered that three of them had forgotten the use of Latin. They hailed me as their benefactor, and this embarrassed me. I did not feel like a benefactor. On the contrary, in an obscure fashion, I felt guilty, and that guilt has remained with me ever since. We initiate great campaigns, and call mighty armies into being for a public purpose that even we who initiate it barely understand.

Our own soldiers are our victims. These men had been deprived of life, even more surely than if they had been killed, for they had retained through the years a consciousness of what they had lost, and the principal cause of this robbery was Marcus Crassus' determination to show that he was as great a man as his colleagues Caesar and Pompey . . . So I made arrangements for them to be returned home and to be settled on land in a veterans' colony in Basilicata. But I have never forgotten them, nor forgotten that war is a terrible necessity. Its triumphs, which I have enjoyed as proper to one of my station and achievements, are illusory. Its disasters are real. There is almost no more to be said about war. I hope never to be involved in it again. I expect to pass the rest of my life here in Rhodes, enjoying the pleasures of the mind, the conversation of intelligent men, and the beauties of the sea and landscape.

EIGHT

No wise man risks incurring the anger of the gods by neglect of religious duties and observances which are properly binding on us. It is well known that the great Scipio was wont to have the shrine of Jupiter Capitolinus unlocked before dawn so that he might enter and commune in solitude – in holy solitude as he would say himself – with the god about affairs of state. The guard-dogs, which barked at other visitors, always treated him with respect. We know also that certain places are in the charge of particular gods; that certain hours of day are propitious for particular actions; and that the wise man invariably consults the gods in order to discover whether they approve a given course of action.

Nevertheless I also recognise that it is impossible for any man to overcome by prayers and sacrifice what is fixed from the beginning and to alter it to his taste or advantage; what has been assigned to us will happen without praying for it; what is not fated will not occur, pray as we may.

Is it possible to reconcile these two beliefs? This is a question I have frequently heard debated by philosophers, and though I have found much of profound interest in the debates – and have indeed, on occasion, ventured to offer contributions of my own, which, I am happy to say, have not been ill-received – I confess that the matters appear to me fundamentally incompatible. The fact is that in this shadowy life, we are incapable of receiving or understanding the full truth about the nature of things in the same way as we are unable to know our own natures thoroughly. What is clear is that on the one hand everyone wishes to know his fortune, while on the other we derive pro-found satisfaction from performing harmonious and time-hallowed actions with the utmost punctiliousness. We all have a desire, an innate desire, to do what is right, and at the same time we are alert for signs which will assure us as to the future. When I first commanded an army, and was marching through Macedonia on my way to Syria, the altars consecrated by the victorious Caesareans at Philippi burst spontaneously into flames; was this not a sign that my fortune would be glorious?

That thought perplexes me still, for I have abandoned ambition. Is it possible, I wonder, that the gods remain ambitious for me? Once at Padua, for instance, I visited Geryon's oracle: I was advised to throw golden dice into the fountain of Aponus, and, in fact, made the highest possible cast. Then, the day after I arrived in Rhodes, an eagle – a bird never before seen on this island – alighted on the roof of my house, remaining there seven nights. Was its arrival witness of a magnificent future, or did its departure suggest that glory had deserted me?

Such questionings are foolish since only experience proves or disproves signs of this nature. Yet, on sleepless nights, I cannot help brooding on them.

I brood on other matters too: on my few years of happiness for instance, which lasted from the date of Agrippa's marriage to Julia to the hour of my father-in-law's death. I felt secure then, my star in the ascendant. Vipsania grew ever dearer to me, we conversed about everything. I saw in the alliance of Augustus and Agrippa, who had been joined with my stepfather in the tribunician power, so that authority in the state was shared between them, a guarantee for the continuing peace and prosperity of Rome, a guarantee strengthened still more by Augustus' love for his grandchildren, Agrippa and Julia's sons and daughters. My own career blossomed. Together with my beloved brother Drusus, I pushed the frontier of the empire north of the Alps: forty-six tribes submitted to the rule of Rome. Augustus erected a trophy commemorating our achievement. In these happy years my son Drusus was born.

Call no man happy till he is dead. The gods are jealous of our felicity. While I was in winter quarters on the Danube I received an anguished letter from my wife. She told me her father had died in his villa in Campania. He had been preparing to join the armies; it had been my pride and concern to see that they were in a state of readiness which he would approve. Vipsania had been with him when he passed into the shades. "He spoke of you near the end," she said. " 'Tiberius,' he said, 'will continue my work. He is a rock' . . . so you see, my dear, that my father respected you as much as I love you, my dear husband . . ."

I wept when I read those words; I am near to tears now as I remember them.

Immersed in an arduous campaign, I had little time to appreciate the personal significance of Agrippa's death. Not even a letter from Vipsania some two months later alarmed me. "Everyone is worried about Julia," she wrote. "It is generally agreed that she must have a husband – and little Gaius and Lucius a father – but it is very difficult to think of anyone who might be suitable. Who can, after all, replace my father? Yet dear Julia's nature is such that she cannot remain single. Your mother is very anxious."

I returned to Rome at the end of the campaigning season, though not before I had ensured that my men were well established in their winter quarters, and that sufficient stores had been accumulated to provision them throughout those months when transport is often difficult in the frontier regions. I had also laid down a training programme, for nothing is so demoralising for soldiers as idleness, and I had instructed my staff-officers to prepare for the next summer's campaign. I did not think of Agrippa while doing all this, but it was he who had taught me that nine-tenths of the science of war rests in adequate preparation. Nor did I give any thought to the problem Vipsania had adumbrated. Why should I have? It was no concern of mine.

Rain was falling heavily as I came within sight of the city, and the steep road that leads from the Forum to the Palatine was awash with running water. It was late afternoon and the wind blew in my face. I made my way to my mother's house, for Vipsania and our son were still lodged in our villa on the coast.

I knelt before Livia and she laid her fingers on my forehead. I rose and we embraced. We exchanged the awkward courtesies of reunion.

"The Princeps is pleased with your achievement, my son."

"Good. He should be. It has been a difficult summer."

"You know," she said, "that he finds it difficult to converse with you . . ."

"My genius rebukes him?"

"Don't scoff. If you want to know, it's your bitter humour that he finds disconcerting. He likes . . ."

"Yes, I know, he likes everything to be comfortable."

"There's no need to be disrespectful. It's been a difficult summer here too. Agrippa's death . . ."

There had been a time, as I knew, when my mother had despised Agrippa. For all her subtle intelligence, she was not altogether free of the prejudices of her class. But she had come to understand his value. They had learned to work together, aware that they pursued the same end: the creation of my stepfather's legend. Moreover, they had understood that while each of them was in important respects far superior to Augustus, and the pair together generally a match for him, nevertheless Augustus emerged, in some fashion which neither could have accounted for, as their master. There are always many observers who put it about that Livia controlled her husband, and she was not unhappy to have this believed, even while she strove to magnify his reputation. Yet she knew that in the last resort, it was not the case. Augustus kept within him a dour capacity for domination. Ultimately he was stubborn, inflexible, adamant; yes, even he, the great politician who twisted and compromised and cajoled and accommodated, yet contrived to impress his will on events. It has always been the paradox of their loving and quarrelsome marriage: that each feared the other. But, despite appearances, Augustus has always been the stronger.

Livia would not talk that evening of Agrippa's death and of its consequences for the state, and I sensed something was wrong, for she had always been eager to engage in political speculation.

* * *

When I met Augustus the next morning, he praised me, and was embarrassed to praise me. I declared my intention of hurrying to my wife and child, and he begged me to delay a few days in Rome. There were matters that had to be discussed when he could spare the hours from the myriad tasks of unavoidable administration, and he wished me to hold myself in readiness. I wrote to Vipsania explaining the situation and apologising for my tardiness. I told her I longed to hold her in my arms. Those were my exact words, I know, though I have no copy of that letter.

It was at the baths a few days later that Iullus Antonius accosted me. I have not mentioned Iullus Antonius hitherto in these scraps of memory, and he deserves a paragraph to himself, as I approach the worst moments of my life.

I had known him since I was a child – indeed we had done lessons together. He was, as his name indicates, the son of Mark Antony, by his first marriage to Fulvia, who had so terrified my own poor father in the long months of the dreadful siege of Perugia. When Antony married Augustus' sister Octavia, that noble and generous woman assumed responsibility for his children by his first marriage, and she continued to care for them even after he deserted her for Cleopatra. There were four, two of whom I came to know well: Iullus and his sister Antonia, who was now married to my brother Drusus. I have always had a warm affection for Antonia, but I never cared for Iullus. Despite my dislike, I felt some sympathy for him. He had been brought up with us, but Augustus never trusted him: he was always mindful of his heredity, and he knew that many of Antony's old adherents, and their connections, regarded Iullus as the natural leader of their party. He therefore permitted him civil office, but declined to allow him any military experience. In an attempt to bind him to the family's interests, he had commanded Iullus to marry Octavia's daughter by her first marriage, Marcella, when she was divorced by Agrippa in order that my father-in-law might marry Julia. No doubt Augustus was wise: Iullus much resembled his father in appearance and in his intemperate character. He was indeed a little drunk when he approached me that afternoon at the baths; he was often a little drunk by that time of day . . .

"So the great general has returned," he said, laying his hand on my shoulder. I brushed it off; I have always detested such manifestations of male camaraderie – all the more so when I know them to be insincere.

"I was surprised that you didn't attend your father-in-law's funeral."

"Marcus Agrippa would have understood my absence."

"And you imply I cannot, because of my ignorance of military affairs. Well, that's not my fault. I think the worse of myself for not being a soldier, and" – he raised his voice – "the worse of the man who has deprived me of that experience, which is properly speaking my birthright."

He stretched himself on the bench beside me and called for a slave to massage him. He ran his hands over his tight curly hair and sighed as the boy's hands worked over his flesh. He must have been almost thirty, but there was still something boyish about his own appearance. His thighs had the smoothness of the athlete who has never sat a horse on campaign in foul climates, and the skin on his face was soft, as a man's is when he is never exposed to wind and rain. The boy worked oil into his legs and I watched his pleasure increase. Then he flopped over on to his belly, inclined his head towards me, and told the boy to go and fetch wine.

"I have been wanting to speak to you," he said. "Now's as good a time as any. We were friends as children, weren't we? I always admired the way you handled my dear late brother-in-law Marcellus. I could see you thought him as great a ninny as I did. But, unlike me, you were clever enough not to let everyone realise this, for you knew how your stepfather doted on him. I couldn't do that, but I admired your . . . reserve, shall we say . . . ?"

I didn't reply. Where there's nothing useful to be said, it is best to remain silent. I may have grunted, for I was interested to see how far he would reveal himself, and it is always foolish to choke off confidences at an early stage, even if the wise man realises that in certain circumstances to receive a confidence may be almost as dangerous as to impart one. These things have to be balanced.

"And then I was married off to his sister, for what that's worth. You did better in that line, though I didn't realise it at the time. There was something to be said for being Agrippa's son-in-law. But there might be more to be said for being his successor again . . ."

"And the father of his sons?" I prompted.

The boy came back with wine. Iullus told him to hand me a cup too. It was sweet and resinous. Iullus rose to his feet, hugging his cup to his breast.

"I have ambitions in that direction," he said. "Julia and I have always been chums . . . if you put in a word for me, I'll not forget it . . ."

He lay down again, called on the curly-headed boy to resume his massage. He sighed with pleasure. I watched his flesh move as the boy's fingers eased themselves to and fro. I thought of his father dying of stupid ambition in the Egyptian sands. I thought of mine fondling the wine-flask on the terrace of his Alban villa while the tears coursed down his fat cheeks. Then I turned on my front, and longed for Vipsania, and dreamed of my own son's future . . .

Augustus was at his most affable when I met him in the next weeks. He treated me to magisterial surveys of the political situation in Rome. I marvelled, as I always did, at his acute evaluation of the political influence exerted by families, individuals and alliances. I admired the judgment with which he balanced this faction against that, showing me how he would sweeten this man's ambition with office or the promotion of some dependant, stifle that man's hopes by the timely detachment of some supporter, how he would keep some dangling in greedy expectation, and drench others with hints of disloyalty and unreliability. I was both entranced and disgusted, for I realised that he used men as counters and that his relish in doing so had in it something of the cruelty of a child.

Then he talked of Agrippa with a tenderness that was affecting. "The best of friends" he called him. "When we were

young," he said, "people used to laugh at his accent, and I
remember Mark Antony telling me that people took my fondness for Agrippa as a sign that I was myself second-rate. He
laughed as he said that, but Antony learned himself how wrong
that judgment was. We would never have triumphed but for
Agrippa. I loved him, you know. He never doubted that our
improbable adventure would end happily. Of course he was
deficient in imagination, but that gave me confidence too. And
now he is gone. It's like having my leg or my right arm cut off.
But our life goes on, that's the terrible thing."

I couldn't imagine Augustus ever thinking that a terrible thing.
I have never known a man who so revelled in existence, or one
who took such pleasure in unravelling problems . . .

"And we who are left," he said, "have to fill the vacancy he
has left behind. I'm happy with the condition of the armies,
thanks to you and to our dear Drusus, I know everything there
is in safe hands. Of course I don't expect either of you to replace
Agrippa in the management of the Republic, that's a task I shall
have to shoulder alone, it would be putting far too much weight
on your young, if capable, shoulders. But there's our darling
Julia. Of course she's overcome with a very proper grief now
but when that subsides, well, it'll be a matter of finding her a
husband. Who shall we choose? And then there are the boys,
my two darlings Gaius and Lucius. Whoever marries Julia must
be a man I trust absolutely, you know, for he will have to act
as their guardian too. Naturally, as long as I am spared, I will
secure their interests, but I'm not immortal, and my health has
never been good. I nearly died ten years ago, you remember,
and my doctor says he couldn't call me a good life. I take care
of myself of course, exercise, and frugality in eating and drinking, but who knows when the gods will call me? So, you see,
my dear Tiberius, the question is worrying. It keeps me awake
at nights, and that's not good for me. Your dear mother shares
my worries, that's a great comfort, but even she can't think of
an ideal solution. We can neither of us think of any solution
which won't hurt somebody. That's the shame of it. I hate
hurting people I am fond of, you know, and yet I don't see how
it can be done otherwise. Have you any suggestions, dear boy?"

Was I expected to answer? I was a blind fool. I did not see the way his thoughts were tending. But even if I had, I do not see how I could have been other than impotent. Augustus has inserted himself into the state in such a manner that his will is always pregnant of the future.

I was kept dangling in Rome. When I announced my intention of leaving the city to join Vipsania, urgent reasons for postponement were produced. Then I was invited to supper by Maecenas. I had always disliked and distrusted my stepfather's Etruscan counsellor; his effeminacy disgusted me, and I could not forget that Agrippa had described him to me as being as "wily as a Spanish banker and vicious as a Corinthian brothel-keeper". My instinct was to refuse the invitation, but the slave who brought it to me coughed to attract my attention and said:

"My master ordered me to add in speech what he chose not to commit in writing: that your future happiness depends on your acceptance. He said you would not immediately believe this, but commanded me to assure you that he has only your best interests at heart, and to say also that the matter concerns your wife.".

The great house on the Esquiline was a mixture of gross luxury and dirt. There was furniture of the utmost extravagance and rich wall-paintings and vases, and a profusion of flowers, but a small dog was lifting its leg against a carved ivory couch as I entered. No one reproved it, and the number of little dogs and cats that swarmed over the palace suggested to me that the action was common. The air was oversweet and perfumed, as if to mask the stench of urine. I knew Maecenas to be in poor health himself. He had retired, as I believed, from public life. His wife Terentia had long abandoned him, and he cohabited with the actor Bathyllus whose behaviour even on the public stage had become a byword for indecency. Maecenas himself had lost whatever reputation he had possessed, and few people mentioned his name without a snigger or an expression of disgust; yet I knew that Augustus still consulted him, and even valued his advice above all others; except my late father-in-law's.

I was ushered into a little dining-room. The table was already spread and Maecenas, in an improbable gown of gold and purple silks, reclined on a couch. He was gazing at a blond boy, who posed, nude, on a stool; his right ankle rested on his left knee and his face was concealed as he leaned forward to examine the sole of his raised foot. An artist across the room was sketching the boy.

Maecenas neither rose when I entered, nor took his eyes from the boy. Instead he stretched out his long bony hand and squeezed the boy's leg. Understanding this to be a command, the boy rose, and, without a backward glance, strolled from the room, trailing a tunic behind him. The artist collected his materials and slipped away. We were left alone, and Maecenas rose and extended both hands in a gesture of greeting. His face was drawn and wasted by disease, and when he spoke, his voice was hoarse and seemed to come from a distance. During the meal he conversed merely of trivialities and plied me with Falernian wine. He ate only some smoked fish and a peach himself. Then he dismissed the slaves.

"I rarely entertain now," he said. "My health does not permit it. You see before you, dear boy, the wreck of a man who has all but exhausted pleasure."

(I thought of the blond model, and dissented tacitly.)

"And yet," he said, fingering a fat purple fig, letting its juice trickle over his fingers which he then licked before dipping them in water and wiping them with a linen cloth, "you are the second supper guest I have had this week. Remarkable. The first was your stepfather . . ."

"Your messenger hinted," I said, "that you had something to say concerning my wife. That is why I came."

"Tiberius, I pray you to allow a sick old man to approach the matter gradually. Display to me, dear boy, the patience with which you are so splendidly equipped, which you practise with such admirable skill in war. It is my affliction that what was once affectation has become so much a part of my nature that I cannot now approach a subject except circuitously. What I have to say would endanger me if I spoke to any man other than yourself. That I choose to ignore the danger is the measure of the respect in which I hold you. Remember that. I have watched you, and watched over you, all your life, and believe me, dear boy, I have your best interests at heart. Yet you despise me, don't you?"

I made no reply. He smiled.

"All my life," he said, "I have made it my business to know men. It is in that knowledge that all my skill lies, and I possess it because I have never neglected the gods' advice: 'Know thyself'. You will know, for all Rome knows it, that I am helpless before the actor Bathyllus. My passion for him has made me an object of mockery. I cannot appear in the street now without enduring insult. What was once pleasant self-indulgence has become addiction. I need Bathyllus and his like – yes, and more, boys like that child you saw here tonight – as a drunkard needs wine. It is what my life has become. Once, I loved my wife, in a manner of speaking. But . . ." he extended his hands, the rings flashed in the light of the lamps, and he laughed, " . . . but they have all been substitutes. There is only one person I have truly loved, and I made it my business to secure him what he most ardently desired: which was Rome. His accession to power, aided by my advice on innumerable occasions, has saved the state, and perhaps the world. I helped to make him a great man for the benefit of all and, in doing so, collaborated with time and the world in the destruction of the boy I loved. I adored Octavius and I still love the boy who survives behind the mask of Augustus. Yet in giving him the world, I lost him. In saving Rome, I taught him to place reasons of state above the claims of ordinary human love. I am proud of what I accomplished, and disgusted by its consequences. My disgust expresses itself in my own enslavement to lust, and it is for me small consolation that the enjoyment of embraces is less damaging to the psyche and the character than the enjoyment of power . . .

"Are you still listening, Tiberius?"

"Yes," I said, "I am listening to your words and to the sound of the gathering night."

"I believe you love Vipsania?"

"I do."

"And she loves you?"

"I believe so."

"And you are happy together."

"We have grown in love, and that love is at least a shield against the realities of the world."

"An insubstantial shield, I fear. Can love armour you against destiny?"

"As to destiny, I have moments of scepticism."

"All wise men are sceptics. I myself am even sceptical of scepticism . . ."

He sighed, and leant back on his cushions.

"Pass me that phial, dear boy. My medicine. And have patience. We approach the point. Forgive my procrastination. I had to be sure things were as I had thought them to be."

He was silent a long time. The sand slipped down the hourglass and moths fluttered round the lamps. A little dog crawled out from under the couch where it had been sleeping and jumped on to his lap. He fondled its ears.

"When Augustus was here the other night, I said to him: if you really loved your daughter, you would let her marry a pretty playboy like Iullus Antonius, and be happy. He replied that he could not let her marry a man who would diminish her. Do you believe he was honest?"

"I believe he would never let her marry Antonius, if not for that exact reason."

"No, you are quite right. He would not trust him as the guardian of Gaius and Lucius. That will be his first concern. But you see, dear boy, for Augustus, people have become objects to be shifted for his advantage which he equates with the advantage of the state. And the terrible thing is he is right to do so. I said to him the other night: everyone has to yield to your monstrous will. It has come to dominate Rome, all of us; it dominates you yourself, it has killed your capacity for imagination and for ordinary human warmth. You, I said, are as much prisoner of your vice as I am of mine. And then, Tiberius, I told him what would happen. This is by way of being a confession. We need more wine."

He picked up a little bell and tinkled it twice. A painted slave in a short tunic brought in a jug of wine and poured a cup for both of us. I drank mine in a gulp and he filled it again. Maecenas held the rim of his own cup to his lips and watched the boy leave us alone.

"I said to him: we end as prisoners of our own character. Shall I tell you what you'll do? You will compel Tiberius to divorce Vipsania . . ."

When he spoke these words it was as if a fear which I had been denying stood erect before me with drawn sword.

"Yes, dear boy . . . after all, I said, Vipsania is no longer of any value since her father is dead. It doesn't matter that she and Tiberius have been happy together, for that happiness has become only an obstacle to your greater intent. You will throw it aside, and force him to marry Julia. He's a strong man, I said, and a man of honour – I do not say this to flatter you now, dear boy, but because I have always found it necessary to explain to Augustus how he makes his will appear reasonable. He will do the right thing by your grandsons, I said . . . As I spoke I could see the clouds slip away from him. He gave me the loving smile I remember from our youth, which he would accord me whenever I resolved a difficulty. For a moment it was as if our old intimacy had been rekindled. I was happy. But later, when he had gone, I was sad to think that this revival of intimacy had been made possible only by my ability to show him what he wanted to do, though he had not yet brought himself to the point of admitting it . . ."

"You know my stepfather very well," I said.

"I think I know him even better than Livia does. You see, unlike her, I remember the boy with whom I laughed and loved before the proscriptions, before he combined with Mark Antony and that imbecile Lepidus to mark down the names of those who must be killed because they had become inconvenient. When once a man has done that, Tiberius, he can excuse himself anything."

"Why do you tell me this? Is it to warn me, so that I can resist?"

"Tiberius, Tiberius, I had thought better of you." He closed his eyes, and, when he spoke again, his voice seemed to me to come from a great distance, across windy deserts of experience. "I had thought better of you. Surely you understand the world Augustus has made, with my help and Agrippa's? The time for effective resistance is over. An act of resistance now is no more than a piece of petulance, like telling the wind to cease blowing."

"I could kill myself rather than submit . . ."

"Tiberius, remember: 'Know thyself' is the command of the gods. Your nature is to serve. You will obey. And you will praise yourself for your obedience."

"Never . . ."

"Then let us say you will console yourself with the thought that you obey in the public interest. And let me add something else: when Augustus unfolds his plan to you, he will assure you that he has consulted me, and that my advice has ever proved to be for the public good. Your submission will then become an act of virtue, just as defiance would be understood as the expression of your selfish and individual will. How, Tiberius, can you put your little marriage above the majesty of the interest of Rome? Together," he sniffed his wine, "we restored the Republic and created a despotism, a world fit for power, ruled by power, a world in which gentle values have become obsolete, a world where one commands and all others serve, a vision of the future in which a hard frost grips men's hearts, and generous sentiments are annulled by the habit of fearful subjection . . ."

I left him and entered into black night, choking with smoke, from which, it sometimes seems, I have never emerged. As I descended the slippery steps of his palace, I was accosted by a whore. I took her, in anger, like a goat, against a wall. I paid her ten times the fee she demanded.

"You must raise your price," I said to her, "for, since all value is destroyed, no measure of worth can survive and you may ask what you choose."

"Oh thank you, sir, I wish all my clients were gentlemen like yourself."

I did not leave my chamber for two days, but lay in sullen torpor, drowning myself in wine. When I received a message summoning me to the Princeps, I sent word that I was sick, and turned my face to the wall.

On the third day a letter came from my wife. I have it here now. It has never been parted from me, all these years . . .

Husband,

It is with a heavy heart that I write that word for the last time. Henceforth it must remain locked up in my grieving heart. I do not blame you, for I understand that you too are a victim, and that you too will suffer. I believe this because I am confident of the virtue of your love for me. And I do not even reproach you, my dear Tiberius, for having lacked the courage to break the news to me yourself. Why, I can imagine you protesting, should I be compelled to do the deed when it is not of my desiring? It is the certainty that you do not desire it which makes it possible for me to bear my sorrow.

My own life is, I now feel, well nigh ended, and I exist only for our son. Yet I cannot quite convince myself that even this is true, for it has been hinted that – of course – I shall be compensated with a new and respectable marriage. I do not want it, but since I do not want what is about to befall me either, what has indeed befallen me, I have no doubt I shall submit. I was brought up to do my duty, and this new departure will be presented to me as duty.

I hesitate to write more, lest my feelings betray me.

I would wish also to warn you. I shall not do so, because my judgment may be mistaken, because I am certain you will share my doubts, and because it would be both improper and unwise to say what I think. I will merely add that my father once remarked that to make Julia happy was work for a god, not a man.

You will, I know, continue to care lovingly for our son, though you will naturally be aware also of the new, and very great, responsibilities you have assumed . . .

Believe me, my dear Tiberius, ever your loving and devoted – but I no longer know how to sign myself . . .

I do not know why I have kept this letter, for I knew it by heart almost from the first. I turn it over in my mind, in self-laceration and for reassurance. It is both a dagger and a talisman.

Perhaps the most remarkable feature of this unholy episode was that I never discussed it with Augustus. He behaved to me in the weeks that followed with benevolence, respect and that evasiveness of which he was the supreme master. There were countless moments when it seemed as if he was about to broach the subject, others when it appeared that I had been granted an opening which would allow me to do so myself; yet nothing was said between us, till the eve of my wedding to Julia when he embraced me – almost without the involuntary shrinking which I had always sensed when he took me in his arms – and assured me of his love and confidence, assurance sweetened by his gift of a villa and estate at Ravello.

"At last," he said, "I can face the future without Agrippa."

But I had raged to my mother, stormed and pleaded. I had howled at the malignity of fortune which deprived me of what I chiefly valued. I had protested that if deprived of Vipsania I would be rendered unfit to prosecute my career. I swore that Livia's connivance in this brutality would destroy my love and respect for her herself. And, in the privacy of my mother's chamber, I cursed my stepfather who had made the world in which I was compelled to live.

She accused me of behaving like a spoiled child; and I was indeed spoiled, I was damaged.

She, my mother, had damaged me. I saw her at that moment, a lean woman with fading hair and a face that grew more chis-elled every year, as if preparing itself to be preserved only in stone, and I saw her as one who had failed me, her son, by her subservience to her husband, by the subordination of her duty to me to his devouring ambition, and her ambition for him. Resentment filled me, tasting of bile. Even as I let bitterness fill my mouth, I knew my reaction was absurd. I knew that every man carries his own destiny with him, and that to blame my mother for my present predicament was as ridiculous as to blame winter for bringing snow to the mountains. I knew too that for a man of my age, for one who had achieved what I had, who had commanded armies and consigned men to death, to experience such resentment was contemptible. Indeed my resentment was as contemptible as my submission; yet I could not resist it.

I soon learned also not to despise myself for submitting. What else could I have done? I had already seen lives wither when men set themselves against Augustus. I have since seen how no considerations of affection, loyalty or decency can deflect him from a course which he has judged expedient or necessary. All men, yes, and all women too, exist for him ultimately as malleable objects: creatures whose lives may be deformed or cut off at his command. I told myself that if I had resisted, if I had opposed my will to his, it would have profited me nothing: I would have been cast into exile, Vipsania would still have been denied me, and my son Drusus' future would have been darkened. My acquiescence was my only means of protecting him.

I told myself this, and knew it to be true; yet still despised my weakness. To appease my troubled mind I transferred my self-contempt to a pervasive scorn for the degeneracy of our times, when, with the loss of our antique Republican virtue, even the nobility of Rome have become the despot's playthings. "O generation fit for slavery," I growled; and those who heard me, and shrank from my harsh speech, did not understand that I included myself among the slaves.

NINE

So we were married. The night before the wedding I sat late over the wine with my friend Gnaeus Piso, a man who has ever been ready to match me bottle for bottle. Piso, as a member of a family almost as distinguished as my own, would later be my colleague in the consulship. We shared more than a taste for good liquor, for, like me, he was a stern critic of the vices of our age, and yearned for the virtue of the free state. A realist however, he recognised that the great days were departed. He had – and indeed, I trust, still has – a talent for making the tart and pertinent observation which had pleased me from the first days of our acquaintance.

"Well, Tiberius," he said that night, "Heracles himself might shrink from the task thrust upon you."

"Heracles' own matrimonial history was unhappy."

"Most people would call you a lucky man, of course. She's not only the Princeps' daughter, but also the most beautiful and seductive woman in Rome."

"She was faithful, I think, to Agrippa."

Piso laughed.

"There's faithfulness and then there's fidelity," he said.

"What do you mean? It's unlike you to play with words."

"When you are faced with women like Julia, what else is there to do with them?"

"I don't understand you, and I think I am happy not to."

"Tiberius, we both know Julia. We have both known Julia. Don't forget that I was once on Marcellus' staff . . . and, old friend, when that pretty boy was alive, what were you to Julia? Can you control her now?"

I pushed the wine-flask in his direction.

"What would you advise?"

"I would advise you not to be in your present position. Seeing as you are, and there's no help for it, then there are only two things to be done. First, you must insist that she accompanies you to the armies, so that she is at least under your eye. Second, keep her in pig. A flighty woman can be anchored only in that way."

I swallowed my wine, and made a face.

"You're forgetting," I said, "that my mother was in just that condition when the Princeps seduced her."

"The situations," I continued, after a pause during which silence and uncertainty filled the room, "are not, of course, analogous. If my stepfather was not yet Princeps and Augustus, he was nevertheless triumvir. There is no one today with that glamour of power . . ."

"Yes, and Livia was already a woman celebrated for her virtue. As you say, the situations are not analogous . . ."

I had not seen Julia for more than two years, and we had held no communication concerning the decision made for our future. I had therefore no idea whether she approved the marriage. In recent years she had shown no sign of the desire she had felt for me when we were young, and I could not believe that I would have been her choice. Iullus Antonius was, of course, a liar, but the confidence with which he had spoken of Julia's feeling for him had been convincing. On the other hand, Julia had always disliked Vipsania and would be pleased to have triumphed over her. These reflections made me nervous, and my evening with Piso had left me ill at ease. I steadied myself with a jug of wine before the ceremony, and then, to ward off criticism from Livia, and perhaps Julia herself – though hers would rather take the form of mockery – I sweetened my breath with a handful of violet pastilles.

My mother summoned me to her apartments. I found her alone, which pleased me, for I had feared that my stepfather would be there too. Then I realised that he would be unwilling to confront me till the marriage had been celebrated: in case I dug my heels in. (He has often remarked on my resemblance to a mule: a poor joke in present circumstances, I thought.)

Livia kissed me on the forehead.

"This is a solemn moment for you, my son," she said.

"Mother, there's no need for dissimulation when we are alone. I take it we are alone – no spies concealed in waiting, no informers behind the screens?"

She snapped her fingers.

"There's no need to take that tone, Tiberius. I can see you are still displeased. Well, sulk if you must but I'm glad that you have the sense to go through with it. I was going to commend you on your sense of duty. Here, come and sit beside me and listen to what I have to say. What have you been eating? There's a nasty smell on your breath."

"Violet pastilles, Mother. My doctor recommends them for heartburn."

"I see. Well, that doesn't matter. You're not making some joke when you mention heartburn, are you?"

"No, Mother."

"I've never liked your jokes. I don't understand them, but there's always been a cruel streak in your idea of humour. However, that's neither here nor there. But I wanted to speak to you before this marriage takes place, since I know you don't like it. Well, I confess I don't like it myself. Julia and I are opposites. That's all there is to it. I can't think of a single matter on which we have ever thought the same. Not even Augustus, for I love him for what he is and she only cares for him on account of what he has to give her. And now he is giving her you, my son, and I am not certain that that is what she wants. So I see trouble ahead . . ."

"In that case, Mother . . ."

"No, don't interrupt. You are wondering why in the end I have approved the marriage. I say in the end because whether you believe me or not – and you have never believed anything that ran counter to your ingrained opinions, I know that well – I have to tell you I opposed it as long as I could. I told Augustus Vipsania made you happy. I even admitted that I was jealous of her as mothers often are of their sons' wives. But . . . no good. The fact is that you are a sacrifice to reason of state. Your domestic happiness is being sacrificed to necessity. And necessity imposes its own rules. Julia must have a husband, and the boys must have a father, and her nature is such that it must be a man who is thoroughly admirable, honourable and reliable. That is why you have been compelled to act dishonourably towards Vipsania that you may act honourably in the interests of Rome. People like us cannot live by private impulses for we cannot live private lives."

"I understand that, Mother . . ." and I did. Political imperatives make sense to me. If that hadn't been true, I would have fought harder.

"I am only sorry," I said, "that it should have to be me . . ."

"There was no one else . . ."

Was the same thought in both our minds? That Drusus could have been chosen? If so, I didn't raise the question. I had always understood that Drusus was different, that he would not be asked to make the same sacrifice of personal interest that was regularly demanded of me. Drusus was different. Everybody liked him. I was devoted to him myself. He was, to use a weak word, nice. But he was nice perhaps because he had never been emotionally challenged. Livia had kept her relationship with him a happy, sunny one. Augustus smiled when he appeared.

Besides, Drusus was married to Antonia, Octavia's daughter, and, even apart from my stepfather's feeling for his sister, her daughter was not expendable as my poor Vipsania was.

No, Drusus was safe.

I did my best. I have nothing with which to reproach myself. For a moment I was even optimistic. For a little time it seemed as if it might work, as if we could live in afternoon contentment.

Julia bestowed her most radiant smile on me. When we were alone, she murmured, as she had used to do, "Old bear, old bear" and stroked my cheeks with fingers light as a flower's touch . . .

"What a hard face, old bear, grizzled and weather-beaten . . ."

She kissed my lips.

"Like Agrippa's," she said. "How strange it will be. Like going back in time and yet coming full circle . . ."

She slipped out of her shift and stood before me in her full ripe loveliness. Moonlight streaked into the room, casting a silvery-gold sheen over her flesh. She knelt before me and thrust her hands under my tunic.

It is night as I write this. I can hear the waves break on the rocks below and silence rises from the town and I see again Julia's upturned face, lips open, and a dewiness under her eyes. She breathed desire, and I was afraid lest I should not be able to satisfy her. She drew me to the bed . . . "Come, husband, come, old bear, you delighted me once, and I . . ." she nuzzled me, "Tiberius, Tiberius, Tiberius . . ."

"Tiberius, Tiberius, Tiberius . . ." I was always anxious. Even when I believed I was giving her pleasure, I was anxious, alert for the comparisons I was certain filled her mind . . . Even when she cried out in ecstasy, my mind seemed to remain apart, and I asked myself whether she was simulating her joy.

Did she try too? I believe she did. I must believe she did. Now that I have nothing urgent to do, I spend hours casting back over my life, weighing my own behaviour and that of others. Too many hours perhaps, for such introspection can become a disease, a potent drug. There are times, however, when I imagine that Julia snatched at the opportunity afforded her by our marriage as a means of escaping the imperatives of her own nature, which she knew well, and sometimes (I think) feared. Like all who experience a strong impulse towards dissipation, a nostalgia for whatever is base and filthy in human existence, she was torn between that attraction and a longing to live a virtuous life, an intermittent longing certainly but one none the less strong for being frequently in abeyance. She lusted after the manifold pleasures of the senses, seeking satisfaction in extremity, yet ever aware of how she received from her debasement diminishing returns. In her best hours she appeared to me as a godlike child of nature, spontaneous, bountiful, joy-giving and joy-enhancing. Yet there was always a desperation in her happiness, as if she pursued pleasure to flee a vision of emptiness. She filled her life with sensation in order not to be compelled to gaze upon a vision of insignificance. Finding no sure foothold in experience, she experienced a sharp and recurrent apprehension that nothing mattered. "We live, we die, and that's that," she said. "Why live except to prolong and intensify pleasure . . . ?" But, when she spoke like that, I seemed to see a dark river mist surround her, chilling the blood and obscuring the future.

She accompanied me, as Piso had recommended, to the armies. She delighted in the life of the camp, and was tireless and uncomplaining on the march. Men and officers adored her, they admired her high spirits and readiness to laugh at discomfort and the accidents inseparable from military life. I found my own popularity – never great, for I had always known that I gained respect rather than affection – grew on her account. To my surprise, Agrippa's widow was more at ease on campaign than Agrippa's daughter had been; for my dear Vipsania's private and retiring nature had been revolted by the inevitable brutality of army life. To some extent Julia shared her feelings, but, whereas Vipsania shrank from them, Julia spoke out against what seemed to her excessively stern punishment. Once I found her rubbing soothing ointment into the back of a soldier who had been flayed for indiscipline. I should have reproved her for her action, which would appear to the soldiers to call in question the justice of the man's punishment, but I could not bring myself to do so, even when the centurion who had flogged the man lodged a complaint.

In other respects the first years of our marriage were less satisfactory. I hesitate even in the privacy of this memoir to write of the intimate details of the bedchamber. It doesn't seem at all the right thing to do. And yet it is impossible to tell the truth about a marriage if one declines to do so, impossible even to confront it. Moreover, one cannot contemplate any marriage – such as, for example, that of Livia and Augustus – without wondering what happens in bed.

Julia never found difficulty in arousing me; yet even when excited to my most ardent, I remained timid, shy or indeed fearful of comparison. I could not then believe that I satisfied her. She flirted with the young officers on my staff and, watching her smile on them and rock with laughter at their callow jokes, I knew that they brought her gifts which I could never match. It went, I was sure, no further than flirtation, though some of the young men were head over heels in love with her. She liked it that way; their admiration delighted her. In the winters we went to the Dalmatian coast, and it was there that our child was conceived.

Something strange happened to me after the birth of our son. I fell in love with my wife. At first I wouldn't admit it even to myself. It seemed disloyal to my memory of Vipsania. Yet it happened, and it began when I saw her lying, exhausted but still radiant, with her hair spread out like a fan on the pillow behind her, and our infant in her arms. I had never thought of Julia as maternal – her attitude to her two boys, Gaius and Lucius, was off-hand and sceptical – she refused to agree with their grandfather's estimate of their abilities. But she cooed over little Tiberius (as she had insisted we call him), and, seeing them there, it came to me, "This thing is mine, this woman too is mine, the most desirable prize in Rome is mine, mine, and properly mine alone" and my heart overflowed with love. I fell on my knee at the bedside, seized her hand and covered it with kisses. I took her in my arms and embraced her, with a tender confidence and ardent desire I had never felt in my life before, not even for Vipsania. I was, that night and for months afterwards, a prince among men.

And Julia responded. That was the remarkable thing. We were, for a brief interlude, lost in each other, as, in mountain country, the clouds can all at once and without warning dispel from the peaks, leaving the wanderer bathed in golden and restoring light.

She said to me: "For the first time, old bear, I feel I am leading the right sort of life. You can't imagine the frustration I have endured. All my bad behaviour is the result of that frustration, and the boredom . . . Oh, how bored I have been! I was forced into marriage with Marcellus, then with Agrippa, oh, I know you admired him, but you can count yourself lucky you

weren't his dutiful wife. My father wonders that I don't love
Gaius and Lucius as he does, and he will be awfully jealous when
he sees how I dote on little Tiberius. He doesn't understand:
it's because that man was their father, and I can't look at them
without hearing his voice droning on and on . . . Maybe I love
you because you're so silent, old bear . . . All I have wanted
was to have fun, and all my life my father has tried to squeeze
that desire out of me."

She would talk like this, lying naked on our bed, and then she
would stretch out her long leg and, with a suppleness that I
found enchanting, paint her toenails shell-pink with a delicate
brush. Or she would rest, warm and damp and relaxed and
happy, in my arms, while her hair tickled my lips and my cheek,
and she sank into sleep. Can life, I wondered, have more to
offer than to lie thus, with the trusting and satisfied proof of
manhood held in sleeping embrace? Can anything equal that drift
into oblivion with your girl in your arms?

As I write these words I feel the renewal of desire, then
regret and misery invade the defences I have so laboriously
constructed.

TEN

In the autumn of that year when we found ourselves in love, my brother Drusus died. We had been engaged in a two-pronged campaign on the northern frontiers of the empire. While I subdued Pannonia, advancing to the banks of the mighty River Danube, Drusus, with a mixture of prudence and audacity which was wonderful, penetrated deep into the mysterious forests of Germany through the territory of the Cherusci and the Marcomanni to the River Elbe, where he erected a trophy to mark the new limit of Roman control. This was no mere raid, for he built a chain of fortresses on the line of his march to secure his rear, while at the same time the Rhine was defended by new, well-garrisoned fortifications. No man of Rome ever deserved better, or did more for our city, than my dear brother in his German campaigns. Then, crossing a river swollen by the October rains, his horse slipped. He struck his head against a jagged rock, and was dragged insensible from the water. Word of his condition was brought to me and pausing only to make necessary arrangements for my own troops, I hastened to his bedside. I covered four hundred miles in less than sixty hours, and arrived to find his doctors ashen-faced and nervous. They were relieved to see me, however, for they knew that I would be able to testify that they had done everything that was possible. Drusus was only intermittently conscious. I sat by his campbed, and prayed useless prayers to the indifferent gods, while he, poor boy, babbled words that I could not understand, and threw himself about in a restless fever.

"He is so weak," the doctors said, "that we do not dare to bleed him further."

Instead they applied compresses of ice to his temples, and sponged his body with water drawn from a deep well.

The sweat dried on his forehead. He opened his eyes, saw me, recognised me, and spoke in a voice which was calm but already sounded as if it came from another world.

"I knew you would come, brother. I have been waiting till you were here . . . Tell our father" – even then I noticed how easily Drusus used that term of Augustus – "that I have done my duty. But I do not believe that we can ever . . ." he broke off. I pressed his hand. Again his eyes opened. "Look after my children, brother, and my dear Antonia. She has always liked you, and . . ." His voice faded and he choked. I held a mug of watered wine to his lips. "I feel like a deserter," he sighed, and closed his eyes, and in a little was no more.

I sat by his bedside as night chilled my bones. I remembered his candour and ease of manner, his probity, his easy affection. Once, he came to me and suggested we should approach Augustus and recommend that the Republic be restored in its antique form. "We both know, brother," he said, "that the restoration our father made was false, and that only a true resuscitation of our ancient institutions can enable Rome to regain its moral health, its old virtue." I placed my hand on his shoulder in agreement, and shook my head, "You are demanding what cannot be," I said. But now, as I heard an owl screech through the long night, I knew that it was Drusus' willingness to attempt the impossible, his refusal to be constrained by the appearance of necessity, which had made me love him.

In the morning his body was disembowelled and embalmed. The next day the funeral cortège began its long journey home. I marched on foot by the wheel of the waggon that carried his coffin. In every village people bared their heads as we passed, for his fame had gone before him. At night I slept on a mattress spread in the waggon beside his coffin. So we crossed the Alps, out of the rains, and marched down through Italy where the peasants were harvesting the vines, and the olive trees groaned under a weight of fruit. We reached Rome, and my brother was laid to rest in the mausoleum which Augustus had constructed for the family; I would have preferred him to lie in a Claudian tomb, but my wishes were not consulted.

Meanwhile Julia had remained at Aquileia in Cisalpine Gaul at the north end of the Adriatic Sea. She was expecting another child and her doctor had forbidden her to travel.

At a dinner-party Augustus spoke of Drusus. He was sincere, and embarrassing. Whenever honey enters his voice, I am aware of what has been cut off. I am made uneasy by my sense of discrepancy: my knowledge that this warm and beautiful voice has spat out orders to kill people and destroy lives. I find myself making excuses for him, saying to myself that it is not his fault he has been put into a position in which he has to make intolerable decisions. And then I remember that he is there because he wanted power.

Now he spoke of all those who had left him: of Agrippa, of the poet Vergil, of Maecenas who was dying, and of Drusus himself. He praised my . . . fidelity, a word you might use of a dog. And then he turned towards his grandsons, my stepsons, who are also – these things become confusing – his adopted sons: Gaius and Lucius. He told them they were the light of his old age, the fire that warmed his heart, and the hope of Rome. Lucius, who is the nicer of the two, and in reality a good and affectionate boy, had the grace to blush.

But the next morning the Princeps was back in charge of Augustus, the sentimentalist who embarrasses me relegated.

"You will have to go to Germany," he said, "to take over from Drusus."

I pointed out that the situation in Pannonia was still unstable.

"You have done wonderfully well there," he said, "and Gnaeus Piso will be competent to consolidate your work. But Germany is another matter. Drusus has made the breach, but all his work will be wasted if we do not follow it up. Don't you see? Germany must be subjugated, the tribes brought within our orbit, or the whole of Drusus' achievement will go for nothing. It will be as if he had never been. And you, Tiberius, are the only man able to achieve the total victory which will be the true memorial to your dear brother, my beloved son . . ."

The note of embarrassing sincerity returned to his voice in this last sentence. It was the sincerity of the actor.

Then he said, "I think you have doubts about the German campaign."

He fidgeted while I remained silent.

"Come on."

"Forgive me, I was gathering my thoughts. Drusus had no doubts . . ."

"Which was why I originally sent him to Germany and you, Tiberius, to Pannonia."

"Yes," I said, "the situation on the two fronts appears to me to be quite different. We have only to look at the map. Pannonia – the Danube frontier – is within a short march of Cisalpine Gaul, and though we still use the term, it seems to me that the province now differs but little from Italy itself . . ."

"So Vergil, who was, you will remember, from Mantua in the north of that province, used to say. And you are both right. So?"

"So we must hold Pannonia and the line of the Danube. But Germany is different. The tribes there do not appear to me to be susceptible to civilisation, while Gaul itself may be adequately protected by the barrier of the Rhine. Therefore I doubt the value of Germany, certainly in relation to the cost of subjugation. I fear some terrible disaster will one day overtake Roman arms in those savage forests. Germany is a wooded desert."

"Nevertheless," he said; and I knew when he pronounced that word that my arguments were vain, that his mind was settled. When he utters that word, it signifies that he accepts the validity of your argument, but will still have his way.

"An empire like Rome's cannot rest. The day it ceases to grow is the day we renege on our duty. The gods promised Aeneas and his descendants an empire without limits. We cannot take on ourselves the responsibility of deciding that we have gone far enough. Of course, for tactical reasons such a decision may be made – for the moment. But no more than that. Besides, it is only our expanding empire which reconciles the Roman nobility to the loss of liberty. Never forget that."

"Which was lost precisely in the cause of empire."

"An undeniable truth, and therefore one better left unsaid."

Augustus will present himself as an enigma to historians. Which of his utterances are they to believe? In one breath he will present himself as the saviour of Rome's liberty and the restorer of the Republic; in the next, confess that liberty has vanished and that the Republican offices are now no more than decoration. Yet he rests his power, or at least its legal expression, on the *tribunicia potestas*, which represents the fullest statement of Republican liberty. How much of what he says does he believe himself?

"A meaningless question," Livia would say. "Your father uses words as counters, which is, ultimately, all they are."

He is a hypocrite deceived by his own hypocrisy. Whatever he says at any moment has the ring of truth for him. This is why he is so adept at deceiving others.

Germany was no place to take Julia. I had myself to hasten there in the middle of winter, for the exigencies of modern war in remote barbarian lands require a degree of preparation such as would have amazed Julius Caesar, that improviser of genius. Lacking genius, I shun improvisation. Moreover, it was necessary that I should learn as much as possible about the tribes by whom I would be opposed. There is of course a close resemblance between one German tribe and another, but not all are equally devoted to war, for that devotion fluctuates according to the temper of the different chiefs. One consequence of this is that, though they fight by tribes, a tribe may often contain a number of outsiders, for high-born youths frequently seek out service with a neighbouring tribe, if their own chiefs are disinclined to make war. Yet, on the whole, peace is unwelcome to the German peoples, and they distinguish themselves more readily in the midst of danger, for, lacking all arts and civil refinements, it is only in war that a man may obtain reputation. Besides, a great retinue, such as their chiefs delight in, since they measure their own status according to the number of their followers, cannot be maintained except by war and violence, for it is to the generosity of their chiefs that they look for the war horse and the spear. Their warriors receive no pay, which is not surprising, for barbarians despise money. On the other hand they accept presents from their chiefs, and they expect to be well fed. They are great drunkards, believing that courage in war goes with a capacity for deep drinking. They are capable of a certain swaggering generosity, but they have more of cruel savagery than wolves. They delight in torturing their prisoners before they kill them.

As I had feared, the morale of our army was low. The soldiers had been cast down by Drusus' death. Moreover, I discovered that the extent of my brother's achievement was less than we had hoped. This was not his fault. It was a measure of the enormity of the task. Though he had advanced through the forests as far as the Elbe, it was only in coastal regions that he had been able to embark on the policy of civilisation which is a necessary part of any conquest that aspires to be enduring. He had constructed a canal through the lakes of Holland, and this had persuaded the tribes resident there, the Frisii and the Batavii, to become allies of the Roman people, for they saw not only our greatness but the prospect of unimagined prosperity open before them. It is trade which greases the wheels of empire, and it is the building of roads, bridges and canals which makes commerce possible.

There were no cities in Germany. Indeed the Germans scarcely live even in villages as we understand them. They prefer to live separately and scattered, and they lay out their villages with open ground, frequently extensive, between the houses. They are therefore averse from learning the arts and manners of civil society; and I saw at once that this was a great problem. It was clear to me that Germany could not be thoroughly and effectively conquered till the land was settled, till cities were built and colonies planted. However, it was difficult to persuade colonists to establish themselves there till the tribes had been thoroughly subdued and brought to recognise the majesty and order of Rome. This was a problem I was unable to solve in my three years in Germany. Indeed, I can hardly claim to have done more than define it, and take a few tentative steps by means of the engineering works I instigated.

Otherwise, every summer was spent in pursuit of an evasive enemy who could rarely be brought to battle. On each occasion that we achieved battle however, the skill and discipline of our armies appalled, dispirited, and defeated the barbarians.

"It will be a slow business," I told Augustus, "and we can offer our young men no hope of glory. I demand sacrifice from them. They must be ready to shed blood and sweat, to toil long hours and to endure hardships without repining. But, if the gods are willing, we shall at last bring these accursed barbarians within the pale of civilisation."

He replied praising my efforts for Rome, " . . . worthy of your Claudian ancestors in their greatest hours, and of your mother's son."

Our second child was stillborn. I had scarcely time to grieve. Julia was depressed by the little girl's death, and her letters were mournful. They were also brief and less and less frequent. I could not reproach her for I had to confess that sometimes days went by without thought of her crossing my mind. Then, in my second summer campaign, little Tiberius caught a fever and died. The news was brought to me as I crouched in my tent on the muddy banks of a tributary of the Elbe. It had been raining for three weeks and our advance was halted. It was difficult to bring up provisions for the troops and horses from our base fifty miles in the rear. Some scouts reported that the enemy had vanished into the uttermost recesses of the forest, but my mind was not appeased by this information. I had a foreboding of danger, even disaster. The forest was too quiet. I called Segestes, the chief of one branch of the Cherusci, a man originally taken prisoner by Drusus and persuaded to ally himself to the Roman people by the eloquence of my brother and the example of his virtue. For a German, Segestes was an honourable man. Yet I was uncertain to what extent I could trust him.

"My scouts report that the enemy has entirely vanished," I said. "Do you think that possible?"

He spat on the ground – an ineradicable German habit that has always disgusted me.

"Is that a commentary on the information?" I asked.

"Your scouts are lying, or they have made a mistake," he said. "If the enemy has vanished, it is because your scouts have been looking in the wrong direction. They should have looked in your rear. That is where they would find my people. That is how they have learned to fight. They intend to cut you off as you retreat, having first prevented supplies from reaching you."

"But a messenger has come through today. I have received letters."

"They would not be interested in letters or in cutting off a small troop. It is in their interest to let you think the road behind is open."

"So what do you recommend?"

"You, a Roman, ask me, a German, what course I would recommend?"

"I ask you as a knowledgeable man, and as one whom experience has taught me I may trust."

He looked at the interpreter as if he wondered whether my answer had been correctly relayed to him. I nodded my head and smiled.

"My noble brother trusted you," I said, "and I trust my brother's judgment."

He received this observation in silence, turned and walked to the open flap of my tent and gazed out into the mist. The rain spattered the canvas, but there was no wind to shift the mist which hung over the meadows towards the invisible river.

"If you return by the route you advanced by, you will march into the trap. Its jaws will close, and then, no Imperator Tiberius, no Roman Army, but much rejoicing among the Cherusci."

"So?"

"So you must find another route, through territory which is unknown to you. You must keep the river on your flank. In that way you can be attacked only on one side. You cannot be surrounded."

"Do we go up the river or down?"

"Down, perhaps, for in that way you will reach the Elbe."

"And if we go up?"

"The mountains eventually."

"And is there a pass there by which we can cross over to the Rhine?"

"I believe there is. But it would be difficult with the waggons. However, if you turn towards the Elbe, you will find yourself required to negotiate a wide tract of marshland."

"And which course will your cousin, the chief for the time being of the Cherusci, expect us to take . . ."

Segestes spat again.

"He is not a clever man. Brave but a fool. He will not be expecting you to do anything but retrace your route. However, there are wise heads among his advisers. They will conclude that you will make for the Elbe, where you have forts and a fleet waiting in the mouth. They will not expect you to take the bold path, because they do not expect boldness from Romans, and they know, general, that you are a cautious man."

I asked my servant to bring us wine. Germans are not accustomed to wine, and many of them affect to regard it as an effeminate drink, since their preference is to swig great jugs of beer or mead. However, Segestes had learned to consider wine as a mark of the civilisation to which he aspired (I had one day found him taking a reading lesson from one of my secretaries) and had even learned to do something which comes naturally to no German: to drink it without evident signs of greed.

"I am honoured, General, that you ask my advice, but how can you know that it is good advice? How can you be certain that I am not intending to take this opportunity to restore my credit with my own people?"

"Segestes," I said, "I could speak much of your honour, and utter a long speech in your praise. I could say I believe, as indeed I do, that you have come to think that it will be to the benefit of your people that they should enter within the embraces of the Roman empire. And there would be much truth in what I would say. But there is another argument which will remind you of what manner of man I am."

I clapped my hands to call back my servant, and whispered a message to him. He departed, to come back in a few moments leading a German youth, who stood before us and glowered.

"When you came over to us," I said, "you did us the honour of entrusting your son, the young Segestes, to us. That showed your faith in Rome. I am sensible of your confidence, and I shall now repay it by making the boy my aide-de-camp. He shall remain by my side throughout this campaign, eat at my table, sleep in my tent. I shall watch over him . . ."

"I see, General," he said. "It is a powerful argument. But I have many sons, seventeen I think, and some of them are in the other army. Why should I trouble myself about the fate of one out of seventeen?"

"Well," I said, "that is a matter for you to decide. You have given me good advice, and I shall ponder it. Do not doubt my gratitude, which I shall extend to this boy also."

And so I threatened Segestes with his son's death, while the death of my own little boy lay like a dead flower pressed in the book of life. Did I give five minutes then to thought of what he might have been? I doubt it. I had been aroused to a sense of the army's danger. Comfort for Julia and mourning for little Tiberius must wait.

I summoned a council, for I have never believed that a general should embark on a course of action without discussing it with his officers. The greater the danger, the more necessary it is that they understand the position. Yet, paradoxically, the greater and more immediate the danger, the more necessary it is that the commander display authority. Debate is then a luxury; yet without granting the opportunity for debate, the commander may lose the chance of obtaining a valuable suggestion. Speed is of the essence, but there is much truth in the proverb *festina lente*: hasten slowly.

I outlined the position, and told them of my conversation with Segestes.

"What reason have we to trust in the word of a barbarian?"

The speaker was Marcus Lollius, a man whom, had I had full freedom to choose my officers, I would never have had on my staff. A few years previously, in Gaul, he had suffered a defeat at the hands of raiding Germans, brought on, in my opinion, by his neglect of security, represented by his failure to keep himself properly informed. However, it seemed the wrong moment to make reference to that episode and I knew I had to treat Lollius with kid gloves, as they say, for he was a favourite of Augustus, whom he flattered absurdly. But no flattery is too absurd for a dynast.

"Drusus trusted Segestes, and I trust my brother's judgment."

This was a politic answer rather than a truthful one; in fact, I had trusted everything about Drusus except his judgment of men, for he was too easily carried away by the generosity of his nature and was therefore apt to take the word for the deed.

"Moreover," I said, "I think Segestes' interest is bound up with the success of our arms and with the fortune of the Roman people."

Lollius threw back his head and laughed, a calculated gesture.

"So, the campaign plan of a Roman army is now to be dictated by a barbarian deserter. I have never heard of such a thing. You would have us march into unknown territory at his word, when we have behind us a fortified line of march, which we know well . . ."

"And which lies through a forest which the enemy know better, and where we cannot deploy . . ."

There was a shifting of feet, as every man imagined the dreams that afflicted us by night in those accursed forests.

We debated the merits of the course open to us. Some were in agreement with Marcus Lollius that we should disregard the advice given by Segestes, and retrace the route by which we had advanced.

"It is only fifty miles to our first base," they insisted.

"You can destroy an army in less time than it takes to march five," I answered.

My reasoning carried weight, though Lollius continued to

sneer. After all, everyone knew that the responsibility was mine, that they would themselves be free of blame even if I chose wrong. Then I outlined the merits of the two courses Segestes had proposed.

"It's clear, isn't it . . . ?" the speaker hesitated, with habitual diffidence. This was Caius Velleius Paterculus, an honest man whose grandfather had fought by my father's side in the terrible siege of Perugia, and then fallen on his sword when all was lost. "It's clear," he repeated. "Segestes thinks you should follow the high route because they will not think of it. But he thought of it himself, and so it seems likely that one of their chiefs will also do so. Therefore we should go downstream to join the Elbe."

"No," said Cossus Cornelius Lentulus, speaking sleepily as was his wont, "have you never played the game the soldiers call 'spoof'? It's a matter of guessing how many coins you each hold in your hand. Well, we are in the same position. We must always take the guessing game one stage further. For that reason I say we take the high road . . ."

There comes a time in war, as in political affairs, when argument falls away. It is a matter then of decision. All courses have been examined, and all found to have their own virtue and their own danger. None possesses any transcendent merit. Very well, the man in command must act and he must follow his course as if there had never been an alternative. I looked round my staff. I saw hesitation, uncertainty, fear. I thought of how both Paterculus and Lentulus were men worthy of the highest admiration. I said:

"Gentlemen, you have considered the problem wisely. You have laid out the arguments for either course with a lucidity which I commend. I will ponder these matters, and issue orders in the morning."

I spoke with an assurance I did not feel – precisely the circumstances in which assurance is necessary. I retired to my tent. I sent for the soothsayer, and drank a cup of wine while I was waiting. The German boy, the young Segestes, crouched in a corner of my tent. He had pulled a blanket round his shoulders and buried his face in it. A mop of yellow hair emerged from its folds, and though the rest of him was hidden I could sense the tension in which he held himself. I put my hand on his head. "Don't be afraid," I said. "Do you speak any Latin?" He shook my hand off.

The soothsayer entered. I asked him if he had taken the omens.

"But not yet interpreted them," he said.

"Good. We shall march by the high road. I trust the omens will be favourable."

There is relief in decision. I retired and slept soundly. But I woke in the darkest hours having dreamed of little Tiberius and of Julia grieving. A whimper came from the corner of the tent where young Segestes was stretched out. I called to him and there was silence. Then I called again and heard him rise to his feet. He stumbled as he crossed the floor and fell on top of me. I held him close and felt him relax and then spring to life. We rejoiced and took comfort in each other's maleness. He smelled of the stable. In the morning he held his head high and smiled at me.

For two days we saw no sign of the enemy but, keeping the river ever on our left hand, climbed high into the mountains. The track was poor, disappearing in places, and very early I gave orders that we should abandon the heavy waggons. For the first day I rode at the head of the column, but on the day following, judging that we had outstripped the enemy, and taken them by surprise, I transferred to the rear, from which direction I now judged an attack most likely to come. It is, moreover, the way of barbarian tribes to wage irregular war, and to try to cut off the rearguard of an army rather than risk frontal assault and wholehearted battle. Meanwhile the scouts who scoured the skirts of the forest reported no movement from the enemy. Our troops grew cheerful, and exchanged the opinion that we had given the Germans the slip. I could not share their confidence and when I consulted the elder Segestes, he declined to commit himself.

Towards evening on the second day it began to rain. The

mist closed in upon us and soon we could see no further than a man can throw a spear in battle. Then one of the light waggons which we had retained slewed across the path, blocking our way. The accident happened in a narrow defile. While men struggled to free the cart, I sent a messenger after the main body of the army to warn them that we should be delayed. At that moment huge rocks descended from our right, blocking the pass. The crash was succeeded by silence broken only by the curses and heaving of our men trying to clear the way. A handful of them scrambled over the rocks, but the main body of the rearguard was held pressed together, unaware of what was happening, in the grip of incipient panic.

The attack came in at an angle on our rear through a beech wood. The steep slope and our unreadiness gave the barbarians an advantage. My first thought was one of shame, not fear, shame and anger. I have always prided myself on my use of intelligence, and it was our intelligence which had let us down, its failure which had exposed us to this risk. I shouted such instructions as I could, but this was not so much a battle as a countless number of individual fights going on at the same time. Only historians, secure in their studies, can make sense of such warfare. For those involved in it there is no comprehensive structure, merely a succession of encounters, one man against one, two against three and so on. It is a story of stabbing spears, swinging or jabbing swords, the clang of metal on armour, cries of anger and howls of pain. There is no possible coherence, no narrative even which can render the whole. Our men first gave way as they were pushed towards the cliff, then, here and there, the surge was checked. All at once I found empty space before me and ran forward to occupy it, shouting commands that no one heard. I thrust at a huge yellow-bearded figure and then almost fell over as I stumbled against his falling body and struggled to extract my sword. A blow on my shoulder sent me sprawling on top of him and I rolled over to see a figure swing an axe above his head and there was a smile of glee on the axeman's face. I struggled to get out of line, and heard a yell and then a shape thrust itself between me and the axe, and axeman and his assailant fell to the ground and rolled over and over. Axeman came uppermost, heaved himself to his knees, his arms rigid as he began to choke the life out of his attacker. I stabbed him in the neck. He toppled forward with a groan. His grip loosened. I put my boot against him and thrust him over, and the boy Segestes struggled out from under him. I held out my hand and raised him to his feet. There was, for a moment, a space around us, and then we were behind our legionaries who were now pursuing the suddenly fleeing enemy towards the wood. I saw worse disaster beckon, grabbed a nearby trumpeter and ordered him to sound the retreat. Legionaries hesitated at the trumpet's note, drew themselves up, drew together and, in almost orderly fashion, still facing the fleeing enemy, halted. Centurions held them in line till order was restored and we could resume the march.

"It seems," I said, to young Segestes, "that there is a new bond between us . . ."

I have been in so many battles, and yet in my solitude it is that little skirmish – and it was no more – that comes to mind. I cannot forget it. When the youth leapt like a wild-cat at my attacker, it was in one sense no more than the sort of selfless action, performed without any reflection, which soldiers commit in every battle. And yet for me it was more than that. Other men have saved my life in other battles, and I have forgotten them. There is an anonymity in the comradeship of war. But this was different. The boy could have been honoured among his own race if he had stood by and cheered, if he had helped kill me and then run with his fellow barbarians. I could not have blamed him. He understood the ruthlessness with which I had been ready to use him, to compel his father's fidelity.

He wept that night and trembled, as I have known others do, when it comes to them that they have felt death's icy fingers. He shook with delayed terror and relief, and his legs and feet were as cold as the river below us. Then we reaffirmed life and he laughed with pleasure, as full of vigour as a young colt or pony. He slept and I stroked his dirty hair and drew sunshine back into my life.

It was tempting to keep him with me, to let myself be sustained and enlivened by his youth and strength and his ready acceptance of things as they are. But that simplicity – the simplicity of the Homeric world – has been corrupted. I could not let him grow to realise that he would become an object of scorn. He saw nothing wrong in it himself of course. Many of the German warriors have their boy-lovers and are said to fight the more bravely by their side. The Gauls too were accustomed to choose their charioteers for their beauty and courage. But, though we tolerate the love of boys, men who indulge in it are despised by others and come properly to despise themselves. Consequently the boys develop effeminate manners and become contemptible. Yet I looked at young Segestes sleeping in the crook of my arm with a smile on his face and thought that life would be better and simpler if we were indeed Achilles and Patroclus, and knew my thought to be absurd. This is not how it is now in our world.

He could not return to his own people, and I did not care to entrust him to his father who might, it occurred to me, have learned to find a use for him of which I would not approve. I told the elder Segestes of the debt of gratitude I owed his son, and of my intention to repay it by advancing the boy to a career within the auxiliary forces of our empire. He was, I said, to regard me henceforth as his patron, and in that role it seemed expedient to me that the boy should go to Rome to study Latin and then Roman Law, which would together fit him for a career either in the army or the civil service. The father was properly appreciative of my intentions and so it was arranged.

Young Segestes was loth to leave me, but I insisted. He told me, to my considerable embarrassment, that he had "fallen in love with his master as a German boy should". I made the break as tenderly as I could, supported by my knowledge that I was acting for his own good. He wept when he took leave of me, and my own eyes were not altogether dry. Unfortunately things did not work out quite as I hoped. Though he studied well, he soon fell into the habit of deep drinking to which Germans are all addicted. Soon after my arrival here, I heard that he had been knifed to death in a tavern brawl. It was sad; he was a boy of promise and virtue. But it would not have done for me to have acted otherwise. I still think of him with pleasure and regret.

ELEVEN

My last campaign in Germany met with unprecedented success. I took 40,000 prisoners, whom I carried across the Rhine and established in colonies in Gaul. The German tribes were themselves thoroughly demoralised and, for the moment at least, subdued. When I returned to Rome, which I had hardly visited for six years, I was greeted as a hero. I was accorded a triumph and granted triumphal regalia. My mother, whose hair had turned white during my years of absence, called me "worthy of my most illustrious ancestors". Augustus embraced me without shrinking and assured me that no man had done more for Rome than I. Clients flocked to my house every morning to do me honour and seek preferment at my hand. Even the common people with whom I had never been popular, since I scorned to court their favour, hailed me with cheers when I appeared in public. I should have been the happiest man in Rome, justified and recognised at last.

I should have been, but things are rarely as they should be, and never for long. I found much to perturb me, in both public and private affairs. When I visited the Senate, I was disgusted to see how the habit of servility had developed in my few years of absence. The assembly of free notables now fawned upon Augustus. Few dared to express an opinion on any matter of importance till they knew his. Complaints reached me, indirectly, in mutterings and whisperings, of how the descendants of great Republican houses were being squeezed from all positions of honour and influence to be replaced by members of the Princeps' family and by those referred to as his "creatures". As a member of his family I might have been satisfied to benefit myself, but I had had no need of Augustus to rise. My position as the head of the Claudian *gens* would have assured me of superiority at any time in Rome's history. I had therefore some sympathy with those who grumbled at the turn things had taken. "For the senator," they murmured, "no hope of glory remains, no hope of a monument to a fame he is no longer permitted to win. No roads or provincial cities may now bear the names of noble families." They complained that no senator might depart from Italy and visit a province without obtaining leave from the Princeps. "We experience a monopoly of power, a concentration of honour and opportunity," men said.

I was aware of these mutterings. Old friends saw to that. They were quick too to point to the honours being showered upon my stepsons Gaius and Lucius.

Gnaeus Calpurnius Piso had been nominated as my colleague in the consulship. He is a man of the utmost integrity and nobility of soul, whom I have long loved dearly. Soon after my return he invited me to supper.

"A serious meal," he said, "not like those dinners given by that old lecher Cestius Gallus – whom, by the way, Augustus has had removed from the Senate – you know the sort of dinners he gives, don't you, served by naked waitresses? They say there's one black girl from the south of Egypt, but never mind. That's not the sort of occasion to which I am inviting you. I want a chance to talk."

He dismissed the slaves when we had eaten and pushed the wine-flask towards me.

"My own wine," he said, "from the hills above Siena where I have a little estate. It is the best wine in Italy, you won't find anything finer."

Everything of Piso's is always "the best".

He plucked at the hairs which grew from a wart on his chin.

"So we are consuls. Very nice, if it meant anything. Of course you have held the office before, so you know how meaningless it has become."

"It carries respect still, and bestows authority on the man who attains it, at least subsequently."

"Precisely. So how would you feel if I told you it was about to be rigged even more shamefully than we have grown accustomed to its being done?"

"What do you mean?"

"I mean that your stepson Gaius will receive the honour in five years' time – at the age of twenty. That should show you how the wind is blowing."

"How do you know this?"

"It's sufficient that I do. Things like that can't be kept secret . . ."

I said, "I was twenty-nine, excused five years, when I was consul for the first time."

"Precisely, and the rest of us are ineligible till we are thirty-three. I'm speaking as a friend, Tiberius, and one whose family has a long association with yours. Our fathers fought side by side at Perugia and both followed Sextus Pompeius to Sicily. You are on the point of being edged out. That's what I have to tell you. And what are you going to do about it?"

The question was, as he knew, unanswerable.

I pondered it all the same as I walked home through the seething city. The night was hot and stuffy. I descended the Quirinale and crossed into the Suburra. Julius Caesar had had a house there, a ploy in his campaign to capture the hearts of the plebeians, for it has always been a popular quarter. It came to me, as I walked, that Rome was no longer a Roman, or even an Italian city. The babble of innumerable tongues assailed my ears. In the space of two hundred yards I heard more than one variety of Greek, the Celtic tongue of Gaul, the harsh language of the Illyrian Highlands, the smooth accents of Syria and Egypt, mellifluous and deceiving, and the incomprehensible murmuring Aramaic of the Jews. A group of them were standing outside a tavern rattling their money-tallies; a man emerged, approached them, conducted a transaction and returned within to resume his pleasure; the Jews gabbled among themselves. A little further on a pork butcher was howling his wares, urging them on the Jews who for some reason think it wrong to eat pig. Nobody understands the laws of their curious religion, with its many prohibitions and requirements but I smiled to think that the pork butcher knew very well that they would take his invitation as an insult. Every second house was a tavern or brothel: through the open window I saw a tawny girl dancing on a table. The sweat glistened on her gyrating thighs and her eyes were blank as if she had swallowed some potion which numbed her consciousness while exciting her animal allure. She paused in her dance, drew her knees together and caressed her thighs with long fingers; a moan of anticipatory and yet ever-to-be-denied pleasure escaped the watching crowd. Then a man wearing a boar's head and a huge false phallus made of leather dyed scarlet mounted the table beside her, threw her over the windowledge so that her long black hair floated round the faces of the panting spectators and began to work his phallus while the girl moaned and bit her lips till a trickle of blood emerged at the corner of her mouth. Meanwhile, standing at the back of the crowd, I observed a brace of pickpockets moving among them, relieving the poor enthralled fools of their purses. "There ought to be a law," a pinch-faced man by my shoulder muttered, "against this filth." "There is," I assured him, and moved on. There is indeed such a law, but it is not enforced. It cannot be enforced, for it is beyond the power of government to make people behave well. When respect for the gods has withered, when families are in disarray, licentiousness prevails; the secret impulses, which men subdue in a decent and well-ordered society, are openly acknowledged.

I paused at the next booth where a little play was being enacted on an open stage. A curly-headed boy reclined on a pile of cushions with a bowl of cherries by his side. He popped one in his mouth and rolled saucy eyes at his audience. Then he uncurled himself, rose to his feet and slipped off his tunic. He did it in the most natural fashion, like a boy preparing to take a bath. The absence of any sense of lasciviousness excited the crowd. He strutted round the stage, then, as if the idea had just occurred to him, began to stroke his cock. He held it out stiff for approval, and then, with supple grace, crouched down and began to suck it. The man beside me – a stout greasy fellow who might have been a pastry cook – hissed, "A proper little contortionist, that bumboy." Then a big strapping woman wearing a red wig bounded on to the stage, a whip in her hand. She swished it around the boy's legs, howling abuse. He skipped and danced and yelped, as if in pain, though it was clear that she manipulated the whip in such a manner that it did not touch him. Then he fell to his knees before her and embraced her thighs, pressing his face against them. She seized his curls with her left hand and pulled his head back. She slipped her right hand down the front of her skirt, grimaced as if she could not find what she was searching for, then, with a cry of triumph, produced a carrot which she thrust into the boy's open mouth. The crowd rocked with laughter. She held the boy there, forcing him to eat the carrot and then lick her fingers like a dog. She pulled him to his feet, and, grabbing his member, led him off the stage. She turned, winked to the audience, and the pair disappeared into the darkness. The crowd howled approval of the obscene buffoonery.

A hand plucked my sleeve. I turned to see a fat shining bald-pated fellow.

"You like boys?" he said. His voice was hoarse and he smelled of onions. "You want a boy? A nice Greek boy?"

He indicated a painted, ringleted wretch who fluttered his eyelashes at me, and wriggled his backside. The image of the young Segestes, brave, upright, clean-limbed, biting his lip to restrain tears when hurt, flashed across my mind.

"Pretty, eh?" wheezed the pimp.

Bile filled my mouth. I thrust the wretch out of the way, and hurried from the noxious place. Yet I returned other nights, to gaze on the shows, to expose myself to a full understanding of the degradation that opened before my eyes, inviting me, in subtle and horrible fashion, to participate. I returned again and again, because I could not do otherwise, and because . . . because . . .

Why do I torture myself with these memories? Why does my mind play upon temptations with fascinated disgust? Why do gross and terrible images invade my mind when I lie down to sleep, in the afternoon and at night? This morning I attended a debate in the school of philosophy here. Two sophists argued the question whether morality was natural to man. One of the Platonic school asserted that since we possessed ideas of truth and justice, absolute truth and absolute justice, though we had never encountered these absolutes in human behaviour, it followed that the idea of truth and justice was innate in us. His opponent, a Cynic, scoffed at this: morality, he said, was a device created by cowards to awe the strong. Ideas meant nothing, it was behaviour that counted, and the superior man disregarded concepts formed by cowards, and acted as he pleased. It was in this exercise of freedom that he proved his superiority. "Then your superior man may be very wicked," said the first sophist.

"Wickedness is a word you have invented," was the reply, "as you have invented truth and justice . . ."

At this point I felt moved to intervene. "It seems to me," I said, "that you two cannot agree because you are talking of absolutes, which we rarely meet. Yet Socrates himself asked his friends, as we are told in the *Phaedo*, whether they had never realised that 'Extreme instances are few and rare, while intermediate ones are many and plentiful', so that if there were to be a competition in wickedness, very few would distinguish themselves even there . . ."

"You have missed the point," cried the Cynic, and at that moment an impudent member of the audience leaped up and abused me for joining in the argument and seeming to support the Platonist.

"It's a fine thing," he cried, "when a Roman prince can't let an intellectual argument flourish without throwing his weight on one side."

I could have said that if he was, as I supposed, a supporter of the Cynic, he could hardly reprove me for my intervention, for I was merely putting his philosopher's principles into suitably unprincipled action. That would have won me a round of applause, and turned the situation off with a laugh. But I was furious at his impertinent presumption, and withdrew with such state as I could muster. I retired to my house, only to reappear with a group of lictors, whom I ordered to arrest the insolent wretch and carry him off to gaol.

My behaviour amazed, and, I think, alarmed the people. It took me by surprise itself, and I am not proud of it. Some nerve was touched I suppose.

When I returned that first evening from the Suburra, Julia was absent. I found a note pinned to my pillow. It was unsigned, and read:

WHAT DOES YOUR WIFE GET UP TO IN THE NIGHT? ARE YOU AFRAID TO ASK HER WHERE SHE HAS BEEN?

I questioned the slaves. All denied any knowledge of the message. It is impossible of course to get the truth from slaves when they are frightened unless you threaten them with torture. I am afraid of doing that, lest I take pleasure in it. Besides, men will say anything under torture and you may be no nearer any truth except what they think you want to hear. Which is rarely the truth.

I had tried to speak to Julia many times since my return. I didn't know how to. It was clear that any love she had felt for me had died with our little son. We made love twice. Then she denied me my bed, and it was not in my nature to compel her to fulfil her marital duties. "I'm bored," she said, "you disgust me, you smell of Germans." I remember I turned away because I felt myself blushing. "I would rather make love to a corpse," she said, "you stink of so many deaths."

"What do you expect of a soldier?"

"War, brutality, delight in slaughter, greed for power, they all disgust me."

"Julia, you know, you must know, that I have never taken pleasure in slaughter, I have only tried to do my duty . . ."

"Oh what a bore you are, what a dismal bore," and there was no laughter in her voice, as there would formerly have been when she uttered that reproach, but she turned instead a gaze on me that was as beautiful and as petrifying as Medusa's.

Livia advised me "to look to my wife".

"You made her that, Mother," I said. "The match was not of my devising. I was happily married before."

"That's not to the point," she said. "I don't know whether you are blind of intention, but doesn't your pride revolt at the thought that her infidelity is now flagrant, that she makes a public fool of you?"

"I hear you, Mother."

"Do you know what they are saying? The joke is that Tiberius may be a match for Germans, but he's no match for Julia, and then they go on to say we could end the German war quicker if instead of sending old Tiberius to subdue them, we sent Julia to seduce them. What do you say to that?"

"Nothing, Mother, you and the Princeps made this marriage, not I. So you can mend it."

"If you were a man you would whip her into good behaviour."

I almost answered: does Augustus whip you? But prudence prevailed. However, I smiled to remember the occasion when he was assuring the Senate that husbands ought to exact obedience from their wives and reproach them if they strayed, only to be interrupted by a senator who cried out "I'd like to see you make Livia toe the line . . ."

I could choose to disregard Livia. When I received a warning from the Praetorian Prefect, I had to take heed. He was polite, circumspect, appalling. He told me my wife was not only unfaithful, but that her behaviour threatened public scandal. She took part in orgies which were not confined to the nobility.

"That would be a private matter, sir, or up to a point. But when all sorts of riff-raff are involved, well, you can see that it's a matter of public order. Of course she's generally masked, but, well, sir, a mask can slip, can't it? And she's not the sort of lady you forget, is she?"

He laid his forefinger along his nose.

"You won't like me for telling you all this, sir, but if you want names and addresses, you shall have them. I ought to pass them on to the Princeps, that's my duty, but frankly, sir, I don't dare to perform it. And I haven't come to the worst of it. A word to the wise, as you might say: some of the nobles she consorts with are what we call in the business 'security risks'. They're the sort of boys who fail our system of 'positive vetting'. I don't know if the Princeps has acquainted you with that, sir?"

"No," I said, "you see I am only his stepson and son-in-law, this year's consul and a general who has been awarded a triumph. I haven't been trusted with information about your system of . . . what did you call it?"

"Positive vetting, sir."

"Positive vetting? A miserable neologism."

"That's as may be, sir. But a necessity, believe you me, the way things are. Well, it's my belief you should know about it, sir, and so I am going to take upon myself the responsibility of at least outlining the system to you."

He then explained that Augustus had become concerned by the possibility of appointing to positions of authority men whose allegiance to the "New Order" was less than it might be. Though he prided himself – rightly, I think – on his judgment of men, he was aware that that judgment was necessarily subjective, and frequently the result of imperfect acquaintance. He had thereby devised a system, after consultation with the Praetorian Prefect and the secret police, whereby every candidate for office was thoroughly investigated: his antecedents were checked, his friendships assessed, slaves were set to report dinner-party conversations, his financial affairs were examined, and his sexual habits and tastes ascertained.

"In this way, sir, a total picture is assembled. Like a mosaic, if I may speak fancifully. No little piece may yield significance on its own, but each one helps to make the total picture comprehensible and comprehensive, sir. It's a wonderful system and you would be amazed at what we come to know."

"No doubt."

"Well, I'm sorry to say, sir, that many of the noblemen with whom the Lady Julia consorts are what we call Category C. Some are even Category D, which means that they are fortunate to be allowed to reside in Rome, sir, and not confined to their country estates, or sent into exile. We get all manner of reports, you understand, from our professional delators –

'sewers' we call them in the firm, for it's their business to draw off all the filth of the city for our inspection – and, believe you me, when I read some of the reports the sewers send in about gentlemen such as Iullus Antonius and Crispinus and young Sempronius Gracchus, well, sir, the hairs on the back of my head stand on end and my blood runs cold. And these are the sort of types your lady wife runs about with, and worse than runs, I'm afraid. Well, sir, if I brought it to the attention of the Princeps, I don't dare to think what mightn't result. That's why I've been so bold as to approach you in the first instance, as you might say. I'll leave you this little list, sir, of her noble lovers. There are others of course who are not noble, and therefore of no political importance."

I could not credit all the names. I had, of course, known the men all my life, some very well, others only by sight and repu-tation. There was my cousin Appius Claudius Pulcher; it seemed unlikely that he was one of her lovers for I believed him to like only virgins, the younger the better; and Publius Cornelius Sci-pio seemed also an improbable choice of lover, for his effemi-nacy was blatant – he had been a dear friend of Maecenas, and was widely despised as a pathic, a degenerate with a taste for mature men. (To such depths had the great house of Scipio sunk.) But the others were only too credible: Antonius had declared his interest to me in unmistakable terms of course, and, since my return from Germany, had bestowed upon me a smile of radiant superiority while remarking: "To some, my dear Tiberius, Mars awards triumphs, to others Venus." And Gracchus, a liar from childhood, a cynic, a debauchee, a man perpetually disgruntled and at odds with the world. And Cris-pinus, one who, it now occurs to me, would certainly at any time in history have distinguished himself in that competition in wickedness which Socrates had imagined; a man who was believed to have compelled his wife to have intercourse with slaves that he might enjoy the spectacle, and to have starved his own son to death when he protested – the thought of Julia abandoning herself to such creatures as she no longer aban-doned herself to me, of their making free of the delights now denied me, that thought, even now, two years later, makes me retch. It persuades me to despair of human nature.

I sent the Prefect on his way, understanding more than ever why the Persians used to slay the bearer of bad news. It would have given me satisfaction to have silenced him forever with a dagger thrust into his mouth; to have cut off that tongue that took such pleasure in relaying this filth.

He had left me with the list. And there was nothing I could do. This Rome to which I had returned contained horrors that made the German forests seem benign as the water-meadows by Clitumnus. I could not speak to Julia; I could not even look at her without seeing the corruption of her beauty. But I smelled danger: these men, her lovers, were hungry, bitter, dissatisfied. Julius Caesar, I recalled, had feared Caius Cassius on account of his lean and hungry look. Such men, he had remarked, are dangerous.

So I had to warn her, and since I could not bring myself to speak of the matter, I wrote her a letter.

Julia,
    I don't know what has gone wrong between us since the death of our beloved son. What I see and hear of your behaviour leads me to believe that his death has disgusted you of everything, and led you to despair of the possibility that there is, or ever can be, any right ordering of things. It grieves me that you seem to include me among your objects of repugnance.
    Our marriage was not of our seeking. It was imposed upon us without consideration of our feelings. I know you would have preferred to marry another, and I sympathise with your sentiments in that direction.
    Nevertheless the marriage was made. I endeavoured from the start to fulfil my obligations as a husband and, in doing so, I was rewarded by the awakening of love for you and the renewal of that physical passion I had felt for you when we were young. I believed that with the birth of little Tiberius, you were, to my great joy, able to reciprocate my feelings.

Time, the exigencies of duty, circumstance and cruel fate have torn us apart, even as little Tiberius was torn from our tender embraces. Such was the harsh will of the gods to which we are compelled to submit. Believe me, I understand your unwillingness to accept the cogency of Fate. I am even able to admire your rebellious will, and to sympathise with what I see to be your unhappiness.

I am prepared to accept your rejection of me as being the expression of impulses which have invaded you and which you cannot control. Your rejection tastes sour as vinegar in my mouth. Nevertheless I accommodate myself to the strength of your repugnance, and only pray that it may abate in time and that affection may grow again from this wintry soil.

But I must say one thing to you which is harsh. I have my pride and I cannot endure dishonour. I am not a Claudian for nothing. If you cannot love me, I accept that, but I must ask you to conduct yourself in a seemly fashion such as becomes a wife of the head of the Claudian *gens*. You owe that duty to me, just as you owe a duty to your father not to bring his moral legislation into disrepute.

And one other thing: you can only hope for happiness if you attain self-respect. I believe you are in danger of losing this. You may even have lost it already. You cannot be at ease till you recover it. There is danger of more than one sort in the course you are pursuing.

Believe me, Julia, I have your interests at heart.

She responded to my attempt at conciliation and my warning with only a brief note.

You always were a prig, now you are stupid as well. You were always cold and self-regarding. Consider the brutality of your own conduct. I have been denied everything all my life, forced to live in accordance with the will of others. I've had enough of it. I'm living for myself now. I prefer it that way. You're a fool to think I am unhappy. And don't threaten me again. I have my own weapons.

When I got this letter, I found in it something that compelled my pity, and softened my heart. I read misery between the lines. I hastened to her private apartments. The slave-girl who was tidying the room told me she had left that morning for a villa at Baiae, given her by her father as a wedding-present when she married Marcellus.

"Did she leave a message for me?"

The girl blushed and stammered.

"Yes, my lord, but I don't dare to repeat it . . ."

"I see. Nothing written?"

"No, my lord."

TWELVE

Pride is a great silencer. It sealed my lips. I spoke to nobody of my distress, and no one could have guessed my state of mind from my demeanour. The letter which I sent after Julia, and of which I no longer possess a copy, was couched in language which could have offered no grounds for suspicion to any government agent who intercepted it. Circumspection in language is the price we pay for civil order.

My stepfather continued to honour me. I was awarded the *tribunicia potestas*, that rag torn from Republican days in which Augustus had dressed himself to disguise his despotism, in which Agrippa also had been clad; the tribuniciary power rendered my person inviolate, gave me authority in Rome, the power to introduce or to veto legislation, and lent my elevation a misleadingly popular touch. By his use of the *tribunicia potestas* Augustus had declared his difference from the common run of senators and was enabled to present himself (pose, some would say) as the defender and protector of the common people. Nothing, not even his command of the armies, so displeased men of Republican sentiments as his use of this rusty piece of the machinery of Republican government.

Yet though he honoured me publicly, and made it clear that I was Rome's premier general, there was no warmth in his commendation. I felt slighted. It was clear to me that he was ready to use me, and as ready to discard me when I had served my turn. That would happen when the boys, Gaius and Lucius, were grown-up. His partiality towards them was extreme. He was even prepared to cheat on their behalf. In a performance of the Troy Game, that simulacrum of war in which well-born youths are given the chance to prove their prowess, Augustus, who acted as a sort of referee of this mimic battle, called foul when a certain stocky and uncouth boy was sitting astride young Lucius and pummelling him in the face. There was nothing in the rules of the game which warranted his interference, and it was obvious that his action was provoked by his desire to save Lucius from the consequences of his own misjudgment. A beating would have done the boy no harm, and taught him much. Augustus' care for the boys has been as excessive as his unrestrained impulse to flatter them has been absurd. I am amazed that Lucius at least has survived this mixture of coddling and admiration, and become such a pleasant and likeable young man. But I am glad to say that my own son, Drusus, has escaped such spoiling and been reared more sensibly.

Augustus' fondness for the boys was grotesque. He never reproved them that I heard of, and told them time and again, in front of other people, that they represented the glorious future of Rome. "Everything that I do is for your sakes," I once heard him say, a sentiment that made nonsense of the great part of his life, and one that reflected ill on his conception of his duty to the Roman people. Of course he was right to encourage youth, and was especially proud of his establishment of Colleges of Youth in all the municipalities of Italy; but he took it too far in the case of his grandsons. I could scarcely believe it when he fondly told them, in my hearing, that at an appropriate date, he would encourage the Senate to accord them the title *principes iuventutis* – Princes of the Youth Movement. This was too much; it smacked of hereditary monarchy.

I expressed my indignation to my mother. She was spinning wool, an affectation, as I had often told her, and one naturally encouraged by her husband. He thought it made for good "public relations" – a vile phrase he had learned from one of his Greek freedmen – to let it be known that his wife engaged in traditional domestic crafts like spinning and weaving.

"You don't really enjoy that, do you, Mother?"

"As a matter of fact I do. It's very soothing. Perhaps you should take it up yourself. You look strained."

"No wonder."

"But you are stupid to fight your father's love for those boys."

"Do I have to remind you that I stand in the same relation to them myself as he does to me? They are not bad boys, but he is in danger of ruining them."

"He is planning for the future, that's all. As we grow older, Tiberius, something strange happens to us. We find the horizon very short one day and stretching out illimitably the next. You can't blame Augustus for being concerned with what happens to the state when he has gone."

"And have I no part in that? Is there no room for me in his plans?"

"Of course there is, of course you have. How could it be otherwise considering your age, achievement and station? Moreover, you might remember that I am capable of making my own plans and carrying them out. For example I am arranging that Gaius should marry your brother's daughter, little Livia Julia."

"Very nice. That will maintain your influence, Mother."

"Don't take that tone with me. I dislike it. I always have. And I know what it means. You are about to sink into a fit of sulks."

"That's ridiculous. I'm concerned of course about my personal position."

"You will be the first man in the state – when your stepfather dies."

"He will live twenty years. And what will I be then? But I am not merely concerned with my own position. I disapprove fundamentally, Mother, of the direction in which things are tending. We are in danger of becoming like an eastern despotism, with a law of succession. It's not Roman."

"Yes, Tiberius, you are a conservative. It is that which makes you unhappy. Well, I share your sentiments but I have the intelligence to know that things have to change if we want them to remain the same. And I know that Augustus' creation is good because unlike you I can remember the civil wars. Don't become like your father, Tiberius, a man for whom all virtue resided only in the past, who viewed the new world as something made for his personal distress."

"There are times I sympathise with him."

"You are foolish. Indeed you are more than foolish. I am glad you have come in this serious mood – not that your mood is often anything else. I am told that you and Julia no longer speak to each other, that you communicate only by letter. Is this true?"

"So you have been spying on us, Mother?"

"So it is true. Do you want to destroy everything?"

I hesitated. It was tempting to answer in the affirmative.

"Julia and I have decided for the time being to go separate ways. That's all."

"All? Do you understand what you are saying? That's all? Your wife is galloping towards public disgrace and you don't realise that you will be stained by it yourself?"

"My wife," I said, "will do as she chooses. She always has. I am powerless."

I retired to the baths. I sweated out my irritation and idled the afternoon away watching young men wrestle in the gymnasium. I dined at home, then sat drinking wine while a slave read to me from Thucydides' account of the Peloponnesian war.

"Foolishness," I said, and dismissed the man.

I drank wine and composed letters to Julia in my head which I knew I would never send. The dawn broke, cold, grey, unpromising. I staggered to my couch and slept badly.

Augustus summoned me.

He jumped up with an expression of pleasure on his face when I entered; it must have cost him an effort, but of course he always took pleasure in his performance.

"My dear boy," he said, "your mother has been talking to me. She is worried. She says you have withdrawn from her. 'I see only what flickers on the surface of the waters, nothing of the dark swirling currents below.' Her precise words, I assure you . . . She believes, she tells me, that you have never recovered from Drusus, your dear dear brother's death." He laid his hand on my sleeve. It hung there like a leech. "Ah which of us has, which indeed . . . ?"

Then his tone changed. It resumed that mastery which I have always respected as he outlined our strategical position. There was a new outbreak of unrest in Armenia – "a country you handled with such deft efficiency in your youth, dear boy". It was necessary to send a strong man to the East. He offered me the job . . . "With *maius imperium* of course – overriding authority . . . I am offering you exactly what Agrippa had. And the job is even more urgent and demanding now . . ."

He gave that radiant and confiding smile which is so essential a part of his famous charm. Then a look of concern crossed his face.

"Are you quite well? You look flushed."

"A touch of headache. No more."

"Good, because the job will demand everything from you."

"No," I said. "No, I'm not going."

"What do you mean? What do you mean you aren't going?"

"Just as I say."

"But this is madness."

He threw his hands into the air, registering incredulity.

"Come, dear boy," he said, "you can't have understood what I am offering you. Agrippa's position. My . . ." he hesitated, swallowed, got the disagreeable medicine down . . . "my partner in the government of the Republic."

"For how long?"

"What do you mean 'for how long'? Listen, dear boy," he patted my arm, squeezed it, "*maius imperium*" – he dwelled on the words like a ham actor, then, in the same manner, smote his forehead with the palm of his hand. "I see what it is. You feel your place is still on the German frontier, you have unfinished business there. Well, dear boy, you were ever conscientious, and I admire you for it. And I am indeed loth, yes loth, to take you from that task. But it can't be helped, dear boy, this matter is too urgent. It is a task of the utmost importance, and one in which you will win great honour . . ."

"No," I said. "I've had enough. I want out."

"What do you mean? Do you understand what you are saying? It is treason."

"No," I said, "it isn't, by no interpretation of the word. And if you don't understand, then that is unfortunate, but my meaning is really as plain as my mind is fixed . . ."

I left him, his jaw hanging open. When, I wondered, had he last been defied in this manner?

To tell the truth I was surprised and puzzled myself. I had planned nothing of what I had said. I had had as little intention to refuse him as expectation that he was going to offer me such a position. My refusal was unpremeditated. It seemed to me all the more convincing for that reason; it had sprung from the deepest recesses of my being: that flat obdurate negative. All my life, I realised, I had wanted to utter that clanging "No". I walked back to my own house through the sunshine of a May morning, with the flower-girls crying their blooms, and the air singing with bird music, and it was as if chains had been lifted from my body.

But I knew I had fought no more than the first battle. Augustus could not compel me to command his army, but he could punish me for disobedience. Moreover, as a senator, I required his permission to quit Italy, and that was, it came to me, what I devoutly wished to do. And I knew where I wanted to go.

I had visited Rhodes on my way back from my early campaign in Armenia, and the memory of that magical island and city, lying like a natural auditorium above a crescent bay, had remained with me, working in my imagination, in, as it were, subterranean fashion, with the sweetness of a summer morning before the sun is high. The Sun is, of course, the patron-god of Rhodes; his huge statue carved by Chares of Lindus adorns the harbour, one of the three thousand statues with which the city is beautified so that even a street empty of people is animated by images of gods and heroes. But my chief memory was of a villa at the western extremity of the city, a villa whose gardens rich in trees – plums, cherries, ilex, oak – and flowers, with red, pink and yellow roses rambling over the stonework, hung over the sea, so that in evening, the scent of roses mingled with the salt tang of the water. There were fountains in garden groves and when the bustle of the city below was stilled, nightingales sang. I had dined there, my host a Greek merchant with a snowy beard, who had greeted my rhapsodic appreciation of his creation of *rus in urbe* with benign complacency. When he died ten years later, he left me the villa; there was a lawsuit in which his son was embroiled, and my advice and countenance were of service. Besides, that merchant had many villas. Thither my mind tended. My resolution to seek repose there was formed before I had attained my own house.

It would not be easy. I therefore wrote to Augustus as follows.

Augustus, esteemed stepfather and father-in-law,

The offer you have made me does me more honour than I am worthy of. It gives me at least the opportunity to express my gratitude for the confidence you have always shown in my abilities. Nevertheless I must decline. I have served Rome and the Republic which you restored for more than twenty years. It is my desire to retire to an island and study philosophy and science. The Republic will manage very well without me, for it is not desirable that one man monopolise honours and commands as you have been kind enough to let me do. Moreover, I think that Gaius and Lucius, my dear and brilliant stepsons, should be able to embark on their public careers, which promise to be glorious, without finding themselves at their commencement in the shadow of my achievement. I have fixed on Rhodes as my place of retirement. It is a place of no importance, other than commercial. I have always been fond of islands, as my revered mother will be able to assure you, and the climate is said to be pleasant. It will benefit the rheumatism I have contracted from the damps of the Danube and the Rhine.

I therefore formally request that permission to retire to Rhodes which I am confident your generous and understanding nature will not deny me.

"Your letter," Livia said, "was ill-judged. It made your father even angrier than he was before."

"And I thought it such a good letter. Civil and well expressed."

"Stop it, Tiberius, it is not in your nature to play games."

"What do you know of my nature, Mother? What does anyone

know of my nature? What do I know myself? What indeed does anyone know of anyone's? Is there even such a thing as a person's nature?"

"There is such a thing as stupidity, no doubt about that. Which you are displaying now. Besides, you don't believe what you are saying. Why in your letter you remarked on Augustus' generous and understanding nature!"

"A form of words. Conventional language, no more than that."

"What do you think is going to happen?"

"Oh Gaius and Lucius will take over."

"Don't be silly. Lucius is only eleven."

"Ten, surely?" I said.

"Eleven."

"Well, that makes Gaius fifteen."

She turned away, throwing her face into half-shadow. "You're breaking my heart," she said. "All my life I have worked and schemed, yes, and sometimes done wrong, on your behalf. I have had such ambitions for you, and now, when you are on the point of fulfilling them, you prefer to throw everything away. Tiberius, why? Why, why?"

She wept. Her tears were the tears of all mothers, of Niobe and Andromeda. My heart softened. Something of my old childish love for her revived. I knelt by her side and put my arms round her. I kissed her cheek, which was pale and a little wrinkled.

"I am sorry to pain you, Mother. Try to understand. I know you love your husband and I respect you for that, and there are moments when I respect him too and others when I even feel a strange and unexpected liking for him. But I do not like what he has done to Rome, and I fear and resent what he would do to me. He has made the whole world his slave, subservient to his terrible will. Men of noble family fawn on him for favours and nobody dares to speak his mind. Even when I wrote to him I flattered him, I was constrained to flatter him. It is contemptible. And as for me, Mother, you have been ambitious for me, as a mother should be for her son, and I am grateful. But what will my achievement signify? In a few years when Gaius and

Lucius are of age, I shall be elbowed into the shadows. I shall have become . . . expendable. Well, let me choose my own moment to withdraw. I am tired of it, simply that. But there is another matter of which we have never been able to speak honestly: my marriage. Yes, my marriage to your husband's daughter. It has become torture to me. I do not blame Julia, for she herself is a victim of his destroying will. But I cannot live like this. I cannot divorce her, can I? I cannot punish her for adultery as a husband is enjoined by law to do. I am condemned by circumstance to live a cuckold and an object of mockery. Don't you see, Mother, I have had enough, enough of hypocrisy and deception, of the demeaning struggle for power, of being bought off with honied words, of . . . all this? I am sorry if I have failed you, but to continue I would fail myself. The world has been corrupted, and I want out . . ."

She stood up. The tears were dry on her face.

"All that," she said, "is very affecting. It reminds me of the sort of speeches your own father used to make. I had thought you a fighter. I should have remembered how you have always been subject to fits of ignoble dejection. I understand you, don't think I don't, better than you understand yourself. You have lost stomach for the struggle but, my son, because you are my son as well as your father's, your appetite will revive. So you have a strumpet for a wife. Well there were cuckolds before Agamemnon, and there will be countless others. What does that matter in the sum of things? You may choose to withdraw but my will, Tiberius, is indomitable. I shall continue to fight on your behalf, whether you would have me do so or not, and one day you will be grateful . . ."

My friends clustered round me, alarmed. I discounted a good part of their concern, for I knew that they had hoped to rise with me, and now feared the effect of my retirement on their future. I understood their disappointment but, since I had made no promises which I had not kept, felt neither guilt nor responsibility. Besides, a man's first duty is to his own peace of mind. As soon as I fully comprehended the depth of my desire to withdraw from public life, I felt as if a black cloud had been blown away. I no longer required wine to let me sleep. My breathing, which had been distressed, improved. My headaches disappeared. At night I dreamed of the wine-dark sea lapping on the rocks below and of the mountains of Asia rising majestic and purple against the evening sky. I could scarcely wait to be gone.

Augustus struggled still to hold me in the captivity of office. He deluged me with letters in which praise, reproof and appeals to my conscience were mixed, higgledy-piggledy. He abandoned dignity and went beyond decorum. When he forced another interview upon me, it ended with him cursing me like a fish-wife, "You are a sack of dung in a man's clothing," he shrieked.

"What a pity that so great a man should have such bad manners," I remarked, smiling, for I knew that I was winning, that his loss of control indicated that the battle was slipping from him.

I exploited my advantage. I knew that Livia's love held him from the violent course to which my obduracy excited him. So I gave out that I was going on hunger strike, till he granted me permission. Naturally, he was bound to yield; my mother saw to that. She made it plain to him that she feared the consequences if he did not grant me leave.

First, however, he took care to let me know what men were saying about me; how some senators saw my wish for retirement as a challenge to his authority; how others declared that I was weary of virtue.

You have been a hypocrite all your life – or so I am told – nursing secret vices which you are ashamed to practise publicly. Now you find such self-control beyond you, and intend to retire to this island to enable you to indulge your vile lusts unhindered by public opinion.

I replied as follows:

Augustus,
How could I wish to challenge an authority which I have served proudly and willingly to the best of my poor abilities these twenty years? I am well aware that your authority,

which I respect, is founded in the decrees of the Conscript Fathers, which no good Roman could wish to challenge.

This was disingenuous; it was founded in his victory in the civil wars, and none now dared to challenge it openly.

The sincerity of my wish for retirement acquits me of the charge of ambition. It would be a stupid manoeuvre to put myself in this position if I were truly ambitious, for you have only to grant my wish for retirement to bring my public career to an end. Besides, if I understand you correctly, you yourself charge me with a lack of that ambition which is proper and laudable in a Roman noble.

The charge of vice is absurd . . .

I paused as I wrote that line. Can any man, I thought, truly rebut such an accusation?

I repeat that I wish to devote the rest of my life to study. My chosen companions in my retreat will be Thrasyllus the distinguished astronomer, and other mathematicians; sober men. They are scarcely the company I should select for an orgy. . .

Should I have added that I was in reality fleeing from orgies? Would it have saved future pain?

I repeat that I am worn out, disturbed, have never recovered from my brother's death, and now there is a new generation ready to serve Rome. My continued presence at the head of the armies would be likely to cause them embarrassment . . .

In reply he asked me:

What sort of example will your miserable and selfish abnegation of duty be to the new generation of whom you speak? I have worked longer for Rome than you, and every bit as hard, but I have never thought to indulge in the luxury of retirement. It would be a fine state of affairs if we could all slip off our responsibilities as you are feebly and selfishly proposing to do. Do you realise how you are hurting your mother and me?

I am afraid that, at the thought of Augustus surrendering power and calling it responsibility, a smile of knowing superiority crossed my face. When I read the letter a second time, I knew that he was beaten.

I embraced my mother before departure – Augustus had declined to say farewell to me. I thanked Livia for her efforts on my behalf and commended my son Drusus to her care. He had expressed a desire to accompany me to Rhodes, but this was of course impossible; it was necessary that he be trained for public life along with his peers.

Livia's cheek was cold.

She said, "I wish you well and happy, dear boy, but I think I shall never be able to forgive you."

"Mother," I said, "I go in search of a happiness I have never known."

"Happiness. An idea for middle-class poets."

As I was sailing past Campania news was brought that Augustus was ill. Naturally I suspected a trick, but it was impossible that I should not give the order to cast anchor. I sat up on deck all night under the stars gazing at the land, wondering if he would cheat me again, this time by dying. Then my friend Lucilius Longus sent me word that my delay was being misinterpreted: that men said I was hoping for my stepfather's death, and intended to seize power.

So little was I understood. Sighing, I gave orders that we should set sail, though the wind was clean contrary.

THIRTEEN

The four years that succeeded my arrival here at Rhodes were the happiest of my life. I had cast aside care, and though I lived in leisure, I abjured mere idleness. I studied for three hours every morning, and read for two every afternoon. I attended lectures and debates in the schools of philosophy and exercised in the gymnasium. I engaged in friendly conversation on terms of equality with the citizens, cultured and generally charming Greeks who showed themselves free of the vices with which those members of their nation who have settled in Rome are wont to disgrace themselves and disgust us. On the contrary, the citizens of Rhodes are distinguished by their learning, common sense and virtue; nobody could reside here without learning that virtue is not, as some suppose, the monopoly of well-born Romans, but a quality innate in all men, which only requires congenial surroundings for its cultivation. The demeanour of the citizens here is such that no wise man can forget that Greece is the cradle of both liberty and law. I was pleased to reflect that through the insensible influence of this enchanted island I was growing in both virtue and wisdom.

My peace of mind owes much to my garden, for a fine garden is, in my opinion, the image of the good life. It was on account of the garden and its situation that I had been so pleased with this villa on my first visit; and residence here has only deepened my delight. It is set round with plane trees, many of them covered with silver-striped ivy. The tops flourish with their own green, but towards the base their verdure is borrowed from the ivy, which spreading around, connects one tree with another. Between the plane trees I have planted box trees, for their aromatic blessing of the evening air, while a grove of laurels blends its shade with that of the planes. There are a number of walks through these groves, some shady, others planted with roses, and the latter connect, by a pleasant contrast, the coolness of the shade with the warmth of Apollo's gift. Having passed through these winding alleys, which are indeed so seductive that I can spend hours in their delight, you come upon a straight walk, which breaks off into a number of others, bordered by little box hedges. There is again a pleasing contrast of regularity with the negligent beauties of rural nature. In the centre of the garden there is a grove of dwarf planes and nearby a clump of acacias, smooth and bending. At the southern extremity of the garden there is an alcove of white marble, shaded with vines and supported by four simple Carystian columns. There is a basin of water here, so skilfully contrived that it is always full, but never overflowing. When I sup here, this basin serves as a table, the larger dishes being placed round the edge, while smaller ones float like vessels or waterfowl. Opposite is a perpetual fountain, the basin of which is supported by four exquisitely carved boys who are holding up tortoises to drink of the water. Facing the alcove is a summer-house, in iridescent marble, which opens into the green shade of an enclosure, cool even at noon when the lizard sleeps on the baking wall. This summer-house is furnished with couches, and, being covered with a trailing vine, enjoys so agreeable a gloom that you may lie there and fancy yourself in a wood. Throughout the garden are other fountains and little marble seats, secluded from the hum of the city below and from the glare of the overmastering sun. In this garden I can echo the Greek poet who exclaims:

> "*Give me beneath the plane tree's shade to rest*
> *While tinkling fountains murmur and caress . . .*"

And when I lift my gaze behind the villa I see mighty pines stride up the hillside. Below, the sea glistens like a shield.

I busy myself improving on perfection. I live simply, eating and drinking little: asparagus, cucumbers, radishes, red mullet, bread, fruit and sheep-milk cheese from the mountain content me; I take no thought for fine wines, the resinated stuff of the locality suffices.

For four years I lived in Arcady, without distractions of war, politics, lust, thought of Rome, power or intrigue. I lived as my nature assures me I was born to live. At night I followed the pure and passionless movement of the stars.

I was completely myself . . .

But, there is always a but in human life. My use of tenses wavers. Do I describe a state, settled as a summer afternoon, or am I struggling to recall, and in recalling to perpetuate, something which, even as I form the conception of my sweet content, is slipping from my possession?

I was not free of disturbance. One day, for example, I had expressed a wish to visit some of the sick people in the city, an obligation I have cheerfully undertaken at regular intervals since coming here. Now a new servant misunderstood my intention, and, when I descended into the town, I was disgusted to discover that a great number of the sick had been collected in a public cloister, at what inconvenience and discomfort I did not care to think. They had even been arranged in separate squads according to their ailments. Naturally I made my apologies as best I could, and the affair passed. But my distress was increased by the realisation that these poor fellows had taken it for granted that they should be put to such inconvenience merely to enable me to display my benevolence. There is something disagreeable, and to my mind immoral, in the social relationships which we have established by our exercise of power. A coarse thought came to me, with a memory. Once, in a temper, Julia flashed at me, "It's all the same whether I get it from a labourer or a nobleman, and, believe me, the former are often better." There is, it struck me, a strange honesty and decency in that judgment.

How ironical that sentence looks.

It was a few months after that incident that disquieting rumours reached me from Rome. The first hint was offered in a cryptic note attached to a letter from Gnaeus Piso; he suggested I

look to my wife. I understood him only too well. I consulted
Thrasyllus, who was evasive. When pressed he admitted that
misfortune threatened; the stars were in ill conjunction. I wrote
to Livia in guarded terms. She ignored my covert questions in
her reply, though I could not imagine that she had failed to
understand them. I hesitated before writing to Julia, for I was
certain that her correspondence would be intercepted and
examined. It so happened, however, that a young officer, Lucius
Aelius Sejanus, whose father L. Seius Strabo had been Prefect
of the Praetorians and was now Proconsul of Egypt, paid a
courtesy call on me while travelling from Antioch to Rome. I
received him, as I did any young Roman who showed me such
respect, and also because his father had served under me on
the Danube.

"There are many in the armies," young Sejanus said, "who
wish for your return, sir."

He spoke in an open manly fashion. His eyes, which were
very blue, met mine and he did not flinch from my assessing
gaze. I liked him for his frank smile, for his ease of body and of
manner. We dined together and he made me laugh with his
accounts of his travels in the East and also because of his evident
dislike of Egypt. When he spoke of that country, a strain of
exaggeration of which he was wholly conscious was evident in
his language. He set out to amuse me, and succeeded. Yet it
was not that which pleased me most, but rather his ingenuous
acceptance of experience. There was something of my brother
Drusus in his manner, and when I looked at him stretched out
on the couch beside me, like an athlete resting between races,
I felt for him that mixture of affection and envy with which I had
been accustomed to regard Drusus, and which I had not known
since my brother's death. The world, and the nature of man,
were less complicated matters for him, and would always be
less complicated, I sensed, than they were for me, and I
responded to his youthful candour. He was little more than a
boy, but he was already worthy of my trust.

"If I asked you," I said, "to do something for me that might
put you at risk, and certainly, if discovered, would endanger
your chances of promotion in the service, but which would

nevertheless be a very valuable service to me, would you be prepared to undertake it?"

He blushed at the question.

"Yes, I should," he said, and then smiled. It was a shy smile, and an uncommonly sweet one. "For I know that you would not ask me to do anything which was dishonourable."

Even so I hesitated. There was shame in my hesitation, which did not distress me, and fear, which did. They were strangely mingled, for one part of my shame rested in my fear to trust him. And this was strange too, for such fear was natural. But I was also ashamed to make use of him, as I intended, though I knew he longed for me to do so. He leaped up, sparkling with youthful life, and fell on his knee before me. He took hold of my hands and pressed them.

"Trust me, sir. I am eager to do you service."

"It is in itself a small thing," I said, "merely to deliver a letter that I dare not send in the normal fashion. But this small thing could destroy you. You must understand that."

"Sir, you already have my answer."

"Yes," I said, "I have your answer, and am grateful for your willingness, but my perplexity nevertheless remains. I do not know whether I dare put you to this trial, or whether I would be justified in making use of you in this manner."

The pressure on my hands tightened.

"Sir," he said speaking in a low and urgent voice, which was yet gentle as that of a woman in love, "I am yours to command. Make such use of me as you please."

His eager smile seemed to mock the seriousness of his words.

"You're only a boy, a boy for whom the sun shines every day, and, if you accept my commission, I am going to introduce you to a world where there is no sunshine. What do you know of my wife?"

The abruptness of my question, and the bitterness of my tone startled him. He got to his feet and turned his back on me. His fingers played on the soft flesh of a ripe peach in the basket on the table.

"I don't know how to answer that, sir."

"I see. Perhaps that is a sufficient reply. It is to my wife that I wish you to convey a letter, and, when she has read it, I warn you that she will be angry with its bearer . . ."

But – I thought – she will look at its bearer, and she will imagine herself caressed by these strong hands and wrestling with these youthful limbs, and she will look at that lock of red-gold hair that falls over his eye, which he brushes back in so negligent a manner . . . and then she will set herself to seduce him; and that is not what I would want for him. But I need someone I can trust, and I think I can trust this boy . . .

"You have nothing to hope for from me," I said. "I am a man on the threshold of old age, who has resigned from the struggle for power. Do you understand that?"

"I hear your words, but I also hear that the stars speak differently, that they promise you a glorious future. And I know also what they say in the armies. So I am happy to accept your commission . . ."

He turned on me with a radiant smile.

"You see, sir," he said, "I have chosen to bind my future with yours. I am, as I told you, yours to command in all affairs."

Tenderness steals on you unawares like the evening breeze that wafts into my garden from the sea. It is not an emotion I have known often: for Vipsania when she would look at me with her plain face beautiful in its response to the pain or unhappiness of others; for Julia as she lay with our little son in her arms; for Drusus as I accompanied his dead body on that long march to the mausoleum; for young Segestes as I held him in my arms against the world. In each case, it seems to me, my experience of tenderness was a form of protest against the cruelty and mindlessness of life. Any rational being knows that the life of man is nasty and brutish, that all our carefully acquired and cherished culture amounts to no more than fragments of defence, work we have made against the reality of existence, against – to coin a phrase – its remorseless nihilism. The gods mock our feeble efforts or are indifferent to them; hence our hearts go out most powerfully to those who struggle against fate, and fail, for in their failure we recognise an ultimate truth

about this life to which we are condemned. "Who," as the poet
says, "would have heard of Hector, if Troy had not been taken?"
When I stood on the cliff-top and watched the sail of the ship
that carried young Sejanus back to Rome dip below the horizon,
I felt a renewal of that strange tenderness, and I could see him
as Hector, that broken hero, dragged behind the chariot of his
destroyer, his long limbs that delighted in movement now flaccid
and streaked with blood, the red-gold hair begrimed with the
dust through which it was dragged, while the vulgar shrieked
execrations, and those of noble mind stood silent, aghast at the
defilement of beauty, courage and virtue.

A sea-bird mewed, dived in search of fish. I shook off my
waking dream. "Ridiculous," I said to myself, and turned from
the glistening mirror of the sea that seemed to foreshadow
death into the sweet shades of evening under the laurels.

FOURTEEN

My letter to Julia had urged restraint, renewed my warning that she was subject to police scrutiny, and advised her that proceedings were being contemplated against her. I dared not say more. In fact events marched faster than I had supposed. Even while Sejanus was with me in Rhodes, information was lodged with Augustus. His distress at this revelation of his daughter's habits was, I am sure, genuine. He must have been the only man in Rome who did not know of her misconduct. Her behaviour had grown more openly scandalous since my departure. The report informed him (he sent me a copy) that "Subject, after a dinner-party, where much wine had been consumed, staggered with her companions into the Forum, and there mounted the Rostra from which position she solicited the custom of chance passers-by, to the pleasure of her associates, who called out, 'Roll up, roll up, for the best-born f— in Rome . . .' "

When I received the letter in which Augustus told me of what had happened, enclosing a copy of the police report, Julia was already doomed. I had only to read the catalogue of her noble lovers again to realise this. It was a political scandal of the first order, as well as a sexual one. Augustus gave no hint in his letter that he now understood my ulterior motive in retiring. On the other hand he did not upbraid me for having done so, so perhaps he guessed.

I could not know how far things had gone while the letter was on its way. Naturally I was also alarmed to think that I had despatched Sejanus with a missive which would compromise me, and might destroy him. I wondered what he had done, was doing, would do, with it. But that was beyond my control, though I wrote to him urging caution in "that matter of which you know" – in itself perhaps a compromising phrase. Meanwhile it was my duty to do whatever I could to rescue Julia from the consequences of her folly. I therefore wrote to Augustus.

> My wife, suffering perhaps from a species of desperation that can, my doctors tell me, afflict women as they approach middle-life, has behaved in a manner which is worse than foolish. The peculiarly public nature of her conduct must touch the bounds of forgiveness, for, as Princeps, you can hardly fail to interpret it as a public challenge to the admirable legislation you have caused to be passed. Yet I appeal to you, in your public and private capacity, to show clemency. Clemency would become you both as father of our country, and as father of your unfortunate daughter. I would beg you to consider that my own absence, the result of my intense weariness of spirit and body, and of my desire to allow Gaius and Lucius to flourish, may have contributed to my wife's aberrations. Clemency is good in itself. The harsh letter of justice will be like a knife which you yourself drive into your own heart . . .

I paused there. There was a further sentence which I knew I ought to write. My gorge rose at the thought of doing so – I gazed with melancholy at the tranquil beauty of my garden – and did what I had to do . . .

> I live in contented exile, remote from public affairs and from the hurly-burly of the city, in an atmosphere free from temptation to excess, ideally suited to the cultivation of a philosophic mind. May I suggest therefore that you command Julia to return to her husband?

It was beyond me to do more than make the flat suggestion, to supplement the recommendation with entreaties which could not be other than insincere, for the thought of Julia again invading the life I had so carefully reconstructed revolted me.

Augustus' reply was brief:

I have received your letter and noted its contents. The course you urge is impractical. When a woman has once become a whore, she is like a dog which has taken to worrying sheep: beyond cure. As her husband you have failed to exercise proper control in the past; I see no reason to suppose you would be more successful in the future. I am therefore arranging for you to divorce her. I do not wish to hear the wretched woman's name from you again . . .

Julia endured no public trial. Judgment descended on her secretly, implacably, stunningly. Her freedwoman Phoebe, a partner in her licentiousness, hanged herself. Julia endured. She was despatched to the island prison of Pandateria, and forbidden wine and male company. Meanwhile retribution was enacted on her lovers. Iullus Antonius was put to death; the others condemned to perpetual exile. I am told that Antonius died in ignoble fashion; the news did not surprise me. He was a man animated by vanity, rather than pride. I found myself agreeably indifferent to Julia's fate. She, after all, had first rejected me. Sejanus wrote to me to say that, in view of what he had discovered on arrival in Rome, he had deemed it wise to destroy my communication. He kissed my hands, and remained my loving and obedient servant. I approved his prudence, and besought him to pay me another visit. Meanwhile I advised him to pursue his military and legal studies with assiduity. "One cannot reach the highest without industry. Therefore, I urge you, in Vergil's words, 'O beautiful boy, trust not too much to complexion'. Study hard therefore, and in the words of another, inferior poet, 'So may the nymphs give thee water to assuage thirst'. Meanwhile, you are aware of my gratitude and good wishes. Though I have withdrawn from public life, I retain influence and friends, and would wish you to regard me henceforth as your father, patron and friend . . ."

Since Julia abandoned me I had felt myself to be, in a profound yet uncertain sense, a superfluous man. Now, in solitude, I brooded on the strangeness of our marriage and of her fate. She had brought her misfortunes on herself; yet she had done

so in the same blithe and regardless manner that had twice, for
periods of my life, delighted and enflamed me. And now that
fire was extinguished, utterly. Even my resentment of her infidelity, and of the shame she had brought on me, withered. It
was almost as if she had never existed. There are loves of
which one retains a fragrant and nostalgic memory. Such had
been mine for Vipsania. I never thought of her without tenderness, but then I rarely thought of her. She had simply belonged
to a stage of my life from which I was separated by the welter
of events, so that it was as if our love had belonged to two quite
different people. My love for Julia had been more intense, as
my emotions had been less pure. I knew now that I had been
awaiting her disgrace as after days of steamy weather you
expect a thunderstorm. And her disgrace had done the work of
the thunder. I felt free to live again.

This realisation perplexed me, for I had imagined myself possessed of a full and satisfying happiness, and had judged that
this rested in my abandonment of ambition and my acceptance
of the meaninglessness of life. Yet though that conviction had
been confirmed by her misfortunes – for what life could in any
scale of values be thought to have less significance than hers?
– I was now assailed with a renewed dissatisfaction, occasioned,
I had to conclude, by the sensation of liberty.

Absurd; hadn't the events in Rome confirmed my scornful
judgment that liberty had been Augustus' principal victim?

I did not entirely escape the effects of Julia's ignominy. It was
reported to me that when men mentioned my name in Rome
they did so without respect. I was a figure who was receding
into the past; of no account. Only a few old friends remained
loyal. Sejanus was almost my only link with the younger generation. There was, however, one other, though tenuous: my stepson Lucius. Whereas his older brother Gaius ignored me
completely, Lucius wrote to me on my birthday, sent me good
wishes, thanked me for the presents I sent him – I sent presents
to Gaius also at appropriate moments, but received no thanks,
though the gifts were not returned. Lucius expressed his distress on his mother's account, though he was honest enough to
add that he had always known she did not care for him. All I

could say in reply was that, as far as I knew, he had nothing
with which to reproach himself: barren comfort, for self-
reproach needs no objective justification. It was ironic however
that Julia's disgrace coincided with Lucius' own appointment,
three years after his brother's, as a Prince of the Youth Movement. He was excited by this elevation; with good cause, for it
confirmed that Augustus intended that the brothers should
share in the government of the empire after his death, even
perhaps in his old age. For the same reason it intensified the
discontent in Rome which had already been fanned by the persecution of those old noble families which had supplied Julia
with her paramours. My own son Drusus sent me only brief,
occasional and uninformative letters; perhaps he felt that I had
abandoned him, though I exercised such care for his education
as was possible at a distance.

My mother remained my stay, supporter and source of news.
She was displeased by the rapid elevation of Gaius and Lucius,
all the more because they were not her blood relations. She did
not dislike them for that reason, though she was certain that
Augustus gravely overestimated their abilities. Her objections
were primarily political. Despite being a woman, and subject to
the characteristic prejudices of her gender, Livia possessed an
acute understanding of the way things are done in the world.
Augustus had owed much to her connections, more to her
sagacity; but now he was, as she put it, "blind with love for the
boys as he was once before in the case of Marcellus". Livia
knew that the Roman nobility would rebel against the semblance
of hereditary monarchy. She knew – none better – that her
husband's claim to have restored the Republic was a figment;
she realised that the secret would be out if power passed to
Gaius and Lucius on account of their birth rather than their
achievement. She urged restraint on Augustus and she urged
me to return to Rome. Yet I still rebelled against doing so.

Then my *tribunicia potestas* lapsed, was not renewed. My
legal authority evaporated. My person was no longer sacrosanct. I had become a mere nobleman, of fading distinction. At
first I was not alarmed; it was, after all, what I had wanted.

Yet very soon I began to feel like a bird trapped in a room.

It is free to fly, but yet confined. It flings itself against the windows, seeing an escape it cannot attain.

Gaius had been appointed to a command in the East, where new troubles were brewing on the Parthian frontier, since the death of King Tigranes of Armenia had encouraged the Parthians to meddle again in that turbulent country. It was a task likely to prove beyond a raw youth, and I wrote to my stepson offering him the benefit of my advice and reminding him of my experience in Armenian–Parthian affairs. He did not grant me the courtesy of a reply. Fortunately, young Sejanus was attached to his staff and ready to keep an eye on my interests. He reported that I was habitually referred to as "the exile", and that my old enemy Marcus Lollius, whom Augustus had entrusted with the responsibility of supervising the Prince of the Youth Movement, lost no opportunity to denigrate me, and drip poison in an ear all too ready to receive it. Sejanus recommended that I pay my stepson (who was in reality my former stepson, since my divorce from his mother) a visit.

I attended him on Samos. It was strange to be in a camp again, stranger still that it should have the air of a court. He received me with marked coldness; as we embraced, Lollius smirked in the background. It disgusted me to see that greedy rapacious face again; besides, he was fatter than ever, and his low-swinging belly gave him a curiously aquatic air – you looked for the webbed feet. He ensured that throughout my visit Gaius and I were never alone together. Meanwhile I kept my eyes open. There was much to disapprove of. Discipline was lax and it was evident that Gaius was one of those commanders who sought to win popularity by condoning misdemeanours rather than to earn it by virtue and efficiency. Lollius, of course, had always been of that type.

In conversation, Lollius was insolent and, shamefully, was encouraged in his insolence by Gaius, who sniggered as his appointed mentor rejected with flat negatives my analysis of the Parthian habit of mind. I declined to enter into argument. It would have been beneath my dignity. Naturally my self-restraint was misinterpreted by Gaius and the young dandies with whom he had surrounded himself. They assumed that I was cowed and timorous – as if a Claudian could be fazed or outfaced by such as Marcus Lollius. However, in these degenerate days, when mere vanity has so often supplanted a proper pride, it is no wonder that virtue and dignity are not recognised, and so become subjects for ill-conditioned levity.

Yet my visit was not without value. It confirmed me, for one thing, in my respect for young Sejanus by granting me opportunities, however brief and fleeting, to further my acquaintance with him in a number of agreeable ways. I admired his tact, the manner in which he neither presumed on my favour nor advertised it. I admired also his intellect, which was powerful, his quick wit and ready understanding.

He made it easy for me too to have confidential discussions with other friends who were attached to Gaius' staff: C. Velleius Paterculus and P. Sulpicius Quirinius. These were men subtle enough to conceal their distrust for Lollius beneath an appearance of affability. They reported that his enmity towards me was fixed: "It blows hard and cold as the north wind. He loses no chance to enflame the Princeps' mind against you."

"A superfluous task," I observed.

"However," Velleius assured me, "Lollius may not be as secure as he thinks. He has been engaged in secret correspondence with the King of Parthia, and I have reason to think that he has taken bribes from him, to subvert Roman policy to Parthian designs. Perhaps the mere suggestion that he has done so would be enough to destroy him."

"No," Sejanus said. "Give him rope. Nothing is to be gained by making an allegation which we cannot substantiate. I have no experience of these matters of course, being only a youth, but it seems to me that in cases of treason it is often better to delay than to strike. In this way you allow the suspect to compromise himself more thoroughly, and are able in time to destroy him utterly."

I nodded approval.

Meanwhile, it was necessary to take precautions on my own behalf. When I returned to Rhodes, I no longer exercised on the parade ground as had been my habit and even took to wearing a Greek cloak and slippers instead of the toga. I wished to emphasise that I had withdrawn altogether from public life and could not be thought a danger to anyone. Despite this, a letter from Sejanus informed me that Lollius had accused me of tampering with the loyalty of Gaius' officers: Sejanus himself had been interrogated, concerning the nature of our conversations. "I gave nothing away," he wrote. This accusation was alarming, all the more so because Sejanus took it seriously enough to have his letter conveyed to me concealed in a box of red mullet which he had a boy from a fishing-boat deliver as a gift. I replied to him in similarly circumspect manner and sent a formal letter to Gaius, explaining that Lollius' charge had been reported to me and that I was accordingly requesting that a close watch be kept on my words, actions and correspondence. This was itself a superfluous demand, for the thing was already being done.

The next letter from Sejanus (arriving this time in a box of figs) was still more disturbing. He reported that a young nobleman at Gaius' table had offered to sail to Rhodes and " 'bring back the exile's head'". The request was refused, but caused much hilarity and the young man was not reproved. Instead Marcus Lollius had a jar of new wine brought to him. "Take care, father and benefactor. Trust in your friends, the least of whom now kisses your hands."

I swallowed the toad of pride, wrote to Augustus, explaining that the causes of my self-inflicted exile having withered, I was ready to resume any duties which he would care to impose upon me, and meanwhile requested permission to return to Rome.

He did not reply to my letter. Instead, he wrote to Gaius asking his opinion. Naturally, with Lollius at his ear, Gaius, who had, poor boy, no mind of his own, declared that I could stay where I was. "He can do no harm there, and no good anywhere else," he wrote. (I have since seen the letter, and recognise the tone and sentiments as being dictated by Lollius.)

I wrote to Livia. She was unable to help. Even she dared not write frankly, knowing that all my correspondence was copied and examined by my enemies. I felt the chill of evening descend around me; it seemed as though my life was to be summed up in the cheat of my marriage and my fractured career. At night I felt myself assailed by temptations to which I did not dare to yield, scarcely even in imagination.

My friends, however, acted on my behalf, without my knowledge. Perhaps on account of my long absence from affairs, I had grown excessively cautious; at any rate I would not have ventured, as they did, to launch an attack against the all-powerful favourite Lollius. The accusations took him by surprise, all the more because they were well founded. He could offer no answer. Gaius withdrew his favour quickly because he was afraid that he might in some way be implicated in Lollius' disgrace. His fear revealed a poor understanding of Augustus, who would have been ready to forgive his beloved grandson anything – as he had in the past forgiven Marcellus. Anyway, Gaius, alarmed, his colour high and his voice rising out of control, upbraided Lollius at a meeting of his general staff, demanded his resignation and threatened him with prosecution. Lollius was unnerved; he did not pause to reflect that his own relations with Augustus had always been good, that he had indeed been an especial favourite of the Princeps. Perhaps, on the other hand, he feared that Augustus would be merciless on account of the favour he had shown the general, that he would interpret Lollius' treason against Rome as an act of personal betrayal also; which indeed it was, especially because it was impossible for Lollius to advance a defence of having acted in the public interest. An examination of his personal accounts showed clearly in whose interest he had acted. His career in ruins, his reputation destroyed by his own greed and folly, the wretched man cut his throat.

The extent of his malign influence was soon apparent. Within a month of his death I was authorised to return to Rome, albeit in the capacity only of a private citizen forbidden to participate in public life.

Livia came to Ostia to greet me. She wept as she embraced me, and I felt the pathos of a mother's love.

"I have missed you," she said, and I wished that I could reply in the same words. But I felt little for her, only a remote and ineffectual tenderness. She had, ever since I grew up, demanded more from me than I was capable of granting her. Now she apologised for the absence of Augustus, offering excuses which I did not believe.

"I didn't expect him to be here to greet me," I said. "This is not a triumphant return after all."

"No," she said, "and whose fault is that, I would like to know? It was not by my wish or my advice that you have wasted so many years of your life. If you have been an exile, it was of your own choice. Nevertheless, my son, it is a return from which triumph may spring."

"I doubt it, mother . . ."

The sun was sinking behind the Alban hills as we mounted the steps of the Capitol to allow me to give thanks to Jupiter for my safe return. The marble shone pink, and Livia cried out that she seemed to see a golden halo over my head. But this was nonsense, and I felt a weariness of spirit as I gazed down on the teeming throng below. I felt more solitary than I had ever been on my island retreat. Within a few days, I retired to a house on the Esquiline Hill, built in gardens which had once belonged to Maecenas. I attended to my duties as head of the Claudian *gens*. I examined my son Drusus, and was pleased to discover that his education was proceeding in a satisfactory fashion. Otherwise I saw only old friends, among them Gnaeus Calpurnius Piso and his brother Lucius, and Cossus Cornelius Lentulus. All three had achieved much; none found satisfaction. All agreed with me about public affairs, and performed their duties without indulging in any illusions concerning either their nature or purpose. Many nights we allowed Bacchus to console us for the death of liberty in Rome, and sought in wine what we could not find in either public or private affairs: a species of joy and some reason for prolonging life, a guard against disappointment and a means of ephemeral freedom from disillusion . . .

The first volume of Tiberius' autobiography breaks off abruptly at this point, and it is impossible to determine whether he abandoned it or whether the pages that cover events up to the death of Augustus in 14 AD have been lost. The former is perhaps more probable since the tone of the last chapters is elegiac. It is probable that he wrote these memoirs partly in Rhodes and partly after his return to Rome while he was living in retirement on the Esquiline. At any rate a brief résumé of events in the following years may be serviceable, in the regrettable absence of Tiberius' own account.

Tiberius returned to Rome in 2 AD. A few weeks later the younger of the princes, Lucius, died at Marseilles on his way to Spain. Tiberius composed an elegy (also lost) for his erstwhile stepson, but Lucius' death made no difference to his political position. However, eighteen months later Gaius also died, as a result of a fever following a wound. This changed everything, destroying all Augustus' plans for the future. Only one of Julia's sons by her marriage to Agrippa survived. This was Agrippa Postumus, so called because he had been born after his father's death. He was unfortunately a brutish imbecile. As he grew up it became apparent that he was unlikely to be fit for office, though this was not yet certain in 4 AD.

The death of Gaius forced Augustus to turn to Tiberius, who had become the necessary man. Augustus adopted him, grudgingly, telling the Senate that he did so for reasons of state, because "cruel fate" had deprived him of his "beloved grandsons". He adopted Agrippa Postumus at the same time, but three years later, on account of his violent behaviour, the wretched young man was confined to an island. Tiberius was himself ordered to adopt his own nephew Germanicus, the son of Drusus and Augustus' niece Antonia. Germanicus was married to Agrippina, a daughter of Julia and Agrippa, and therefore Augustus' grand-daughter. In this way Augustus hoped that the succession would revert to his own blood relatives. The sufferer in this instance was of course Tiberius' own son Drusus.

Tiberius spent most of the next decade away from Rome, campaigning on the Danube frontier and in Germany. He achieved great success. The period, however, saw one of the greatest disasters in the history of Rome when P. Quintilius Varus lost three legions in the German forests. Again Tiberius had to restore the situation, retrieve the disaster. His achievement was formidable. Nevertheless the defeat of Varus persuaded Augustus that Germany could never be conquered and that the Roman Empire should not be extended further. Tiberius concurred in this decision.

In 13 AD Tiberius was formally associated with Augustus in the government of the empire, sharing his *imperium* as Agrippa had done long ago. The following year Augustus died at the age of seventy-six.

PART TWO

ONE

Old age is a shipwreck. I saw that in Augustus and indeed heard the phrase on his lips, though, if I remember, he did not apply it to himself. Now I recognise its truth for me. I am breaking on the sharp rocks, buffeted by cruel winds. Peace of mind and ease of body both desert me. The Greek poet Callimachus complained of being assailed by the Telchines – a cannibal tribe ready to tear your liver out. I had thought to erect a barricade by study, collecting the wisdom of ages as found in books. It offers no defence. Philosophy, I conclude, offers comfort only to minds that are not disturbed, which have, therefore, no need of it. Philosophy cannot quiet the maledictory and maleficent demons who torment me. I am, men say, the emperor of the world. Some fools in Asia are even ready to worship me as a god. When I was told this, I remarked to myself that the only resemblance I could see between the gods and myself lay in our indifference to humanity, and contempt for men.

Augustus died in his seventy-seventh year. I had grown fonder of him in his old age, as he became aware of the depth of his failure. There were moments, I even thought, when he realised how he had corrupted Rome, breeding a generation of slaves, therefore of liars, since no slave can be trusted to tell the truth, but must always say what he believes his master wishes to hear. He fell ill when I was about to return to the army. Naturally I changed my plans and hastened back. He was still conscious and lucid. He entrusted Rome, and Livia, to my care. I knew that it was not what he would have wished to do, but I knew also that he had come to value me in his last years. In a letter he once wrote "If you were to fall ill, the news would kill your mother and me, and the whole country would be in danger." The first part of the apodosis was characteristically hyperbolic, but he knew the second part to be true, and I welcomed his recognition of my worth.

We buried his ashes in the mausoleum he had constructed for the family. I pronounced the funeral eulogy, avoiding the direct lie, not eschewing polite fictions. A couple of days later, the former praetor Numerius Atticus obligingly informed the Senate that during the cremation ceremony he had seen my stepfather's spirit soaring up to Heaven through the flames. Nobody chose to express doubt.

Augustus was declared to be a god.

What would they have said if they had known that almost his last act had been to despatch orders that his only surviving grandson Agrippa Postumus should . . . cease to survive?

Nothing, I suppose. They would not have dared.

I owed Augustus some gratitude for taking that decision on himself. Unfortunately the timing was such that the boy was not killed till a few days after his grandfather's death, and then there were naturally many ready to believe that I had ordered his execution. I would in fact have had no authority to do so.

The question of authority had to be settled immediately. Augustus claimed in his political testament, the *res gestae*, which I published at his request, that after the expiry of the peculiar powers granted him by the law which established the Triumvirate with Mark Antony and Manius Aemilius Lepidus, he had possessed "no more power than the others who were my colleagues in each magistracy, though I excelled all in authority".

This was disingenuous. He had ensured that a superior overriding *imperium* was granted to him, which, in effect, meant that his legal power was unquestioned in all affairs, even within those provinces of the empire which are nominally within the charge of the Senate. He had devised a constitution which obscured his power, but did not prevent him from exercising it wherever he chose. It was his wish that I should inherit his position.

I had no doubt of that. He had revealed it in numerous conversations in his last years. Livia was certain that was his intention. When she returned from watching over her husband's ashes, she embraced me, and said: "At last, my son, you have everything which I have striven for years to obtain for you."

"Mother," I said, "if I have anything, it is as a result of my own labours, and anyway I am not certain what I wish to have."

"What you wish . . ." she repeated my words, and shook her head. "Don't you understand, my dear, that your wishes have never entered into the matter? You have what is yours, what the gods have awarded you, what I have for forty years worked to bring about."

"We shall see."

"Oh no, you will see sense. You will see that you have no choice. Go down to the Senate by all means, and offer to restore the Republic in its old form. You won't find anyone to understand what you mean."

Gnaeus Piso gave me the same advice.

"Of course you're a Republican," he said. "So am I. Of course you detest the tyranny which has been imposed on Rome. So do I. But that's all there is to it. It's not a choice between the empire and the Republic. It's a choice between Tiberius and some other emperor. You must grab the empire by the balls, my friend, or someone else will take a tight and painful grip of yours."

I did not sleep the night before I attended the Senate. It was a calm night in September. The moon was up and the city silent. A cat brushed against my legs as I stood on the terrace of my house gazing beyond the city to the invisible sea. I bent down, picked up the cat and held it in my arms, stroking its back and listening to its contented purr. Everything Livia and Piso said was true; yet I rebelled against the despotism of fact.

I sought to be dull, yet to impress the Senate with the magnitude of empire. I read to them the account of the empire which Augustus had prepared. I deluged them with statistics concerning the number of regular and auxiliary troops serving in the armies, the strength of the navy; details concerning the provinces and dependent kingdoms; the tax receipts, both direct and indirect; the annual expenditure. It was an audit of empire, impressive and daunting in scale. The last sentence repeated the judgment at which Augustus and I myself had independently arrived following the disaster in Germany: that the empire should not be extended beyond its present frontiers.

Then I laid the document aside, and spoke as follows.

"Conscript Fathers, we are all of us heirs of the great history of Rome, children of the great Republic. My own family, as you all know, has played a major part in the development of Rome's greatness. My late father Augustus has overseen the security of the empire, and guided its destiny, for more than forty years, longer than some of you have been alive. You have known no other father of the country. He restored peace within the territories of the Republic. After the civil wars he restored the institutions of the Republic. He extended the frontiers of the empire into lands where the arms of Rome had been unknown. In the words of the poet whom he delighted to honour, he made the world cry: 'Behold them, conquerors, all clad in Roman togas.' He followed the Roman custom: to spare the subject and subdue the proud.

"But now, fellow citizens, we must ask, not only where shall we find his like but, more urgently, whether it is proper that any one man, lacking his supreme qualities, should wield the same degree of power. For my part, I think it is a task beyond any of us. It is certainly beyond me. I was honoured in his last years to be permitted to share his burdens, and, believe me, I know their weight. I know what hard, demanding, hazardous work it is to rule such an empire as Rome's.

"Besides, I would urge you to consider whether it is proper that a state like ours, which can rely on so many distinguished personages, should commit such power to one man, and concentrate the management of the empire in the hands of a single person. Would it not be better, Conscript Fathers, to share it among a number of us?"

The previous night Livia had asked me to rehearse my speech. I had declined to do so, saying that twice-cooked meat never tastes good, but I had given her the gist.

"They won't know what you mean," she said, "and they will

be afraid you are trying to trick them. Besides, though you don't know it, they stand rather in awe of you. You've been away so much, you're practically a stranger in Rome, and consequently you have become an enigma. They will be seeking to uncover the secret meaning of your discourse."

"There is no secret meaning," I said, "I am giving them their chance. Over the years I have heard, or come to know of, so many mutterings, so many protests at his concentration of power, so many complaints that the path of honour and glory in which our ancestors delighted is now closed, blocked off, that I wish to give them the opportunity to explore it. That's all."

"All?" she said. "They will be scared stiff."

Now, when I finished speaking, there was a prolonged silence in the Curia. It was broken only by a shifting of bodies and a few coughs. I resumed my seat, and waited. Nothing happened. When I looked at a senator, his gaze slipped away.

I sighed. Suddenly I was beset by abject appeals to take Augustus' place . . . "There was no alternative" it was cried. I rose again and, making an effort to speak courteously, and not to reveal the disgust I felt, I explained that while I did not feel myself capable of assuming the whole burden of government, I was naturally ready to take on any branch of it that they might choose to entrust to me.

C. Asinius Gallus then rose to speak. I knew him for an ambitious man, but an imprudent one. His father had been one of Augustus' generals, but Augustus had never entrusted an army to the son. Moreover, I had cause to dislike, as well as distrust him: he had married my dear Vipsania after our divorce, and treated her badly, partly because his taste ran to very young virgins, and he often proclaimed that the body of a mature woman disgusted him. So, when he got to his feet, I prepared for something disagreeable.

"Tell us, Caesar," he said, "which branch you desire to have handed to you."

"That is not for me to say," I replied. "Frankly, I would be happy to retire altogether from affairs of state. Yet I am ready to accept any duty which the Senate cares to impose upon me."

"That's not good enough," Gallus said, "and we all know it. For if we nominate a branch which does not please you, then we shall offend you and since you already have the power, by reason of your tribune's status, to annul any decision we take, and since you have already shown your willingness to employ the power entrusted to you by the fact that you have accepted a bodyguard of the Praetorians, none of us is likely to make the sort of specific proposal you call for. Besides, you have misunderstood the nature of my question. It was never my intention that we should parcel out functions which, frankly, are indivisible. I only put forward my question in order to make it quite clear that the state is a single organic whole which requires that it be directed by a single mind. And who, Conscript Fathers, better than Tiberius, who has won such great honours, denied the rest of us, in war, and who has done the state, and Augustus, such service in peace?"

After this speech there was a general confused babble, as one senator after another (and sometimes more than one at the same time) protested that they had no wish but to surrender the power that belonged to them into my hands. Quintus Haterius even went so far as to cry out: "How long, Caesar, will you allow the state to have no head?" – as if Augustus had been dead for years rather than a few days.

Finally, Mamercus Aemilius Scaurus, a man never without a sneer on his lips, remarked that since I had not used my tribune's power to veto the motion which suggested I should replace Augustus, he hoped that the Senate's prayers would not go unrewarded. His comment was greeted with acclamation. He smiled, pleased to be the object of general attention and to have forced me towards the unwelcome chalice. For Scaurus was one of the few senators intelligent enough to understand that I was sincere and it pleased him to destroy my hope that someone would consent to take up part of the burden, and so make it possible to attempt to restore the Republic.

I was beaten. Driven to power by a generation fit for slavery, there was bitterness in my heart as I indicated my acceptance. What was I accepting? Misery and back-breaking labour. What was I setting aside? The hope of happiness. "I shall do as you ask," I growled, "until I grow so old that you may be good enough to grant me a respite."

That evening I was prostrated by a migraine. I dismissed the slaves whose remedies were vain. Sejanus stroked my head with a napkin soaked in vinegar.

"You shouldn't work yourself into these states," he said. "It's because you live in a world formed by your own imagination, a world where men still seek to practise virtue. But it's not like that. In your heart you know it isn't. It's just your obstinate Claudian pride that insists that other men ought to have standards like yours. You don't understand human nature. It's made up of wolves, jackals and lambs. And the occasional lion such as you."

"What are you yourself, dear boy?"

"When I'm with you, I feel I might be a lion's cub. On my own I recognise myself as a wolf."

He soaked the napkin again.

"Is that any better? In the same way you won't admit the truth about the empire, though you know in your heart of hearts what it is. It's impossible that we should be an empire beyond Italy and the Republic at home. The two forms of government don't mix, and the Republic could never administer the empire."

He wiped my brow again.

"There," he sighed, "you're committed to it. You can't escape ever. Now you must sleep. I'll put out the light."

TWO

Sejanus comforted me as no other could. He was no longer the happy, if circumspect, boy I had first known on Rhodes, but a man in the prime of life, of matchless vigour and capacity. His judgment was admirable, his industry extraordinary. But it was his buoyancy that I valued most. I am by nature melancholic, given to brooding and depression, forever conscious of dangers and difficulties. His sanguine temperament uplifted me. I had only to see him stride towards me, that frank and confident smile on his face, his whole air one of athletic well-being, to feel the clouds lift. He had, moreover, one other great virtue: he always, it seemed to me, told me the truth. This is rare, for truth is what men like to conceal from those who exercise power.

Of course, people were jealous and tried to turn me against him. My niece Agrippina, for instance, despised him for his comparatively humble birth, and lack of ancestors – as if Sejanus was not at least as well born as her father Marcus Agrippa. She was also forever complaining of his manners, merely because he did not practise polite insincerity. Others denounced him in anonymous letters, and Scaurus drew me aside to inform me that he "knew for a fact" that, in his youth, Sejanus had been the catamite of the debauched moneylender Marcus Gavius Apicius, and that his fortunes were founded on this liaison.

"What's more," he said, "Apicius still makes him an allowance and in return Sejanus procures young guardsmen for him. What do you think of that, Tiberius?"

"You seem to forget," I replied, "that Sejanus is married to Apicius' daughter, Apicata, and is the father of her two children. I think that contradicts your malicious assertions."

Nevertheless my denial did not entirely convince me myself, for I knew Apicius and could imagine how desirable he would have found the youthful Sejanus. Nor did I believe that, as a boy, Sejanus would have resisted the temptation of physical pleasure. The second part of the accusation seemed merely spiteful. However, I arranged that a watch be kept on Apicius' acquaintance.

Concern with such matters was abruptly thrust aside. Word came that the army in Pannonia had mutinied. This was especially painful to me, since the legions stationed there had long been under my own command. Their complaints were manifold, also long-standing, for they were experiencing one of those periodic revulsions from service which may afflict even veteran soldiers. The ringleader was a fellow called Percennius who, having worked as a professional cheerleader in the theatre before becoming a soldier (to escape the just wrath of an offended father, as discovered later), knew how to incite crowds with his insolent tongue. To their subsequent shame, many of the soldiers listened to him, indulging in the vain hope of oversetting the reality of their existence; even those who knew better were either carried away for the moment, or did not dare to argue with their intoxicated comrades. Some of the officers were beaten, others fled in panic; one, a company-commander called Lucilius, noted for his strict discipline, had his throat cut.

Mutiny is as simple as it is serious. Whatever the grievances of mutineers, however justified they may be, they cannot be appeased till order is restored. That is a fundamental condition of military life. I therefore had no hesitation in acting to restore order.

I entrusted the task to my son Drusus. He was, of course, young for the job, but I had every confidence in his good sense. Moreover it seemed to me that the despatch of my own son would convince the sensible element in the legions of my benevolence and confidence. I sent two battalions of the Praetorian Guard with him, strengthened beyond their normal numbers by picked drafts and with them, three troops of horse guards and four companies of my most trusted German auxiliaries. Naturally Sejanus, whom I had appointed joint commander of the

Guard, with his distinguished father L. Seius Strabo, led these troops and, to enhance his authority, I made him Drusus' chief of staff.

Before they set off, I said to them: "There is nobody I trust more than you, Drusus, my only son, and you Sejanus, for whom I have the most tender fatherly feelings. You are going to the place of honour and danger. I cannot give you precise instructions. You must exercise your judgment according to the circumstances in which you find yourself. But keep two things in mind: first, many of the soldiers' grievances will be legitimate, and ought to be satisfied. Second, you cannot safely satisfy them till they have submitted to their ancient discipline, and order has been restored. Take this letter and read it to them as a preliminary. It states that the heroic soldiers of Rome, who have been my comrades in so many arduous, yet glorious campaigns, are dear to my heart, and that, as soon as I have recovered from the shock of my bereavement – I refer of course to the death of Augustus – I shall refer their grievances to the Senate. Meanwhile, you, Drusus, have the authority to grant any concessions that may be safely granted. Make the soldiers understand that the Senate is capable of generosity as well as of severity . . ."

I embraced them both and watched them ride off with hearts that were lighter than my own. This was natural: they were young and proceeding to the point of action; I was old and condemned to remain in Rome, unable further to influence events. The next weeks were anxious for me.

They were made more anxious by news from the Rhine. Possibly inspired by news of the Danube mutinies, the legions there followed suit. These were the responsibility of my nephew and adopted son Germanicus. Since he was supreme commander in Gaul and on the Rhine frontier, I had no choice but to entrust the suppression of the mutinies to him, setting aside whatever doubts I might have myself as to his ability to do so. These doubts were real, for Germanicus, though a young man of great charm and enterprise, was cursed with the itch of popularity. Moreover, it was soon reported to me that certain elements among the mutineers hoped to persuade him to lead

them in civil war, even though he had taken an oath of loyalty
to me as Augustus' successor.

The response of the three young men to the dangers into
which they were thrust was significant. Drusus and Sejanus
behaved with diplomatic skill, and exemplary fortitude; Germanicus like an actor. The accounts each gave reveal much of
their individual characters, and hint at future difficulties I was
to experience.

Drusus wrote as follows:

When we arrived here, Father, the situation was even worse
than I had imagined. The soldiers, as I preferred always to
think even of the mutineers, met us at the gate of the camp.
It was shocking to see their disarray. The men were disgustingly dirty, but they were not as disorganised as they looked,
for as soon as we were gathered in the camp, they picketed
the gates and placed armed outposts at key points. It was
almost as if we were their prisoners; certainly we were in a
sense hostages. Nevertheless I mounted the rostrum and
read your letter to them. This calmed them for a moment
and they put forward an officer, Julius Clemens, whom you
will remember as skilful in staff-work, to present their
demands. Clemens, I should say, had agreed to be associated
with the mutineers in order to try to act as a bridge between
them and the authorities. I should say that he showed considerable courage and public spirit in undertaking this dangerous role, which he performed in a manner that won my
admiration. He now presented demands concerning conditions of service – asking that this be limited to sixteen
years, that pay be increased to four sesterces a day, and that
they should be guaranteed freedom from recall after release.
I replied that these demands did not seem altogether
unreasonable, but that they were matters which would
require to be referred to the emperor and Senate. I added
that I would urge you, my father, and the Senate to look
sympathetically on them.

This answer appeased a great part of the crowd. Unfortunately, however, one of the ringleaders, a private named Vibulenius, realised that the mutiny in which he and his like so delighted, since it gave them a sense of power that they had never previously experienced, was in danger of withering away. So he fanned the flames.

"Why is it," he cried, "that when it comes to decisions about our conditions of service, the emperor calls in the Senate? But when it's a matter of punishment or battles we don't hear anything about the Senate. In the old days Tiberius used to shelter behind Augustus when it came to denying us satisfaction for our grievances; now Drusus has come here to hide behind Tiberius . . ."

Well, the meeting broke up with nothing decided, but at least without the outbreak of violence which seemed likely at one point. All the same, the situation was extremely tense. Any officer or member of the Guard whom the mutineers encountered was insulted and some were attacked. Gnaeus Cornelius Lentulus, for instance, was hit on the head by a stone, and would have been lynched but for the arrival of a troop of the Guards. Still, we got to our huts and were able to take counsel.

It was obvious to us that most of the men were reasonable, as men usually are, individually, but that they were incited to a sort of temporary madness by a subversive minority, who did not have the men's welfare at heart, but sought only to enjoy their unexpected power and licence. Someone remarked that what we had to do was to divide the sheep from the goats, as it were, or rather the sheep from the wild dogs. "Divide and rule" should be our game-plan. I therefore agreed that officers of my staff should venture into the camp, holding as many private discussions as they deemed safe, in an attempt to identify the wild dogs and to persuade the sheep that we would urge careful consideration of their grievances, always reminding them of the care you have always shown for their welfare, and pointing out also that it would be difficult to treat honourably soldiers who seemed to have abandoned the discipline and sense of duty characteristic of their calling. I may say that the courage of those officers who undertook this perilous assignment was remarkable; their skill in carrying it out wholly commendable, for during that night the good soldiers gradually disengaged themselves from those who had incited them. A sense of obedience gradually crept over the camp, like the first light of dawn. The soldiers withdrew themselves from the gates, and the eagles and standards set up at the outbreak of the mutiny were returned to their proper place.

This was encouraging, and the next morning I called another meeting. I found the men in a new, amenable frame of mind. I spoke severely at first. Caesar, I said, had once addressed mutinous troops by the name of civilians, rather than of soldiers. The previous day I had been unable to accord them even that less dignified term. (For you know better than I how soldiers despise civilians, even as citizens, except when danger runs high, affect to despise soldiers.) Now, I said, it seemed that reason had prevailed, that the gods had withdrawn their madness from the soldiers and that they were therefore ready to resume their proper bearing. Threats and intimidation could make no impression on me or on my father or on the dignity of the Roman Senate. If, however, they were now pleading for pardon, then I would recommend mercy to you, and, as I had promised yesterday, a careful hearing of their grievances, for which I did not lack sympathy. They begged me to write to you at once. I despatched the delegation which has brought you this letter. The mutiny is over, for the moment, and we propose to arrest and isolate the ringleaders. But the men have been harshly treated in the last months. They are now cowed, but if their grievances remain unattended, they will become resentful.

I could not have behaved better than Drusus myself, and my heart glowed with pride in my son.

A letter from Sejanus arrived a few days later.

You will have heard from Drusus how worthily he behaved, in a manner that showed him to be a true son of his father.

The mutiny is over. My own part in its suspension was necessarily secondary, and may be judged small. I should like, however, to draw your attention to the admirable manner in which the Guards conducted themselves. I have no doubt that the example of their discipline contributed to the collapse of the mutiny.

The confusion when we arrived was indescribable but, for me, the most interesting moments came during that first night when we conducted an exercise in propaganda which ought to become a model for the education of officers. I must say it taught me a bit about human nature. It was interesting to see how completely morale can collapse when one sets oneself to prey on natural anxieties. The men had committed themselves to a course which at heart alarmed them. As soon as I realised this, I started putting the question: "Are you going to swear loyalty to Percennius and Vibulenius? Do you really imagine they can do anything for you? Do you suppose this ex-cheerleader and crazy private are going to replace Tiberius and Drusus as leaders and lords of the Roman world?" You could see these were questions they had been asking in their own hearts. Then I said: "You want more money? Right? Do you think these two clowns are going to be able to pay you? How can they raise money when the stores in the camp run out? And are they going to provide you with land when you retire? I hadn't heard they had farms to give away. Where are their own estates? Don't you see they have led you by the nose?"

It was great fun. I assure you, Tiberius, I saw one of the poor fools touch his nose, as if feeling the ring they were leading him by.

If Drusus has a fault it is the reflection of his noble and generous nature. That's why I insisted that the ringleaders should be dealt with in summary fashion as soon as the bulk of the men had returned to their senses, for it would only have required a fresh puff of wind to drive them mad again. He hesitated, fearing that punishment of their delinquent leaders would dismay the men. But I knew better. I knew it would please them, and at the same time frighten them. So, without telling Drusus and disturbing his conscience, I sent a contingent of guards to arrest Percennius and Vibulenius, and had them executed. Their bodies were put on show and the effect was remarkable. Some of the other chief men in the mutiny tried to run away, and were easily picked up by my guardsmen. Others were actually surrendered voluntarily by their units, who were only too anxious to disassociate themselves from these wretches.

It is astonishing how a combination of sympathy and terror can undermine even the most formidable-seeming of movements.

Drusus was at first not entirely content with my decisive action, but he was pleasingly appreciative when he saw how effective it had been.

The news from Germany is distressing. I am sure you can trust your nephew, but I receive reports which make me uncertain about some of his methods.

I trust you are taking care of yourself. The health of Rome and the empire depends on the preservation of yours. I pray that you are not suffering from migraines, when your devoted servant is not there to ease them away.

The news from Germany was indeed worrying. The mutiny took a different form there, for some of the men clamoured for Germanicus to lead them. If he wanted the throne, they said, then they would back him. This was more rebellion than mutiny. Germanicus was tempted. He admitted that later. A report from a young knight, Marcus Friso, whom I had attached to his staff, convinced me of this. But either his loyalty held, or he deemed the risk too great and lacked the nerve to play the part of Caesar or Sulla. At any rate, he behaved as if they had insulted him, shouting that death was better than disloyalty.

Friso reported that:

He pulled his sword from his belt and pointed it at his own throat. "You will force me to kill myself if you press these demands," he cried. Not everyone was convinced that he meant it. One private soldier named Calusidius called his bluff, for he drew his own sword and offered it to the general remarking that it was a good deal sharper. I can tell you Germanicus turned pale at the offer, and what would have happened next must be uncertain, if some of his friends hadn't managed to hurry him away. It was not an edifying scene.

Naturally Friso's report disturbed me. I couldn't but reflect how ashamed my dear brother Drusus would have been of his son's theatrical display.

And the next day Germanicus made another absurd speech in which he proclaimed:

"When you pulled away the sword I was preparing to thrust into my heart" (it had actually, according to reports, been aimed at his neck, where more soldiers could see it) "your friendly care for me was unwelcome. A better, truer friend was the man who offered me his own sword, for I should then have died with my conscience free of the crimes my own soldiers have committed and are contemplating."

Then he called on the gods, and invoked the memory of Augustus and his own father Drusus and, in Friso's words, ". . . spouted windy rhetoric about washing clean the stain of criminal disloyalty . . . I tell you it again made me ashamed to listen to him . . ."

And yet he had already by chance delivered the master stroke which brought the soldiers to their senses. Some of those who were present have told me he did it through timidity, others have praised his policy. In such matters there is seldom unanimity of opinion, for no man knows the secret impulses which determine men's actions. He himself ascribed it (naturally) in his letter to me as policy. Perhaps it was.

By his account then:

It had become apparent to me that my wife, my dear Agrippina, though she has the heart of a lioness, was not safe in the camp, and neither were my beloved children. So I determined to send them away under heavily armed escort. Agrippina was loth to go. As you know, her courage is matchless. She reminded me that she was the grand-daughter of the divine Augustus and the daughter of the great Agrippa, and would be worthy of her blood, whatever the danger. But I could not permit her to stay, in her condition (she is with child again, you will be delighted to hear) and with our youngest son, little Gaius, in attendance. So I insisted.

Then a miracle occurred. A miracle – I say without boasting – which I had foreseen. As soon as I had convinced my wife that she must depart, she burst out into tears of lamentation which rang through the camp, as the wails of Andromache, crouching over the murdered body of her lord, Hector, echoed over the plains of windy Troy. Why did she weep? I answered that she wept because I could no longer trust her or our son, little Gaius, born in the camp and the soldiers' darling. (They call him Caligula – little boots – you know – isn't it charming?) I could no longer trust them, I repeated, to the care and protection of Roman soldiers, but must send them forth, to our allies, the Treviri.

This, as I had guessed it would, broke the men's hearts. "Will Caligula go?" they cried. "Can we not be trusted to care for our little darling?"

"No," I said, "you cannot. Not while you act as ravening wolves rather than Roman soldiers." I held my ground. I did not know I had such words in me . . .

So judgment or fortune favoured him. The men submitted. Then followed an extraordinary scene. They themselves arrested the leading rebels and punished them in their own ferocious manner. The men, with drawn swords, stood in a circle. The prisoners were paraded in turn on a platform. If the soldiers shouted guilty, their victim was thrown to them and butchered on the spot. The men revelled in the massacre; it seemed, Friso said, " . . . as if it purged them of their former guilt. Germanicus meanwhile did nothing. My opinion is that he judged that when the men grew ashamed of this latest manifestation of their own savagery, he would escape blame, though he benefited from it."

*   *   *

There was much that was disquieting in these accounts. Germanicus had triumphed. The result was good. But the manner of its achievement did not inspire me with confidence in my nephew and, by Augustus' will, prospective heir. Certainly his histrionic behaviour contrasted unfavourably with the calm good sense and resolution displayed by Drusus and, of course, Sejanus.

I had myself to endure much criticism for remaining in Rome while these troubles were afoot. Two half-grown boys, men muttered, could not control these mutinous soldiers. I should have gone myself to confront them with the imperial dignity. Or I should have despatched an experienced marshal. I was aware of what was said, saw no cause to answer my critics. If they could not see that I might inspire more awe at a distance, while I could also without deceit revoke any unwise concessions the young generals granted, as soon as it was safe to do so, well, I could not be blamed for my critics' lack of perception. As for the suggestion that I should have sent an experienced marshal, it wasn't for me to point out the danger of such a course. Not on your life. But I had read Roman history if my critics hadn't, and I wasn't prepared to set up a new disturber of the peace, a new Caesar or Antony, backed by an army which he had bribed to return to order by lavish promises of future rewards and favours. I had learned from Augustus to distrust generals who had contrived to extract personal oaths of loyalty, and I saw only too well the danger that such men might offer to the state. Our equilibrium was precarious. I wasn't going to disturb it by offering the opportunity for new dynasts to emerge.

And my strategy worked. The mutinies were suppressed. The frontier was secure again. All the same, I couldn't escape the awareness that Germanicus himself, for all his protestations of loyalty, would have to be watched. There was a rashness, an intemperance about his behaviour which I could not approve.

I remembered Sulla's prescient comment when he was persuaded to allow the young Julius Caesar to escape his proscription and so escape the fate of the other followers and connections of Gaius Marius: "In that young man there are many Mariuses . . ."

Yes, Germanicus would have to be watched. Fortunately, I had young Friso to hand; and Sejanus in reserve.

THREE

I was in my middle fifties when the burden of empire was laid
upon me. Naturally I looked for assistance; to my regret I
failed to find it. Nobody who has not been responsible for the
administration of such a vast and unwieldy body as the Roman
Empire can imagine the demands it makes. Augustus had frequently complained of his labours; but, unlike me, he had sought
his position. He was a man who would have been lost without
power. I am different and not a day passed when I did not groan
at my responsibilities, when I did not look back with nostalgia
to the years of my retirement on Rhodes and forward with
longing to the day when I could relinquish the reins and be
myself again.

The hope was vain. I knew that from the start. I had accepted
a commission which I could not lay down.

Livia did not understand my repugnance. She assailed me
with suggestions and advice, warnings and encouragement. I
grew to dread the sound of her voice, the announcement of her
arrival, the summons to her house.

I felt myself alone. A few weeks after Augustus' death, while
I was still wrestling with the consequences of my inheritance,
Julia died on the island of Pandateria to which her father had
consigned her. We had had no communication for years; what
could we have said to each other? Could I have apologised for
the destruction of her life which had not been my work? Could
she have brought herself to ask my forgiveness? Nevertheless
I ordered that her ashes be brought back to her father's mausoleum. I owed her that, but I made certain that they would be
consigned there secretly and without ceremony.

Hoping to please me, the Governor of North Africa, Lucius

Nonias Asprenas, arranged for the execution of Julia's lover, Sempronius Gracchus, who had spent fourteen years imprisoned on the African island of Cercina. He thought to please me by this action, but the only pleasure I derived was in the news that Gracchus had died in a manner more worthy of his ancestors than he had lived.

These two deaths drew a line under the past.

Yet the past would not let go. Germanicus had resumed war with the Germans. I approved this for two reasons: it was necessary to strengthen the Rhine frontier, and it would be good for the lately mutinous legions to be engaged in real soldiering. Moreover, there was a case for reminding the Germans of the power of Rome, for they were still flushed by their triumph over Varus six years previously.

Germanicus therefore advanced deep into the forests and, driving the divided enemy before him, approached the Teutoberg Wood where Varus had been destroyed. They came to the defeated general's first camp, and then to a half-ruined breastwork where the remnants of the legions had fought. The day was wet and windy, as it had been then. Around them the desolate marshes mocked the ambition of mortals. Beyond a shallow ditch were whitening bones, ghastly in the failing light, which showed where Romans had fallen; there were little heaps where scattered troops had come together and made a last stand. Fragments of spears, abandoned armour, and horses' limbs lay about, and there were skulls fastened to tree-trunks by the barbarians. They even found the altars at which Roman officers had been slaughtered in a parody of religious ceremonies.

My nephew gave orders that the bones should be interred, an order which I subsequently and naturally approved. He cut the first turf himself, even though, as a member of the ancient priesthood of Augurs, he should not have handled objects belonging to the dead, as he did. Nevertheless I approved this also; it showed a proper reverence. I was less pleased to be informed by Friso that Germanicus had not only lamented the long years in which the bodies had lain unburied, but had added that the failure to make the attempt to penetrate the forests to accord them decent burial was, as he put it, "shameful". He had little idea of course of the extent of the disaster and of the difficulties I had experienced in trying to restore a modicum of stability on the Rhine frontier, or of the impossibility, in the circumstances of the time, of doing what he thought ought to have been done.

Some of those who heard his words were shocked to realise the limits of his understanding, and disapproved his implied criticism of my own conduct, which, for my part, I attributed to his youth rather than to any more sinister cause.

His ambitions were, however, worrying. He believed that it was desirable that we should bring all the Germans residing to the west of the Elbe within the empire. I could understand the attraction of the proposal, for I had felt it myself, years ago. Both Augustus and I had become convinced of its impracticality. We feared too that the conditions were such that any commander might experience the same fate as Varus, a fate which Germanicus himself only narrowly escaped the following year.

There could be no doubt about his ardour, more concerning his judgment. It seemed strange too when reports came of the prominent part his wife, my former stepdaughter Agrippina, was playing behind the scenes. She was unnaturally conspicuous.

I had asked Sejanus to make a tour of inspection of the northern frontier in order to establish the truth, or otherwise, of what was said. For security reasons, I told him to report to me in person. If there was something untoward afoot, it was better that he should not, for his own sake, commit his suspicions to writing.

Sejanus came to me straight from the road, without even pausing to bathe, and lay (as was his wont) stretched out on a couch, his thighs flecked with mud.

"They're up to something," he said.

"What do you mean?"

"Wish I knew, wish I could say exactly. There's a strange mood in the army, not exactly elation, such as you might expect after victory, more as if they are nerving themselves for some-

thing big and dangerous. Of course Agrippina can't stand me,
so I don't make much of her rudeness to me. She has always
looked at me as if I were a bad smell. But Friso told me that,
when her husband was on campaign, she acted as commander-
in-chief, every order was referred to her. Your letter of con-
gratulation was suppressed. Instead she personally thanked the
men for what they had done on behalf of the Roman state and
Germanicus, no mention of you. When you add to that the
accounts I received of how she went round visiting the sick and
wounded, how she dispensed presents of money, food and wine,
and of how she took little Caligula with her everywhere, and
seemed to be trying to inspire a personal loyalty among the
soldiers, well . . . I know what conclusions I draw."

"Let me hear them."

He pushed back a lock of hair that had fallen over his eyes,
and smiled.

"I'm not sure that I dare."

"What do you mean?"

"Look," he said, "I owe everything to you. I'm very conscious
of that. And I know you have an affection for me, and I'm utterly
loyal to you. I've got to be, apart from anything else, for I am
committed to you. You understand that, don't you?"

"I look on you as a son and my dearest friend."

"That's just as well," he said, "because if I had any doubt
about your feeling for me, I would be afraid to express my
opinion, even though it is my duty to do so. I believe that
Germanicus and Agrippina are playing the part of Caesar, and
have cast you as Pompey. They think that if they can attach the
legions to themselves, personally, they can defy you, and even
seize the throne."

"I don't like that word," I said.

"Very well, then, power . . ."

"But why should they . . . ?"

I broke off. He smiled again.

"You don't mean that," he said. "You know better . . ."

I could not meet his eye.

"I am grateful," I said. "Grateful and terrified . . ."

"I accept the gratitude. Remember this. Augustus had you

adopt Germanicus as your heir, but you have your own son
Drusus. Your nephew can't forget that . . ."

Sejanus had used a potent word to waken my fears: the name
of Caesar terrifies all Romans. Caesar, the destroyer of liberty,
the man who unleashed civil war on Rome. Of course Caesar
was, in reality, more than that and less than that. He was
perhaps an instrument of history, for, in the circumstances,
there would have been civil war even without his ambition. And
that ambition, one may say now, was not entirely selfish (though
my mother would disagree). It is even possible to maintain that
Caesar had some sort of vision of regeneration, that, in some
sense, he perceived, even if only dimly, how the state had to
be reformed. Nevertheless, whatever one grants him, and none
denies him genius, Caesar the wolf, the destroyer, the rebel
who would make himself king, is still the figure who fills one's
eye.

Rome has never recovered from the catastrophe into which
his ambition plunged the state. I who now, by a stroke of irony,
find myself his heir, know that better than anyone. I am the
most unfortunate of men: a reluctant ruler who despises those
he rules. Caesar let slip the dogs of war, of civil war, the worst
of wars; his murderers and his heirs fought another, a bloody
and divisive series of wars. Augustus emerged sole victor, and
set himself to repair the state. Sometimes he deceived himself
that he had in fact done so. In his heart he knew better, as Livia
knows, and as I try all too often to hide from myself. Behind
the façade of Republican respectability which he erected, he
established the ultimate reality: power breeding fear. And I
have inherited that reality, that power and that fear. I hoped to
reanimate the Republican spirit, and found it corrupted by fear.

On the surface things are different. We debate in the Senate
with a degree of freedom. The law-courts operate according to
ancient practice. Elections are held. Armies are banished from
Italy (except for the Praetorians). Trade flourishes. Men go
about their business in ease and safety. The harvests come
and go, gathered and fruitful. Italy basks in sunlight. Wealth
accumulates. The pleasures of art, of the theatre and of the

circus are widely enjoyed. Everything has been, to use a favourite word of Augustus', consolidated.

And yet the basic question should be asked, though I dare
only to put it in the silence of my own mind: why are people
behaving in the way they do? Why do they do all these things,
which, taken together, give the impression that we have
achieved a united society, giving happy and willing support to a
benevolent government? Any wise man must find the answer
self-evident: they are driven to this simulation of content by
fear. We are dominated by fear: fear of the barbarians without
and within. It is fear which compels men, even of great family,
to perform degrading acts of self-criticism and self-abnegation,
fear which informs the insincerity of our public life. It is fear
which prevents men, even senators – perhaps most of all senators – from saying what they think, even in private; they are
afraid someone might inform against them.

Of course this is no ordinary fear. We are not all shaking with
daily terror. On the contrary, the surface of our life is just
what it seems; look at the Senate and you see rich, happy,
self-confident citizens. No, we can take nothing for granted, not
even love, affection, the loyalty of one's own family and friends.
Rome throbs with a pervasive anxiety. There is no one who is
not vulnerable.

Not even the emperor. It was fear that drove Augustus to
turn so savagely on his daughter and her lovers; fear for his
own creation that caused him to arrange the murder of his
grandson Agrippa Postumus, so that, as a result of his prudence, I inherited a legacy of blood. And Agrippina, Sejanus
assures me, holds me responsible for her brother's death, which
she ascribes to my order, rather than her grandfather's.

"She is, according to Friso," Sejanus said, "forever hinting
to Germanicus that you are the enemy of her branch of the
family, and persuading him that he cannot trust you."

So the corrupting fear infects even what men have started to
call the imperial family.

The fear is widespread. Hardly a day passes that I am not
assailed by anonymous and scurrilous verses. Daily, while I
resided in Rome, informers found means to approach me with

evidence of seditious talk and plotting. For the most part I paid
no attention. When I was told that a man had been speaking
against me, I replied that the ability to think and speak as one
wished was the test of a free country. What was the result of
my enunciation of this impeccably Republican sentiment?
According to Romanius Hispo, a man of obscure birth but some
merit whom I found useful on account of the store of information
he habitually collected, men saw my reply as a sign of dissimulation. I was encouraging free speech, they said, in order to be
able to identify my enemies. It was a lure to encourage them
to betray themselves. Such was the demoralising effect of fear.
But is it any wonder, in these circumstances, if I too began to
see enemies on every side?

Of course people were ready to use the treason laws for their
own advantage, hoping either simply to ruin those they disliked
or envied, or to profit from the rewards which the law decreed
should go to informers. Some of the accusations brought were
in themselves trivial. For instance, a charge was brought against
one Falanius, a member of the equestrian order, of insulting the
divinity of Augustus. He had, it was said, admitted among the
worshippers of Augustus a certain actor in musical comedies
named Cassius, who was, notoriously, also a male prostitute,
and he was accused, secondly, of disposing of a statue of Augustus, when selling some garden property. At the same time a
friend of his, Rubrius, was charged with blasphemy against the
divinity of Augustus.

I deprecated such charges, and informed the consuls, who
were considering them, that in my opinion Augustus had not
been voted divine honours in order to ruin Roman citizens. I
pointed out that Cassius, however deplorable his private life,
was an accomplished actor, who had taken part in the games
organised by my mother, the Augusta, in her late husband's
honour. As for the blasphemy, I said, the gods must see to
their own wrongs.

Could anyone take exception to my common sense? Of course
they could. I was accused of displaying jealousy of Augustus.
Tiberius would be a damned sight quicker to avenge insults to
his own honour, they said.

In fact I wasn't. Romanius Hispo informed me that the senator
Marcus Granius Marcellus was spreading the rumour that I had
dismissed the charges against Falanius merely because Cassius
was my own catamite. He added that Marcellus had placed his
own effigy above that of Augustus and myself and was saying
that I had prepared a plan to send leading senators such as
Scaurus and Gallus into exile. Though I demurred, Romanius
insisted on bringing a charge of treason against Marcellus. I
announced that I would hear the evidence in the Senate, and,
on this occasion, vote openly and on oath, for I hoped that
such a statement would check merely malicious accusations
by exposing those who brought them to public obloquy. What
happened? My friend Gnaeus Calpurnius Piso exposed the
hypocrisy of the Senate in a couple of sentences. "Caesar," he
said, "will you vote first or last? If first, I shall have your lead
to follow. If last, I am afraid that I may inadvertently vote against
you." I was grateful to him for his intervention; it convinced me
that it was impossible that the Senate should give a fair trial to
anyone accused of treason. Fear would hold them back from
expressing their true opinions. In disgust, I voted that Marcellus
be acquitted of treason, though, technically, he was guilty.

These were all minor worries, though symptomatic of the
disease which gripped the state, when compared with the problem that Germanicus posed me. His victories in Germany
secured no solid or enduring advantage, though to do him honour and enhance his reputation I was prepared to exaggerate
their value, and so decreed him a triumph. I hoped also, I
confess, that so public a statement of my regard might reconcile
him and Agrippina to me, and at least dilute the suspicion with
which they regarded me. Vain hope.

I had another reason however. My nephew was eager to
prosecute the war further and launch another expedition – his
fourth – against the Germans. There was no prospect that he
would meet with substantial success. His campaigns to date
had fortified me in the opinion at which Augustus and I had
independently arrived: that the prudent limits of empire had
been attained, and that plans for further expansion should be
abandoned. Now the ardour of an impetuous youth was calling

our judgment into question. It was intolerable, and could not be permitted.

Livia was for a sharp response. "He must be put in his place, compelled to understand that his position is subsidiary. How dare this callow youth set his opinion up against yours . . . ?"

She sat upright in her chair, and rapped the ferrule of her ebony cane on the floor. Her knuckles gleamed white, her head, more than ever like that of a noble bird of prey, quivered. That, and a certain tremor in her voice, betrayed her age.

"Germanicus has friends, admirers, supporters," I said. "He may also have secured the personal allegiance of his soldiers."

"That itself is treason."

"I do not say he has done so formally by extracting a personal oath. But it has amounted to that."

"Your father would never have permitted it."

Perhaps not, but Livia now lived in the imagination, where all things are possible and difficulties dissolve of their own accord, or are dispelled by an act of will. If only, I thought, I understood Germanicus as well as I understood my mother. But I had no difficulty in understanding Agrippina: she was filled with implacable hostility towards me.

I poured out honours upon the young man. I caused an arch to be dedicated beside the Temple of Saturn, in celebration of the recapture, under his leadership and my auspices, of the eagles lost with Varus. I arranged that his triumph should be celebrated the following May with unrivalled splendour. The procession included spoils, prisoners, and pictures of mountains, rivers and battles. To my displeasure, Agrippina insisted on accompanying her husband in his chariot; everyone commented on the noble sight they presented surrounded by their five children, smiling to be the centre of such adulation. In my nephew's name I distributed three hundred sesterces a head to the population, and Rome rang that evening with wine and song. I announced that to do the young man further honour, I myself would share his consulship.

Germanicus was flattered by all this attention; he revelled in his popularity. Everyone fawned upon him, and he believed they meant what they said. Some did, of course; but the generality was prompted by fear. People thought he was the coming man. They were awed by the power which they believed he could deploy.

But, though flattered, he was not diverted from his argument that the German war should be renewed. Agrippina urged this course, feeding his vanity. She gave dinner-parties at which she strove to seduce senators into agreement. She did not do so by the charm of her person. Her features were sharp and her voice harsh; she had none of her mother's sensual nature. She was indeed ostentatiously faithful to her husband, and cruelly critical of ladies who lapsed from monogamous chastity. The truth is, she was a prig.

I did all I could to appease the hostility of the young couple. I consulted Germanicus' mother, Antonia, with whom I had always been on good terms, a woman of exemplary sense and virtue. She confessed to me that she found her daughter-in-law "difficult".

"I know," she said, "that you have acted fairly, and indeed with great generosity towards my son. It wasn't easy for you to accept Augustus' will and favour him above your own boy, Drusus. Believe me, my dear Tiberius, I am grateful for your even-handedness in this matter, and I understand that the only dispute between the two of you is over a matter of public policy, in which it is likely that a man of your experience judges more wisely than a youth, however brilliant. I trust your love for Germanicus as I trusted your love for your brother, my dear husband Drusus."

Antonia then proposed that we should publicly display our concord by arranging a marriage between my son Drusus and her elder daughter Julia Livilla, who, as a little girl, had been betrothed to Gaius Caesar.

"She is a few years older than the dear boy," she said, "but I never think that a bad thing. Surely such a marriage will convince my son that you feel nothing but benevolence for our part of the family."

I agreed. The marriage was arranged and celebrated. What was the result? Agrippina at once began telling anyone who would listen that this was all part of my scheme to displace Germanicus, and ensure that Drusus succeeded me. What could you do with such a woman?

"You could stop her mouth," Sejanus suggested, laughing at the idea. "You could remind her there are islands in the sea reserved for the female members of her family."

He was not serious. Germanicus' position alone would have made it impossible for me to serve his wife as Augustus had served her mother and her elder sister; the latter, named Julia like her mother, had suffered the same sentence for similar offences. The scurrilous poet Ovid, it may be remembered, was among those who shared her crimes and her disgrace.

FOUR

Fortunately, developments elsewhere offered a temporary solution to the problems Germanicus raised. I had been compelled to arraign the aged King of Cappadocia, Archelaus, before the Senate, and it had been decided to incorporate his kingdom within the empire, so that it came under direct rule. This did not displease me, for Archelaus had insulted me during my residence at Rhodes, when he felt himself safe to do so, on account of what he conceived to be my own fall from favour. The supervision of the transformation of Cappadocia from one status to another was important work, and I judged that Germanicus would acquit himself excellently in the role required.

I had already made this decision when news arrived that King Vonones of Armenia had been expelled by a faction that favoured Parthia to Rome. Since the strategic importance of Armenia is so great, this was a situation fraught with peril. I therefore resolved that Germanicus should assume supreme authority over the Eastern provinces of the empire, and proposed to ask the Senate to grant him *maius imperium*. I could not have expressed my confidence in his abilities more fully. Even so, Agrippina found cause for complaint, though Germanicus seemed pleased enough. She, however, let it be known that he was being denied glory in Germany, and persisted in describing the arduous task to which I had called him as "a mere police action".

She also criticised my decision at the same time to appoint Gnaeus Calpurnius Piso Governor of Syria. Yet this seemed to me prudent. Piso was a man I had trusted, of vast experience and, hitherto, distinguished for common sense and virtue. Syria was a responsible position, since the Governor there com-

manded four legions. It was necessary, given the instability in
the East, that the Governorship be held by a man capable of
independent action. Agrippina let it be known that I had
appointed Piso to act as my "spy" – she actually used that word.
In fact, I had done no more than suggest that he might find it
necessary to act as a brake on Germanicus' noble impetuosity.
I was afraid that the young man's lust for military glory might
embroil us in a full-scale war with Parthia . . .

So, before he set out, I said to Piso, "Your task, my friend,
is to hold yourself ready to bridle the colt."

That was the limit of my instructions.

Germanicus' progress towards Armenia resembled that of a
candidate for office, rather than a general. He visited Drusus in
Dalmatia, and spoke to him, "in confidence, of course, brother",
in a manner which my son later described as "approaching the
borders of sedition". He told Drusus that my judgment was
failing, and the day might not be far off when they would have
to declare me incompetent to rule. "He said it with that laugh
of his, you know, so that it could be passed off as a joke if
necessary. But I don't think he intended it as a jest."

He proceeded down the Dalmatian coast, through Albania and
into Greece, till he reached the gulf of Nicepolis. There he
surveyed the scene of Actium, and reminded me in a letter that
it must arouse mixed emotions in his breast, since he was the
grand-nephew of Augustus (and married to his grand-daughter)
but also the grandson of Antony. "I am proud to think," he
wrote to me, "that in my children the feud between those two
great men is reconciled."

He visited Athens, ostentatiously approaching the city with
only a single attendant, out of regard for our ancient treaty of
alliance. The Athenians, always delighted, in their giddy-headed
manner, with something new, received him with rapture; they
scattered flowers before him, and regaled him with feats of
oratory, which he bore with an equanimity that was not perhaps
entirely insincere. His subsequent progress through Asia was
slow: judging from his letters he was travelling as a tourist
rather than a man on an urgent mission. I received three pages
of vapid but euphoric descriptions of the site of Troy, which I

had in any case visited myself. At Clarus he consulted the oracle of Apollo, where the priest, though illiterate and ignorant of metre, is accustomed to emerge from a cave, where he has drunk from a sacred spring, with a set of appropriate verses. Since neither Germanicus nor Agrippina broadcast their import, they cannot have pleased the young couple.

By the time he eventually reached Armenia, he found the immediate danger over. Certain Armenian noblemen – persons whom I had known myself or whose fathers had known me – had had the wit and enterprise to seek my advice directly. Letters were exchanged, presents were despatched according to their advice, and by the time my nephew came on the scene, I had arranged that he should crown Zeno, the son of King Ptolemo of Pontus, as their king. Zeno had long adopted the habits of Armenian noblemen, and he was devoted to hunting, feasting and such barbarian practices. Nevertheless, though the immediate danger was, as I say, past, the arrival of my nephew lent dignity to the occasion and mightily impressed the impressionable Armenians. Nor would I wish to deny that Germanicus carried out his duties in an altogether exemplary fashion.

Piso, meanwhile, had arrived in Syria, and was behaving in a manner which was not at all what I had intended. It may be that his elevation had gone to his head. Possibly he was prompted by his wife Plancina, a protégée, as it happened, of my mother; Plancina detested Agrippina and was determined to outshine her. At any rate a quarrel soon broke out between Piso and Germanicus. It was some time before I heard of it, and I was displeased. I had asked Piso to supervise Germanicus, not to thwart him; but by every mail I received complaints from my nephew. Piso, he said, was trying to secure the allegiance of his four legions for himself, rather than for Rome. Moreover he had refused to send Germanicus a legion when requested to do so; this was an infringement of Germanicus' *maius imperium*. In defence, Piso suggested that he was suspicious of Germanicus' intentions and was therefore unwilling to surrender one of his legions. As for allowing his men to call him "father of the army", of which Germanicus had complained: well, he couldn't prevent his popularity, could he? Besides, he said, he was suspicious of Germanicus' own intentions. I knew how he had behaved in Germany, and he was carrying on in the same way now. Piso was afraid that Germanicus intended mischief; "Think of Caesar," he said. Piso's letters were copious and detailed. I cannot quote them exactly or at length, for I later deemed it prudent to destroy them, but I remember that warning.

In the autumn Germanicus visited Egypt. He had no right to do so, as I reminded the Senate, for a senator, even a connection of the divine Augustus, required my permission in order to enter my private domain. I said this principally so that no other senator should feel free to follow my nephew's example, and the reproof I directed at him was mild; I merely pointed out that he should have asked my permission, which would, of course, have been granted, and that his failure to do so had set a bad example. Naturally he was interested in seeing the Egyptian sites. I remember I even asked him if he had seen the stone statue of Memnon, a remarkable object which gives out the sound of a voice when the sun's rays strike it. I advised him also to visit the great library of the Museum in Alexandria, and asked him to convey my regards to the great scholar Apion, whom I described as "the cymbal of the world"; his Egyptian history is full not only of recondite information but of sage reflections; his pamphlet *Against the Jews*, though perhaps intemperate, argues the case against that curious people's obstinate monotheism with acuity and vigour. These memories, unimportant in themselves, may serve to convince sceptics of my generally friendly relations with my nephew. However his with Piso had deteriorated abruptly. There were faults on both sides. Piso believed that Germanicus was employing his *maius imperium* in a manner that prejudiced his own authority. Germanicus complained that Piso had reversed orders he had given to divisional commanders. In a fit of pique he ordered him out of Syria, and Piso, though furious, finding his position intolerable, obeyed; he retired to the island of Cos. All this happened abruptly, without consultation with me.

Then Germanicus fell ill, of a fever common in these parts. He seemed to recover, then had a relapse. It was reported that he accused Piso and Plancina of having poisoned him. Agrippina, in no condition to judge anything, was vociferous in accusation. She ordered her slaves to seek evidence of poison and magic; naturally they found what they were required to find, as slaves will. Examination of the floor and walls of his bedroom revealed human bones, signs of spells, curses, and invocations; there were lead tablets inscribed with my nephew's name, charred and bloody ashes, and other "malignant objects effective to consign souls to the powers of the tomb", as they put it.

According to Marcus Friso, who subsequently made a full report of the circumstances to me, Germanicus then said, "Even if I were dying a natural death, I should have a legitimate grudge against the gods for parting me from wife, children, country and friends, and for denying me the due rewards of my virtue. But it is not the gods, but rather those demons in human shape, Piso and Plancina, whom I accuse. Tell my father, the emperor, of the vile conspiracy which has brought about my death. You will have the opportunity to protest to the Senate and invoke the law. The chief duty of a friend is not to walk in grief behind a corpse, but rather to remember the dead man's desires and carry out his will. Even strangers will mourn Germanicus. But if it was me you loved, not merely my rank, then I charge you to avenge me."

A slave wiped his brow with a cool napkin, while Agrippina stood by, dry-eyed and with a harsh expression on her face.

Germanicus raised himself on his elbow and continued: "Show Rome my wife, the grand-daughter of the divine Augustus. Display the weeping faces of our six children. Sympathy will go to the accusers. Any tale of criminal instructions given to Piso will be hard to believe; but if believed, far harder to forgive."

This was a remarkable speech from a dying man, or would have been if Friso had actually heard it. In fact, as he made clear, he was repeating only the version sanctioned by Agrippina. The only authentic touch was the contrast between the concerned care of the slave and her dry eyes. Friso added that Agrippina had also told her intimates that Germanicus had advised her to tread warily where I myself was concerned.

*   *   *

He died. In his funeral eulogy he was compared to Alexander. No one is on oath on such occasions, but this was absurd. It was said that after defeating the Germans many times, he had not been allowed to complete their subjugation. If he had been in sole control, he would have equalled Alexander in military renown as easily as he surpassed him in decency, self-control and every good quality.

It was easy to see at whom the eulogy was aimed, by whom it had been inspired.

His body lay in state in the main piazza of Antioch. Some of those who examined it found indubitable evidence of poisoning, which must be accounted a medical miracle. Then it was cremated, not embalmed, as one might have thought proper in such circumstances. Agrippina appointed Gnaeus Sentius Saturninus commander of her late husband's legions, and, in effect, Governor of Syria; then she sailed for Italy with her children and the ashes of her husband. I say "she appointed" because that was actually, as Friso told me, what happened, though of course it was dressed up in a more suitable manner, and it was given out that the decision had been made by senior officials, officers and senators. Sentius then fortified the province against Piso. He also arrested and sent to Rome a woman called Martina who was known to be a friend of Plancina and who was, he reported, a notorious poisoner.

Piso, confident that he was still rightful Governor of Syria, on the strength of his original appointment by me, which I had not had either the occasion or indeed the opportunity to revoke, now attempted to re-enter his province. Sentius resisted him. There was a brief scuffle or passage of arms, and Piso, lacking support even from those legions he had formerly commanded (whose officers had mostly been suspended either by Germanicus or by Sentius), surrendered. He was placed under arrest and despatched to Rome, charged with making war against Roman forces.

This news came in piecemeal as Agrippina journeyed slowly, with many stops, across wintry seas to Italy. I was horrified to learn of Germanicus' death. I mourned him as a young man of infinite promise and the son of my beloved brother Drusus. Yet our emotions are rarely single, and my grief was not unmixed with the sense that the gods had done Rome a favour. I regretted also the disgrace of my old friend Piso, and could not believe the accusations being brought against him. Nevertheless these had to be investigated and if they were proved then I had to confess myself sorely deceived in Piso. I could never forgive the murder of my nephew – if it had been murder. My mind was confused, flickering between darkness and light. It was impossible to know what to do for the best.

Naturally I ordered official mourning for the young man. People fell over themselves to express the depth of their loss, in language which was understandable, if excessive. On such occasions exaggeration becomes the norm. Even sensible people are caught up in the general mood, and imagine that public affairs affect them more nearly than they actually do. It is easy to suppose that one's life is blighted by events which in reality trouble only the imagination.

I sent two battalions of the Praetorian Guard to greet Agrippina at Brindisi. I hesitated at first to put my dear Sejanus in charge for I knew the depths of the woman's antipathy towards him. On reflection, however, I decided that it was necessary to have a man there whom I could trust; and there was no one, except Drusus, in whom I reposed more trust than Sejanus. This was just as well, for the public mood was such that even the Guards themselves might have been infected. As it was, a curious incident took place at Brindisi. The alleged poisoner, Martina, arrived there about the same time, in a different ship. The next day, she was found dead, while Agrippina was still in the city. There were no marks of violence, but poison was found in the roots of her hair. Naturally some people said she had killed herself; others that she had been murdered for fear of what she might reveal. Human nature being as it is, the worst possible construction was put on this. Few reflected that the motive for her murder (if she was indeed murdered) might have been the knowledge that the wretch had nothing to reveal.

Agrippina's journey to Rome with her husband's ashes was superbly stage-managed. She held, or was accorded, a reception in every town, and lost no opportunity to win sympathy and

applause, and to present herself as a sorely aggrieved woman.
Sejanus was powerless to do anything but observe and report.
His natural prudence told him that it was impossible to stem
the surge of sympathy even though at every step it threatened
to boil over into sedition.

Germanicus' own mother, Antonia, was so disgusted by her
daughter-in-law's histrionics that she refused to leave her house
and greet the arrival of the cortège in Rome. Naturally I did not
do so either. For one thing, Sejanus warned me that my presence might provoke disorder. His advice was good, but my
absence was criticised. Drusus, however, approved it; his wife,
Julia Livilla, though Agrippina's sister-in-law, suggested that the
thing to do with the grieving widow was to chuck a bucket of
cold water over her. "Even in the nursery," she told Drusus,
"she was always acting. And as for her love for my brother,
she made his life a perfect misery by her constant nagging and
complaining." Of course the crowds were ignorant of this; they
revered Agrippina as the model of what a woman should be.

I myself arranged that Germanicus' ashes should be laid in
the mausoleum near those of Augustus. A huge crowd turned
out, the Field of Mars was ablaze with torches. Agrippina stimu-
lated the mob to orgies of grief; she had taken care to distribute
a quantity of gold, and her paid creatures exerted themselves
in eulogies of her virtue and bitter accusations directed against
Piso and those who had "encouraged" him. They had their
effect; there were disgraceful riots in the Suburra, Trastevere
and the Field of Mars itself. It seemed to me that the situation
was getting absurdly out of hand, and I issued the following
statement to try to persuade people to return to their senses.

Famous Romans have died before, but none has been so
ardently mourned. I commend your devotion to the memory
of Germanicus, my dear son and nephew. But moderation
should be observed. The conduct of ordinary families or com-
munities should not be the model for an imperial people. After
the first tears, we should observe calm. Remember with what
restrained dignity Julius Caesar mourned his daughter and
Augustus his beloved grandsons. Remember how our fore-

fathers courageously endured the loss of armies, the death of generals and the destruction of great families, eschewing the tears and lamentations which are suitable only to women. It is not for Romans to resemble hysterical and effeminate Orientals. Great men die; the country lives for ever. So I request citizens to return to their ordinary occupations, and since the Megalesian Games are due to start, to their proper pleasures.

My words had their desired effect. People were ashamed of their extravagances. Normal life was resumed – to Agrippina's indignation.

It could not, unfortunately, last. What we call normal is all too often what we aspire to, rather than what we actually experience. In this instance, the lull was short. There was Piso to be considered. He had returned to Rome and was now under a species of restriction in his own house. It overlooked the Forum, and Plancina soon attracted unwelcome attention by the lavish dinner-parties she organised in an attempt to drum up support for her beleaguered husband.

His case was desperate, and appeared the more so to me as I received more information about his rash and indisciplined conduct. My mother urged me to prevent any trial taking place.

"Plancina is a good friend of mine," she said, "and I have talked with her at length. I am convinced that the accusations levelled at her and her husband are unfounded. It is impossible that they should have murdered Germanicus. Do you really imagine that if I believed otherwise I should hold any conversation with my grandson's murderer? But it is all the product of Agrippina's warped imagination. She is beside herself with grief, spite and disappointment."

"I can't stop a trial," I said. "It would give substance to the rumours that make me worse than their accomplice. The whole thing must be aired in court and I am sure they will be acquitted of the charge of murder."

"Nothing good will come of it," Livia said. "I know people better than you do. If a trial takes place, it will merely give people the opportunity to spread worse and more lurid rumours.

For the plebeians find it impossible to distinguish between putting a man on trial and finding him guilty. You will regret this
trial if you permit it."

She was right of course, but I could not prevent the trial.
Livia's logic was merely abstract; she had withdrawn from the
realities of political affairs, where contingency rules, and one
has to act in response to pressures. To have prevented the trial
would have been tantamount to declaring not only that Piso was
guilty of the worst crimes with which he was charged, but that
rumour was right, and he had acted at my behest. Otherwise –
men would say – why should I choose to protect him?

Besides, I did not wish to do so. I had trusted Piso, and in
one way or another, he had betrayed that trust. I had thought
him competent and sagacious, and he had proved a fool.

When the Senate met charges were brought against him, first
by Lucius Fulcinius Trio, then by two members of Germanicus'
staff, Publius Vitellius and Quintus Vernaius. I was asked to
take over the enquiry, but urged that it should be heard by the
whole Senate. However, I outlined my view of the case.

"Gnaeus Piso," I said, "was trusted and admired by Augustus, and by me myself. With your approval, Conscript Fathers,
I made him Germanicus' helper in his Eastern duties. Unfortunately, as the world knows, they did not see eye to eye, and
unwelcome and unforeseen developments took place. Now it is
your duty to decide, objectively and without malice, whether,
having upset Germanicus by disobedience and quarrelling, he
merely rejoiced at his death (about his rejoicing there is no
dispute) or whether he did worse than that, and actually com-
passed his death.

"Now, if you decide the former, and conclude that Piso
exceeded his position and then exulted at Germanicus' death –
and at my sorrow, bear that in mind – then I shall renounce his
friendship and close my doors against him. But I shall not use
those powers which you have chosen to confer upon me merely
to avenge private wrongs.

"If, on the other hand, you find proof of murder, a crime
which would require vengeance whatever the victim's rank, it
will be your duty to give satisfaction to the children of Ger-

manicus and to us, his parents and family. There are also other matters which you must consider.

"First, did Piso incite his troops to mutiny and rebellion?

"Second, did he bribe them to support him?

"Third, did he make rash and illegal war to recover his province . . . ?

"But you must also ask yourselves whether these are lies spread and elaborated by those whose grief has dislodged their reason.

"In this context, I must say that the excessive vigour displayed by some who are eager to fasten a crime on Piso has given me cause for irritation. For to strip my son's body and expose it to the vulgar gaze, thus encouraging – even among foreigners – the report that he had been poisoned, served no good purpose, since this question is still undecided, and is indeed the object of your enquiry.

"I would remind you, Conscript Fathers, that sensationalism is the enemy of justice; and that justice is the fruit of reason, not emotion.

"I grieve for my son, Germanicus, and always shall, till death releases me in my turn. But I offer the accused every opportunity of producing evidence which may establish his innocence, or proof that Germanicus provoked and maltreated him, if that was the case. I go so far as to say that I hope he may be able to clear himself, since, for my part, the discovery that a Roman nobleman in whom I had put my trust should have proved so unworthy of my confidence would be yet another bitter draught to swallow.

"I implore you not to regard charges as proofs merely because you are conscious of my personal grief.

"Those whose relationship to Piso, or loyalty towards him have made them his defenders should help him without fear in his hour of need . . ."

Such was my speech, and I do not regret it. It would have been dishonourable to have spoken in any other way. Yet night fell, and I knew that I had failed. My measured words were condemned on every side. Those who believed that Germanicus

had been the victim of Piso and Plancina angrily complained that
I had invited the Senate to acquit him. Their adherents, on the
other hand, accused me of having abandoned them. Livia said,
"I never thought a son of mine could have been such a coward:
to desert your friends in such an attempt to appease your invet-
erate enemies. It's worse than a crime, it's a blunder, and the
consequences will hound you to the grave." Yet I could not
have spoken otherwise, though it was pointless to offer that
argument to my mother.

The trial was conducted during foul weather. The *tramontana*
blew cold, gusting round the Senate House and making the
canopies of stalls and litters flap furiously. The weather did not
deter the mob. They also blew like an angry tempest, jostling
senators and threatening them with violence if they did not vote
to their satisfaction. They swarmed round the litter that carried
the wretched Piso to his daily ordeal, screaming out that he
might escape the Senate, but never them; they would string
him up if he was acquitted. Some of them seized his statue and
began to haul it to the Gemonian Steps, but I sent in the guards
to arrest them. I was determined that the city should not be
given over to the violence of the mob.

Rumours abounded. The most dangerous was the suggestion, put out by some of Piso's supporters and eagerly believed
by my enemies, that he would produce a letter from me which
would justify all his actions. No such letter existed. Yet I was
disturbed by the rumours, not only because they were so widely
believed, but also because I feared that a letter might indeed
have been forged. I therefore ordered Sejanus to interrogate
Piso and search his house.

Sejanus threw himself back in the chair and stretched his arms
above his head. He laughed. I have seen lions, in the arena
which I detest, move like Sejanus, with the same grace and
menace. He laughed again.

"Poor Piso," he said, "poor bugger, he knows it's all up with
him."

"But the document, the letter."

"There is no letter. You know there isn't."

"And none has been forged?"

"My men turned the place upside down. Piso was indignant. He told me, 'You know perfectly well there's nothing to be found'. The fact is, in his strange way, he has thought of forging a document, of course he has, but something held him back."

"Honour?"

"Perhaps. Fear more likely. He still hopes you will halt the prosecution. He still maintains he never went beyond what he understood your intentions to be. Not till the last moment, when he invaded Syria. He knows he did wrong there. He knows they have got him on that count."

"Sejanus," I hesitated, embarrassed as I had never been with him before, "when you saw Piso before he took up his appointment, how far did you go?"

He smiled, yawned, stretched himself again.

"It's a bit late to ask that," he said. "Tiberius," he continued. "There's nothing for you to get tense about. All you have to do is let the law take its course."

"Let the law take its course?" Livia snapped her fan shut. "Are you mad? When you start sacrificing your friends to your enemies, I believe you to have taken leave of your senses. Don't you understand, child, that woman is implacable? When she attacks Piso, that's only the first step. You are her real target. Besides, it's absurd to think Plancina could be guilty of murder. I've known her since she was a little girl."

There was no evidence of murder, nothing but spiteful rumours. Some were ridiculous. It was suggested that Piso had first tried to poison Germanicus on an occasion when they had been neighbours at dinner. Even some of Germanicus' friends found it too fantastic to suppose that he should have attempted this in front of witnesses which included Germanicus himself and his slaves. Piso scoffed at the charge and offered his own slaves for torture, demanding too that the waiters at that dinner-party should be put to the question. But the defence faltered everywhere else. Evidence that Piso had bribed troops, subverted discipline and invaded the province was overwhelming. Realising this, Plancina, who had sworn that she would share his fate, now desperate only to save herself, resolved to conduct a separate defence. That evening it was necessary to double the number of guards who escorted him home.

Towards nightfall I was informed that Piso's secretary was seeking an audience. I declined to see him. There was nothing I could do, and I had no wish to compromise my own position by entertaining such an emissary in conversation. I therefore returned the message that I was confident Piso would act in a manner worthy of his ancestors.

I do not know how Piso received my message. At some point during the night he abandoned hope. He gave a note to one of his slaves and, announcing that he was ready for sleep, dismissed Plancina and his attendants from his chamber. He was found in the morning with his throat cut. A bloody sword lay on the floor beside his body.

The news was brought to me in the cold morning. Black clouds scudded across the sky. I watched a procession of worshippers, heads covered, move towards the Temple of Mars the Avenger. Jackdaws were flung in wild flight by the winds. The slave fell on the ground before me, extending a hand which clutched a sealed document.

Piso had written:

Conspiracy and hatred have ruined me. There is no place left for innocence and honesty. I call the gods to witness, Caesar, that I have always been loyal to you, and dutiful to the Augusta. I beg you both to protect my children. Marcus accompanied me to Syria, but had first advised me against doing so; his brother Gnaeus has never left Rome. I pray that they who are innocent should not share in my misfortune. By my forty-five years of loyalty, by our joint consulship, by the memory of our friendship, I, whom your father the divine Augustus honoured, and whom you befriended, implore you to spare my unfortunate son. It is the last thing I shall ask of anyone.

I passed the letter to Sejanus.

"He doesn't once mention Plancina," I said. "Well, all friendship is but a memory now, but we shall see that his son does not suffer . . ."

To please my mother, I argued Plancina's case before the Senate.

Piso was rash, but he was murdered by public opinion as surely as if the mob had lynched him as they threatened to do. On the day of his funeral Agrippina gave a dinner-party. I declined an invitation to attend.

How many nights I have gazed at the majesty of the skies, and thought of Piso during his last hours on earth, deserted, empty of hope, finally absolute for death. There have been many times I have envied him.

FIVE

There was a moment of joy: Drusus' wife Livilla gave birth to twins. I had hoped this would draw them together. It failed to do so. I accused Drusus of neglecting his wife.

"I thought I'd given her enough to occupy her, Father," he replied. "Anyway, it's easy for you to give such advice. You don't have to put up with her bad temper."

"Perhaps, but it is not seemly that I should hear constant reports of your quarrels."

"Who brings them to you? Sejanus, I suppose. You put too much trust in that man. Indeed, it grieves me, Father, that you seem to rely more on him than on me, your own son."

He had no reason to think that, and I told him so. But this awareness of ill-feeling between Drusus and Sejanus was a new cause of distress.

There was soon another, though it brought Drusus and myself together. His mother, my poor Vipsania, was dying. I had never thought of her dying before me. Though we had only once seen each other since our divorce, she had been a warm presence in the background of my life, like a place where you have been happy. Drusus and I travelled in wet weather to Velletri, where she had been living in a villa inherited from her father; she had been long separated from her husband, Gallus.

Vipsania took her leave of Drusus first. Then he told me to go in. I had not in the end been certain that she would wish to see me.

I would not at first have recognised her, for disease had eaten her away, the flesh had fallen from her face, and her eyes spoke of the pain she suffered. She stretched out her hand. I took it in mine, kissed it and fell to my knees by the bedside. We remained like that for a long time. There was a peculiar musty smell in the room, and the air was close and heavy.

"Don't try to speak," I said. "It's enough that we are together again."

She disengaged her hand and stroked my brow . . .

Did it happen like that? Or does my memory deceive me? Sometimes these few minutes with Vipsania have the clarity of a dream, the kind from which one awakens with a calm assurance of having been granted a vision of a more profound reality than that in which daily life is spent. There is a re-ordering of experience, as if a veil has been lifted. And yet her chamber was already a gateway to the tomb. Drusus felt none of this. He wept to lose his mother, while I remained dry-eyed. Yet my loss of what I had long ago lost was sharper: I was given a glimpse of what had been denied me. When I leaned over and kissed her cheek, from which life was already fleeing, I sealed our acknowledgment, with which we had lived for thirty years, that love and tenderness are hopeless against the fact of power. I turned out of her chamber and set my face to a funeral as bald as a winter mountain-face.

"It's odd to think," Drusus said, "that my mother was the half-sister of that hell-cat Agrippina."

"I hadn't realised you dislike Agrippina so."

"Dislike her? Surely you understand, father? She's determined to destroy us both."

"I no longer know what I understand."

"What's more, she will bring up her children as our enemies."

Drusus pushed the wine towards me. We both drank.

"It seems to me," he said, "that our family is overstocked with impossible women."

"Your mother was never impossible."

"No," he agreed, and called for more wine.

"But my wife is," he said, "and Agrippina, and my grandmother, and as I recall, my stepmother Julia. What have we done to deserve them?"

A little later he fell asleep. This was how we mourned Vipsania: in drunkenness and self-pity. But it wasn't only Vipsania we mourned, I thought. Our sadness had deeper roots than mortality. Death, after all, can come as a friend; death brings welcome relief from pain, as in the case of Vipsania, perhaps from dishonour, as with Piso; perhaps from the tyranny of the eternal 'I'.

"Would you like more wine, my lord?"

I looked up. One of Drusus' slaves was leaning over me. He was called Lygdus, a eunuch from Syria, a gift, I recalled, from Piso. He smiled, nervous but eager to please. The scent of attar of roses floated towards me. He placed a pale brown, thin-fingered hand on the flask. I felt a surge of cruelty, which disgusted and excited me. These creatures, I thought, are completely in our power. But then, who isn't in mine? Am I not the master of the world? Isn't that what they say? A master who despises men, fears assassination (but why, when I long for death to release me from my responsibilities?) and shuns company. The boy waited. I looked at him; he dropped his gaze. Apprehension expelled the desire to please. He waited.

I had had reports on this Lygdus of course. Such things have become necessary. He was said to be familiar with his master, a cherished favourite. There is always someone like that in the household of any man of virtue. It is our way of sweetening our arrangement of things, which by its nature offends notions of humanity. And men are rarely indifferent to eunuchs; they either despise them or desire them, sometimes both. A eunuch occupies a peculiar status in our imagination; he is a sort of object on which we can lavish irresponsible tenderness or employ to satisfy our innate cruelty.

"Are you fond of your master?"

I spoke in Greek, to put him at his ease. He replied in the same language, haltingly.

"My lord is very good to me."

His fingers plucked the fringe of his short tunic.

"Is he often in this condition?"

"Oh no, my lord, this is exceptional. He is distressed on

account of his mother's death. Shall I fetch you more wine, my
lord?"

"No," I said, "wine is no answer tonight. Look after your
master. He is very dear to me."

He bent over to ease Drusus' head, which had slipped off the
couch, into a more comfortable position. The short gold-fringed
tunic rose up his buttocks. The sand-coloured legs were long
and shapely.

"Go to bed," I said, and twisted my fingers hard till the
knuckles ached. "I will tend to your master tonight."

Drusus was dear to me; so was Sejanus; and the animosity
between them intensified. Each was jealous of what he supposed to be the other's influence over me. My efforts to dispel
the suspicion each entertained for the other were vain. My only
comfort lay in my certainty that both were utterly loyal.

Their quarrels, however, disturbed me. On one occasion at
least, Drusus lost his temper – I cannot recall the cause, if
indeed I ever knew it – and struck Sejanus in the face. He
complained – it was reported – that Sejanus was a threat to the
security of the empire, citing as an example my decision that
the Praetorian Guard, whose commander Sejanus still was,
should be concentrated in a new camp on the north side of the
city. I had approved the suggestion for two reasons. In the first
place it relieved citizens from the burden of having the Guard
billeted in their houses; second, it was an aid to discipline and
efficiency. There was nothing sinister in the proposal in any
way.

I was irritated by their quarrels because both were vital to
the administration of the empire. As Augustus had frequently
remarked, this is too great a task for a single man, and it is
necessary that the Princeps should have helpers whom he can
trust and who are willing to collaborate with each other. Drusus'
jealousy of Sejanus impeded the smooth functioning of the
machinery of state. There was no dispute as to policy. Indeed,
as I pointed out to Drusus, Sejanus was barely concerned with
the formulation of policy, and had never evinced a wish to be
saddled with that responsibility. He was content with an execu-

tive role. "My forte," he fequently said to me, "is carrying out your policy. I am here to help you by making things run smoothly. I am sorry that Drusus distrusts me, and I wish he could see that he has no occasion to do so." Indeed, Sejanus was so disturbed by his consciousness of my son's ever-growing hostility, and his knowledge of how this affected me, that he more than once offered to resign all his offices and retire into private life. "For the last thing I desire," he assured me, "is to be a cause of friction between you and Drusus, and for that reason it may be better that I remove myself from the scene, since I am convinced that the animosity which Drusus now entertains is ineradicable."

Naturally I refused his generous self-sacrifice, and assured him I could not do without him.

"I rely utterly on Drusus in some matters, and on you, dear boy, in others," I said. "I have told Drusus this, and advised him not to listen to those who have poisoned his mind against you."

Sejanus wiped a tear from his eye.

"I am more moved by your confidence in me than I can say. But your trust emboldens me to add something which I would prefer not to feel obliged to tell you. All is not well between Drusus and Julia Livilla. That noble lady has confided her distress to my own dear wife, Apicata. She says that since the death of one of the twins, Drusus has turned his face against her. In particular she is distressed that he denies her his bedchamber, summoning in her stead the eunuch Lygdus. I would not mention something which is bound to pain you, if I did not hope that, fortified by the knowledge, you might find the means to set things right."

I was touched by his innocent confidence in my abilities, but I did nothing. Bitter experience has taught me that neither prudence, a sense of decency, nor advantage, can overcome sexual repugnance or check the direction of lust.

These were distractions, but the business of government was incessant. I strove to make the Senate true partners in the state again, and insisted that I was, at most, first among equals.

When one obsequious fellow had the ill-taste to address me as "My Lord and Master" I warned him never to insult me in such manner again. I referred all public business to the Senate, including much that Augustus had been accustomed to handle himself, and asked for the Senate's advice in every matter that concerned the national revenue, the allocation of monopolies, and the construction or repair of public buildings. I even consulted them about the recruitment and discharge of soldiers, the stationing of legions and auxiliaries, the extension of military commands, the selection of generals, and how to answer letters which I had received from foreign potentates; all matters which Augustus had reserved to himself. I encouraged argument in the Senate and assured its members that "When a right-minded and true-hearted statesman has had as much sovereign power placed in his hands as you have put in mine, he should regard himself as the servant of the Senate; and often of the people as a whole, and even of private citizens too."

These were not mere words, spoken for show. On the contrary; I was pleased when decisions were taken in defiance of my wishes, and abstained from complaint, even when I knew I was right and the majority wrong. Once for example I had insisted that city magistrates should be resident throughout their term of office, but the Senate permitted a praetor to travel to Africa, and even paid his expenses. Moreover, I allowed the senators to disregard my advice if they chose to do so. When, for example, Manius Aemilius Lepidus was proposed as Governor of Asia, Sextus Pompeius Tertius declared that he was quite unfit for the post, being, as he said, "a lazy degenerate pauper". I didn't altogether disagree with Pompey and let my feelings be known. Nevertheless I acquiesced in the Senate's decision to appoint Lepidus, believing that this display of independence was valuable in itself.

In other matters, however, I was sceptical of the Senate's zeal. One year, for instance, the aediles urged me to speak out against extravagance. There was a great cry in the Senate that laws against lavish expenditure were disregarded, and that consequently food prices were increasing daily. I was aware of this and deplored it. I tried to set an example of austerity, on

one occasion serving up a half-side of boar at dinner, for
instance, and remarking that it tasted just as good as the other
side. But I knew that such laws, like those against sexual
immorality, were unavailing. Frugality and chastity used to pre-
vail because people had self-control. Law is incompetent in reg-
ulating moral behaviour. The remedy lies with the individual. If
we are decent, then we behave well; if we are not, we shall
always find some means of gratifying sordid and discreditable
passions.

Nothing caused me more trouble in these years than the flood
of accusations brought by informers. Even when the charges
which they laid were well founded, the general consequence
was despicable. Rome was in danger of becoming a city where
every man spied on another, and no man dared trust his neigh-
bour. I did what I could to check them. When two members of
the equestrian order, Considius Aequus and Caelius Cursor,
accused the praetor Magius Caecilianus of treason, I not only
saw to it that the charges were dismissed but also had the
accusers heavily fined. I hoped that if men realised that an
accusation might involve them in financial loss, this would make
the hope of profit from a successful charge somewhat less alluring. Alas, I underestimated men's cupidity and talent for self-
deception. Accusations of one sort or another, many ridiculous,
continued to flood in. One result of this was the demand from
the Senate that candidates for public office, especially provincial
governorships, should be more closely scrutinised, and that
those rumoured to be of scandalous life should be excluded.
One senator urged that the emperor alone should judge this
matter. Superficially, this had something to commend it, but
the proposal was fundamentally flawed. I was not prepared to
accept such a burden, and argued instead that an emperor's
knowledge cannot be all-embracing. "If you adopt this scheme,"
I said, "then you will merely encourage slanders and scurrilous
rumours, as intriguers try to influence my choice. The law is
concerned only with acts which have been committed. What will
be done is unknown. Many governors have belied either hopes
or fears; responsibility stimulates some natures and blunts
others. You cannot judge a man in advance. Besides, I ask you

to reflect on this. Emperors have enough burdens already – and quite enough power. Strengthen the executive and you weaken the law. That is a fundamental principle of politics. When it is possible to act according to due legal process, then the exercise of official authority is a mistake."

I believed that then; I believe it still. Yet the nature of man is such that the very people who clamour for action on the part of the government are among the first to deplore it – whenever that action appears to affect their own interests.

The longer I exercised the supreme authority, the harder it became for me to know the truth of any matter. I was learning the horrid isolation of office. No man addressed me without his own interest in mind. No man therefore spoke to me in open honesty. If anyone brought me a story which reflected ill on someone else, I had to ask myself what my informant hoped to gain, by what greed or resentment he was animated, and estimate this, before I could consider the objective truth of what he told me. Moreover, I learned that, even when not actuated by malice, men were inclined to say to me only what I wished to hear. It was on account of his freedom from these vices that I valued Sejanus, as Augustus had valued Agrippa. Sejanus, I believed, was not afraid to speak the truth, and since I was confident that he had no ambition to be more than he was, and was moreover imbued with feelings of affection for me, I trusted the advice he offered.

Throughout this time I was disturbed by the hostility which I knew that Agrippina entertained for me. I did all that was possible, all within my power, to appease it. I took her sons under my personal protection. There were three: Nero, Drusus and Caligula. None was altogether satisfactory. Nero had been a delightful small boy, intelligent, quick-witted, and possessed of a lightness of spirit that seemed to owe nothing to his parents. Indeed, in looks he resembled his grandmother Julia – he had her suddenly joyous smile, and her way also of pouting his lips when displeased. Germanicus had been inclined to be severe with him and, after her husband's death, Agrippina tried to force her eldest son to assume a responsibility against which his nature rebelled. She would berate him furiously whenever he fell below the impossible standard she demanded; this was in contrast to her treatment of the other boys whom she spoiled outrageously. Perhaps in reaction, perhaps in response to the deepest impulses of his nature, Nero took refuge in absurd affectations of manner, which, as he approached what should have been manhood, resolved itself into a blatant and degraded effeminacy: he painted his lips and eyelids, rouged his cheeks, daubed himself with Syrian scent, and was said to wear silk undergarments. At the baths, as a boy of fourteen or fifteen, he would ogle senators, and invite them into his cubicle. Naturally enough many were sufficiently allured by this pretty and dissolute child to risk immoral association with a member of the imperial family. To avoid embarrassment, I asked Drusus to reprove him; Nero then attempted to seduce his uncle. At the age of seventeen he fell madly in love with an actor, who was so notorious a pederast that he had once been pelted with dung in the street. I put a stop to that by sending the comedian into exile. But I continued to receive reports that made it quite clear that Nero was incorrigible.

All the same I persevered. I was, I admit, susceptible myself to the boy's undoubted charm. My heart softened when I saw in his gestures the Julia who had entranced me. There was even, I felt, a certain gallantry in his debauched behaviour; it was a response to an innate misery. He was never malicious, and in the right mood his wit flashed radiantly forth. Nevertheless he presented a problem. When he appeared in the imperial box at the games, a section of the crowd, which did not share the sentimental attachment to Germanicus' family which was common, would be sure to yell insults at him such as "fairy prince", "ganymede" and "pansy". On account of the rouge, you couldn't tell whether he blushed to hear himself so mocked. My mother, who detested him, refused to attend the games in his company. My only pleasure was to see Agrippina bite her lip to restrain her fury.

His brother Drusus loathed him also. Drusus was a prig, like his father Germanicus, and with none of the charm which Nero had inherited from Julia, and perhaps also from his great-grandfather Mark Antony. Drusus was mean, jealous and scheming. None of this showed in his looks – in this respect, he took after his grandfather Agrippa. Drusus was a consummate hypocrite, so accomplished that he deceived me for years. He was also intensely ambitious, and realising that the path to power lay through my favour, set himself to win my regard. This disturbed Agrippina, and I had reports of terrible quarrels between them. Eventually, however, he persuaded her that he was insincere in the court he paid me. When she warned him not to trust me, he looked her in the eye, and said, "Believe me, mother, I could never trust a man responsible for the murder of my father and for insults such as those he has directed against you." Yet the very same day, he would approach me with protestations of devotion and, more to the point, with requests for advice about affairs of state and the art of war, for, he said, "None knows better than I the value of your experience as Rome's greatest general, and hence I am eager to sit at your feet." Drusus was always quick to inform me of Nero's latest extravagances of behaviour, always, of course, shaking his head with pretended sorrow. "I really don't understand how my brother can allow creatures like X or Y to take such liberties with him. I'm afraid he must be deranged." It was fortunate that Sejanus supplied me with this information which led me to discern Drusus' true and untrustworthy character.

As for the youngest of the boys, Gaius Caligula, he was simply abhorrent. I have never myself liked gladiator shows, and would willingly ban them if the people would accept such a deprivation of pleasure, but even men who delighted in them were disgusted by the relish with which Caligula would view cruelty and death, even as a child. To see a boy of ten lick his lips at the sight of blood and squirm as if experiencing an orgasm in his enjoyment of the pain of unfortunate men was disgusting.

"A fine family," I often thought. "I thank the gods that Drusus and his son stand between them and power."

SIX

And then Drusus fell ill. He complained of lassitude and frequent bouts of nausea. His limbs ached and felt heavy. The merest motion was torture to him. I brought doctors hastening from Corinth and Alexandria to supplement the skills already resident in Rome. It was useless. Daily I watched my son weaken; daily I saw his appetite for life ebb away. In these circumstances even Sejanus was no comfort to me. Though I trusted him absolutely, I could not help reflecting that he would not mourn my son's death. I could not tolerate the company of Drusus' wife, Julia Livilla, for her indifference to her husband's condition was all too obvious. The eunuch Lygdus tended his master with sedulous care; one morning I found him in floods of bitter tears because Drusus had had a bad night, and I was not so cynical as to suppose that he was weeping merely because he feared to lose a master who loved him. My mother brought me no comfort either; old age had transported her to a realm where present griefs meant little. She irritated me by talking all the time about the joy which Agrippina would feel at Drusus' death. Curiously, my only solace came from young Nero Caesar. Though he was unable to cast aside his effeminate affectations, he nevertheless possessed an imaginative sympathy which let him understand my misery. Others reproached me – behind my back, but not without my knowledge – because I continued to attend the Senate throughout the long and wretched course of my son's illness; Nero, meeting me as I returned one morning from the Curia, embraced me with a spontaneous tenderness, and said: "At the moment you must feel that work and responsibility alone give your life any meaning." Then he stroked my cheek saying, "But I wish you could weep for Drusus, for your own sake." Strangely, I was irritated neither by his tears nor by the scent of bergamot with which he had bedewed himself. I could find no words to thank him. I embraced the boy, holding him close a long minute, drawing strength and comfort from his youth and sympathy.

Drusus died. When I entered the Senate the next day, the consuls sat on the ordinary benches as a sign of mourning. I thanked them, but reminded them of their dignity and rank, and requested that they resumed their proper station. Many senators wept, some with the aid of onions applied surreptitiously to their eyes. I raised my hand in a gesture to silence the display of grief.

"I know," I said, "that some will criticise me for appearing here while my son's body awaits burial, and my affliction is fresh. Many mourners can scarcely endure even the condolence of their families, and prefer to shut themselves away from the light of day. I understand such conduct and would never censure it. For me however seclusion is the worst temptation, and so I resist it, seeking a sterner solace. The arms in which I have taken refuge are those of the state."

I paused and then spoke of my family.

"My son's death is but the latest affliction in my mother's long and glorious life," I said. "Drusus was her grandson, and married to her grand-daughter, my brother's child Julia Livilla. Judge therefore how the Augusta grieves. Her only surviving male descendant apart from myself is my little grandson Tiberius Gemellus. After sixty years and more in the service of the Republic my mother, the Augusta, sees only this child as the heir of her labours, though I must not forget that he has, of course, an elder sister Livia Julia.

"As for me, my son's death, following so soon on that of his adopted brother, our dear Germanicus, is a blow from which I do not now feel I shall ever recover. At such moments it is of little comfort to recall the nobility and virtue of the dead, for, to tell you the truth, Conscript Fathers, such reflections only sharpen the pain, by reminding us of what we have been deprived. So now, I must tell you, that apart from little Tiberius Gemellus, only the sons of Germanicus remain to comfort my declining years . . ."

Then I had them called before the Senate, and the three
stood there: Nero shy, ill at ease, but with a dignity which I
had never previously known him to assume; Drusus proud,
even arrogant, yet sullen, as if he suspected my intentions and
would charge me with insincerity; and Gaius Caligula squinting
horribly and unable to stop fidgeting . . .

"When these boys lost their father," I said, "I entrusted them
to their uncle Drusus, begging him – though he had children of
his own – to treat them as though they were his own seed, and,
for posterity's sake, to fashion them in his image. Now Drusus
has gone. So my plea is directed to you. The gods and our
country are my witnesses.

"Senators, on my behalf as well as your own, adopt and guide
these youths, whose birth is so glorious – these great-
grandsons of Augustus. Nero, Drusus and Gaius" – I continued,
taking each in turn by the hand, and then embracing each –
"these senators will take the place of your parents. For in the
station to which you are born, the good and bad in you is of
national concern . . ."

I quote this speech in full, because, in the light of what later
happened, I would wish that posterity should fully understand
the sincerity of my benevolence towards the sons of Germanicus. If things turned out otherwise subsequently, it was
the gods that willed it, not I.

My mother grew ever more insupportable in her old age. No
sooner had I finished addressing the Senate than I received a
summons from her. I found her dressed in mourning, but with
the light of battle in her eye. She at once reproached me for
the speech which had been fully reported to her.

"It was not enough," she said, "for you to allow that woman"
– she meant Agrippina – "to destroy your loyal confederate Piso
and attempt to destroy my dearest friend Plancina, by her lies
and malice; but now you have to elevate her children in this
rash manner. How do you know that Agrippina didn't poison
Drusus? Have you thought of that possibility? Certainly his
symptoms resemble those of certain poisons, and who had a
better motive?"

"Mother," I said, "this is truly nonsense. There is no reason to suppose that Drusus was murdered. Do you think the suspicion has not crossed my mind, and been rejected? Besides, Agrippina and Drusus were never enemies. If she was going to poison anyone, don't you think she would have started with me?"

"And now," she continued, paying no attention at all to what I said, "you choose to make yourself ridiculous by speaking in this manner about the woman's children? Do you think that will appease her?"

"They are members of the family," I said, "and the great-grandsons of your husband. Don't you think I have a duty to them?"

"I have no patience with your folly. But you were always as obstinate as a pig. When I think how Augustus used to complain of you! And of how I would defend you! Here, listen to what he said," and, saying this, she drew a letter from her bosom, and began to read: "I can never be easy with Tiberius, because I never know what he is thinking and therefore find it difficult to trust him. Moreover, besides his obstinacy – and I agree with you there – he is a bad judge of character. Like you, I have noted with distress his susceptibility . . ."

But I cannot bring myself, even in the privacy of my chamber, to quote further, or to allow myself to dwell on the charges my stepfather brought against me, charges which, I can only say, derived from a more profound misunderstanding of my nature than I believed him capable . . .

"If you bring forward that disgusting little creature, Nero, who is in my opinion no better than a catamite, you will make yourself an object of public mockery and contempt," my mother said.

"Nero," I said, "has obvious faults, but I believe he is capable of outgrowing them. There is a fundamental goodness in his character. Believe me, I have seen evidence of it . . ."

But Livia had reached a stage in life when her attention wandered. She could no longer sustain an argument. Instead she now began to reprove me for offences, many of them imaginary, which lay in the distant past. She accused me of neglecting her.

She accused me of having conspired with Julia – yes, Julia – against her. In the next breath she told me she had "adored" Julia, "the best of daughters", and never been able to forgive me for the failure of our marriage, "directly caused by your vices. Julia was distressed by what she heard of your infatuation for that German boy, and everything that went wrong stemmed from that . . ."

Since I knew that Livia's dislike of Julia had been fixed from the start, and since I could remember how she had time and again warned me against her, I could only wonder at the tricks which old age can play with memory. I was pained to be compelled to observe the decay of my mother's faculties. Every meeting in the months that followed gave rise to new reproaches, new fantasies, new tirades. The confusion of her mind was betrayed in the intemperance of her language and in her willingness to give me pain, a willingness that might better be described as a compulsion.

Livia's confusion exasperated me. I could no longer tolerate her society. Yet I have to confess that it was no wonder she had grown confused: it would have been no wonder even if she had lacked the excuse of great age. Her confusion was a proper response to the corruption of the times. If I put the most generous interpretation on what she and Augustus thought they had achieved, then I would say, that in bringing to an end the civil wars that had gnawed at Rome's body politic, they believed that they created an opportunity for the revival of virtue. Of course, Augustus, being a man of the world, was aware, from time to time at least, that he deceived himself in nursing such a hope; nevertheless the hope was there, and not ignoble. But it was cheated. Augustus greatly admired the poet Vergil, who celebrated the perfect order of Italy in his *Georgics* and promised a resumption of the Golden Age in his sixth *Eclogue*, and throughout his *Aeneid*. When Augustus spoke of Vergil, a wholly unaccustomed tone – a mixture of warmth and reverence – invaded his voice. There were moments when he really believed it was his destiny to make the Vergilian vision real. I don't say that Livia felt in exactly the same way; hers was never a poetic nature, but she still responded to the underlying impulse, and at certain moments both thought it came within the scope of the possible. There was thus, for all his personal ruthlessness and duplicity, something altogether admirable about my step-father's ambition. Without his capacity for self-deception, I could throb to the same music. All my life I have been entranced by a vision of virtue, and always it has receded into the obscurity of reality. Plato teaches that this life is at best a dusty reflection of what is ideal. Our experience is a flickering of figments, shadows dancing on the wall of the cave in which we are imprisoned. Yes, indeed; but these are figments that torment, shadows that lie and steal and stab and betray. We envision an ideal Republic; we expound principles of civic virtue; we extol law. Experience matches none of this. Augustus, with a sunnier nature than mine, contrived till near the end to give himself the illusion of faith. I have had to cling to it by my fingernails, like a man scrabbling to save himself from tumbling from a cliff-face into the void.

Perplexed, dismayed, deceived, my mind in the months after Drusus' death entered into turmoil. His loss hit me harder than I could have imagined; indeed, I had never imagined it. I descended into a narrow cleft in the rocks, and, no matter where I turned my gaze, found nothing to comfort, only the dark-grey and slimy rock. In those nights I came to know the grief of Hecuba, carried as a slave to Greece, who saw her son dead and her daughter a sacrifice, and then, driven out of her senses, barked like a dog on the deserted beach, as the winds howled. The same winds howled around me.

I had never had much faith in humanity. Now I lost those shreds which remained. There was a case came before the Senate, in which a certain Vibius Serenus charged his father of the same name with treason. The elder Serenus had been exiled some eight years previously, on what charge I now forget. Now he was brought back and stood before the Senate, in chains, shabby and exhausted by illness, fear or neglect. His son, a brisk and elegant young man, accused him of plots against my life. Subversive agents, he explained, had been sent to foment a rebellion in Gaul; they had been financed by the ex-praetor Marcus Caecilius Cornutus. Substance was given to the charge by the suicide of Cornutus, but the elder Serenus denied everything. He shook his manacles in his son's face, and challenged him to produce his accomplices. "Surely," he said, "an old man like myself cannot be thought to have plotted the emperor's murder with the help of a single confederate, and him a man so weak-spirited as to kill himself because of a lying charge?" His son smiled, and named Gnaeus Cornelius Lentulus and Lucius Seius Tubero, friends of mine, whose loyalty I had always considered certain. I said that the accusation was absurd. The elder Serenus' slaves were then tortured, and revealed nothing. Sejanus supervised their examination, and assured me there was no case to answer. Serenus the younger then panicked; he feared the Tarpeian Rock, the reward of attempted parricide, and fled from Rome. I had him fetched back from Ravenna. "Continue your prosecution," I said, intending that his ignominy should be exposed to all. Certain senators, however, misinterpreted my intention; they thought I was certain of the father's guilt, and, to oblige me – yes, such was their notion of what would oblige me! – demanded that the father should suffer the ancient punishment for treason, and be flogged to death. I declined to allow this motion to be put to the vote, and was ready to dismiss the charge and punish the son. At this point Sejanus came to me and said that though the slaves had revealed nothing to prove their master guilty of this treason, nevertheless there was cause to believe that the accusation was not altogether unfounded. I was perplexed, divided between suspicion of the father and loathing for the son's impious zeal. Both were consigned to exile.

Scarcely a week passed without some charge being brought against some man, and though I struggled to preserve my indifference, my disgust intensified. The spectacle of greed, fear, resentment and vindictiveness, that was offered again and again to my eyes, was altogether repellent.

Nor was I appeased by the arrival of a delegation from Further Spain requesting to be permitted to build a shrine to me and to my mother. I refused angrily, dismayed by this new evidence of servility: "Let me assure you," I said, "that I am human and mortal, performing merely human tasks and content to occupy the first place among men to which the Senate has chosen to appoint me. Future generations will do me justice if they judge me worthy of my ancestors, careful of your interests, steadfast in danger, and fearless of animosities incurred in the public service . . ."

Sejanus reported, "You shouldn't have spoken like that. It doesn't have the effect you hope for. When you reject veneration, people assume that you are either insincere or genuinely unworthy of it."

I considered carefully the character of Agrippina's sons. Despite his effeminacy, there was more true virtue, I thought, in Nero than in his brothers, both of whom showed a relish for cruelty that disgusted and frightened me. I resolved therefore to cultivate him. I was now in my middle sixties and, though my health was good, apart from painful rheumatism, knew that I could not count on many years. My own grandson Tiberius Gemellus was still a child, and I was anyway conscious of the promise I had made first to Augustus concerning Germanicus, then to the Senate concerning his children. Nero pleased me by his wit and intelligence; also by an innate melancholy, which suggested to me that he had no exaggerated hopes of his fellow men.

"My father was everything that I am not," he said to me, "and I have always been unhappily conscious that men consider him a hero."

"Why unhappily?"

"Because . . ." he pushed back a curl that had fallen damply over his face, ". . . I don't really know why. I only know that this knowledge makes me feel ill at ease."

I understood that. If at that moment I had asked him, "Why do you go with men?" perhaps everything would have been different. Perhaps a rare moment of honesty would have diverted us into another path. But I dared not ask that question, in case the answer destroyed such intimacy as we enjoyed. There is a limit, I told myself, to the frankness proper between an old man and a youth. Instead, I shied away and talked instead of the duties and burdens of power.

"Burdens," I said, "which I hope you will yourself assume."

"You can't think me suitable . . . ?" He blushed. "For one thing I am no soldier and could never be one."

"I believe you to be honest," I said, "and, in the fashion of your generation, honourable."

He squirmed, perhaps with embarrassment.

"It pains me," I said, "that your mother so distrusts me."

He blushed again. It was clear that he would wish to defend Agrippina but, aware of the injustice of her attitude towards me, could summon up no argument.

"To demonstrate to her and to the world that I have confidence in you," I said, "I am proposing that you should marry my grand-daughter Livia Julia, the only sister of Tiberius Gemellus. I believe that you are the only person I can trust to do right by the boy, and I believe that marriage to his sister is not only the best way of displaying my regard for you, but will itself be of benefit to you."

He was taken aback, protested that he was unfit for such an honour. For a moment I savoured his terror, then hastened to reassure him. He had been the victim, I said, of evil rumours; it was time to silence them. My grand-daughter was a sweet girl, whom I was sure he would come to love. I watched his mouth tremble; then, with an effort, he smiled. He looked like my Julia caught out in a lie. I kissed him. "We understand each other," I said.

The proposal of this marriage took Agrippina aback. She could not oppose it; yet she feared that it represented in some way which she could not fathom a plot aimed at her. She was correct. It was my intention to lure Nero from her malign influence.

In the same week that the marriage between Nero and Livia Julia was celebrated, my mother fell ill, and Sejanus requested my permission to divorce his wife Apicata. "We no longer find each other agreeable," was all he said. "That is sufficient explanation."

I called to see my mother. She looked at me as if she did not
know me, and refused to speak. I besought her not to die in a
rage, and performed a sacrifice in her bedchamber in order that
the gods might restore her health and reason. But even as I
moved my hands over the altar I knew that I wished her dead.
I had in fact wished that for years though it was only now when
death was imminent that I found myself able to confess it even
to my own heart.

It was raining as I left her house for the last time, and stood
looking down into the bustle of the Forum. It rained as I had
wept in childhood whenever she seemed to withdraw her love
from me. Nothing lasts, except memory with its shadowy and
ghostly truths.

Agrippina raged. She accused me of stealing her son, of thwart-
ing her in every endeavour. The tip of her long nose trembled.
That nose, which destroyed her pretensions to beauty, and
which was not even imperious, invaded my imagination. I saw
it quivering over my every act.

"Is it my fault," I answered her, "that you are not queen?"

"Queen?" she replied, failing to understand that I was quoting
Sophocles. "We have no queens in Rome."

"Except my dear brother Nero," said Drusus.

"That's no way to speak. He will outgrow his affectations.
There is much good in the boy. Come, Agrippina, we have both
suffered much. There's no cause for us to be enemies. Let us
at least have a truce. Come to dinner with me tomorrow."

She consented; but at the table, when I passed her an apple,
she held it in her hand a moment, squinting at it, then passed
it back to me.

"You eat it," she said. "I would like to see you eat it. You
chose it so carefully."

"I selected it as the best apple," I replied, and bit into the
fruit.

"Did you understand the significance?" I asked Sejanus.

"Of course I did. She as good as accused you of attempting
to poison her. What's more, when she tells the story, I'll bet

she doesn't mention that you actually ate the apple. I've told you before, I'll tell you again: that woman spares no effort to slander you. Of course nobody really believes the specific accusations, but, as the proverb has it, 'Much water weareth away stone . . .' The sum of her accusations has an effect."

I turned away in misery, back to my desk and the never-ending series of decisions to be made, reports to be considered, questions to be debated, problems to be confronted.

"Work," I found myself muttering too often, "is the surest anodyne."

But when I retired to bed, and sleep did not come, as so many nights it denied itself to me, my thoughts turned back to my villa and gardens in Rhodes. It seemed to me, or so I persuaded myself, that I had come closer to content, and to an understanding of the purpose of life, in my retirement there, than at any time since I had been thrust back into the maelstrom of action. I could not of course retire again; if Drusus had not died, it might have been possible, as I had intended, to associate him with myself in the government of the empire, as Augustus had done with me in his last years; and then, I promised myself, I would be able to lean on my son, depart from Rome confident of his virtue, and, in retirement, exercise no more than a general power of supervision. That dream had been as seductive as a ripe peach. Now it had withered.

I turned to wine; to no avail. It brought neither joy nor comfort.

And yet I heard the sea lapping against the rocks, smelled its tangy odour mingled with the scent of roses, myrtle and honeysuckle. And I remembered a story which a Greek scholar had once told me.

He was a freedman called Philip, in Julia's household, and he had married, with his mistress's blessing, a free-born Greek girl from the island of Capri, where Augustus had had a villa. He told me of his wife's uncle, an unmarried man against whom, nevertheless, no accusation of vice had ever been brought. He was revered in the family for his wisdom and calm philosophy, though my informant was for long ignorant of any justification for the high regard in which the old man was held.

"Indeed it seemed strange to me," he said, "for Xenophon, as he was called, seemed in human relations the most cantankerous of fellows. He rarely spoke at family gatherings, and when he did it was generally to express his disapproval of the younger generation. I can't now recall what incident encouraged him to take an interest in me. Perhaps there was no incident. Perhaps he merely detected in me some communion of feeling. I can't say. At any rate it so happened that I developed the habit of sitting with the old man in the afternoons which he spent on a terrace under a vine-wreathed arbour while the rest of the household took its siesta. We would drink the yellow wine from the family's own vineyard, sharp acidulous stuff, nevertheless with a piquant and memorable flavour to which I had become happily accustomed. Forgive me these details, which I offer you because they bring back to me so vividly the memory of these afternoons when I was aware of an utter stillness, as of death; yet simultaneously of the sound of the waves below and of lizards scurrying over the ancient wall that surrounded the terrace. Xenophon would eat sea-urchins, which he put whole into his mouth and chewed noisily with much spitting. He was generally silent and would spend hours on end gazing out to sea. I noticed at last that his eyes were fixed on some rocks which thrust themselves out of the water a little further from land than a man could swim with comfort.

"'Is there something about these rocks?' I asked one afternoon, when his gaze had been more than usually fixed.

"'Do these fools in there ever speculate before you on the reasons why I have never married?' he replied.

"I hesitated.

"'You're a sensible fellow,' he said. 'Doesn't it disgust you to copulate with human beings?'

"I adored my wife, and if she had not disliked sex in the afternoon would happily have been in her bed.

"'But then, why should you? You're like the rest. You don't know anything better.'

"And he popped another sea-urchin into his mouth, and spat vigorously.

"'You do then?' I said.

"He paid no attention to the impudence in my tone, but smiled. I have never seen such a smile. It had such an assurance of bliss.

"'When I was a young man – oh younger than you,' he said, 'I learned better. I was vouchsafed an experience which I can only call miraculous, and which altered my whole life. You ask me why I gaze at these rocks. It is for the same reason that I keep a rowing-boat tied up in the cove below. I was betrothed then to a cousin. One afternoon as I sat in this same place the air was filled with music such as I had never heard. It was a music both melancholy and uncanny, yet with an undercurrent of joy, like the movement of deep water. I left the terrace and made for my boat and steered towards the sound. And so I came to these rocks where the music seemed close, yet no louder than it had been at a distance. Like one in a trance, I mounted the rock to the girl who reclined there making the music though she had no instrument and her lips were still. It seemed to me that she was the music. She took me in her arms and the music hummed around us, and I knew delight beyond the limits of imagination. I became one with her, achieving an ethereal perfection of unity compared to which any human coupling is an obscene shadowy representation of reality. I say girl, but of course she was no human thing, but a spirit, a nymph, the plenitude of what may be desired. We made love while the sun sank in the west, and through the darkness and till it rose in a pink-dappled sky behind the mountains of Campania. And the music never left us. Then she closed my eyes with a kiss, and murmured to me that she was of my life forever, and that we would come together again. And I woke, with the sun beating on the rock, and no sound but the sea, and found myself alone. These sea-urchins have the taste of her, for she belonged to the sea, and returned to it, and will one day call me thence. So do you wonder, young man, that I look on your couplings with the same scorn you might feel for cocks mounting fowls in the yard?'"

Philip paused.

"It was a Siren he had met and loved. There is no other conclusion possible."

"You believed him?" I asked.

"For a long time I didn't. But I have never forgotten his words."

"What song did the Siren sing him?"

"A song that is beyond imitation. Evidently."

"For a long time you didn't believe him?"

"That is right."

"And then? What is the end of the story?"

"Oh, it has no end. Don't you know that, Emperor? No story ever has an end. All narratives are circular. They couldn't be otherwise. But I can tell you another stage in the journey. One day old Xenophon was sitting on the terrace as usual, while the other members of the family slept in the afternoon. There had been a week of scirocco, but the skies had cleared and the air was gentle. They left him with his flask of wine and a basket of sea-urchins. Nobody ever saw him again. When they woke, he had vanished."

"And his boat? That had vanished too?"

"Of course. There was consternation. It was assumed that for some reason nobody could fathom he had descended the cliff, embarked in his little boat, and sailed into . . . what? The void, perhaps?"

"But you don't believe that?"

Philip smiled. "I wasn't there at the time. I have never spoken to anyone except you, Emperor, about these matters. This is the first time I have repeated Xenophon's story . . ."

"So there are Sirens . . . the calm under the winds . . ."

"It may have been a delusion, Emperor. He was a very old man, and perhaps not right in his wits."

SEVEN

Some three weeks after this conversation I occupied the imperial box at the Games. I had gone reluctantly, as usual. I believe no man of taste and sensibility can take pleasure in gladiatorial contests. Moreover, thirty years' experience of warfare has schooled me to view this contrived carnage with disgust. I have seen too much courage and suffering and terror to take any pleasure in their compulsory exhibition by wretches condemned to fight for the amusement of the mob. It is even more disgusting to see educated men of good birth – and even women – salivating gleefully at these shows. Few things fortified my respect for Sejanus more than the contempt he felt for those who delighted in these contests.

Duty, however, compelled me on occasions to attend. And on this day almost the whole family was present, from the unfortunate slobbering Claudius, my poor brother Drusus' younger son, whose wayward wits and physical disabilities might excuse the morbid pleasure he took in the battles in the arena, to Agrippina and her brood. As usual Agrippina maintained a quasi-regal air of superiority; she scarcely deigned to acknowledge the cheers with which she was greeted; yet by the merest twitch of her lips and inclination of her head conveyed the sense of her immeasurable pride. Instead of offending the populace, her hauteur encouraged their enthusiasm. It was strange. I have always known that the mob resented what they took to be my own awareness of my superiority; yet their adoration of Agrippina swelled in proportion to the distance she set between herself and them.

That afternoon the third contest was between a swarthy Anatolian mountaineer, armed with net and spear, and a

flaxen-haired German boy with short sword and shield. If the
German had been schooled by the gladiator-master, terror or
desperation had deprived him of all memory of his training. He
launched a succession of wild attacks on his opponent who
evaded them with ease, in return offering only light jabs with
his spear at the discomfited boy, whose arms were soon pink
with his own blood. After each of his clumsy assaults had been
avoided he paused for a moment, his chest heaving and his legs,
which still retained the soft fleshiness of youth in contrast to
the Anatolian's sinewy hardness, quivering. Then he pushed
back a lock of hair which had fallen over his left eye, and charged
again. This went on for some minutes, and it was obvious that
the two were reprehensibly ill-matched. The Anatolian was
playing with his opponent, following the instructions given to
gladiators by their cynical trainers "to let the crowd see them
sweat". Then one of the boy's wild swings caught the Anatolian
on the shoulder. He was hit only with the flat of the sword, and
not cut, but the power of the blow sent him hurtling to the sand.
His spear and his net flew from his grasp. He crouched on all
fours gazing at the boy, who, perhaps horrified by his achievement, perhaps merely surprised, stood still, incapable of action.
The Anatolian shook his head from side to side. The crowd
howled for his death. The boy did not move. Then he lowered
his sword and pushed its point into the sand, and his opponent
scrabbled like a crab, but keeping his gaze fixed on the boy,
towards his spear and net. He retrieved them and got to his
feet. Still the boy did not move. And now the Anatolian, as if
stirred by the disgrace of his fall, began to tease him. He
whisked his net about the boy, making him jump and look foolish. With deft swirls of the net he pursued the German round
the ring. Once the boy's nerve cracked and he turned his back
on his opponent and tried to flee. But there was no refuge from
the swirling net. Its mesh swung in the air before him, and he
turned again. The crowd shrieked. The boy rubbed his forearm
across his brow to wipe away the sweat, and left a streak of
blood there. He looked up. It seemed to me he was looking
straight at me, imploring mercy, but I doubt if he saw anything
but a mist of fear and danger. Summoning up what was left of

his courage, he hurled himself on his opponent, with a wild cry and upraised sword. There was no one there. The Anatolian skipped aside, and thrusting out his foot, sent the boy tumbling to the sand. In a trice he was enveloped in the net, and the spear pressed against his throat. The contest was over.

Next to me Gaius Caligula jumped out of his seat, screaming, "Kill him, kill him . . ."

The crowd roared approval.

I looked along the row. Agrippina remained impassive, as if what was happening in the arena had no meaning for her. Nero's lips trembled; he shared the boy's terror and yet could not prevent himself from responding to the cruelty of the spectacle. Claudius jabbed Drusus in the ribs and showered excited spittle on him as he jabbered his enthusiasm, stuttering, I suppose, even worse than usual. Drusus himself assumed the air of a triumphant general; so might his father have looked on that dreadful day when he permitted the repentant mutineers to expiate their own crimes by the judicial murder of those who had led them into rebellion.

And I looked down on the bloody sand, and saw the boy's limbs relax as if he consented to death, while his eyes were still dilated with the terror of realisation. I knew that look. I had seen it often in battle. I had seen men and boys make that same astonished discovery, in an instant of revelation, that everything they thought of as being essentially themselves, everything they knew through their senses – what they knew best of all, their own body – could be snuffed out, as if life was no more than a dream now turned nightmare. His lips moved, his tongue touched his lower lip and I turned my thumb up, to save his life.

I saved not only him, but myself, and my own reason. I had acted without calculation. I left the arena amidst a storm of boos and catcalls, as the mob howled their disappointed blood-lust. I was trembling. I took a glass of wine to calm myself.

"The crowd will hate you for this," Sejanus said.

"They hate me already. Let them hate; provided they fear."

I quoted the line lightly. It was inaccurate, for I had no wish to be feared, only obeyed. Even that is not accurate, as an expression of my sentiments. I would rather there had been no need even for such obedience, and I would have preferred that people obeyed the dictates of reason and virtue rather than of any man. I might, more appropriately, have quoted Horace: *odi profanum vulgus et arceo* – I loathe and shun the profane rabble . . . The words sounded in my mind, but I kept them to myself. Yet in that instant my resolution, slowly formed in the dim recesses of my determination, was complete: it was possible to shun them forever. Still, even now, I did not acquaint Sejanus with my purpose. Instead I sent him back to the circus to offer some anodynic and hypocritical explanation of my departure.

"And my excuses. Don't forget to offer my excuses to our masters, the people."

"Of course."

"The public wishes to be fooled," I said, "therefore let it be fooled."

"I don't understand."

"No matter. Nothing is any matter."

"Are you sure you are all right?"

"Yes," I said, "I have seen deliverance." And with these words I dismissed him.

Then I sent one of my freedmen to the gladiators' school to purchase the defeated German, and bring him to me.

He entered, puffy-eyed, in a short tunic of grey wool, with sandals on his feet. He threw himself prostrate before me. I told him, in his own language, to get up.

"You are a free-born German," I said, "and perhaps of good birth. I know it is not the custom of your people to abase themselves in this manner."

"I have been torn from the customs of my people, and compelled to practise other manners."

"Of what tribe are you?"

"Of a branch of the Cherusci."

"The Cherusci? But they have not been at war with us. How does it come about that you are a prisoner and a slave?"

He explained that he was the son of a chief and had been sent, according to the German fashion, to complete his education with another tribe and, finding them engaged in frontier warfare with the legions, had been captured in a skirmish.

"And so, by a series of accidents, I arrived where I found myself today. Why did you save my life?"

He guessed – I could tell from the nature of his glance – one answer, which was not the whole answer, and to have embarked on a full analysis of my reason for acting would have led me into areas I neither understood, nor wished to understand, myself. So I merely smiled and said, "I thought you were too young to die."

"Too young, or . . ."

"Too young to die in that manner at any rate . . ."

"I am grateful."

"Once long ago," I said, "a German boy, who looked rather like you, saved my life in battle. Perhaps that was why. Perhaps it is to that boy who has been dead many years that you should be grateful. I don't know. I felt this afternoon that there had been too much blood. I have had more than my fill of it. Have your wounds been dressed?"

"Those that can be have been. What will you do with me now?"

I could not answer. Instead I passed him a cup of wine. He looked startled, then drank it back in one go, in the German manner, of which, I remembered, I had cured the young Segestes and his father.

"For the moment," I said, "you had better remain in my household."

I spoke without reflection. The boy blushed.

"Of course," I said, "I daresay you would rather I returned you to your own people, but it might not serve. I have seen how your people treat returned slaves. They regard them as having been degraded by their experience. No, you will do better to remain with me."

Naturally, when the word went round that I had taken the boy whom I had rescued from the arena into my own household, the worst construction was put on my actions. The boy was said to be my catamite, and insulting graffiti appeared throughout the city declaring that I had been moved by lust, not humanity. Agrippina was reported by Sejanus' agents as expressing her revulsion and contempt for my "debauched senility". "Will the

Roman people be content to be governed by an old man who cheats them of satisfaction in order to gratify his immoral impulses?" she was even heard to enquire.

Alone, in the starry watches, on the camp-bed which I had retained since my soldiering days, I knew the truth of these accusations. Who can disentangle the network of emotions which prompt action? My mind, searching in vain for sleep – for I had long been a victim of the most desolate insomnia – played with images, simultaneously painful and pleasant, of the boy Sigmund's limbs stretched out on the bloody sand, of his trembling lips and of the blond hair that flopped over his left eye. I could not deny to myself what I felt, nor the delight which I took in having the boy about my person. But I was impressed also by his manly character, by his reserve and dignity. The embraces of an old man with foul breath and a scrawny chicken neck could not fail to disgust him. I would not compel him to debase himself. He had a sense of decency which I could have believed vanished from the world. It pleased me to have him in my household, to engage him in conversation, instruct him in virtue and knowledge of the world, to be able to rely on him for little services which he performed with punctilious respect.

For a few brief months I approached happiness. It was disturbed only by my miserable consciousness of Livia's decline into a species of madness often associated with extreme age, and by my consciousness of Agrippina's malice and unremitting hostility. Scarcely a week passed without Sejanus bringing me evidence of her zeal in poisoning men's minds against me, even of encouraging plots against my life. Mindful of her popularity, and of the respect due her as Julia's daughter and Germanicus' widow, I declined to permit him to act against her, hoping always that she would in time desist from her malignant folly. I did not realise that it was in her blood, that she was possessed of the same impulse to self-destruction that had maddened Julia herself.

Meanwhile I reposed all my trust in Sejanus. He was the one man living who had never let me down. Then one day he approached me with a request, an unprecedented act, for he had previously been content to accept what I offered and never to ask anything for himself. But this request was startling. To emphasise its importance, he put it in epistolary form, though we had long been accustomed to discuss everything freely and without formality.

> The many kindnesses of your father Augustus, and the still more numerous marks of favour and friendship I have received at your hand, have accustomed me to bring my hopes and desires to the imperial ear as readily as to the gods. I have never asked for anything for myself, neither money nor great office. I would prefer, like any other soldier, to work for the emperor's safety, which I am ready to secure with my own life. Yet I have now, to my astonishment, won the greatest of privileges – to be thought worthy by a certain great lady of alliance in marriage with your family. I speak of Julia Livilla, the widow of your lamented son. The consciousness of what Rome has lost by his untimely death drew us together: we discovered a common sympathy and comforted each other in our grief. Her sentiments towards me have encouraged me to hope for what I would not otherwise have dreamed of as being within the realms of possibility. Besides, she has reminded me that Augustus himself, when choosing a husband for his daughter, did not regard men of my equestrian order as beneath consideration. Therefore, I humbly request you to bear in mind, if you should now be thinking of a husband for Julia Livilla, your devoted friend who would gain nothing but prestige from the relationship. I ask nothing more. I am content with the duties I perform; satisfied – for my children's sake – if my family is safeguarded against the unfounded spite and malevolence of Agrippina. For myself, to live out my life under so great an emperor represents the summit of my ambitions . . .

The request surprised me. On reflection however it seemed natural that Julia Livilla, deprived by cruel fate of her husband, should have turned for consolation to the only man of comparable quality with whom she was acquainted, more especially since Sejanus' own marriage to Apicata had failed, to his evident distress. Yet there were issues other than personal happiness to be considered. I therefore replied in cautious and non-committal manner.

My dear Sejanus,

There is no one, as you know, for whom I feel more affection, and in whom I repose greater trust, than yourself. I have proved this again and again. If we were all private persons, then I would not hesitate.

However, while such men's decisions may be based on their own interests and affections, rulers are situated differently, since in important matters they need to consult public opinion. So I can't fall back on an easy answer and merely say that Julia Livilla can decide for herself whether she wants to marry again or not. (And of course if she does, she could find no one more worthy as a person than yourself.) I shan't even say that she has a noble mother, Antonia, who is more properly her intimate adviser than I am myself. No, I shall be more frank with you, as you deserve.

First then, Agrippina's ill-feelings (to use a mild term) will be greatly intensified if Julia Livilla, who is – I don't need to remind you – her sister-in-law, should be joined with you in marriage. This would virtually split the imperial family in two. (As you know, I detest the expression "the imperial family", as being incompatible with our Republican inheritance, but nevertheless facts are facts, and this is one, however disagreeable.) Even now, the women's rivalry can't be repressed, and my grandsons are torn between them. What would be the consequences if the proposed marriage made the feud worse?

Second, you are mistaken, dear boy, if you think that Julia Livilla, after being married to Gaius Caesar and then to my beloved Drusus, would be content to grow old as the wife of a mere knight – or that you could retain that status. Even if I allowed it, do you think it would be tolerated by those who have seen her brother and father, and our ancestors, holding the great offices of state? Your elevation would be necessary.

You say you do not want to rise above your present rank. I honour that sentiment, though it is the general opinion that you have long ago eclipsed all other knights. You are even now an object of envy and, in envying you, people criticise me. I am already criticised for the favours I have granted you. Don't you see that the envy and criticism would be intensified by this marriage?

You remark quite correctly that Augustus considered marrying his daughter to a knight. But he foresaw that any man distinguished by such an alliance would be enormously elevated, and so those he had in mind were men like Gaius Proculeius, a close friend of his, who took no part in public affairs. The two positions are not comparable. Moreover, in the end you must remember, the sons-in-law whom he actually chose were, first, Marcus Agrippa, and then myself.

I have spoken openly as your friend. Ultimately I shall not oppose any decision that you and Julia Livilla come to. Of certain projects of my own, and additional ties by which I plan to link you to me, I shall not speak now. I shall only say this: your own personal merits, and my consciousness of your profound devotion to my interests and to my person, convince me that no elevation would be too high. When the time is ripe I shall speak frankly to the Senate . . .

Sejanus declared himself deeply touched by my letter. He acknowledged the justice of my observations and promised to consider them carefully.

"Nothing," he said, "must be done to give any further cause for the vile and unjustified criticisms directed at you, or that will encourage Agrippina in her seditious manoeuvrings."

But I knew from the look in his eye that he had not abandoned his hopes. That was natural, for the prospect of marriage to my son's widow was alluring. Moreover, Julia Livilla herself was eager for the match; and she had no fear of antagonising Agrippina further. Indeed she welcomed the prospect.

The same autumn saw two disturbing trials which contributed to the resolution I was secretly forming.

A case was brought against a senator, Votienus Montanus, who was accused of slandering me and the constitution Rome had inherited from Augustus. With incredible folly, he called a common soldier, by name Aemilius, as one of his witnesses. This man, who had been dishonourably discharged from the service some time previously, had apparently been deprived of his wits by a sense of grievance. He poured out a stream of abusive filth, mostly directed against me. I can scarcely, even now, bring myself to list the slanders. The least was habitual immorality. I was accused also of having been an accessory to the murder of Germanicus – a murder which was, of course, wholly imaginary and which had been disproved in poor Piso's trial. Impiety towards the gods and the memory of Augustus, participation in orgies and magic rites involving the prostitution of free-born virgins and even the ritual sacrifice of servile children – such monstrosities stood out from the stream of filth with which my ears were assailed. Perhaps the demented man had been encouraged to speak like this – though he probably needed little encouragement – in the hope that the court would be distracted from consideration of the crimes with which Votienus himself was charged.

The second case was even more serious and distressing. It was first brought to my notice by Sejanus. Compelled as any ruler must be in our unhappy times, to operate a system of surveillance, I had nevertheless found this requirement so distasteful that, unlike Augustus, who kept a close eye on such matters himself, I had delegated full responsibility to Sejanus, as the only man in whose honour and scrupulosity I could trust. One morning he approached me frowning, his face a study in gloom and perturbation.

"Something extremely unpleasant has come to light," he said. "It concerns a noble lady, Claudia Pulchra."

Then he recounted how this lady, a cousin of mine and also of Agrippina's, whose close friend she also was, had made her house on the Aventine a hive of sedition. The first rumours had been brought to Sejanus by Gnaeus Domitius Afer, a recent praetor, whom Claudia had attempted to seduce.

"Indeed," Sejanus said, with that frank and sceptical smile

which he was accustomed to bring to any story of depravity, "I rather think she succeeded, and the wretched Afer believed himself the chosen of fortune. He was certainly greatly flattered by her attentions. But then he discovered that she was indulging herself with another adulterous relationship, with Caius Furnius, and this displeased him."

"Furnius?" I said. "A difficult and disagreeable fellow, yet not without ability."

"Quite."

The name alarmed me, though I chose not to let Sejanus see this. I knew Furnius for a malcontent. He was a man of considerable merit whom I had denied responsibility on account of his wayward character, ungovernable temper, and suspect associates. His grandfather had been a friend of Mark Antony: his father had had the good sense to adhere to Augustus, and had indeed held a consulship towards the end of Augustus' life. But I had been unable to honour Furnius as he would have wished. There could be no doubt that he was disaffected.

"When I learned this," Sejanus said, "I naturally took such steps as I thought necessary to investigate affairs. I placed a trusted agent in Claudia's household. His reports convinced me not only of her uncontrollable, or at least uncontrolled, immorality – her habitual adultery which exposes her to the penalties decreed by the *lex papia poppaea*, but of still more heinous crimes. Here, would you like to read the full reports, or shall I summarise them . . . ?"

I shook my head. My spirit was invaded by gloom as a sea-fog creeps inland.

"Naturally," Sejanus said, "I don't rely on these reports alone. As you have often reminded me there is a danger that agents will tell you what they think you want to hear, though of course I have done everything in my power, by the example of punishments meted out to any falsifiers, to convince them that what we want is nothing but the truth. At any rate, I am certain that the wretched woman has conspired against your life, both by suborning professional poisoners and by employing sorcerers to practise their black arts to your harm. Here for example" – he delved into the sheaf of reports which lay on the table before him – "I have an affidavit from one of her freedwomen, detailing how, at the last full moon, an Egyptian sorceress – but you don't want to sicken yourself with the details, which I can tell you are so disgusting that they have cost me a night's sleep . . ."

"No," I said, "I don't want to know. You had better arrange for the law to take its course."

"Yes," he said, "I think I might get Afer to conduct the prosecution. He has an interest in its success."

"I am beginning to understand you Romans," Sigmund said. "When they made me into a gladiator, I thought, this is all wrong, life isn't like this. I thought that, because it was all so different from life as I knew it. But I know better now. I'm not good at expressing myself, despite your kindness in trying to teach me, but it seems to me that the arena is a sort of mirror to the life you all lead. You are the most powerful man in the world, but you can't escape the net. I haven't angered you, I hope."

"No," I said, "the truth should never make you angry. And I am pleased you are learning how things are . . ."

I averted my gaze from his candid eyes, and looked over the roof-tops of the turbulent city. A red kite swooped in low circles over the temples of the Capitol.

Agrippina wrote to me, protesting at the trial of her friend.

Claudia Pulchra is nothing but a pretext. I know that the accusations levelled against her are really directed at me. You sacrifice to Augustus, as the law ordains, but you persecute his descendants. It is not in mute statues that his divine spirit has lodged – I, born of his sacred blood, am its incarnation. Nothing can alter that. So I see my danger. Claudia Pulchra's only offence is that she has had the recklessness to choose the persecuted Agrippina as her friend.

Sejanus handed me back the letter.

"She really is deranged, poor woman," he said. "Who knows

what she may attempt in her delirium? I'm not sure that it's
safe to leave her at liberty."

The trial followed its predictable course. The case against
Claudia Pulchra was unanswerable. By my request, certain
articles – those concerning her conspiracy against my life –
were deleted. The adultery was enough; she and her paramour
were both exiled by order of the Senate.

Agrippina fell ill, or gave out that she was ill. It is possible that
this trial had let her see, for a moment, the dangers of the
course on which she had so thoughtlessly and maliciously
embarked. I do not know; I never understood the cause of her
terrible anger, or plumbed the depths of her aggrieved self-pity.
She asked to see me. I attended her sick-room where she lay,
her eyes swollen by weeping; she held a cold compress against
her temples, and she frequently interrupted her disordered
speech with bouts of sobbing. I pitied her, and remembered
that she was Julia's daughter, and that, in the early years of my
marriage to her mother, I had taken pleasure in her childish
intensity of feeling.

"I am lonely," she sobbed. "My children, for whom I have
sacrificed everything since the death of my husband, are almost
grown-up. My mother was torn from me when I was little more
than a child. Now you who were my stepfather persecute me.
Why do you do that, Tiberius? What harm have I ever done you?
You were jealous of Germanicus? Is that a reason to pursue me
as you do?"

"I was never jealous of Germanicus," I said. "He was my
dear brother's son, and I admired him. Sometimes I thought
him injudicious, and then I intervened, but I never accused him
of anything worse than inexperience and the impetuosity of
youth. Agrippina, we have – perhaps with neither of us willing
it – drifted into misunderstandings and suspicions. There is no
need for them. You know I detest talk of the imperial succession, since it is a matter for the Senate as to who should
hold the first place in the Republic. But I know that there must
be a Princeps, and that he must come from our family. Don't

you realise that I see your sons, Nero and Drusus, as my immediate heirs? I am an old man, almost seventy, and few summers remain to me. Can't we set aside our animosities and be friends?''

I stretched out my hand to her, but she shrank from its touch. Nevertheless I felt that my words had moved her, and waited for a reply. She was silent a long time. Then she said:

"I am so miserable, so alone, neglected and misunderstood. And I am lonely. You cannot imagine how lonely I have been since my husband was torn from me. Not a night has passed that I have not wept to feel his place empty beside me. My youth is fleeing, and I see only a dark future. Help me, Tiberius, let me marry again. Indeed, I beg you to choose me a husband. I am still young enough. Marriage . . . marriage is the only respectable consolation open to me. Surely Rome contains men who would be proud to marry Germanicus' widow and become the father of his children . . . ?''

"Don't you see," Sejanus said, "she is laying a trap for you? Her appeal to your pity is only a device. If you choose a husband acceptable to her, you immediately raise up a rival to yourself. And if your choice settles on one whom she rejects, this will be further evidence of your persecution. She will say that you are insulting the memory of Germanicus by proposing a husband unworthy of her rank and his reputation.''

Sejanus knew Agrippina well, better than I. I had thought her sincere in her request. Even now, I sometimes wonder if she was in truth sincere when she asked me; it seemed that her distress was genuine. And indeed I still believe it was. Yet she was torn by conflicting desires. I was moved by her emotion, wary of her volatile passions. We understand our own natures but little, and then usually in retrospect; the spontaneity of speech and action puzzles our understanding. It is not therefore strange that other people should be so unfathomable in their inconsistency.

I put myself about to do as she had asked. I selected two candidates, both worthy men of good family, both distinguished for public service, both trustworthy. Either would have made a distinguished husband; either would have been seen as an acceptable successor to Germanicus by any unprejudiced critic. I shall not name either, because I have no wish to reveal to the future shame of their family how contemptuously Agrippina responded to their names. One was "a sack of dung"; the other "a servile coward to whom Germanicus would not have given the time of day". Both judgments were absurd. But what could I do, especially when she accused me – as Sejanus had predicted – of having chosen them merely to insult her? That was not my intention, though I grant that it might appear so in the case of the second candidate, for Sejanus told me subsequently that the man was one of young Nero's lovers. But I was ignorant of that when I recommended him.

EIGHT

In my sixty-ninth year I left Rome. I hope never to see the city again. It has become ugly to me. I could not attend the Senate without experiencing nausea, occasioned by my awareness of that body's degeneracy. A day spent there – no, even a morning – left me oppressed with an intolerable heaviness, a lassitude, the sensation that I had lost all sense of freedom, that I was seized with painful and disabling cramps, even to the point of paralysis. The smell of the place disgusted me; it reeked of decomposition. I was smothered with words. In all talk, I reflected, there is a grain of contempt. Whatever we have words for, that we have already gone beyond. Language, even the language of poets in the modern world, serves only what is average, mediocre, communicable. I felt a profound desire to escape all that and, in escaping, to resume my long-abandoned search for something beyond daily existence, mere existence, for something which might justify its tedium.

The value of anything does not lie in whatever one attains by it, but in what one pays for it – what it costs us. My assumption of the imperial role cost me happiness, even self-respect, for, in the shifts and manoeuvres necessary to maintain my authority, I abandoned any sense of my own virtue. I had become the slave of Augustus' legacy. Perhaps I might even in old age achieve freedom.

I removed to Capri. Why that island? Because it pleased me. Simply that? Because I could settle on it as my abode without the agony of introspection and self-justification. Because of the colour of the sea.

Sejanus approved my choice. He said: "You will be safe there. There is only one landing-stage."

I told the Senate I should communicate by letter and that they should consider Sejanus my mouthpiece. But I was not rash enough to grant him the *maius imperium*, which I alone possessed. I would not put that temptation before him, nor make him such a mark for the envy of others. He threw back his head and laughed when I explained my reasons.

"Is it any wonder," he said, "that I have served you so long and with such content?"

"You old fox," he said later.

I trusted Sejanus, but I no longer found any pleasure in his company. That was another reason for my departure from Rome. His presence no longer invigorated me. He was a middle-aged man, with a bald spot, running to fat, and dominated by ambition, a calculating man, without that blithe acceptance of being in which I had taken such delight. I embraced him on embarkation, and said to myself, "It's over. I no longer need Sejanus, except in a political sense." But there, thanks to my abdication, I needed him more than ever.

Augustus had left me a villa which I immediately occupied. But I set myself to build a new villa, to my own taste, higher up the mountain.

"Why have you come here?" Sigmund asked. "Is it rest you seek, master?"

"No," I said, though I longed for rest, "beauty. In the end only beauty offers consolation. The only rest is to be found in the experience of beauty. I don't say 'contemplation', because that is passive. The experience of beauty must be active."

The poor boy looked at me, and shook his head.

I invited some old friends to accompany me: Marcus Cocceius Nerva, an ex-consul; Curtius Atticus, the distinguished knight; and my mathematical philosopher, Thrasyllus. I took also the Greek freedman Philip, and of course Sigmund. It was a small household, and such as I trusted would not weary me with importunate demands. There was no point in going to say goodbye to my mother; she no longer recognised anyone, but would sit and rail and weep for death. I prayed that she would soon be released, and in fact this happened within six months of my departure.

Those first months were the happiest I had known since I left Rhodes. The sea air let me breathe more easily, and in the early morning, before the heat of the day caused me to surrender my terrace to the lizards, I felt ten years younger. Best of all was the awareness of freedom. Of course I was still bound to my official boxes. Not a day passed that did not require me to take twenty decisions concerning the welfare of the empire, or write twenty letters. But I was able to do so, calmly, without the agitation of spirit which had so disturbed me in Rome, without the pressing consciousness of a greedy and untrustworthy humanity, without the fear that I was doing nothing more than shore up a barrier against the corruption of the age; for, strange to say, all that oppressiveness and disquiet were lifted from me. Others sensed my unwonted contentment.

"It is as if the world stops at the water's edge," Atticus said, "and yet I feel as if the world is waiting for some great sign, as if we had reached a stage of history pregnant with possibility."

"That is as true now as at any time in the history of our people," I replied.

In the late afternoon I would sometimes have myself rowed out into the bay. I kept my gaze on those rocks where Philip's uncle by marriage had encountered his Siren lover. But the rocks were deserted and there was no music in my ears. Nevertheless somewhere, I knew, the Sirens rested, nursing promises of bliss.

One day a wind blew up, and the boat was unable to make its way round a headland. Instead we found ourselves forced back to land. An opening yawned before us, and our helmsman steered towards it. For a moment my bodyguard shifted his hand to his sword-hilt, but I smiled and told him there was no danger.

"Where are we going?" I asked.

"I am going to show Caesar one of the wonders of the island," said the helmsman, and guided the little boat under a shelf of rock and into a cave. All at once the world and daylight disappeared, and we found ourselves in a twilight that was intensely blue. The water lapped against the boat, and shimmered caerulean, shot with violet streaks. The walls glistened a deep azure, and the bubbles of the water sparkled darker than any sky or sea that yet remained blue, with little gleams of ruby red and emerald. The boat paused in the middle of the violet water that was as still as a summer lake. There was silence. An air of freedom from earthly concerns breathed over me.

"This is peace."

I sighed to leave the place of enchantment, but when we came back to the world of men, and I saw by the landing-stage bronzed boys, naked to the waist, their tunics kirtled, wade thigh-deep in the water to drag nets of fish to the shore, and heard their girls cry encouragement, and saw pride in their mothers' eyes, I gave myself up for a little to the illusion that life is good.

Of course it is an illusion. At best, life has good moments. But the atmosphere of Capri nursed my pain and grief, as nothing had done since my marriage to Vipsania was severed by politics.

One other afternoon, dismissing my attendants, I climbed the hill behind my villa. A narrow lane led to a little temple. The walls were covered with ivy and wild honeysuckle and, as I approached, an owl rose on silent wings from a broken column, and flew towards a grove of cypresses. The sun was still hot and, weary from my climb, I rested there, leaning my back against the temple walls and watching the lizards dart to and fro. Far below the sea murmured, and there was no wind. Finches twittered among the nearby pines, and the crackle of crickets was the only other sound to disturb the tranquillity. I think I fell asleep.

A boy was standing before me, his golden limbs moulded like the finest carving. Flowers were twined in his dark hair, and his brow was smooth as one untroubled by dreams, or one whose dreams are only of delight. I found I could not speak.

"What are you doing here?" he asked.

When I made no reply, he touched my lips with a wand he carried, and repeated his question.

"Men do not usually dare to make such an enquiry of me," I said.

He smiled.

"Oh men," he said: "Mortal men."

"Are you not mortal then that you speak of men and death so lightly?"

"No, why should you think that?"

He smiled again.

"What are you seeking?" he said.

"Oblivion."

"You cannot enjoy that in your life."

"Peace, then. And the experience of beauty."

"You are not moderate in your requests."

"Who are you," I said, "that you speak so confidently, despite your youth?"

"I am a youth only because I choose to appear to you as such, because I choose not to age. I am the genius of this place, and I am here because you summoned me."

"Did I do that?"

"Certainly."

"And can you grant me what I seek?"

"Only if you are prepared to pay the price."

"Is there a price?" I asked. "But of course there must be a price. Well, beautiful boy, tell me what it is . . ."

"It is a price that few would pay, and which most would think themselves dishonoured by paying. But, since I know that your misery is great, I shall make you an offer."

His mouth, which was shaped like a bow, curved in mockery, in which, nevertheless, I discerned a sympathy such as I have never known and which I yearned for deeply.

"This beautiful island," he said, "is yours for consolation. Isn't that enough, without extracting my price from me, and submitting to it?"

"Tell me what it is," I said.

"Very well, you may enjoy such beauty, peace and oblivion

as is within your means, if you consent to let your name be branded with infamy down the ages of time . . ."

"Such beauty, peace and oblivion as is within my means? How much is that?"

"Not as much as you would wish, more than you would achieve without my aid."

"And my name infamous?"

"You will be denounced as a monster, a murderer, a brute and satyr, a deified beast . . ."

"And if I say no?"

"Then you will never see me again. I shall depart, and leave you to your nightmares, your fears, and memories . . ."

He smiled, a radiant smile, mischievous as the God of Love . . .

"Good," he said, "you accept my bargain . . ."

"I have not said so . . ."

"Words are not needed . . ."

The owl cried. The bird of Minerva, it is said, flies only by night; and then I saw that the moon was up, a thin young moon like a golden horn. I was alone, and knew the cold of solitude.

So I made a bargain which would disgrace me in the eyes of my ancestors, and will make my descendants – if any long survive me – blush to recall my name. And I have done so for a promise that may never be redeemed, in which I do not truly believe, for I cannot grant the existence of a power that will still my memory. Finally, the circumstances of my bargain perplex me; it is possible that I saw the boy only in a dream. Yet who would be so bold as to deny that what we experience in a dream may not be true reality? There are philosophers who argue that we dream this life. It is certainly at moments as vivid as a dream.

I might escape the past; I could not escape the present. Every courier brought me news of depravities and conspiracies in Rome. Agrippina, forgetting her plea and my promise, had launched herself in new tirades of slander against me; she reiterated the old lie that I had been privy to Germanicus' murder. Sejanus reported that her agents were active in the army. "I fear what they are plotting," he said. "Allow me, pray, to take the necessary preventive measures." But I declined.

Then he crossed to the island to confront me with his evidence.

"I dared not entrust this to any courier," he said to me, "for in the current atmosphere of suspicion and treachery, I did not know anyone on whom I could absolutely depend. The fact is, Tiberius, that that woman and her son have so corrupted the legions that rigorous investigation is going to be necessary before we know who is trustworthy. And I must tell you that even such investigation may prove unreliable, for one has to trust the investigators, who may be unworthy of our confidence. Do you understand the morass through which I wade?"

"You say, her son. Which of her sons?"

"Nero."

"Nero, I would be sorry to believe him guilty. He is a boy on whom I have lavished kindness."

"Nevertheless, he has been heard to say that it was time the old man was dead. I give you his exact words."

"They don't seem so very dreadful. I have often thought that myself."

"Caesar," he said, "you don't understand."

He threw himself back in his chair, and clapped his hands, and despatched a slave to fetch wine. He had long been accustomed to use such freedom in my presence, and I had delighted in it. Now, for the first time, it seemed presumptuous; yet I knew the depth of his loyalty towards me. He waited in silence for the wine, drank a cup of it, and wiped his lips. Sweat glistened on his brow.

"You must listen," he said. "I know you don't want to, but you must, or we are both dead men, and Rome is in turmoil. You are Augustus' heir, you have often told me so and, whatever you think of him secretly, you have always granted him one great achievement: he brought the civil wars to an end. Do you want them to break out again?"

Then he marshalled his facts or information. It was not just a matter of loose or seditious talk, though that was bad enough. But Agrippina had been holding dinner-parties attended by senators whom she supposed to be disaffected and, worse than that, she and Nero had been concocting plans to slip away from Rome and join the legions in Germany, where Germanicus' memory was still especially revered. Then it would be, Sejanus said, like Caesar crossing the Rubicon into Italy. With the German legions behind them, they could march on the capital and dictate terms.

"We are as close to civil war as that."

I hesitated.

"Your agents," I said. "You know how I distrust espionage, for agents have a habit of telling their masters what they think will please them."

"True, but I have two agents whose evidence is, I think you will agree, incontrovertible."

"If that is so, then . . . who are they?"

"The first is Drusus."

"Drusus? Why should he inform against his mother and brother?"

Sejanus smiled, like a great cat playing with a mouse.

"Oh he has several reasons. One, he is jealous, because Nero is the elder. Two, he hates his brother and is disgusted by his addiction to vice. Our Drusus is a nasty little prig, you know. Three, he is ambitious. He hopes, with Nero out of the way, that he himself may be your successor."

"I would rather be succeeded by a pig than by Drusus. It seems to me that his evidence is suspect, Sejanus, for it is founded on animosity and chimes too well with what he thinks are his own interests."

"That's as may be. And it might be suspect, if it was not corroborated."

"By whom?"

"By his sister-in-law, Livia Julia, little Nero's wife. Her husband does not love her of course, but they are apparently on friendly terms. I should say perhaps they are on friendly terms by my instructions, relayed through my dear Julia Livilla, the girl's mother. She early realised that little Livvy was disgusted by her husband's preference for men, and regarded it as an insult to her own charms. And what girl wouldn't? But she has the sense, and the self-control, not to show her feelings, and little Nero is a blabbermouth, with no more idea of security than a pigeon. She knows about his dealings with the German armies and whatever she knows she tells her mother, who passes it on to me. So, you see, Caesar, it's not just a matter of paid informers this time. And don't forget that, though we dropped the poisoning charge laid against Agrippina's friend Claudia Pulchra, I have always said that was a mistake. You can't know what a relief it is to me to have you here, on this island, but even here, you may not be completely safe."

"Why should I care about safety when I long for death?"

"You have been asking that question for twenty years. The answer is still the same. Because you care for Rome."

"A stinking hole."

"Granted, you think that. But an idea. You don't want to go down in History as the man in whose hands the empire broke. And empires are frangible. Think of how Alexander's dissolved within a few years of his death. You don't want historians to write that Tiberius, through a supine idleness and a feeble irresolution which overtook him in old age and corrupted his judgment of men and affairs, allowed the empire bequeathed by Augustus to be destroyed in civil war and internecine feuds. Better to strike now to avert disaster. It is sometimes necessary to be brutal in order to do good . . ."

But I hesitated. I heard the waves lap on the rocks, and saw the moon lie on the waters. My judgment had been called in question; but I remembered how young Nero had embraced me after my son's death and told me he wished I could weep for my own sake. His emotion had embarrassed me but I could not believe that a boy capable of such sympathy was also capable of plotting my death.

"Let us eat first," I said.

Sejanus settled himself on his couch, and broke off a crab's claw.

"Of course," he said, "young Nero is a consummate hypocrite."

In the end I compromised. I compromised because I could not bring myself either to believe the reports Sejanus had brought

me, or to dismiss them. So I sent him back to Rome with a
letter to the Senate in which I complained in careful phrases
and opaque terms of the seditious implications of Agrippina's
animosity towards me; if a lady of her status, I observed, was
permitted to speak with the licence she was reported habitually
to allow herself, then others, lacking her intimate connection to
me, would feel themselves at liberty to express insubordinate
and disobedient thoughts. All authority would soon be called in
question and, without authority, the Republic would be endan-
gered. Insults directed at my person were no matter to me, for
I had long accustomed myself to endure them. Half a century
of public life had inured me to mere personal abuse. But I had
been entrusted with responsibilities by the Senate, and I could
not acquit myself properly of the duties thus laid upon me if my
authority was so freely questioned. As for Nero, I contented
myself with drawing the Senate's attention to the political consequences of his licentious self-indulgence.

We are honoured only as we behave honourably, and the
decency of public life depends on the decency of the private
conduct of those whom the Senate has entrusted with authority, and of those around them, including members of their
own family. I have in the past endeavoured in private conversation to persuade this young man, for whom I have much
affection, to conduct himself in a more seemly manner. I
arranged that he marry my dear grand-daughter, hoping, as
I did so, that her charms and virtues would succeed where
my earlier pleas had failed. Now, to my sorrow, I learn that
the experience of marriage has not persuaded him to turn
away from the practice of vices, which, if indulged in the
public gaze, cannot fail to bring the young man himself into
contempt, and which will, in its turn, be transferred to other
members of my family, even perhaps to me myself, and also,
by extension, to you, Conscript Fathers, and thus to the
whole structure of legitimate authority. Therefore, I address
this letter to you, in the hope that my public reproof, supported as I trust it will be by your unanimous expression of
your very natural and proper abhorrence, will succeed where

my private urgings have failed, and so persuade this young man, who possesses so many talents, and in whom I discern – setting aside this particular matter – so much natural virtue – to amend his way of life, discard the vices which corrupt his character and tarnish his reputation, and so live in a manner more worthy of his status as a Roman nobleman and the great-grandson of the Divine Augustus.

Sejanus was not satisfied with this letter. He complained of my moderation, even timidity. He told me that I would destroy myself through my own benevolence.

I am not certain how my letter was received, for I have had conflicting reports. It seems that it puzzled the senators. They did not know what I wanted them to do, though I should have thought it was clear. One, Messalinus, leaped up to demand that Agrippina and Nero should be put to death, but omitted to say on what charge. Then Julius Rusticus, a man I had long revered and whom I had appointed to keep the minutes of senatorial proceedings, tried to calm the assembly by arguing – quite correctly as my account must have made clear – that the motion should not be put to the vote. It was inconceivable, he said, that I should wish to eliminate Germanicus' family. All that was required of the Senate was to note the arrival of the letter and its contents, in the hope that its measured and dignified language would serve as a public warning to the two errant members of the imperial family. That was all the emperor wished.

News of the letter alarmed the mob. They crowded round the Senate House, baying support for Nero and Agrippina. This unsettled the senators further. I doubt now whether the appearance of the mob was spontaneous. It was reported that some of them shouted that my letter was a forgery – Tiberius could not favour plots to destroy his family. If this report was true, it sounded to me as if someone's agents had implanted that idea in their minds.

But whose? I was already aware that my retirement to Capri had made it more difficult for me to know what was happening.

I was more than ever at the mercy of the information I received.

My letter did not have the desired effect of persuading either Agrippina or Nero to mend their ways. Indeed, it may have had the contrary effect. Within a month of its appearance, Sejanus sent me word of new communications between the pair and the German legions.

He appeared on Capri without a prior announcement, something he had never done before.

"The situation," he said, "is critical."

It was a beautiful morning. I had bathed early, and was break-fasting with Sigmund and other members of my household when news was brought that a ship was approaching the island. Un-announced arrivals were always agitating, and Sigmund exerted himself to calm my suspicions. It was a relief when I learned that Sejanus was on board. Nevertheless I reproved him for having taken me by surprise.

"The situation is critical," he repeated. He spoke without geniality. He was insensible to the beauty of the scene and of the morning. "You don't understand," he said, "you refuse to understand the danger we are in. Conspiracies are afoot all around us. To speak frankly, I don't know that I can trust the security of your own household. If I let my movements be known in advance, then it becomes more difficult to protect you. Think what your position would be if I were assassinated. And there's nothing they would like better. Without me, you would be quite helpless here. You would actually be a prisoner. It wouldn't be necessary to kill you, or even arrest you, though of course they would get rid of you as soon as they felt it safe to do so. And that wouldn't be long."

He sat in the sun, sweating. He had dismissed all my attend-ants, and posted guards at the doorway which led to the terrace, and more guards in the anteroom by which the terrace was approached.

"I've taken a risk leaving Rome," he said.

I told him I didn't understand why he had come.

He sighed. He got to his feet and strode to the corner of the terrace looking down on the beautiful bay which I was quite sure he did not see. He stood with his back to me while the silence prolonged itself. Then he turned, frowning.

"Anything may happen while I'm away," he said. "I have left good men in charge, but even good men may be suborned. What's brewing is more than a plot, more than a revolt. It's a revolution. Agrippina dines half a dozen different senators every day. Letters fly to and fro between her and the legions in Germany. Here's an example."

The letter he passed was evidently seditious. It called on the commander of the legions there to hold himself in readiness for the day which would soon be upon them. "As soon as we act against the Bull, or are ready to act against him, I shall let you know. I understand of course that you do not dare to commit yourself till you are certain he has been eliminated."

Sejanus threw back his head in that defiant gesture I had once loved.

"I am the Bull," he said.

"And this is genuine?"

"Yes."

"You are certain?"

"Yes."

Four weeks earlier, one of Agrippina's trusted freedmen had left her house disguised as an Egyptian dealer in precious stones. He had given Sejanus' agent the slip in Ostia, but the agent discovered that he had embarked on a ship bound for Marseille. Messages had been sent to the governor of the city to intercept the merchant, but they had been delayed, and Agrippina's man had escaped the city. A cavalry troop had set off in pursuit, and he had been apprehended at the Augustan gate of Lyon. The letter had been found on his person. It bore no direction, but the freedman had been put to the question and, under torture, had revealed the name of its intended recipient.

Sejanus said, "It is unlikely that Agrippina will act till she has had an acknowledgment but, if none comes, she may be minded to move for fear it has been discovered. She will not dare to move directly against you in such circumstances, but she will certainly act against me. As you can see, that does not depend on the assurance of help from the German legions. Here, however, is the second sheet of the letter."

It read:

As for the old man himself, it will be time enough when we are in control of the machinery of the state to determine his fate. I know you have tender feelings of residual loyalty, and these shall be respected. Therefore you yourself may conclude, in conversation with my son, who to some extent shares your sentiments, whether he shall be imprisoned where he is, or in some less salubrious island, such as that to which my mother was confined, or whether he shall be more conclusively disposed of. I am bound to say that, for our general security, I favour the last course, since who can tell the number of adherents he may still have, or how his survival might act as a focus for disaffection?

Sejanus smiled for the first time that morning. I lifted my eyes from the page, compelled by his smiling stare.

"I do not think this is her handwriting," I said.

"No. She has dictated it."

"Would she trust a slave or freedman with such matter?"

"Evidently. Since she has done so. Who else could have composed it? I grant you it was imprudent . . ."

"Strangely imprudent . . ."

"Imprudent, yes, but not strangely so. I have always known that you have never understood Agrippina. She thinks normal rules don't apply to her, and consequently she disdains precautions that any sensible person would take. Moreover she is so swollen with pride in her own popularity that she cannot imagine one of her own people capable of acting against her. Besides which, in this case, she has been justified. She wasn't betrayed . . ."

His impatience and assurance both disturbed me. Early in my military career I learned to be suspicious of any course of action which was vehemently advanced. Whenever a man shows unusual ardour in urging a policy, you may be certain that something is wrong somewhere. Sejanus had always been alert to my moods; he caught a whiff of my doubts.

"You hesitate," he said, "because you are unwilling to believe Agrippina could desire your death, though you have evidence enough that she has long wanted that more than anything in the world. You have never accepted that she really believes Piso murdered Germanicus, and that you instigated the crime. She has been mad for revenge ever since . . ."

I did not answer. I felt the power of his stare. I had made Sejanus by my own choice and now it seemed to me that he had escaped my influence, achieved an autonomous force. I felt my age, and the weakness and irresolution of age. I looked down at the sea. The sun sparkled on the water and there were children playing, with happy cries, in the shallows. Sejanus followed the direction of my gaze.

"I can see it is a temptation," he said, "to pretend in this island paradise that you have escaped the world."

He sat on the terrace wall and crumbled fragments of rubble between his fingers. A cat brushed against my legs and I bent down to run my hand along the soft fur. Sejanus dropped pebbles over the wall, and seemed to listen for a sound that never came.

"I'm not out of the world," he said. "I am right in the centre of the horrible gory mess. You rescued that German boy from the arena but you left me to fight your battles there. Well, I've a confession to make. I'm afraid. There, you never thought to hear me admit to that. I'm as fearful as that German boy was when he lay on the sand while the world hurtled away from him and left him face to face with death. You may be indifferent to death, Tiberius, and I would be indifferent to death in battle, but this fear is different. It's the terror that stalks by night. Whenever any petitioner approaches me, I wonder if he is the murderer they have despatched. I try to reassure myself: 'He's been searched by my guards' I say. 'He can't possibly have a weapon'. And then I wonder if my guards have perhaps been suborned. It is to such imaginings unworthy of a man that my devotion to your person and your interests has condemned me."

"Very well," I said, "but I do not wish them put to death . . . I shall write in suitable terms to the Senate."

"Now," he said.

I watched his boat shrink into invisibility. There were pink roses on my terrace, I called for wine. I waited.

The Senate, now certain of my intentions, was only too happy to order the arrest of Agrippina and Nero. A vote of thanks for my deliverance from vile conspiracy was passed. Some ardent spirits, hoping to please me, called for the death penalty. This time no mob swirled around the Senate House. Rome was quiet as the grave. Agrippina was sent to the island of Pandateria to be confined in the villa where her mother, my poor Julia, had been lodged. Nero was imprisoned on the island of Pontia, where several of Julia's lovers had dragged out existence. I thanked the Senate for their vigilance on my behalf, and commended Sejanus to them as "the partner of my labours". When he wrote renewing his request to be allowed to marry my daughter-in-law, Julia Livilla, I made no objection. Let him please himself, if it still pleased the lady. I asked him only to maintain his care for the children he had had by Apicata.

A few weeks after his mother's arrest, Drusus visited me on Capri. I had not invited him for I detested the thought that this young man, who had been so zealous in the destruction of his brother Nero, should be seen by so many as my ostensible heir. He demanded praise for his loyalty and eagerly begged a reward. It was time he was granted command of an army, he said. I replied that I entrusted military commands to experienced and trusted soldiers, not to ignorant boys. He flushed.

"Furthermore," I said, "I find your expressions of loyalty to me less striking than your indifference to your mother's fate. Where natural affections wither, it is hard to trust noble sentiments."

*　　*　　*

"You have made an enemy of that young man," Sejanus wrote. "He returned to Rome inspired by malice directed at your person."

I could not help that. I saw in Drusus the fierce and cunning servility which has been the bane of Rome. It is the Ides of March today, the anniversary of Caesar's murder. Of course the corruption of virtue long preceded that, which was indeed a vain attempt at its purification. Marcus Brutus at least, a man who won the admiration of almost all those opposed to his actions, certainly saw that murder as a necessary cleansing deed. I am told he looked down on Caesar's mangled corpse, and muttered, "Cruel imperative". There was one exception to the general approval of Brutus: my stepfather always described him as a prig, fool and ingrate; he called the conspiracy against Caesar "a mad dream of disappointed careerists given a spurious respectability by Brutus who lacked any understanding of how the Republic had changed since the Punic Wars".

Augustus was right. Yet I have often wondered whether I would not myself have been among the self-styled Liberators. I am sure at some moments that I would have been, for I would have found the rule of a single person – a rule then in its infancy – as repugnant as . . . as I find it now when I am myself that person. And yet, if I have any consistent virtue, clarity of mind must be granted me. Would I not then have looked around the Senate as I do now and have found a generation fit for slavery, no longer capable of exercising the restraint of the passions on which the enjoyment of true liberty depends?

It is not only a question of morality, though ultimately all political questions must be seen as that. It is a question of consistent authority. Rome has been destroyed by its empire; the doom of the Republic was written in the conquest of Greece, Asia, Africa, Gaul and Spain. My whole life, animated by Republican sentiments, has yet been devoted to making the re-establishment of the Republic impossible. And it is thanks to Brutus and his friends that the inevitable principate had its origins in murder and civil war.

*   *   *

These thoughts have been with me a long time. I looked around
and saw no man but Sejanus capable of governing the empire.
Drusus was a scoundrel. I doubted the mental balance of his
younger brother, Gaius Caligula. My own grandson Tiberius
Gemellus was a sweet child, but nothing in his nature promised
that he would be a man of character. Perhaps the best security
for him was indeed that Sejanus should marry his mother and
be entrusted with his care, as Augustus had entrusted me with
the rearing of Gaius and Lucius. Surely, I thought, I could trust
Sejanus? The nobility, jealous of his comparatively humble birth,
would rebel if he was openly elevated to the position which
Augustus had enjoyed, and I had endured; but he could be the
power, as it were, behind the throne, my grandson's throne. I
announced that as he had long been the partner of my labours,
I would honour him by making him my partner in the consulship
for the following year.

That announcement proved to Drusus that he had gained nothing by his betrayal of his mother and brother. He collected
about him a group of giddy-minded, dissipated and discontented
nobles. Their dinner-table talk was rank sedition. This was
reported to me; I relayed it to the Senate, who ordered Drusus'
arrest. Pending full investigation, he was held under house
arrest. I ordered that he be strictly guarded, and forbidden
company.

Agrippina, hearing the news, embarked on a hunger strike.
Orders were given that she be forcibly fed. She resisted the
attempt. Struggling with her guards, she received a blow which
cost her the sight of her left eye.

NINE

Does chance govern all? I had a letter from Antonia, my brother's widow, Germanicus' mother, saying she hoped to visit me, perhaps for a few days while she was holidaying at her villa on the Bay of Naples. I was minded to refuse, though I have always liked and admired Antonia. I was afraid that she would plead for her grandsons Nero and Drusus; not for her daughter-in-law Agrippina, I was sure of that, for she had never cared for her. It would have been embarrassing to endure her intercession on their behalf. So I wrote a letter saying I was unwell and unable to receive visitors.

But I did not send it. I was distracted by another letter I had received. This was from Sejanus. He requested that I accord him the tribunician power, that Republican status which Augustus had employed as a device to enable him to initiate and veto legislation and to ensure that his person was sacrosanct, which I had, of course, been granted by him. In fact I had been considering whether this should not be accorded Sejanus; I had hesitated because I knew how much a grant would stimulate discontent and envy. Yet the matter was on my mind. Now, on the other hand, there was something in the tone of Sejanus' letter which was displeasing, a peremptory note, as if he had only to ask to be given what he demanded. There was an underlying suggestion that with this power he would be free of my authority. It was not stated. Perhaps Sejanus himself did not know that it was there, but I caught a whiff of arrogance and impatience and this disquieted me.

In my perturbation, nostalgia invaded me. When I thought of Antonia, I set aside my fears as to what she would request. I was able to forget the sink of political Rome, with its private bureaux of espionage, its stench of conspiracy, its atmosphere infected by suspicion and fear; instead the memory came to me of conversations under chestnut trees, conversations that stretched towards the setting sun, and covered in the most friendly and sincere manner the whole range of human experience. In talking with Antonia, I reflected, I would share again some species of communion with my long-dead brother. And I remembered that in those distant days Antonia and I had been bound together by the purest sort of affection, that between a man and a woman, into which is breathed only the lightest breeze of sexual desire – a desire which, for imperative reasons, will never be translated into action; an affection which floats like a raft on a lake in the sunshine of a summer afternoon that can never end.

There was to be a happy day before she arrived. Sigmund had fallen in love with a local girl, a Greek called Euphrosyne, whose father practised as a doctor in Naples, but owned a little villa on Capri, given to him by Augustus in return for some service he had rendered. It would have been a quite unsuitable marriage but for my patronage. Miltiades (the father) would never have consented that his adored daughter should marry anyone so unsuitable as a German freedman, who had, moreover, been a gladiator, if that freedman had not also been my favourite. For my part I was delighted by the match. Euphrosyne was an enchanting girl, with black eyes and a mass of dark curls, a creature made for pleasure, yet tender-hearted and witty. To see them together was a justification of empire, for what but Rome could have brought these two perfect, but contrasting, physical types together? Their happiness and the delight they took in each other enfolded us all. I blessed the marriage, asking only that both remained in my household.

Antonia arrived early, while we were still celebrating. Her hair was white but she retained that serene beauty which she had inherited from her mother, Octavia.

"You must forgive me," she said, "I never keep to my plans exactly, for reasons I shall later explain. Meanwhile, Tiberius, how delightful it is to see you again, looking so well and happy."

"You have come in the middle of a happy occasion," I said, "and your arrival, Antonia, adds to the pleasure."

"Ah," she said, "if Rome could see you now, so innocently engaged as a sort of godfather, people would be ashamed of the scurrilous stories they are so fond of retailing."

"You risk spoiling my pleasure by mentioning that place."

"That's the last thing I want to do," she replied, but her face clouded.

"It's strange," she said, "how we have remained friends."

"We have our dear Drusus and many memories in common."

"And yet I cannot turn anywhere without being told that you are the enemy of my family."

"We could never be enemies, Antonia. I remember with the greatest gratitude how you refused to heed the vile rumours about Germanicus' death."

"I knew they were all lies. I knew you could never have a hand in the death of your brother's son. Now two of his grandsons have been imprisoned by your command."

"By order of the Senate."

"At your request . . ."

"If you had seen the evidence . . ."

She looked away, her grey eyes filled with tears. A little wind blew whispers of the ocean towards us. The blue-veined marble of the terrace shone like a dull shield in the noon sun. We sat in the shade under an arbour of trailing roses.

"I came a day early," she said, "because I no longer choose to advertise my movements exactly. More than that, I do not dare. And I brought Gaius Caligula with me because . . ." she paused, and looked me in the eyes with a candid gaze which I was reluctant to meet but from which I could not turn away, "because I am afraid of what may happen to him if he is not with you."

She then spoke of Gaius. He was an unsatisfactory youth, moody, disorganised, given to apparently unprovoked outbursts of cackling laughter and fits of temper. He had, she was afraid, a streak of cruelty. (I pictured the boy, his tow-coloured hair wild as a slum-child's, leaping from his seat in the theatre and shrieking, "Kill him, kill him!" as Sigmund lay helpless and terrified on the sand.) Nevertheless, and perhaps precisely because he was difficult, awkward, and given to nervous terrors at night, Antonia loved him; Agrippina, who, having once spoiled him, had come to detest him, had long ago consigned his upbringing to her care, and she felt the special responsibility for him that good women so often feel for their most unsatisfactory child. Now she was afraid on his account.

He had friends, a year or two older than himself for the most part, of good family, but given to dissipation and wild talk. She disapproved of their influence, but her alarm ran deeper.

"I don't know how to say this," she said, "without angering you."

"Antonia, you won't anger me, because I appreciate that you speak out of friendship."

She laid her hand on mine. The bones of old age met in mutual reassurance.

She was suspicious of these friends, some of whom had appeared suddenly, and all the more because she had come to know that much wild talk was exchanged at their drunken suppers. So she had taken steps to enquire about them, and had been alarmed to discover – she hesitated on the word "alarmed" – that two of them had also been intimates of Sejanus. "They were described to me as his protégés. Or else as his creatures." And they maintained relations with him. She had had one of them followed on several mornings after he had attended supper-parties with Gaius, either at her house, or at the home of another member of the group, or at a tavern. On each occasion, he had gone straight to Sejanus' house on the Esquiline, and remained there a long time. "I could only conclude that he had gone there to make a report . . ."

"Tiberius," she said, "my boy is wild and uncontrolled in his language. He is easily led, because he has no confidence in himself and so is open to flattery. It wouldn't be difficult to lure him into saying stupid things, even engaging in stupid . . . conspiracies. I am afraid for him, because I believe that one day soon, Sejanus will come to you with evidence, and witnesses to support it, all showing that he has engaged in sedition. That's why I want you to take him into your own household. Permanently."

When I didn't answer, she said:

"Tiberius, did all the evidence against his brothers, Nero and Drusus, come to you by way of Sejanus . . . ?"

"I trust Sejanus . . ."

"Where there is the most trust, there is also the greatest treachery."

She cleared her throat, a polite preparatory noise. She folded her hands in her lap and sat very straight.

"Nobody else," she said, "will dare to tell you what I am going to say. In giving such entire confidence to that man, you have isolated yourself. He has made of you a mystery at Rome, and mysteries are always feared. You made him what he is, but are you sure he has not escaped your control? When he claims to act in your interests, are you always certain that he is not in reality preferring his own? Agrippina has been your enemy – certainly – she is a foolish and bitter woman – but are you so sure that her sons were not made to appear your enemies, by the contrivance, indeed by the order, of that man? What reason do you have to believe the evidence he offers, when I can show you how that evidence has been concocted?"

"He has never told me a lie."

"He has never told you a lie which you have discovered. My poor Tiberius," again she placed her hand on mine, "this is not the first time you have been betrayed by affection, and trusted beyond the moment when reason for trust had vanished. You don't like to hear what I am saying, but if these same thoughts have not come to you in dark moments and been then thrust aside because you find them intolerable, then, mindless of our old, long-enduring friendship, you will act against me. I too will follow the other women of our family to an island prison, and Sejanus will be left master of the field and of your mind. But if I speak to you doubts which you have already entertained in your secret heart, then you will know that they are not vain and unworthy imaginings since they are shared by another. You will know that you are as much his victim as Nero and Drusus or as my poor chick Gaius Caligula may be. If you are not convinced, ask him for a report about the boy. I will wager that he will, with expressions of sorrow, present you with all the evidence he thinks necessary to destroy him. Has it not occurred to you that the chief beneficiary of my grandsons' pretended plots has been that man: Lucius Aelius Sejanus, and none other?"

Night closed in about me like a blanket of wet mist. Sleep was denied me; through the dead hours questions, fear and hesitations afflicted me, like nails hammered into my brain. At dawn the chorus of sea-birds circling the cliffs mocked my red-eyed restlessness. Before we separated, Antonia had said: "In Rome men now talk of you as a monster, given over to nameless vices which everyone is yet ready to name. These stories are spread and believed. At a dinner-party the other day, someone remarked that one day, when sacrificing, you took a fancy to the acolyte who carried the casket with the incense, and could hardly wait for the ceremony to end before you hurried the lad out of the temple and assaulted him; then you did the same for his brother, the sacred trumpeter . . . Who spreads such stories?"

"The Roman people," I said, turning away to hide my feelings, "have ever been scurrilous."

"I grant you that."

"They are the kind of stories people invent about men in positions of authority, and which others love to spread. They told like tales of Augustus himself, though nobody who knew him believed them."

"But people choose to believe them of you. Why is that?"

For a moment I was tempted to tell her of the vision I had had on the mountainside, and of the promise which the divine boy had made to me. But that promise seemed already a cheat; I was no nearer the peace of mind he had offered me in exchange for my reputation. Besides, Antonia might think I was suffering from the delusions of old age, such as had afflicted Livia.

"Perhaps simply because I have withdrawn here," I said.

"That certainly is one cause for credulity. But there is

another. When I first heard that story told, I made it my business to track it down. It was said to have come from Quintus Junius Blaesus, who is, as you know, Sejanus' uncle. Do you think such a man – for he is of very little merit and a known coward – would dare to invent such a story, or if he did, would he not be certain that his nephew would support him?"

"But I cannot see that it is in Sejanus' interest to imperil my authority in this manner."

Antonia sighed. "Tiberius," she said. "You are too reasonable. That has always been your fault. You have acquired a reputation for duplicity simply by telling the truth. Don't you see that you consider Sejanus truthful because he has consistently lied to you? As to your question: it is in his interest to have you thought unstable, capricious and cruel, near to madness. In this way anything vicious or unpopular can be laid at your door, while Sejanus acquires the reputation of being the only man capable of restraining your savagery.

"There," she said, "I have proved my own confidence in your continuing virtue, for if I had spoken in this manner to a man who was really as they describe, I fear I should not see tomorrow."

"If you have spoken truth, Antonia," I said, "I would wish that I might not."

I yielded nothing to her suspicions in our conversation, and struggled to yield nothing in my sleepless hours. If Sejanus were false then the rock on which I had built my life – not the certainty of his loyalty, but rather my own faith in my knowledge of men – would crumble. For two days I could not bring myself to do anything either to confirm or disprove Antonia's allegations. I pretended that she was here simply on a friendly visit, but I also took the opportunity to watch Gaius Caligula closely. My scrutiny failed to reassure me. Apart from anything else, the boy was obviously unreliable; he would argue a point vehemently, and a few hours later – at the next meal for instance – assert the contrary, without seeming to be aware of any contradiction. So at lunch he quoted Homer, and remarked that there was "Nothing on earth finer than Homeric verse or a Homeric hero", and at dinner remarked that the best thing he knew about Plato was his decision to exclude Homer from *The Republic* because, as the boy put it, "Poets are liars who tell us life is noble".

Perhaps it isn't, but it is better that young men should think it so, and Gaius was very young, only nineteen.

Then he said that no one should enter marriage a virgin, only to state with quite unnecessary ardour a few hours later that if he discovered that his bride was not a virgin, he would smother her with the pillow of the marriage bed.

I could not ignore Antonia's words, simply because the young man had an unpleasant character. (Another displeasing aspect of this was that, as a result of being educated at Rome with a number of Thracian princes, he had imbibed all sorts of notions about a royal state, and what was due to royalty, that I found offensive.) Accordingly, I wrote to Sejanus in guarded terms. Antonia had brought Gaius here on a visit, I said, and I would be grateful if Sejanus would send me, under seal, a copy of the lad's dossier. There were things about him which I found disturbing, I said.

The courier returned directly. Sejanus wrote that he was alarmed to hear of Gaius' visit. I would see that he was not to be trusted. He was ill-disposed towards me and had often talked of his longing for my death. I should be on my guard against assassination.

He named his witnesses. They were those young noblemen whom, according to Antonia, he had employed to spy on Gaius and, as she insisted, to provoke him to treasonable utterances. "These young men," Sejanus wrote, "were so shocked by the language of the young prince (as he chooses to style himself) that without any prompting on my part, they came voluntarily forward to denounce him."

Once, campaigning in Illyria, I came on a village which had just suffered a small earthquake. Not many people had been killed, but the physical damage was still astonishing. I remember one old woman gazing in wonder at a crevasse which had appeared in the floor of her cottage. The walls still stood, the roof had remained in place, but there was this chasm, but two feet wide, and more than a spear-length deep; her hens and a

cockerel had been swallowed up. Some of them had perhaps
been smothered; others clucked and squawked in indignant
puzzlement, which reproduced, as it were, exactly the
expression on the old woman's face. I now shared the sen-
sations of the old woman and her cockerel; life had lost its
foundation.

It came to me that I was isolated as never before. I was
myself a prisoner, for I had put myself in Sejanus' power. There
was not an officer on my staff whom he had not appointed. I
could not be certain that my correspondence with provincial
governors and military commanders was not subject to scrutiny
by Sejanus' agents. Nor indeed could I have any confidence that
I received all the letters addressed to me; it was possible that
any which Sejanus deemed unsuitable for one reason or another
were intercepted and destroyed. Almost everything I knew was
what he had allowed me to know, and my knowledge of the
world was his.

He had nurtured my every suspicion and now I found myself,
as a result of the revelation Antonia had forced upon me,
redoubling suspicions. I realised I could be certain of nothing.
A few months previously, for example, I had invited an old
friend, Pomponius Flaccus, whom I had formerly made Governor of Syria, to spend a few weeks of his retirement as my
guest. The invitation was declined: Flaccus was too ill to travel.
Now I found myself wondering whether the invitation had been
received, or the reply concocted. My suspicions might be unjust
in this case; that made no difference to the fact that they were
there.

He had taught me to fear others. We had hardly had a single
conversation in recent years in which he had not raised the
problem of my security or offered me the names of those who
were plotting my assassination. Now I learned to fear him in
his turn.

I had only one advantage. Sejanus had to believe that I still
trusted him absolutely. It was necessary to confirm him in his
confidence. I therefore wrote thanking him for warning me
against Gaius and his friends, and for his continued efforts on

my behalf. "The only thing," I said, "which enables me to bear the ingratitude and unreliability of men is the trust which I repose in you – the one man who has never let me down." In the same letter I confirmed that he would be my partner in the consulship the following year, and reminded him that I had been sparing in my assumption of that dignity: sharing consulships only with Germanicus and my son Drusus. The implication was, I hoped, clear; they had been my chosen, indeed designated, successors. I had no need to spell out the import of this honour to Sejanus. I held out hints of the tribunician power – "when the time is ripe". I was tempted to satisfy his desire to be granted this, in the hope that such a gift would swathe him in grateful security; but I hesitated, held back by a new fear. Sejanus had schemed to isolate and control me; might he not decide, if protected by this power and assured of this authority, that I had become redundant, and could be safely eliminated? So I promised more than I performed; let him still, I said to myself, have something to hope for from my hand.

It was necessary to reanimate support for my person among the senators. I therefore ordered that the trial of Lucius Arruntius, accused by Sejanus' agents of treason, should be abandoned. There was not, I wrote, sufficient evidence. Taking a risk, I had this letter conveyed to Rome by Sigmund and handed to the consul Memmius in person. Since Memmius was a cousin by marriage of Arruntius I trusted he would obey my instructions without consulting Sejanus. But I had days of alarm till I learned that he had done so, and even more till Sigmund returned safe to Capri.

Let me confess too that I had hesitated before trusting even Sigmund with this message. I felt a warm and tender love for the young man, in the happiness of whose marriage I delighted, and of course I was sure that my confidence in his virtue was well founded. And yet at the same time, I could not be sure. I tormented myself by elaborating methods, cajolements and threats which Sejanus might have employed to suborn the boy. When Sigmund returned, I called him before me in private and heard his report, and embraced him with a warmth that sprang from relief as much as from affection.

I wrote to Sejanus saying that I had heard rumours of mutterings against my authority, even of conspiracies against my person, among the officers of the Praetorians. I would be grateful to him if he would investigate this matter and, before acting, supply me with the names of any whom he had reason to suspect of such disaffection. He replied that he had absolute confidence in almost all these officers whom, he reminded me, he had himself appointed after the most careful scrutiny. Nevertheless any barrel might contain a bad apple, and he could not deny the presence of such. He mentioned a number of names, the chief of which, he said, was one Macro, a Calabrian, ". . . the sort of man who is discontented with life because no regard which he is paid can ever measure up to his own estimation of his qualities". Moreover, he added, this Macro had been a familiar of first Nero and now Gaius. He was an associate of some of those turbulent young men who had been inciting Gaius to disaffection, and to that treasonable course which he had been pursuing till my invitation to Capri temporarily removed him from such evil influences.

"Sigmund," I said, and paused, unable to bring myself to ask him if he loved me, if I could trust him, if he would risk his life on my behalf. It has never been in my nature to make such requests of people; never since I was deprived of Vipsania.

"Master," he replied, and waited. His lips curved into a smile.

"Not 'Master'," I said. "Call no man 'Master', dear boy."

I lay in bed, weak as from a nervous fever. The sunlight streamed into the chamber. It illuminated the golden down of the boy's cheek. I longed for the comfort of his strength, the reassurance of what I could never demand from him. I patted the bed, and indicated that he should perch there.

"You are troubled," he said. "I have known that for a long time. Remember one thing: I owe everything I possess to you, even my life. I can never forget that. Whatever you desire of me, I shall do."

His words shamed me. I think I wept to hear him speak like this. Certainly the easy tears of old age filled my eyes. For a little, I could not speak.

"It is your life," I said, "that I may be asking of you again.
But there is no one else whom I dare to trust. Do you fear
Sejanus?"

I did not look at him as I asked the question, so that I do not
know if his face paled or his eye flashed.

"No," he said, "I hate him, but that is different."

"You hate him?"

"He forced himself upon me. He made me do things which
disgusted me." Sigmund blushed at the memory. "He told me
that if I didn't, then he would tell you things which were not
true but which he would make you believe. I said you wouldn't,
but he assured me that he could always make you believe what
he wanted you to believe even when you didn't want to. So, so
he made a woman of me, and worse than a woman."

There was nothing I could say of comfort. Things remain with
you and cannot be cured by words. But my new anger with
Sejanus was fiercer and it was enflamed or corrupted by jealousy
or envy, for he had done what I had denied myself. And so I
abandoned prudence and told Sigmund what I wanted him to
do.

Sigmund left the island the next day and journeyed to Rome.
He travelled alone, and in disguise. I had given him an imperial
pass as protection but told him that he must not use it except
in extremity. It was better that his connection with me should
be unsuspected. I gave him also my seal ring, and warned him
that he would be in danger if it was found on his person, for it
would be too easy to charge him with theft.

He smiled: "I'll stick it up my arse," he said.

I wished I could have brought myself to return his smile.

In his absence I received another letter from Sejanus. He purred
with pleasure at the honours I had showered on him, the most
recent of which was his appointment to the priesthood of the
Arval Brethren. He said he was overwhelmed by the honour I
had paid him by proposing him as the successor of Germanicus
and Drusus as my partner in the consulship. He hinted that
the award of the tribunician power would make his satisfaction

complete. He spoke of the delight he experienced in his marriage to Julia Livilla and his consciousness of his unworthiness to be a member of the imperial family. Then he announced that Nero was dead:

> The wretched prince seduced one of his guards and persuaded him to abet his escape from Pontia. The other guards suspected the liaison however and reported it to me. I commanded that a closer watch be kept, and the pair were apprehended as they embarked in a boat. A struggle ensued in which both were killed. I regret to have to inform you that Nero displayed lamentable cowardice in his last moments, and died pleading for his life like a woman.

The arrogance of the letter disgusted me.

"It seems," I said to Antonia, "that he no longer troubles himself even to make his story consistent."

"Drusus will be next," she said, "then my poor Gaius, unless you act . . ."

"What can I do?" I said, for I dared not reveal my plans even to Antonia. Nor could I bring myself to tell her that it was superfluous to murder Drusus. If the reports I received were to be believed, his sufferings had deprived him of his wits. He raved – foul-mouthed filth, mostly directed at me, but also at his mother Agrippina – and refused to eat.

When Sigmund arrived in the city he went to a tavern in the Suburra kept by a German of his own tribe, who had been one of my slaves and whom I had established in this occupation after twenty years of honest, if infuriatingly stupid, service. (It is not true, by the way, that all Germans are stupid – some have a tiresome cunning, and some are, like Sigmund, indeed intelligent; yet Romans always think them stupid because even the most intelligent retain a naïvety which is foreign to our nature. It arises, I think, from an inability to comprehend the complexity of civilised life and civilised beings, and manifests itself in a dreamy mooniness, which is certainly irritating, and of which even Sigmund is not innocent.)

Sigmund explained to Armin the tavern-keeper that he was in hiding from the police. He knew that Armin would accept this as sufficient reason for subterfuge, but would be alarmed if Sigmund gave any hint of the importance of his mission. Then he explained that the matter could be cleared up if Armin would undertake to get a message to the Praetorian camp. This puzzled Armin who couldn't understand why a fugitive from the law should wish to make such a contact, but when Sigmund said his trouble was all a matter of misunderstanding, Armin nodded his head and agreed to arrange for an intermediary; misunderstandings were the sort of things which Armin could understand. Indeed misunderstandings had always seemed to permeate his life.

So the message was delivered and Sigmund endured anxious hours while he waited to see if the fish would bite. I had instructed him to make the message cryptic; it was framed in such a way as to suggest to Macro that Gaius was threatened with danger and in his terror would denounce him unless he came to his assistance. I told him to put it in this way because there was always – I was sure – a germ of truth in the allegations which Sejanus brought against those whom he had determined to destroy, and I thought Macro would be frightened. I wanted him frightened. He would not dare to be my tool if he was not afraid.

He arrived at the tavern by night, suspicious, heavy-eyed, still crapulous from last night's drinking-bout. When he found only a young German there, he suspected a trick and called for his guards. Sigmund, however, produced my ring. This, I had warned him, was his moment of greatest danger, for Macro might refuse to consider the implications of its being in his possession. Macro's first reaction was indeed to arrest him for theft. He began babbling of treason.

"If you talk like that," Sigmund said, "you are baring your own neck for the sword. Sit down."

The Praetorian sub-prefect obeyed.

"If I had stolen it," Sigmund said, "I wouldn't be such a fool as to have made arrangements for you to come here, would I?"

Macro scratched his head, and said he would like some wine.

"This is a German house," Sigmund said, "you can have a mug of beer."

Then he told him that Sejanus had written to me accusing him of treasonable conspiracy; he was involved in a plot with Gaius against my life.

There was enough truth in this for Macro to start trembling.

"The emperor instructed me to inform you," Sigmund said, "that he believes less than half of what he has been told. He has sent me to fetch you to give you an opportunity to put yourself in the right. He says you must immediately arrange for leave and accompany me secretly to Capri."

"Secretly?"

"Of course . . ."

Macro scratched his cheek and took a long pull of his beer.

"Don't you have a letter?"

"That's a foolish question."

"How do I know this is not a trick?"

"You don't, but you will be in worse trouble if you think it is. If you choose not to accompany me –" Sigmund spread his hands wide – "then he asked me to assure you that he will tell Sejanus to subject you to interrogation."

"When I mentioned that, he was like wax in my hands," Sigmund reported. "The difficult part of our conversation was the first five minutes, as you predicted. But I am not sure, I am not sure that he is the man for you, since he is both a bully and a coward."

"He's the only man there is," I replied.

Macro was a lean curly-headed fellow, with an eye that might sparkle, I thought, in other circumstances, and a discontented twist to his mouth. When he spoke of Sejanus, a bitter note entered his voice, which trembled a little, whether with fear or anger or a combination of these two closely allied emotions I could not say. But I could see that he was afraid of me also, and that was good. Indeed, my only danger was that his fear of Sejanus was such that he would betray me to him, despite the prospect of power and glory which I dangled before him.

He assured me that, even among the Praetorians, feelings against Sejanus ran high.

"Men say, 'Why is he favoured above us, when he is not better born?' Others, like myself, if I may say so, my lord . . . ?"

"Don't address me in that manner."

"I'm sorry, I respect your sentiments of course. Well then, General, others like myself who have transferred to the Praetorians after long service with the northern legions are conscious that we have campaign medals and wide military experience, and are yet subservient to a man whose career has scarcely taken him to the front, who has never seen a real battle, but who has risen by, if you will forgive me, my lord – I mean, General – by political arts."

And then I summoned up courage – the hesitant, self-doubting courage of old age – and told him what I required of him.

He was both excited and terrified by the prospect, and I felt like a man who requires a six on a single throw of the dice.

When Macro left the island, I had Sigmund arrange with the master of a fishing-boat that it be held in readiness for me, if necessary; for I knew that, if Macro failed in his enterprise, I would have to flee my home, take refuge with the armies, and hope that I would there find a sufficient remnant of loyalty to rescue the position.

It was a beautiful October, my favourite month. I woke early on the appointed day. By that time Macro should have effected his liaison with the captain of the night-guard, Laco. He had asserted Laco was a man he would trust with his life, which is why we had chosen his term of duty. It was, of course, just what he was doing. I could eat nothing. The sun sparkled on the water below, and the air was crisp. Birds still sang in the gardens. The Senate would meet, I knew, in the Temple of Apollo on the Palatine, since the Senate House was being refurbished. Did this beautiful morning indicate that Apollo favoured our enterprise?

I had not written to Sejanus for ten days. That might have worried him. I had not been able to bring myself to write despite the necessity of keeping him easy. I could not trust myself to write, for memories of what I had felt for him assailed me. Anger would have entered my words. So I took this risk. But Macro would assure him that he had delivered a letter to the consul Memmius, who would act as president of the Senate, and that that letter announced the grant of the tribunician power for which he lusted. He would make his way to the Senate in expectation of glory.

Sigmund appeared on the terrace to tell me that the fishing-boat would be at my service from the middle of that after-noon.

"How will you fill the day?" he asked.

I had no answer, then or for any subsequent day.

He ordered that a litter be prepared and, without troubling himself to secure my assent, arranged that the household should picnic by the little temple of Apollo which stood on the mountain-top. The air is sweet there, with the scent of thyme, myrtle, marjoram and pine-needles. I let him have his way, but could eat nothing but a few black olives and some cheese. I dared not drink wine.

Memmius would read my letter aloud. Would he have the presence of mind to adapt it, as I had instructed, according to his perception of the mood of the Senate? I pictured Sejanus lolling in his seat, a proud confident lion, as my words of praise buzzed round his head. And then, alert, as I voiced my first criticism. How would the senators react to that?

Gaius began to laugh, an uncontrolled cackle. I glanced across. A lizard was trapped in a little crevasse. It had fallen in backwards, and its forepaws scrabbled desperately at the edge. Gaius prodded at them with a little jewelled dagger, and con-tinued to laugh. I gestured to Sigmund, and he lifted the beast by its neck and shoulders and set it on top of a broken wall; it glanced around, alarmed, and then scurried out of sight. Gaius scowled.

After escorting Sejanus to the Senate, Macro had been instructed to hurry across the city to the Praetorian camp in the old Gardens of Lucullus, and reveal his commission as their new commander. On his way across Rome he would have picked up gold to deliver as the first instalment of a donative, from my banker. He had been nervous about this, but I insisted that it was necessary to give the soldiers tangible proof that I would reward their loyalty. Besides, any man who accepted the gold would be thoroughly compromised and would know that there was no turning back.

The sun climbed to its zenith. The air shimmered. It was the last heat of the year. I plucked a rose and pricked my finger on its thorn. Sigmund stretched out beside me in the shade of the pine trees. He lay on his back, looking up at the latticed sky. Then he closed his eyes and slept. Others of our party slept too. Gaius wandered off towards a shepherd's cottage. A dog barked in the distance, and a cock crew.

It would be over now, one way or another. My heart raced. I pressed my fingers against each other, taking a fierce satisfaction from the skeletal sensation.

To a man the senators, the majority of whom owed him favours and had fawned on his greatness, deserted my falling and former friend. They shrank back from him as if they saw in his disgrace the reflection of their own ignominy. But even so Memmius did not dare put my abrupt denunciation to the vote. Then Memmius called on Sejanus to stand. He did not move. The Senate sat in silent terror. The call was repeated. Sejanus remained motionless. At the third demand he stumbled to his feet to find Laco, the captain of the night-watch, ready at his side. Only when Laco placed a restraining arm on him did abuse break out. Then, the spell broken, the senators burst into a babble of accusation and insult.

I like to think he did not understand fully what was happening, that his comprehension was numbed by shock.

He was hustled out, down the ilex-fringed Clivus Palatinus, along the Sacred Way, with the mob apprised, as mobs always quickly are of great and terrible events, jostling him, cursing his tyranny, delighting in his disgrace. Women, it was reported, spat at him, men hurled horse-dung with their abuse. In this way he was bundled into the Mamertine prison under the Capitol and thrust down that narrow twisting stair to the ancient execution chamber of Rome.

By the order of the Senate, after a vote, he was strangled at the fourth hour after noon.

But I could not know this as the sun sank and the air grew cold, and I was jolted down the hillside, with my gaze fixed on the sea and the little harbour where the fishing-smack was pulled up on the shore.

I had requested that Sejanus be arrested. The Senate, without prompting, embarked on an orgy of revenge for the indignities they had so sychophantically endured at the hand of my fallen favourite. Neither his family nor his close associates were safe. Even his children were put to death at the Senate's command. After debate it was decided that his thirteen-year-old daughter should first be raped by the public executioner because the law forbade the execution of free-born virgins and, as one senator – a descendant, you will not be surprised to hear, of that pillar of Republican virtue, Marcus Porcius Cato – argued, to transgress this law would carry with it the risk of bringing misfortune on the city. As if we were not all steeped in misfortune!

TEN

On the day after I received news of Sejanus' death, I mounted
the little hill behind my villa to the place where I had encountered the godlike boy who had promised me peace of mind in
exchange for my reputation. I wished to upbraid him for cheating
me, since I had sacrificed one without gaining the other. But he
did not attend me on this occasion. Instead a chill wind blew
from the north, and the sky turned grey as a pigeon's back.

Sejanus appeared to me in dreams, his swollen tongue pro-
truding through black lips, and the reproach in his eyes which
he could not utter. I woke weeping, and trembling. The half-
sleep which was permitted me was disturbed and made miserable by dreams in which beauty was cruelly tortured and men
and women shrieked accusations at me. I crouched in a corner,
a blanket pulled over my head, while the tramp of angry feet
sounded around me, and voices demanded a painful and ignom-
inious death.

Sejanus' body had been exposed three days on the Gemonian
Steps, open to the insults of the mob, and the same mob would
have had mine exposed by his side. And there was a part of me
which cried that I deserved no better fate. "To the Tiber with
Tiberius!" shrieked the mob.

I wrote to the Senate:

If I know what to write to you at this time, Senators, or how
to write it, or what not to write, may the gods plunge me in
a worse ruin than I find overtaking me every day . . .

When they sent a mission of consolation, I refused to receive
it.

Worse, still worse, followed. When I was ready to say I have known the worst, I found even this was not true. Apicata, Sejanus' discarded wife, wrote me a letter.

> . . . which I could not have dared, Tiberius, to write before now. I have lived, with terrible knowledge for some years now, and it is right and proper that I share it with you. Prepare yourself there for a grief such as even you have not yet known, for what must indeed be the extremity of grief and pain. You believe that your noble son Drusus died a natural, though lamented death. It is not so. He was murdered, at the instigation of his wife Julia Livilla, by my false husband Sejanus whom that woman had bewitched. You will not wish to believe this, but why should you be spared the terrible knowledge which has been locked up in me for years . . . ? If you seek proof, question the slaves who attended him on his deathbed.

I did not wish proof. Yet I sought it. The wretches were put to the question, and confessed. When this news was brought to Julia Livilla, whom I had hitherto thought guilty of nothing worse than lust and depravity, she recognised the peril of her position, and took poison. So this woman who was the daughter of my beloved brother Drusus and of Antonia whom I had always revered, and whom I had so proudly seen married to my dear son Drusus, died in squalor and ignominy. These revelations and her suicide so distressed me that I have never since been able to bring myself to converse with Antonia.

Everything that I held good has been tarnished and made to seem filthy and disgusting.

In the city, that sink of iniquity, the senators busied themselves with accusations and revenge. I scarcely cared now what charges were brought against whom. Let them kill each other, like starving rats in a trap, I thought.

Agrippina died, raving, two years to the day after Sejanus' execution. Her son Drusus, even more demented, died, cursing me and accusing me of the most monstrous list of crimes. I commanded that the account of his last months be read to the

Senate. It was reported that many wept while others shuddered with disgust. I did not care. Let them see what they had made of Rome. Let them realise to what sort of empire they had condemned me.

Two or three times I set off to visit Rome. On each occasion I was overcome by nausea and turned back. Once I found that my pet snake, a creature I had adopted on account of the revulsion which snakes generally inspire in men and women, had died and was being eaten by ants. A soothsayer helpfully interpreted this as meaning that I should beware of the mob. I answered that I needed no such warning.

Work was the only anodyne, for even the beauty of the island seemed to be a sort of mockery of my experience. I therefore spent hours poring over the accounts which the Treasury sent me, studying the reports of governors, checking the supplies for the army, considering building projects, correcting the abuses of officials. A financial crisis arose; I settled it by making interest-free loans available. I took measures to calm alarms on the eastern frontier. I worked long hours, as if everything mattered, though I no longer believed in anything that could.

Sometimes in the afternoon I catch glimpses of happiness, when I gaze over the tops of shimmering olive trees to the ocean, or when the infant child of Sigmund and Euphrosyne crawls across the terrace to tug at the hem of my toga. But, as the sun sinks, I look across the bay to the Siren rocks, and weep that I have never heard the Sirens' song, and never will.

Memories flicker like shadows cast by the flames. Maecenas telling me of how he had collaborated with time and the world in the destruction of the boy he loved . . . Agrippa throwing his head back and swearing, and then clapping his hand on my shoulder and telling me I was at least a man . . . Vipsania's cool eyes and soft voice . . . Julia stroking the long line of her thigh and calling on me to admire it . . . Augustus with his lying and cajoling tongue . . . Livia whipping me till I confessed that I was hers . . . Young Segestes and Sigmund and the promise of release . . . Sejanus, yes, even Sejanus, as he had been when he first appeared to me on Rhodes and threw his head back, exposing his smooth throat, as he laughed at difficulties and exulted in his being . . .

In the night I listen for the owl, Minerva's bird, but hear the cocks cry instead, and the dogs bark.

My life has been consecrated to duty.

"Why prolong life save to prolong pleasure?" my poor father would sigh as tears trickled down his fat cheek.

Duty . . . and what is the end? Gaius will rule Rome in my place. If I cared for Rome, I would have him disposed of. But they deserve him. The other day I found him shrieking with fury at my grandson, little Tiberius Gemellus, though he is not little now, but a tall, willowy and handsome boy of fifteen.

"Restrain yourself," I said to Gaius. "I shall be dead soon, and then you will be free to kill him. And someone else will kill you. It's the way of the world . . ."

In Rome this man charges that with treason, and so it goes on. If we had really restored the Republic, we would have lost empire, but might have . . .

A trite reflection. There is no point continuing with this account of my life, which is ending as it began, in fear, treachery, misery and contempt.

Another flask of wine. Perhaps the nightingale will sing before I retire . . . retire to rest my body, but nothing else.

I have written nothing for months, but now do so again, if only to record for posterity the reason for my last act, which posterity will see otherwise (I have no doubt) as the last judgment of my long-drawn-out drama of revenge against the family of Germanicus.

This evening Sigmund approached me. He was trembling. I asked him what was wrong and he did not hesitate.

Yesterday, my great-nephew and presumptive successor to this hell of empire, Gaius Caligula, son of the hero Germanicus, raped Euphrosyne, who is in her sixth month of pregnancy. This morning she miscarried. Sigmund fell on his knees before me, and took my hands in his, and implored revenge. I looked him in the eye. His face, which is fat now and no longer beauti-

ful, was wet with tears and loose with grief. His voice shook
as he spoke.

"Euphrosyne," he said, "shudders even at my touch. I do not
know if all can ever be well again. I do not know if what is
broken can be mended. I beg you, Master."

All my life I have refused that word, but when I looked at
him, and knew his misery, I did not refuse it, but put my arm
round him and drew him to me.

I have commanded Gaius to appear before me in the morning,
and have meanwhile arranged with Macro to have guards on
hand to arrest him.

POSTSCRIPT

This deposition is made by Stephen, formerly known as Sigismond, first a free-born German prince, than a captive compelled to serve as a gladiator, who was rescued from shameful death by the Emperor Tiberius and served subsequently as his slave, freedman and friend, to Timotheus, pastor of the Christian Church at Corinth, to whom I entrust this manuscript for safe and perpetual keeping.

I do so in the knowledge that my earthly master, the Emperor Tiberius, is reviled by the followers of my heavenly master, the King of Kings, on account of the fact that Jesus Christ was crucified in Jerusalem during Tiberius' reign, with the connivance of the procurator of Judaea, Pontius Pilate. Nevertheless I take this opportunity to affirm that the emperor bore no responsibility for this crime, and was indeed wholly ignorant in his innocence. I have no memory of the death of the Saviour even being mentioned by Pontius Pilate in his reports, and, since I frequently acted as the emperor's secretary, it is likely that my memory is correct.

Moreover, I take this opportunity to lay a personal calumny which has made my life difficult even among Christians who preach the doctine of the repentance and forgiveness of sins and are comforted by such knowledge. For it is wrong to repent of sins which have not been committed as I have often been urged to do. Therefore I wish to put it on record that I was never the emperor's catamite, though he loved me, for this love was pure and paternal, and I owe much to him.

For this reason I have guarded this manuscript which is his memoirs, since his untimely death, when I confess that

I stole it. But I did so to preserve it, and for the most honourable reasons. And I entreat this same Timotheus before whom I make this deposition to guard it in like manner as I have done, for my sake and for the sake of truth, that also the reputation of my earthly master may some day be redeemed from the calumnies with which it has been assailed.

It is concerning the circumstances of his death that I wish to speak.

The conclusion of his account of his life records how I myself approached him with an accusation levelled against the future emperor, Gaius, a man notorious for the wickedness and depravity of his life.

This accusation that he had enjoyed carnal knowledge of my wife Euphrosyne in despite of her will and her efforts to prevent him was true. Tiberius believed me, and promised to take action.

Perhaps the information disturbed him, for he was as fond of Euphrosyne as he was of me and, being an old man, he fell ill. However, he soon showed signs of recovery and assured me he was determined to see justice done. That was our last conversation, and I insist that Tiberius was at that moment regaining strength.

Two hours later he was dead.

What happened was this.

Gaius had been alarmed by the summons to attend the emperor for he knew his guilt and feared that the emperor would punish him. He therefore rejoiced when he heard the news of Tiberius' illness, which was brought him by Macro, the Praetorian Prefect, a partner, also I regret to say, in sin with Gaius. Macro assured him that on account of Tiberius' illness he need have no fear, and the pair indulged in an evening of heavy drinking. Some time in the night word was brought that Tiberius had died, and Gaius was drunkenly hailed as emperor.

Imagine their terror when they heard that Tiberius had recovered and wished to see Macro. Both men were now overcome by guilt and fear on an additional count. Macro, however, obeyed the summons and dismissed the guards who attended on the emperor. He was closeted with him about an hour. (When I heard this news I made ready to leave the palace, for I feared the worst.) Eventually Macro emerged from the emperor's chamber with a smile on his face, announced that the old man was no more and that they could all proceed to enjoy Gaius' reign.

Now Tiberius was alive and recovering when he entered, dead when he emerged. I have always believed that Macro killed him, probably by smothering him with a pillow.

As for myself, having anticipated that my dear master might not have long to live, I had some time previously made plans to escape, for I realised that as a favourite of the old emperor, I would be antipathetic to the new régime; furthermore Macro had long detested me, for reasons that may be clear to anyone who reads the emperor's own memoirs.

My father-in-law, a worthy Greek doctor of medicine, co-operated with me in my escape, and we were passed from one friendly set of hosts to another till we arrived here at Corinth where I have remained ever since. My first years were passed in hiding till the news of Gaius' murder, after a short reign disgraced by vice and all sorts of unspeakable cruelties, released me from my terror.

It was my good fortune a few years subsequently to be granted the grace to hear the gospel of Jesus Christ and to be received into his fellowship. Some of my comrades in Christ Jesus, who know of my association with Tiberius, would urge me to repent that life utterly. I cannot bring myself to do so, for I am conscious that there was virtue, albeit a pagan virtue, in it, and I am furthermore persuaded that my master, Tiberius, though ignorant of Christ and his teaching, was nevertheless possessed of as Christian a disposition as any unbaptised pagan may exhibit. And I have preserved this manuscript for the reasons stated above.

Given at Corinth in the Year of Our Lord 60 and in the hope of
salvation through the resurrection of the body and the faith in
our Lord Jesus Christ.

ALLAN MASSIE
Thirladean House
Selkirk
March 1990